D1824230

The Battle for The Four Realms

Book 1: Dragon Bone

By

Aldrea Johnson

"The Battle for The Four Realms" Book 1: Dragon Bone
Copyright © Aldrea Johnson 2017
Publisher: Imzadi Publishing LLC
ImzadiPublishing.com

Cover Art: Anita Dugan-Moore

ACKNOWLEDGMENTS

I would like to thank everyone who has helped me along the way. My family obviously; who clearly believe in me even when I didn't believe in myself.

I would also like to thank the wonderfully talented Vivian Foster, who turned my manuscript into something readable, Katherine Tate for polishing it even further with proofreading and editing; and my thanks also have to go to Anita Dugan-Moore for turning a sentence into cover artwork.

In addition I would also like to thank everyone at Imzadi Publishing for all their support and hard work, for seeing what I didn't, and for getting this book out there.

CONTENTS

Foreword

Before they came to be, they were the whispers of the wind, the sparks of the fire, the mist of the ice and the dust of the caves. They dwelt within the caves of magic and were happy as they danced like sparks caught in the breeze and faded away only to bloom brighter again. Before they had form, before they had thoughts, before they could breathe, before they awoke, they were of fire, ice, wind and dust. Then they were given form, breath, and life and they carried inside themselves the elements of their birthplace.

They grew too big for the caves and ventured forth in search of new homes. Four Elements in the shape of dragons North, East, West and South they were the first, the brothers and sisters of the elements floating away on the breeze of the wind cave. As they floated and fluttered in the breeze the wind split their sides and wings grew from the lacerations. The dragons grew more beautiful as they flew, and as they flew elements dropped to earth. From each breath, great mountain ranges sprang up, while great lakes, rivers, ponds and streams were formed from the melting ice.

The breath of the wind dragon became the breeze and the breath of the fire dragon became the sun. From the gentle breath of the fourth dragon, trees, flowers, plants and animals were formed and all four dragons breathed life into them. Each dragon found a new home and settled. Their homes became their namesake and they lived happily. After many thousands of years, the four dragons returned to their birthplace to rest and reverted to what they had once been. The caves of magic saw what their firstborn had created and sent forth new life. Anterian led her people from the caves of elements into the Realm.

Chapter 1

Aliedori moved her hand before her face as if she was brushing away something only she could see. Maldar waited for her to speak. He clasped and unclasped the large knife. Surely she should be saying something by now, his sister's calm, pretty face gave nothing away. One of Keidrop's pointed golden ears flickered as if she too was becoming impatient; she was taking far too long. Maldar dropped his eyes to the campfire and waited some more.

"You know," he said, more than a little anxious now, "it shouldn't take that long, I need you on my side against the Olds."

"Our parents are not that old." Aliedori brushed her black hair from her face, pushing it roughly behind her ears, and surveyed her surroundings. Her green eyes often held a dreamy remote look when they scanned the surroundings, but this time it was with purpose. Maldar allowed his mind to drift while trying to ignore the mirth clearly visible in those emerald green eyes ever since he had told her what he had done.

"Well...!" Sometimes there was no telling what she was thinking but this time… this time he knew what was coming. Finally she lost her struggle and the laughter she had been trying to keep suppressed bubbled up spilling out of her mouth and rippled across the quiet landscape.

"I love you very much, dear brother, but really, was it not just last cycle you were the toast of the dragon towers. You never struck me as the handfast type. Aren't you both too young?" Sobering slightly, she watched him carefully. He was nervous she could tell by the way he was playing with the knife but something had caught her attention.

"Okay," Maldar replied, a little disappointed. "Laugh as much as you want just as long as you are on my side when it comes to the Olds." A small smile played around his mouth as he drifted off into his own private Realm.

Aliedori had her palm pressed flat on the ground, and then she lifted her hand, curling her fingers slowly drawing in the elements before making a fist.

"What's wrong?" Maldar's smile vanished, replaced with a frown. He had a growing sense of unease; his mind had been elsewhere,

3

but now it was fully focused on her. He gripped his boyhood sword, using it as a long knife. Aliedori didn't respond. Instead, she waved an invisible annoyance away with her left hand while her right fist held the elements. She glanced first to her right and then to her left; Maldar knew that even with such a quick glance she had taken in everything.

"What is it?" Maldar asked again.

He could sense nothing, but that didn't mean there wasn't something wrong.

"Something is not right.' She stood.

Maldar shivered as a feeling of dread crawled through his stomach. Keidrop, who had been resting peacefully, her golden wings drawn close to her body as she slept, now unfurled her wings and looked up the moment Aliedori got to her feet.

"At the risk of repeating myself, what is it?" Maldar said also standing up.

There was a sliver of steel in his voice as he replaced his knife in its sheath, but it was when he brought his arm up and across his body to draw his sword that he sensed it. The hairs on the back of his neck bristled as he felt all the air being sucked out of the forest; he could neither move nor speak. Aliedori remained still for a moment or two then opened her fist and the light-filled sphere exploded, sending a brilliant illumination around the forest. The light found a shadow and chased it.

"Maldar, you go that side I will take this side. Keidrop, see if you can catch whoever that is, but be aware they are extremely fast."

Aliedori spun on her heels; the illumination followed her, and together they gave chase as the shape disappeared into the distance. It dodged through trees, always slightly ahead just out of the light. Slowing her pace to enable her to draw her seax, she suddenly realised that she could no longer hear Maldar or Keidrop. She risked a glance over her shoulder as she picked up the pace again. An arc of lightning hit her taking the ground from beneath her feet. *Magic*, she thought, as she landed on her back, winded and dazed. She pulled herself quickly to her feet, ready to give chase again, but the shape was gone. She could feel the residue spell and taste it on her tongue; the bitter sick taste of dark magic. It caught in the back of her throat, making her gag. She leaned forward losing her supper; then wiped away the beads of sweat that had gathered on her forehead. Her stomach settled and the pain in her chest where the lightning had made contact ceased instantly as she placed her palm against the nearest tree. From a bush close by she pulled off three leaves, brought them to her lips and whispered. Then, opening her palm, she commanded, "Seek." Two leaves fell at her feet while the third fluttered in a zigzag motion through the trees; she followed it at high speed before it fell to the ground ahead of her.

Here the bitter taste on her tongue increased and so did her unease that something or someone had been watching her; watching them. She searched the area where the third leaf had landed but found nothing; the shape had disappeared into the darkness. She sent the light sphere high into the treetops illuminating a larger area, but all she saw were shadows and dark areas where the light could not reach.

"Where did you go or are you still here?" She scanned the shadows, but despondent that her search revealed nothing she retraced her steps running farther than she realised.

She emerged from the trees, her light orb floating above her head "Did you see anything?" she asked as she came to a stop beside the dragon. "There was a lot of powerful magic," she continued as she caught the dragon's reins. Her action caused the dragon to move.

Maldar still wasn't moving; he was caught motionless in mid-action, reaching for his sword, his right arm across his body. His face was frozen in a look of fury and his blue eyes were like ice. Aliedori knew that the binding spell was only partly responsible, her action had played its part in that look, but this was not the time; they would come back to it sooner rather than later.

Aliedori said in a stern voice hiding her fear, "Mal move yourself, we need to get to Skellglade."

In an instant Maldar completed the action of drawing his sword and looked around him wildly.

"You won't see anything, we – you and Keidrop – were caught in a binding spell, I think it came from the centre of Skellglade. A charm powerful enough to stop a dragon."

Still Maldar did not move, "What did you chase?"

"I do not know. A mage perhaps," she shrugged.

"From Skellglade?" He arched a brow questioningly.

In a couple of strides, he was by Aliedori's side. He took Keidrop's reins and mounted his dragon, reaching out for his sister's hand.

She allowed herself to be helped onto Keidrop's back, the dragon spread her wings and rose rapidly barely stirring the fallen leaves. They dropped down almost instantly on the spot where the shadow had vanished. Aliedori felt the power ripple through Keidrop's powerful body as her feet touched the ground.

"What are you doing we need to get to Skellglade?"

"Skellglade can wait we need to find this mage," he said. "Why didn't you take Keidrop with you?" Maldar finished.

Aliedori frowned.

"I did not realise that you were both caught in the spell," she said dismounting. The bitter taste burned the back of her throat like acid and she swallowed as she scanned the darkened trees and bushes beyond the illumination. The light spheres carefully chased the darkness wherever it was found, but it never went far enough, there was always a dark spot just out of reach of the light.

"Something or someone is out there." She visibly flinched and stepped behind a tree. She drew her seax; the earlier static storm was playing havoc with her senses

"Do you think this is part of our coming of age test?" Maldar was standing over her. She pushed herself up into a standing position and almost gagged. She breathed deeply and slowly; surely this couldn't just be her reaction to the use of the elements in dark magic.

"No one has coming of age tests any more. It is dying out even among the traditionalists; there are just those ridiculous ceremonies now." She was having problems controlling the growing nausea. The smell of burning incense was mixing with the bitter taste of the dark magic and Aliedori was struggling not to be sick.

"I hate that smell," she said, but Maldar could smell nothing.

Suddenly a phanthora materialised, its wings close to its body, its glowing claws swinging perilously as it appeared before them. Aliedori pushed Maldar out of the way and dived in the opposite direction. Landing hard on the ground she sprang to her feet instantly drawing energy from the earth as her palm made contact.

"I thought those things never left the sacred forest." Maldar replied, slightly breathless, but springing to his feet his sword at the ready

"Well, apparently they do tonight. Perhaps you are right it could be a test, but somehow it does not feel like one."

She was moving as she spoke, her seax in one hand and a silver bolt in the other. Maldar matched her speed as they attacked from both sides. Aliedori was met with a powerful force and found herself flying through the air again. A searing pain ran from her head to her toes as her back and head made impact with the hard ground. The silver bolt dissolved into nothing. Winded, she stood a little slower this time; her head hurt, she felt drowsy, her eyes grew heavy and her feet and arms grew weak. Despite the energy she drew as her body touched the ground, her seax slipped from her hand. She was unable to focus as she bent over to retrieve her sword; she felt the warm handle with a finger.

"Aliedori!" Maldar screamed her name.

She grabbed the seax and brought it up blindly. The phanthora let out an agonising roar and the light spheres splintered and perished like the embers of a dying fire. Darkness engulfed them and the red eyes glowed brighter.

"I think you only made it angrier." Maldar grabbed his sister's hand and pulled her out of the way of the springing feline. The forest was too dense for it to use its wings effectively.

They hid behind a large tree, breathing deeply.

"Where is that damn dragon when you need her?" Maldar said trying to catch his breath; they both peered cautiously around the tree.

"Whatever it is, it is not a true phanthora," Aliedori said pulling Maldar out of the way just as the giant tree splintered showering them both in fragments from the tree trunk. The creature sprang again, and this time Aliedori was ready, using an incantation she snapped off and lit a branch before handing it to Maldar. She lit another branch, and they both charged at the creature. It faltered as they came hurtling towards it, swerving to avoid the flames and colliding with a bolder. Aliedori tore through forest with the seax in her hand. Then, using the boulder to elevate herself, she opened a gash in the creature's side and watched as luminous fluid oozed from the wound.

"How do you know it's not a true phanthora?"

Aliedori pointed to the ground; the luminous ooze was fading fast instead of setting everything alight.

"It can be hurt, and if that is the case, then we can send it back to the ancestors." Maldar struck the creature with his own sword and more luminous fluid exploded onto the ground. The phanthora howled again.

"I think it's getting bigger, Aliedori. I think each time we wound it, it grows." Aliedori said nothing. A pale shape moved in the shadows. Hurriedly Aliedori dragged Maldar into the dense foliage of the fallen tree.

"There are more of those creatures. Look," she indicated with her sword.

"What's the plan again... send it back to the ancestors?" he sighed as he surveyed the area quickly.

She stood and pulled Maldar to his feet and touched a branch of the tree.

"Return to your place," she commanded, "and tell your sisters of the gift I gave you." Maldar stood still beside her as the splintered bark began to stir.

The sound they heard was like the Realm groaning under the combined weight of a thousand phanthora creeping along the ground, shaking everything; even the mighty oaks trembled and shuddered. When Maldar looked back to the tree, the old oak was standing firm as if it had never been touched. He stumbled and grabbed a small tree to steady himself. From out of the shadows the phanthora appeared. Maldar spun round, his blue eyes now large with fear.

They were surrounded!

He glanced towards his sister who did not appear to notice; her attention was still taken up by the newly reformed tree.

"Whatever you are thinking Alie, please think faster."

"You're right Maldar, this could be a test. If the phanthora's intention is to send us to the ancestors we would be with them by now."

"Test or not, we can still be sent home to the ancest..." Maldar's words died in a scream as a mighty mouth came down and picked him up, flung him into the air then caught him and tossed him again. This time, he was hurled sideways. He spun round in the air and started to fall rapidly. He stopped with a sudden jolt and felt himself being pulled back. Then he was by her side, Aliedori had never used her abilities like that on him before. He collapsed onto his knees and knelt there for a while trembling. He felt her hand on his shoulder, a small comfort, but as she withdrew her hand and he attempted to stand, a slight tremor passed through him.

"A circular pit," he said, "and we are on the inside, trapped." He hoped she had built an escape route into her plans.

"Maldar hold on to me." He did as he was told placing one arm around her waist while the other kept hold of his sword even though it was useless against the magical phanthora. In a last desperate attempt, Maldar slashed out at the approaching creature. Luminous fluid oozed out of each gash and sent a rancid, bitter smoke into the air each time the slime hit the ground. Maldar coughed, clearing the taste from the back of his throat. It was too dark to see the phanthora clearly, only the luminous slime and the red eyes shone in the gloom.

"Maldar, stop doing that! You said yourself that they grow when wounded." Her voice was calm and even, without fear. With renewed strength and purpose Aliedori raised her seax to her lips and Maldar felt a new tremor rock the ground as she uttered the incantation. The serrated, long horn of the drac glowed brightly as did his sword; she dropped the seax.

"Throw your sword into the pit."

"I liked my sword, that was my favourite," he said as he watched it fall.

"We are sending them back home to the ancestors." Jagged rocks, shaped like his sword and her seax appeared like teeth in the pit. The earth around them began to crumble, and broad fissures snaked out in four directions; the jagged razor-like teeth ran through each one.

"Why are we not moving?" It had taken him a while to come to his senses.

She ignored the question and instead wrapped her arm around his waist.

"This would be a good time for Keidrop to be here, hold on." The pit of steel and bone became an endless grinding mouth.

"Return to the Ancestors!" she commanded.

The grinding increased. The ground was disappearing at an alarming rate. The phanthora took their chances and sprang into the air as one.

"Hold on," she said, again her voice still calm, still strong. Maldar did not feel the same so he shut eyes and brought his free arm up to cover his head as a phanthora's gaping maw opened ready to swallow them whole. Maldar felt something wrap around his waist, binding him to Aliedori, then he was swung up, and he felt weightless and small.

When he opened his eyes again he was suspended high above the pit. Aliedori was clutching a vine, and her other arm was wrapped around his waist. He looked down, the ground had disappeared and the last of the phanthora was struggling to get free of the grinding teeth.

Aliedori gripped the vine tighter and turned her face upwards. The moon hit her face covering it in a silver light. She closed her eyes against the cold rays of the moon and drew the silver light into her lungs letting the light restore her energy.

"Take us down," Aliedori commanded.

"Are you sure?"

"Well, we cannot stay up here forever; we still need to get to Skellglade."

"You think the phanthorans are the work of the man-child?" Maldar asked in disbelief.

They were being gently lowered and by the time the ground came up to meet them there were no mouths of steel and bone and no phanthorans, just an abundance of green leaves blanketing the ground with their swords lying on top.

"Poor trees," Aliedori said, not answering his question. She picked up their sword. Maldar took his and replaced it in its sheath. When he looked up she had her palm pressed again an old oak tree that had stood for centuries in the fabled Forest of Souls. Her incantation was, as always, strange but beautiful to his ears. Her voice… her words… came from the breeze, the earth, the moon and the water… all speaking in one voice through her.

"New leaves?" Maldar whispered in awe. He would never get used to her abilities. She said something else, this time she was talking to the trees; he would never get used to that strange secret language either.

"Heal yourself Maldar". We need to free Keidrop."

He rested against a tree and drew on the restorative energy. He felt better, reinvigorated,

"Thank you," he said talking to the tree. Then he turned to Aliedori, "What do you mean, free her?" he demanded.

Maldar turned and rushed back to the spot where he had last seen his golden dragon.

"In the name of the Ancestors," he cried in disbelief as hot fury stung his insides. His beautiful golden dragon was ensnared in a trap of vines and giant makka bushes that had pierced her skin. Wherever they touched her body, small spirals of smoke emitted and blood was dripping from the wounds.

"They are burning her alive!" Aliedori do something!" he shouted, anguish evident in his voice.

"Move back Maldar." When her brother didn't move she shoved past him, took a deep breath and gathered her strength. Her mind was swimming with strange images, each one more violent than the next. She knew she had to stop this; she could not let those images take control, and so gripping her seax she strode forward. She shook her head, trying to eradicate the images from her mind. Her green eyes flashed gold. Aliedori moved through the darkening trees until she was in front of Keidrop who was suspended too high by the vines and thorny bushes for Aliedori to reach her.

"It burns," the dragon said as her golden eyes fluttered open. Her wings were folded at an odd angle and her voice was sharp and filled with pain. There was the smell of burning flesh, unpleasant and cloying in her nostrils.

"Hold still Kei, I will get you free. Maldar I need your help. "Put your hands together like this." She put one booted foot on his interlaced fingers and one hand on his shoulder for balance as he hoisted her up to reached Keidrop. With some difficulty, Aliedori placed a palm against the dragon's face. She held it there for a short while until the dragon visibly relaxed. Her nostrils flared, and smoke was added to the gloom of the forest.

"Put me down now."

Aliedori released a healing light sphere, momentarily penetrating the darkness. It splintered round her, sending shards of light like glowing stars that floated up and settled on the dragon. They worked their way onto her skin and under her scales, healing wherever they touched. Hundreds of giant thorns fell at their feet; they were as long as Maldar's arm, and they watched as they melted into the ground and disappeared. A low rumble of relief was emitted from somewhere deep within the dragon. Aliedori shifted and placed one hand on a vine and the other on the ground and called to the earth to release Keidrop.

Nothing happened.

She tried again, but the vines remained steadfastly green; then she remembered something touching the largest tree.

"Ask your sisters to release my dragon," she commanded and stood back, but Keidrop was sill suspended in the tight coils of vines and bushes that were pulling ever tighter.

"You know me, and you know I did not do this. I did not bring those creatures here." She glanced behind her, and Maldar saw her green eyes flecked with gold for an instant.

"Release my dragon!" she said again. This time, Maldar did not recognise the voice; it seemed to come from somewhere else. Suddenly the vines and thorny bushes sprang back releasing the dragon.

Keidrop crashed to the ground with a mighty thud. Maldar rushed to the side of the motionless dragon, noticing that the burns and cuts were already healing.

"I can't believe you actually argued with trees," Maldar laughed. "And I don't believe that the man-child is responsible for this."

The dragon was breathing easier now and Maldar ran his finger over the dragon's rough scales and down under the chin to his soft spot.

"Neither do I, but a spell did come from Skellglade. We still need to know if it was intended for our mother's people."

"Don't you mean *your* people?" Keidrop was stirring and Aliedori sat down beside them frowning. She waved Maldar's words away with an elegant movement of her slender hand that was run through with steel.

"Besides, I saw the mage responsible, he was still here.
Come on, Keidrop, open your eyes. We have things to do."

The dragon opened her large golden eyes and looked at her two charges curiously but said nothing.

"He is gone, I saw him watching us fight," Aliedori said, replacing her sword in its sheath. As she stood up Keidrop and Maldar also got to their feet. Keidrop unfurled her golden wings, flapped them twice creating a leaf storm; they had healed completely and were free from any scars. Before the small leaf storm could gather momentum, Keidrop and her riders were gone heading west.

The only evidence of a battle was the green blanket of leaves that covered the ground and the few dancing in the draught caused by the dragon.

Chapter 2

The distance from the ridge where Aliedori and Maldar were camping to the settlement was several days' walk. However, Keidrop' back, that distance was covered in no time at all, even with two riders.

Night had fully arrived; the stars were blazing in the sky and the moon was hanging low when Keidrop began her descent to the settlement of Skellglade. She circled once, affording Aliedori ample time to assess whether there was still any danger. Skellglade was a medium-sized settlement with between four and five thousand dwellers, but it was growing all the time thanks to the birth of a mage sixteen cycles of the seasons ago.

The settlement was unnaturally quiet even though it was night; at this time, dwellers would usually be preparing evening meals, drinking at the tavern, partaking in noisy social gatherings in the square, or debating in the community house after a day at their trade. Many outlying settlements chose to model themselves on the city of Fengardia: however, Skellglade retained the traditional layout with the main long house being in the centre.

Tonight it should have been full of the noise and music of dwellers socialising, drinking and debating loudly, but instead it stood quiet. There were lights shining onto the square from the windows, and some of the open doors and smoke drifted up through the chimneys. It was natural for some of the dwellers to be indoors for the night but there should have been plenty of people still in the open square.

The square was large and paved with red, baked bricks. Trees and hanging vines provided shade on seats placed below them, and highly scented flowerbeds offered a welcome distraction.

Where there should have been laughter, noise, and music drifting on the cool evening air, there was silence. There was no movement that Aliedori could see but as Keidrop came closer to the treetops, she saw several figures lying prone on the ground.

"Are they dead?" Maldar asked.

"No," Aliedori said jumping off Keidrop's back before she could land. She walked towards the nearest body, stared for a second and said,

"Just a sleeping incantation, which appears to have been cast over the whole settlement." She bent down to touch the young woman lying at her feet.

"Where is everyone? It's far too early for everyone to be indoors." Maldar walked towards another prone figure with his hand on the hilt of his sword.

"I was thinking the same thing and you won't need that," Aliedori said as she glanced up and saw Maldar was about to unsheathe his sword.

"You won't, but I might," Maldar said kneeling down beside the sleeping form of a very young man. He knew if she said he did not need his sword then he didn't need it, but it was a comfort to feel the hilt in his hand.

"Who could have done this and why?" he asked.

Maldar was looking down at the golden haired man-child who was no more than fifteen.

"This isn't a binding incantation, it's a sleep incantation, and it was placed over a binding one. They were put to sleep after the binding incantation had dispersed." Aliedori didn't answer Maldar's question; she could not answer it yet. The dwellers had retreated inside in fear, with the hope that locking their doors would keep out whatever was happening outside.

Aliedori looked towards one of the dwellings, which had its door open, spilling light out into the yard. The settlement was built around a quadrangle, with the main dwelling, the home of the mage, in the centre. Next to this was the community building. The other dwellings were built around the two main buildings; beyond this was farmland and dwellings stretching into the far distance. The distant fields were full of green wheat, the first of the season that would be ready for harvesting in a few more weeks.

To the left of the dwellings stood several enclosures for messenger animals and beyond these were bare pastures and the fruit orchards. A large and glorious tower was under construction, its foundation a combination of red, baked bricks and strong saplings. The roots, infused with magic, were beginning to thicken; the saplings would grow with each added layer of bricks. The dragon tower was on the opposite side of the riverbank and it showed the growing importance of Skellglade.

Some of the houses were built in the traditional style of wood, moss and reeds – wooden frames with mud and moss walls and reed roofs. The vast majority of the other dwellings were built of either air-fired bricks made from the local red clay soil, sand and water or timber framed.

However, the dwellings still retained a simple rustic look. Rectangles were cut into one of the walls and polished crystal sheets were fitted into smaller rectangles for windows. For the doors, two or three solid planks of wood studded with metal balls were hung from metal hinges with dragon leather.

Aliedori noted with interest that all the dwellings were constructed with a hint of magic. She smiled, the man-child was good, very good indeed, even the older dwellings constructed long before he was born contained magic at their base. Some dwellings were more ornately decorated than others, but they were all simple buildings, built from nature and a little magic for people who made their living from their natural surroundings.

Each dwelling housed a family unit; some were large, three generations living together, while others housed just one or two settlers. The largest house was of fired bricks, ornately decorated with dragons above the entrance. This house belonged to the village leader and Aliedori took it all in.

"Let's see what we can find out from that one over there," she said pointing towards an open door as she moved towards the entrance of the house furthest from the centre. Maldar followed, his sword still in hand; even though Aliedori said it wasn't necessary he felt better having his trusty friend close by. Aliedori looked back at Keidrop; the dragon had found a lump of coke stone under the ground and had started rooting it out.

A low growl emanated from deep within her; she was contented but alert and would strike at a moment's notice. Maldar stepped into the dwelling after Aliedori.

It was simply furnished but with solid and well-crafted wooden furniture. There was a fire set in a large, round, clay pit in the centre of the one-room dwelling; it was surrounded by a double ring of red, baked bricks to prevent the wooden floor from catching fire. The logs were still blazing and the covered pot still bubbling. At one end of the dwelling below the open window stood a table set for two, with a pewter jug of plum wine in the centre. The occupant of this dwelling was not wealthy but they certainly were not poor either. Beneath the table was a chest with a large black dragon clasp that was firmly closed, Aliedori noted with interest. At the other end of the room was a bunk large enough to sleep two and thrown across the end of the bunk was a beautifully print-ed cape. Beside the bunk was a simple but well-made wooden cabinet on top of which lay the brooch that held the cape in place and an ornate comb made from dragon's bone. Aliedori noted these things carefully as they were clear evidence that these people had settled in for the night and were preparing their evening meal, yet now they were gone.

Maldar removed the pot from the fire and doused the flames then followed Aliedori out into the square and into another dwelling. Here the occupants were all asleep; some had collapsed where they stood and fallen to the floor, while others had fallen asleep where they were sitting.

"The sleep charm worked very well, so why use a binding charm as well?" Aliedori asked.

They moved on to another dwelling, its occupants were all pres-ent, it appeared only two houses were empty. They approached the vil-lage leader's house.

"I will wake the settlers." Maldar noticed that Keidrop was no longer eating but lying down by the long house, trying to make herself as comfortable as possible as a prelude to sleep. Her small ears twitched in irritation as Maldar rang out the first toll. A new bridge spanned the river, and on the opposite bank new dwellings were being constructed, more proof that the settlement was growing and would one day be a large, thriving provincial town. Maldar rang the bell that was placed on a plinth in the centre of the square. Aliedori's right hand made the sign of the eight and cast it away. The young male nearest to Maldar began to stir then pulled himself onto his knees, looking around dazed and con-fused. Standing up, he first looked at Maldar and then at Aliedori, but in the twilight he could not make out their features even when Maldar offered him a steadying hand.

The other occupants came out of their houses, some carrying lamps that illuminate the square. Others carried swords and any weap-ons that came to hand as they woke and left their dwellings. Keidrop stirred, raised her golden head, and surveyed the waking settlers. De-ciding that there was no immediate danger she rested her head again on her front legs, pulled her wings over her head and went back to sleep.

Maldar was alert and ready, his right foot planted firmly on the ground and his left leg pivoting in a fighting stance, sword in his hand, poised. When he saw that Aliedori remained unconcerned, her body still relaxed, he crept closer as she had not moved since breaking the incantation.

"Sheath your weapons," Aliedori said. "We are not a threat… Maldar please."

Reluctantly Maldar sheathed his sword but continued to stand by her side.

"I am Avery Le Masson, the appointed. I lead this settlement in the name of the Grand Naturalist. Please name yourself." She still carried a seax and had not sheathed it as requested. Aliedori inclined her head as a sign of natural respect and Maldar followed suit. Avery had been appointed by the Grand Naturalist, Aliedori's mother – appointees were in place to relay edicts, provide order and protect the settlements. In turn the appointee and the people were under the protectorate of the Southern Realm's mandates and laws and the Grand Naturalist's protection.

"I am Aliedori….' she began, but Maldar stopped her.

"Don't, Dori, we will be here all night and don't even start with my name, they might just fall asleep again and this time they won't need a charm." Aliedori turned to him, trying to look stern but a smile crept in turning up the corners of her mouth.

She turned back to the villagers, "I am Aliedori, Intendant and Regent to the Grand Naturalist of the Southern Realm. This is my brother Maldar, dragon knight, also of the Southern Realm."

The villagers all inclined their heads as a sign of respect; they all knew the name and recognised the Grand Naturalist sign that Aliedori wore around her neck. They also recognised the crest of a dragon knight when they saw one, as a great lady had sent her own daughter at their request for an envoy. They were very honoured indeed.

Avery spoke again, "We thought that the settlement was under attack again. Forgive us Intendant, we were not able to identify you in the twilight."

Avery lowered her eyes and began to bend at the waist, but Aliedori stopped her.

"We were on the ridge at Dragon's Rest when we were caught by a binding incantation," Aliedori said. Maldar silently thanked her for her generosity.

"We were attacked earlier despite taking every precaution, and it would seem all barriers have been breached."

"Yes I know," Aliedori said, "it would seem that villagers have been taken from their beds. This time two appear to have been taken; how many others are missing and why was Fengard not informed of the raiders?"

"It is unusual for settlers to go missing," Avery said. "It is even more unusual for them to be taken from their beds."

When Aliedori did not respond, Avery continued, "Strange events have occurred since this new moon; a number of the settlers have vanished during the hours of darkness. We have woken to empty beds and dwellings, unable to explain where they have gone."

Aliedori began to pace, her arms behind her back, head down. The settlers mumbled amongst themselves; Avery hushed them and moved towards the community hall. They followed her in, leaving Aliedori, Maldar and the man-child alone in the yard. Aliedori continued to pace and the man-child moved towards her, but Maldar put a hand on his shoulder stopping him. After a while Aliedori paused, looking at them both, then resting her eyes on the mage she said, "Hello Athelstan Le Masson, do you remember me?"

When the young man said nothing, Aliedori gestured with her hand, "Shall we go and join your mother and the others?"

Chapter 3

Aliedori strode away, but the man-child remained where he was until Maldar gave him a gentle push on the shoulder to get him moving. They entered the long, two-storey building, which, like the dwelling houses, had a wooden floor and clay-baked brick walls. But, unlike the other houses, the hall was highly decorated and had a minstrel gallery overlooking a huge fire pit. The ground floor was one large room and on the upper floor, apart from the minstrel gallery, there was a balcony that ran halfway around the wall and was accessed by a wide wooden staircase leading from the floor below.

Hanging from the minstrel gallery were two large tapestries, one, a portrait of the Mother, the first Naturalist of Fengardia, the other of her mother. The ground floor was where the dwellers met with the appointee to resolve conflicts, to celebrate handfast ceremonies, new life and to pass on information and instructions from the Grand Naturalist.

Upstairs, was a place that travellers and traders could use as a resting place and have a welcome break. A fire had been burning in the central clay pit and the embers were still smouldering. Aliedori tossed several logs on the fire. The charm ensured that the wood caught instantly to illuminate the centre of the hall and spread quickly out as far as it could reach; the fire was for illumination rather than warmth. She raised her arm and the candles attached to the wall-mounted sconces around the room ignited in unison. Once the hall was lit, she could see everyone and every one could see her and Maldar clearly for the first time. Maldar, who had seen this trick so many times before, raised an eyebrow at her. It was also part of what she had been trying to teach him since they were children. Aliedori and Maldar waited patiently for the settlers to take in their surroundings. Aliedori did not wear a head covering but dark green silken ribbon wrapped in circles round two thick plaits that hung down each shoulder. She wore a choker of gold that tapered down into the shape of an eye and rested on her chest bone.

The emerald green jewellery in the centre was the same colour as her eyes. Her clothes were made from pelt, the softly malleable second skin of a dragon. Once cured, the dragon second skin was soft enough to wear against the skin of even a new born baby, but it was almost impenetrable as well as waterproof.

Aliedori was wearing the dragon pelt over a thin linen tunic that ended mid-thigh, held at the waist by a dragon pelt belt. Attached to the belt were two small pouches and a long knife called a seax, as well as a small curved sword worn in a scabbard. The scabbard was decorated with the same emerald green stones as the eye in her choker. Beneath the over tunic Aliedori wore dragon pelt leggings as closely fitting as the dragon pelt top, and on her feet she wore dragon leather boots held in place by straps crisscrossing around her legs and tied in place by a buckle just below her knees.

Maldar was dressed in a similar vein, except his tunic stopped short of his thighs and he wore an ankle length sleeveless dragon pelt over his tunic, which was slit at the back and held together by the belt of his scabbard. Neither wore capes, the warm weather precluding the need for them.

Maldar was well built, standing six foot four inches, with gentle features and, like his sister, his nose was small.

He had clean, shaven, light brown complexion with dark brown hair, loose strands of which perfectly framed his handsome oval face. His wide, blue eyes were framed by thick brown brows set in a face of contentment. Broad shoulders tapered to a narrow waist and he was blessed with well-muscled arms and a torso, which was testament to many hours of training with the blade. The tunic that clung to his body as he moved enhanced Maldar's wide shoulders and flat stomach, making him appear more powerfully built then he really was.

As they entered Avery's dwelling, Aliedori saw the protective rune displayed on one wall. Like the rest of the settlement, the displayed runes carried her mother's markings. Her mother was protector and leader of the Southern Realm and for her runes to have failed the settlers when they needed them the most was unthinkable.

Yet the runes, Aliedori could see, appeared to be working well, and they were undamaged. She would inspect them before leaving and reinforce their protectiveness by casting an incantation. The runes carried her mother's magic; they protected the settlement from bandits and raiders and no one should have been able to break the charm. Yet someone was powerful enough to override her mother's incantation, enter the settlement and take her people. It didn't make sense – there were no bandits or raiders out there who commanded such power. In order to break the charm, the runes must be broken and their magic siphoned off. Who would dare do such a thing? Aliedori's eyes rested on her mother's runes for a few seconds then, she turned the same emerald gaze to the man-child standing before her. Aliedori placed a hand on his shoulder.

"Can you tell us what happened?" she asked.

"Come and sit, please." Avery offered Aliedori an ornate seat on the raised dais at the head of the long table. Aliedori thanked her and took a seat but not the seat offered. She sat and with an open palm gesture and an inclination of her head as she asked the others to join her. Avery took her rightful seat; Maldar took a seat between Aliedori and the young mage. The settlement elders were all seated and as the hall began to fill, the chatter became louder as everyone was eager for their stories to be heard. Someone tossed another piece of wood on the fire and stoked it before taking their place amongst the dwellers. Aliedori watched the sparks fly and for a moment she thought she saw something in those sparks.

Food and drinks began to appear as if from nowhere and were placed on the table; cold cuts of meat, pickles, and fruit were joined by meats of the ocean. Aliedori wasn't hungry, but she knew it was part of the welcome. She and Maldar had not so long ago finished off a meal enough for four people and had drunk at least as much berry wine. She was after all the daughter of the Grand Naturalist.

A silver goblet was placed in front of her and filled with fruit wine. She raised the goblet along with the others, a blessing was offered to the ancestors, and she and her mother accepted it. The wine was refreshing and she drank with good grace. Slightly light-headed, she turned over the empty goblet in front of her indicating that she did not want more.

Aliedori took a breath and turned to the young mage, smiling, her head already clearing.

"So, a binding spell Athelstan, very well thought out," she said.

The man-child flushed. He was used to having the attention; as a mage he was expected to provide a public service. But he was a naturally quiet boy who was more interested in his studies; to have such a pretty woman's full attention was a little overwhelming. She was the daughter of the Grand Naturalist and all the eyes of the settlement were gleaming with pride, as a compliment paid to the mage was indeed a compliment to them all. Although Avery was his mother, he was also the child of all the settlers. Athelstan knew what he wanted to say but still fumbled for the right words. He was about to speak when he realised that she knew his name and that it was the second time she had addressed him by his given name. She knew who he was. He was almost struck dumb again by the knowledge and he turned to his mother. She seemed so far away at the head of the table, but he looked to her for guidance as he always did, and she smiled. Athelstan would only be seventeen at the next cycle of the season, and he was already showing signs of becoming a powerful mage. Unlike Aliedori, Athelstan was not born with magic; he had developed the ability while still a yearling. But the power to control some aspect of nature was in his blood, magic ran through his very being. The Realm had many mages, but few were born with magic.

It was said that when Aliedori was born her first cries almost caused the palace to flood. Such was her distress at leaving the watery home of her mother's womb that she wanted to return. Athelstan developed the ability to cast simple spells by the time he could talk, but Aliedori's abilities started the moment she was born. As with all mages, he was introduced at court once his abilities began to appear. By the time Athelstan was eight cycles, he and Avery made their third journey to Fengardia for classification and registration. There were three classifications: one – nature was used as a source of power, thus the user had a limitless supply of magic; two – the user drew magic from within but could use aspects of nature to replenish themselves; and three – the user's magic was achieved through alchemy. Athelstan was classified as a two, but Aliedori was not sure that was the correct classification.

"Do you remember?" she asks again. Every aspect of the journey had overwhelmed Athelstan; in particular the vast shining city and the merriment he had seen at the court. He did remember, however, the Intendant, she had sat with him talking, doing tricks and making him laugh and that memory would remain with him forever. At the time the Intendant was almost the age Athelstan was now.

Athelstan nodded and Aliedori winked at him, making him flush all over again. He spoke before he lost the ability.

"The binding spell was to capture the dragon riders that came out of the West," Athelstan spoke softly.

"Do you know for sure that they came out of the West?" Maldar asked the young mage, who nodded again and continued.

"A message was sent out to Fengardia after the first riders appeared and while we waited for a response the raiders returned. The binding spell was my attempt to keep the raiders here until help came."

Maldar was listening attentively and heard the uncertainty in the mage's voice. He patted him on the shoulder and, looking directly into the man-child's eyes, he said, "You cast an amazing incantation, the only problem is it rebounded and we... well, I was caught by it. Aliedori freed me as she did with the sleeping spell. Never doubt your abilities Athelstan," he praised the young mage. Aliedori explained that the city had not received the message and they were only there because of the binding charm.

"Athelstan, the binding spell was a good idea and would have worked well, but the mage who cast the sleep spell was very powerful," Aliedori told him.

"What is known about the rider, can you tell me about him?

"Riders," Athelstan corrected her. "I think that I may be the only one who has seen them," he said after a brief pause while he gathered his thoughts.

"Work had ceased for the day, and everyone was preparing for the night as it began to get dark. I left by the east gate to the sound of laughter, families in the square, ordinary daily life. I checked the runes as I always do then went to collect night balms and other flowers that only bloom at night. I crossed the bridge to talk to the tower builders and infuse the saplings. I was collecting some plants that only grow on the branches of other trees. I was about to climb down from the tree when I saw the first dragon." Athelstan paused for a while, lost in thought. "I remember thinking how wonderful it would be when our first dragon tower is completed. The dragons appeared black against the full moon as I sat in the crook of the tall tree watching. I was not worried when they did not fly over, even though I was uneasy as I watched them. They hovered for some time then swooped down in the middle of the settlement, when they took off again they had settlers with them."

Uneasiness fell over the hall, and the settlers began to mumble amongst themselves. Avery put up her hand silencing them at once. The implication was now clear to them as it had been to Aliedori for some time.

Athelstan continued, "It took me a moment or two to realise that I could no longer hear music. The music had followed me when I crossed the bridge and out into the forest, but now there was silence. I cast a binding spell and climbed from the tree. It took all my powers to keep awake and then return home.

But the dragons and riders were caught, or so I thought. I rushed to the bell to summon the settlers and wake them from their unnatural sleep. But I fell under the charm before I could break the incantation," Athelstan finished.

Aliedori and Maldar exchanged a meaningful glance but did not speak. No one else spoke and the entire group sat in silence until an older settler stood and spoke.

"I saw them also. I was out beyond the wall on the other side of the bridge when I spotted them. They were not black, they were something else altogether and so were the riders," the old man said.

"Thank you, Morton," said Avery and Aliedori inclined her head towards the settler also.

"Where did they come from and where did they go?" Aliedori asked, but before she could get a reply someone else asked a question.

"How did you come to be here?" The voice came from dwellers near the door and Maldar answered.

"As I explained earlier, I was caught in Athelstan's binding incantation, we came here as Aliedori believed it could only have come from this settlement," he said. He turned to continue speaking but Aliedori stopped him by drawing the conversation back to Athelstan.

"So young mage," her voice slightly raised until she got the settlers attention again.

However, before she could continue, Avery spoke, "Athelstan shows great talent in the natural arts. I can remember the first time his laughter brought fresh stem growth from his baby basket."

It was not just a mother's boast, or an appointee trying to defend the actions of the young mage, it was a reminder that Athelstan was still only a child and the expectation of him was always great.

"Already this season we had to extend the settlement across the river as another five hundred new settlers arrived and I believe that more are on their way." Aliedori raised her hand as a sign to placate Avery, Skellglade was still called a settlement but it had long since stopped being one. It was now the size of a small town, and the larger it grew the more demands would be made on the mage and the appointee. Skellglade had doubled and tripled in size since Athelstan's birth and very soon the Southern Realm would have a second city.

Aliedori raised her hand again, "Athelstan did very well; not only did he bind the riders he bound the dragons too. The Ancestors have smiled on this settlement and we must offer tributes in thanks. But sometimes it would be nice if they asked if you wanted it or at least warned you first."

This brought much needed laughter and broke the tension in the hall. Maldar gave Aliedori's hand a secret squeeze. To be the vessel for magic was a great responsibility, and sometimes it was a responsibility Aliedori didn't want, though she had never said as much and had always accepted her faith with grace.

"It is good that the settlement is growing. It will be of considerable note and I give my blessing upon the settlement and its settlers old and new and those who come in peace."

Aliedori finished and picked up a plum and, biting into it, closed her eyes. The hall fell silent and Aliedori opened her eyes. What had she done, had she broken some protocol by biting into the fruit? She sat up in the chair. She had been sinking farther and farther down as Athelstan told his tale and now she sat to attention again. She turned to Maldar for guidance but he was looking towards the head of the table. Avery was smiling and thanking the Intendant for her generous blessing bestowed on the people and the settlement. Avery's face, though, clearly showed surprise at having a blessing bestowed upon them, but she accepted it with good grace and allowed the settlers to do the same. Maldar wondered if Aliedori should have blessed the settlement, as a naturalist as powerful as her meant the blessings could be more than just words.

Chapter 4

Maldar knew that Aliedori would sometimes have to be careful what she said. Because words are not always just words, not for his sister, sometimes words were actions. Fear, pain, hate – sometimes her words were so big and powerful it could change things forever. He had been sitting next to her all evening; he had felt her barely contained emotions; pent up anger at the dragon raiders. Pride, she was very proud of Athelstan and she was proud of their mother's people, but frustrated too with herself for not following her instincts when she first sensed something was wrong.

This blessing gave her heightened emotions, which could go way beyond simple words. He felt it and he was sure the settlers could feel the blessing spreading, carried by the breeze amongst the trees, to the crops and plants surrounding the settlement. Moving beneath their feet into the earth and spilling into the river, the blessing reverberated through the settlement bringing the settlers into the square. Illumination spheres sited high on poles lit paths to and from the square and even across the river. Bright spheres were strung over the bridges connecting the older part of the settlement with the new development. The bridges reminded Maldar of Fengardia, but instead of white marble they were made of red bricks. Maldar was sure that most of the settlers were now crammed into the hall and was glad to be outside, even though the square was now full too as those who could not fit in the hall had spilled out into the square. The settlement was alive with songs, harps and all manner of musical instruments. He could take no more of the din inside and had slipped out with some of the elders. The minstrels had started a song and now everyone joined in… well, almost everyone. Athelstan, Avery and Aliedori were still sitting at the table in silence while the other elders of the settlement joined in the celebration. Athelstan had studied Aliedori's face carefully when she gave the blessing; the words had come from her heart and he wondered if she realised what she had done.

Athelstan had seen the light sparked in her eyes as it had done when she lit the hall. The vision had frightened him and scared him even more as he felt the blessing spread. He was sure that no one else was able to feel it until he saw Maldar's face. Athelstan felt and saw the fine hair on the back of his hand rise and a strange feeling almost overwhelmed him; he had to close his eyes for a second to calm himself. He was the mage of this settlement, and not all settlements were lucky enough to have one born within their walls. That was blessing enough, and Aliedori's small blessing made him realise that no matter how powerful he became, he would never possess even a quarter of the power she had now. He whispered her name, and he knew she heard him even though his voice was barely audible to himself, because Aliedori looked at him,

"You are a good and competent mage Athelstan, and your incantations will get more powerful, it's only a matter of time. Please tell me again what happened, we need to know in which direction they were taken."

Aliedori paused waiting for Athelstan to speak, and when he did not she placed a palm over his and said, "Tell me?"

Athelstan looked directly at his mother for the first time since the two visitors had appeared.

"I can't be sure, but when the first settlers went missing, along with my best friend, I sent trackers."

"Trackers? Where are your trackers? Please can I talk to them?" Aliedori asked. Avery sent a messenger to get the keepers of trackers to bring them to the community house. While they waited Athelstan continued with his tale.

"I know they went into the West because I commanded a Gem to follow the raiders." Aliedori acknowledged that without Athelstan's swift action no one would know where the settlers were taken. Athelstan was silent now and remained looking at his mother for a while, then turned his gaze towards the flickering flames in the centre of the room.

Aliedori spoke, "The runes were drained by powerful dark magic, but I will restore them before we leave. The blessing and the runes will make the settlement safe from those who may come with intent to cause harm," she said. Her hand behind back she continued, "After we talk to the trackers I think we should take a look to see if we can find out anything."

Athelstan nodded, knowing without her needing to say that she was not going to return to Fengardia without first trying to find out more. They walked out into the night air, and youngsters who were all vying for his attention soon surrounded Maldar. The keepers brought the trackers into the square and they approached Aliedori as Maldar joined her. Aliedori attempted to find out what had happened, but was not able get much more from them than Athelstan except: *"The raiders flew into the West and when they landed we followed them but then the raiders disappeared. We searched the area where they landed but we could not find any trace of them. The air crackled with magic but the place was dank and evil,"* the young blue Gem explained.

"Can you remember where this place was?" Maldar asked.

"About four days flight into the West. There is nothing there in that part of the forest now, even the nymphs do not go there."

Aliedori thanked the keeper, and the little gems. Turning to Avery and Athelstan she asks if they have seen any nymphs in the area. Both confirmed that it was unusual to see nymphs outside the neutral forest. Aliedori said goodbye to Avery before she and Athelstan went off to restore her mother's runes with magic.

Athelstan was unhappy to be left, as he did not trust his powers and wondered if he could really protect the settlers. Aliedori assured him that he could, with the aid of the fully restored runes and the blessing. She also promised to make sure that her mother sent help, even though she knew that he did not really need it.

Aliedori found Maldar with Keidrop who was being fed coke stone by the children of the settlers. Maldar shooed the children away, sending them scurrying back to their parents and the celebration. A blessing should be celebrated every time, especially such a powerful one.

They were about to mount Keidrop when Athelstan came into view and walked towards Aliedori. With hands together, he bowed deeply before she could stop him. She thought all this bowing and scraping would have to stop, but said out loud,

"You are a fine mage Athelstan; you will be finer still with time. It only becomes a problem if you cannot find the solution, and that is yours and yours alone to find."

The man-child thought for a moment, then smiled knowingly as if he had already discovered the solution to the problem. He thanked her, but his thanks were lost in the beat of the powerful dragon wings.

Athelstan stood alone on the bank of the river, the draught caused by the beating of the dragon's wings almost knocked him off his feet. He swayed but remained strong as he knew he would have to in the coming weeks and months. Soon the Intendant and the dragon knight were airborne and he watched until they were just tiny specks disappearing towards the Western skies. He turned and walked back through the gate into the settlement and the questioning eyes of his mother. Tomorrow would be a good time to answer questions he thought and walked in the opposite direction in search of a new best friend.

Chapter 5

It was not unusual for the people of the Southern Realm to tell stories about the West, especially as its borders were firmly closed to the other Realms. Wild tales could be heard at dragon's tower and harbour's side at any time across the Realm, especially when the storytellers were spiced with ales and fruit wines. Aliedori had heard some of these tales. The Western mages had chosen to withdraw from the other Realms long before they tried to take the Eastern Realm's magic by petrifying their forest. They might have been closed as far back as their war on magical creatures; that had been the when many dragons and other beautiful creatures were almost lost forever.

But stories begat stories, each one wilder than the last and so the West had become a narrative for the chroniclers. The vast swathe of land was double protected on some sides and triple protected on one side by the Trees of Souls. Few ventured out and even less crossed into the West. Those that did were mostly traders. But traders were prohibited from entering the inner walls and trading posts were set up either outside the walls or between the inner and outer walls, thus keeping contact to a minimum.

Aliedori knew very little about the West except traders' tales, children's stories designed to keep children from misbehaving. She had also heard her parents' stories and some tales from Wulfgar of the Last Battle. But it was her father's role in the Last Battle that captured the imagination of the chroniclers and the storytellers alike. The battle to hold the Dragon's Gate was known throughout the Realm and was celebrated in the Eastern Realm. Sometimes Aliedori got the impression that all her father wanted was to forget that it had ever happened. Her father did not think of the victory and the small part he had played. What her father thought of most of all was the senseless loss of lives and his fallen comrades and friends in the Dragon Watch. Her father had told her once that The Last Battle was not a magical war.

While many mages and naturalists were used to enhance weapons and warriors' abilities, the battle was mainly of warriors' strength and determination, and the West only lost because they underestimated the East's desire to remain free. Her father's small band of dragon lords and knights had held the gate until reinforcement arrived. They did not come from the allies but from the warriors of the Eastern Realm itself.

The moon hung low, and the sky was a blanket of bright, dancing, tiny spheres. The three had been flying for some time, and Aliedori had lapsed into an uneasy silence. Maldar wondered how the talk of a planned night camping in the forest with his sister had turned into a hunt for stolen settlers in the West.

All he'd wanted to do was to tell Aliedori about his proposal and get her on his side. Together they would tell their parents about his intended pair bond to a wood nymph. In the morning, they would have returned home, and with Aliedori as his ally, their parents wouldn't have stood a chance against the two of them. Both sets of parents would spend the remainder of this cycle planning a feast to celebrate the bonding ceremony for the next spring. What could be simpler, Maldar wondered? Aliedori's voice came to him suddenly, full of empathy and understanding as if she knew his thoughts. "I'm sorry, Mally," it was the name she called him when she knew he was angry with her, or when she wanted him on her side.

He had used the same term of endearment with her name only this morning. He had asked her to go with him and Keidrop to camp in the woods. She had looked up from what she was doing, her green eyes full of suspicion after he had called her Dori, not once but for the second time. She instantly said "yes" before knowing what he wanted. That was why he loved her so much. She was his sister, his ally and his best friend. She was not the future ruler of the Southern Realm; she was just his sister and would always be. They would do anything for each other, so later in the afternoon when she showed up with an overnight pack he was not surprised. Aliedori rested her forehead against his left shoulder and her remaining words, if there were any, were lost in his clothes. He picked up her hand bringing it to his lips to give it a gentle kiss, followed by a squeeze before releasing it.

"What did you tell Athelstan?" he wanted to know.

"Nothing," she sighed, her forehead still resting against him, "just about his own binding spell."

"Oh, I see you showed him what needed fixing but not how to fix it. What else was there, something else was said, I saw it in your faces?"

"How could you possibly see it in my face when your back was to me?" Aliedori responded.

"What else, Dori?" Maldar demanded.

"Athelstan believes that the settlers will not be returning," Aliedori said sadly.

"Do you think so too... no, you know that for certain. Down, Keidrop," Maldar commanded.

Keidrop descended as Aliedori tried to protest, but Maldar ignored her.

"Find a clearing and take us down Keidrop."

A sudden wave of anger washed over Maldar as he swung his legs over Keidrop's neck to dismount and jumped the last few feet. He was on the ground, pacing, before the dragon had landed.

Maldar didn't know why he was so angry. His sister had done nothing wrong. Aliedori had always had magical powers but there was so much that had changed since her last name day and she continued to change. Her powers were magnifying and developing, and new powers were manifesting themselves almost daily. Maldar witnessed these changes in his sister, not only because she gave him an almost daily update, but because he could perceive them himself, and he was almost overwhelmed by them.

If *he* felt overwhelmed by them, then how was *she* feeling? Maldar calmed a little. He watched Aliedori as she slid off Keidrop's back then patted the great dragon's neck and sent her off to rest or root around for tasty coke stone. Aliedori turned to Maldar, her usual calm and serene features showing confusion, sympathy and sadness in equal measure.

"First of all brother, Athelstan is a mage; he can see aspects of what is happening, just as I do. He has not told his mother or the other settlers that their loved ones are lost, and he asked my advice. And secondly, why are you so mad at me? What did I do? Stand still, will you?"

Maldar stopped, her command bringing him to complete standstill in mid-stride. Realising her mistake she mumbled, "I didn't mean it that way." She really would have to start learning to differentiate between a command and a request.

Maldar completed the stride, and he was about to turn and pace in the opposite direction when he caught a glimpse of his sister's face.

"What did you do?" he asked, no longer angry, his anger having disappeared as quickly as it had arrived.

"Nothing, something small, very small, really... really tiny... small, tiny," she measured it with her index finger and thumb.

Then Maldar remembered what she had said.

"You stopped me... really Aliedori you will have to control your magic more successfully. If it happens again I'm telling mother, you are not allowed to use magic if you can't control it. Maldar sounded like a petulant kid, but it was all a put on.

"I didn't mean it," Aliedori said, more than a little ashamed. "I didn't know it was a command until it came out, but you made me so, so..."

Her voice trailed off under the assault of her brother's blue-eyed gaze. Unable to keep a straight face any longer, Maldar grinned. They had never been able to be angry at each other for long.

"You should have seen your face," he laughed. "You owe me big time, Dori."

"What about all the times you owe me," she countered.

"Well, they don't all count."

"Yes, they do, they all count. I don't see why they shouldn't count; think of all the times I've bailed you out."

"You are my big sister; you should be looking out for me."

When Aliedori did not reply, Maldar realised that she was in the midst of two conversations at the same time, one with him and the other with the owl sitting on a low branch just above their heads.

"We can stop here for the night; Kastillion is going south and has agreed to take a message to our parents of our whereabouts and what has happened."

Maldar was about to comment when the owl hooted and flew off. He watched it quickly disappear amongst the trees.

"So we are going into the West?" Maldar asked, throwing himself onto the ground.

It wasn't a question, it was more of a statement of fact, and she nodded her head, watching him. Aliedori knew that Maldar was not as calm as he appeared. Like his sister, there were times when his outward calm belied the fire inside, and this was one of those moments. Aliedori knew her brother well and knew when to challenge and when to ignore it.

Maldar had calmed somewhat but she knew that it would not take much for his fury to spill out again. This time she chose a third option, but first said, "There is a place the trackers spoke of, we need to go there." When Maldar said nothing she tried again, this time with a goblet of fruit wine.

"Finish telling me about your intended," Maldar smiled and Aliedori knew that her tact had worked, at least for a while anyway. Maldar needed her on his side to face their parents.

"Okay, you build a shelter and I will collect firewood and build a fire," Maldar said and reached around where he was sitting to pick up the dry wood.

"Or I can do both. After all, I owe you 'big time'." Maldar watched as vines and saplings began to entwine, moving until they were completely interwoven with each other around the trunks of the surrounding trees creating a structure with sides and a roof. The moss inside the shelter appeared to thicken, and at the same time dry wood, twigs and leaves gathered in a pile and appeared to light themselves. Maldar stared at her.

"You suck the fun out of everything," he said, poking fun at his sister and in return, she stuck her tongue out at him. Maldar had always been in awe of her, even as a small child, but he was also very proud.

Her power was beyond anything he had ever known, and somehow he knew that she was capable of so much more... more than any naturalist or mage that had gone before, even their mother. Aliedori had asked him to talk about Waifyn, but that could wait, there was a more pressing matter at hand.

"Whoever is doing this, taking the settlers I mean, need to be stopped. I am sure that Skellglade is not the only settlement where settlers have been taken." The fire was now blazing and he watched it for a while. "The place the trackers spoke of could be where the settlers have been taken."

Aliedori said nothing; of course she was sure that Skellglade was not the only place to have lost its settlers. There were other settlements on the Western boarders and closer, too. She sent an image of what she had taken from the trackers mind. Maldar would have been impressed if he wasn't trying so hard and failing to suppress a shudder.

"We need to visit Stornvale and the other settlements along the borders, but we first need to make sure that our people are safe," Alie-dori said. Maldar nodded in agreement, but what he really wanted to do was to climb on Keidrop's back and head into the West. However, he wanted to put off venturing into the place Aliedori had shown him for as long as possible.

If he arrived and the settlers weren't there he would get back on Keidrop and fly to Fengardia. He knew that the last thing he should do was fly off into unknown danger into the path of an unknown enemy. In order to find the settlers they needed a plan of action and more information. Maldar knew that Aliedori was right; first make sure that the other settlements were protected then find out who was taking them and where.

"So we fly to Stornvale now?" Maldar asked signalling for Kei-drop. Aliedori stopped him with one look and spoke as if to a child.

"If the settlers are taken by bandits on dragons at night, then us appearing on a dragon larger than…" Maldar did not let Aliedori finish.

"Okay, okay, I know!" Maldar said pacing, sometimes he hated Aliedori's serenity and calmness but that was the way she approached everything. He could not remember the last time he had seen her angry and he sometimes wondered if indeed she ever got angry. At other times her anger could shake the ground if she allowed it. At the moment they had no idea who the enemy was except that they may have come out of the West.

Maldar knew that the outward apparent calmness and serenity hid her true feelings. He also knew that she was worried about what they would find when they reached the settlements. She worried also about the strange '*dead*' place the trackers '*showed*' her but most of all she was frightened for his safety. Maldar believed that there were still many aspects of her new, emerging magic that she could not control fully, and flying into an area where there were almost certainly bandits was dangerous and very unwise. While they were battle-trained and skilled with their swords, neither of them had ever used their skills against another being other than in practise.

Chapter 6

The West was a closed Realm. It had chosen its isolation; or rather the grand mage Erostol had ordered its closure, after his people collected saplings from the heart of the Tree of Souls and planted them along its borders. Within a week, with the aid of spells and magic siphoned from the slain magical creatures, the trees had grown into an impenetrable barrier. The chroniclers were never sure whether Erostol erected the barriers to keep the Realms out or his people in. All those on the wrong side of the fortress were given just four days to return or be locked out forever.

Only those with magical powers – mages and naturalists – were allowed in after the allotted four days. Many lost families, homes and businesses. Settlers from other Realms were given the same allotted time to leave. They became self-contained and self-sufficient and trading with the other Realms was only done with the agreement from the Grand Mage, Erostol. The last brutal attack the Western Realm led was against the Eastern Realm. When the battle was over and the dead had been sent to the ancestors it was discovered that the Western warriors had taken all their dead with them. Erostol led the war against magical creatures many centuries before and therefore could not still be the leader of the Western Realm. Human life was long, and humans with magical powers could live even longer. Could Erostol still be alive?

Aliedori looked at Maldar. His chin was touching his chest and he appeared to be asleep, but she knew he was not, he was thinking and she did not need to draw an image from his mind to know what he was thinking about. They were going into the unknown. Dark magic was being used to steal settlers from their beds, and the raiders were using dragons. They were using what appeared to be black dragons. Aliedori knew that whatever colour the raiders' dragons were they could not be black, but the significance was not lost on her and neither would it be on other people.

She pulled her legs up and rested her chin on her knees as she continued to watch her brother through half-closed lids. Powerful magic was certainly being used to change the dragons' colours. The chronicles of the black dragons of the Petrified Forest were well known to everyone and whichever side the dragons took, victory was sure to follow. While the black dragons were not of the Petrified Forest, they were the guardian symbols of the Eastern Realm. They, nonetheless, came to be identified with the protection of the forest. The dragons would not, could not, be influenced by magic. As magical creatures themselves, it would take a very powerful mage to harness that enchantment. The black dragons of the Eastern Realm were powerful symbols that gave hope and inspiration to all. They were the true protectors of the Eastern Realm, and whoever was stealing settlers wanted the Realms to believe that the East was behind it.

It didn't matter at this point who was taking the settlers, what mattered was why. Were they stealing Southern settlers and implicating the East for the purpose of starting a conflict between allies? Could it be that simple? With the East isolated from its only ally, it would be ripe for the taking and the West could walk in and take it. But they had tried before, and it had not worked even after freezing the forest where most of the Eastern magic came from. It had not worked then, and it would not work this time, but what had changed? What was so different this time that the Western Realm felt that they could strike another blow?

These were questions that Aliedori did not have the answers to, but the first part was easy. The colour was meant to fool people into believing that the raiders were from the East. Thanks to Athelstan's quick thinking in using Gems to track their bigger cousins, no one would know where to start to search for answers. Aliedori tried to remember if there was ever a time when black dragons did not feature in parables of truth, honesty and loyalty. Someone was trying to destroy, or at least raise doubt, about the reputation of the protectors of the legendary Petrified Forest of the East. For the Guardians to switch allegiance meant that they had given up hope of the forest ever returning to life. Therefore all hope for the Eastern magic was lost forever. Aliedori refused to believe that this was the case. Of course while magic was mainly associated with the life of the forests, magic was found in everything and everywhere and all classifications but only naturalists or mages knew how to harness it.

"Black dragon," Maldar said slowly.

Aliedori smiled and raised her eyes, then her head and looked at him. He had clearly been thinking along the same lines as her.

"Would they leave the East and the forest to petrifaction? Honesty and friendship are surely about remaining until the forest is restored."

"Truth, honesty and above all loyalty," she corrected, "is the motto. Have you ever read the chronicles?"

He looked at her.

"Are you sure we are related?"

As soon as she said it, she wondered if it was a mistake. This was not the time to remind Maldar he was a foundling. He was already angry, not with her but at the disappearance of the settlers. Not that it mattered to her that they were not blood, she loved Maldar beyond words, and he could not be closer to her heart if he were blood. He was as close as any blood brother could be. He had stopped his pacing sometime ago and thrown himself in frustration on a tree trunk, planting his chin on his chest. The pacing was Aliedori's thing, not his, and he had soon warned himself. He stood deliberately and with purpose and walked towards her, stopping directly in front of her. He offered her his hand; it hung before her just out of eye level. When she did not move, he offered it again, this time more forcefully. She took his hand and ended up holding it in hers. Maldar wondered how she managed to do that.

He said, "Look at me."

She looked up and into his eyes.

"You are my sister, no matter that your parents' skin is a different shade from mine, you are the only family I have. I know and will always know that I belong," he continued to hold Aliedori's gaze. "You found me and took me into your home, but most importantly into your hearts. I have never doubted for one moment of my life that I was loved. Even those rare occasions when I made it impossible to love me, you loved me more."

Aliedori released his hand but said nothing. Maldar leaned forward, grabbed her shoulders and dragged her to her feet. He caught her face between his hands and kissed her forehead before pulling her plait in fun. "And yes, we are related," he said, "beyond blood." Aliedori laughed nodding her head. "Wow, my brother the big speech maker, not just a dumb dragon lord."

"And don't you forget it," Maldar swelled and threw his shoulders back, his chest out and lifted his head high and began to strut around like that until Aliedori spoke in a quiet voice. "I know you sometimes wonder where you came from. That is why we visit Dragon's Rest so often; there is that small part of you that wants answers". Maldar suddenly became deflated and stopped in mid stride. She never failed to surprise him.

"Should we know each other so well?" he asked. She did not reply but then he was not expecting her to.

"Anyway, as I was saying, if you'd ever pick up a chronicle once in a while you would realise the black dragons were the ones who helped save many of the people when the forest was first petrified. Had it not been for the mages, many settlers would have perished along with the forest or so the legend goes.

As you know, the legend has it that the mages were able to assume the shapes of whatever creatures they wanted. When the forest was frozen those mages took the shape of dragons and because they were wearing black, the dragons became black also. Before the great magical purge the mages could change shape between human and other forms as often as they chose.

However, after the purge there was only enough magic for one transformation a year. The mages agreed that they would use whatever magic was left to protect the Realm in whatever way possible, so they swore to guard the Eastern Realm until all life returned to the forest. They swore to always tell the truth and be loyal to the people, the forest and to each other. Hence, truth, honesty and loyalty."

Aliedori paused catching her breath, still watching Maldar and resting her elbow against Keidrop. She patted the ground beside her and Maldar joined her. She did not want him to forget about the invitation to talk about Waifyn, but for the moment, there were other things on both their minds. If the dragons were truly black then there was a mage powerful enough to control ten ancient mages with the power to change shapes. The Eastern Realm would certainly be lost if the black dragons were set to a new purpose. But who was so powerful that they impelled the dragons to change allegiance? To cause them to leave their sacred duty, forest and the people they were sworn to protect.

This was all speculation, of course, fragments of information to fit the Daemon of the West. Either the chroniclers were wrong and dragons do change alliances or Athelstan had been mistaken. Maldar doubted the young mage was wrong, and he knew that the chroniclers were beyond question. An extremely powerful naturalist had to be using very dark magic to command the black dragons. Commanding a creature of magic was not an easy task; magical creatures must have a willingness to submit their will. To command them to go against their nature was virtually impossible, and could even be beyond the power of Aliedori. Somehow, it appeared that was exactly what had been done, or were these different dragons or the offspring of the forest guardians? The black dragons of the Eastern Realm would not have given up their eggs without a fight to the death. Maldar had not read enough of the chronicles to know whether the guardians produced offspring as dragons or human. Either way, if anyone had attempted to remove the guardian offspring, all four Realms would know of it.

True black dragons were as rare as true golden dragons. He had only ever heard of one true golden dragon hatching and he owned her. He had never heard of the hatching of a true black dragon.

Maldar sighed, a long, drawn out sound, tempered with lost opportunity and resignation.

"We need to find out more about what is going on Aliedori," he said finally. He wanted to stop thinking.

"I know," Aliedori sighed, she sounded weary. Maldar's head was full of thoughts but their parents' last words to them came to the forefront, in particular their mother's words which still burned in his ears: "Keep away from trouble. I can never tell whether trouble finds you two or if it's you two who find trouble."

Their mother was smiling as she said this.

"Oh, mother, what kind of trouble can we get into?" Aliedori had asked innocently. "We are only going to Dragon's Rest." Their mother had laughed and said that if there were trouble out there, they would find a way to get into it, and then told them to enjoy themselves. Whatever this was, it wasn't enjoyment Maldar thought as he looked around him. This place was not as familiar as Dragon's Rest; he hadn't ridden or flown to this part of the forest for a long time. Feelings of unease crept over him and he shuddered, not from the cold as it was still a very warm night. The cold he felt was dread and it came from within; he felt it in the pit of his stomach.

"Get some rest and dream of Dragon's Rest, it will do you good," said the calming voice of his sister.

He glanced at her, but she was looking down into the fire. Dragon's Rest was where they had set their stall for the night, or so Maldar thought. A part of the forest that was less than half a day's flying, close enough to the city where dragons tame and wild had come to drink, feed, find mates, lay their eggs and hatch their young for thousands of years. There were numerous streams and rivers, and an abundance of coke stones ensured that there was plenty of food and fresh water. Dragon's Rest was a place where wild and tame existed in the same social group. Their ancestors had followed the first dragons to the Southern Realms millions of years ago, led by the naturalist Anterian out of the wind cave deep in the heart of the of it. After the fire cave had created four beautiful dragons, the wind cave breathed life into them and sent them forth. Dragons had returned with news of the world beyond the fire and wind caves. It was said that all life came from the Tree of Souls; a place where all the Realms had grown and became an extension of the Tree of Souls. As children, Aliedori and Maldar made the many annual pilgrimages to the heart of their ancestors' home, though, strictly speaking, it was no longer possible to enter into the heart of the Tree of Souls. Anterian had taken her people and settled them by the large body of water and quickly established a settlement that grew and grew into the city it was today.

Anterian and her people lived in harmony for thousands of years and yet to the community it seemed as though they were only sent from the cave just days before. The dragons of Dragon's Rest had moved on many hundreds of cycles of the sun and moon ago, seeking out new breeding and feeding grounds. The coke stones, streams, rivers and people remained and for many thousands of years the local coke stones in the area sustained the herds. They would return again in the future, hence the name Dragon's Rest; the dragons were allowing one of their feeding grounds to recover fully before returning.

As a young Dragon, Keidrop needed frequent flights to strengthen and build stamina. She would take to the skies often to exercise her wings, lungs, heart muscles, and to breathe fire freely. Maldar took to the skies with her at every opportunity; it was on one of these jaunts that he met Waifyn, bathing in one of the crystal blue lagoons. Maldar thought that the Nymph was the most beautiful creature he had ever seen and had told the Nymph so when he surfaced. The Nymph had said nothing for a while, simply smiled, looking Maldar up and down several times before disappearing under the water. The Nymph was gone for so long that Maldar wondered if some danger had befallen the creature. He was thinking about diving in when the Nymph resurfaced, grinning with water dripping off his body as he climbed on the bank beside Maldar. By the time he stood up and took Maldar's hand, placing in his palm the pale blue stone he was carrying concealed in his closed fist, Maldar was in love.

Keidrop came and curled herself around them. At almost thirty-five feet, she could do so easily. She built a solid living wall of muscle, sinew and fire-breathing defence around them. Maldar reached out and patted her head, stroking the only soft spot on a dragon, just below her jaw line at the centre of her throat. Keidrop snorted steam through her nostrils, and Maldar could not imagine life without her in it. Nor could he imagine Keidrop changing allegiance anymore than he could imagine not being in love with Waifyn.

"So with the rising of the sun we travel farther into the West?" Maldar asked looking into Aliedori's eyes, challenging her to say differently. When she did not he continued, "Athelstan thinks his friend and the other settlers are dead, but you think differently."

Aliedori did not speak for a moment, then she said sadly, "He saw, or thinks he saw, their death, but what I think he saw was the death of themselves." Maldar looked at her, puzzled.

"What do you mean?" he asked.

Aliedori gazed off into the middle distance for a while before she replied, "They have been changed somehow, the old selves are gone and a new ones reborn, and before you ask, I don't know how, I just know."

Maldar knew that Aliedori understood her people in the same way that he understood dragons, and if he had lost Waifyn or Keidrop he would know, he would feel the loss in the depths of his being.

"How does it work?" he asked softly. "How do you keep it all in and stop yourself from... you know?" His voice trailed off, he wasn't sure quite what he was asking. But it was a question that had to be asked and sooner was better than later.

Aliedori looked up at him. She had been lost in thought for a second or two, but now her full focus was on him. Maldar felt strange, not because she understood his unspoken question but because he knew that, if she wanted, she could see into the depths of his being. Aliedori scratched her head; she was thinking how to phrase her words so they made sense to her brother.

"Maldar, I was born with magic, and every day it's more powerful, and every day I learn a new way to contain it and use it." She scratched her head again, and her face took on that strange lop- sided look. It was the look she only got when she was thinking of the best way to explain magic.

"Take this for instance." She opened her fist, and in her palm was his beautiful blue stone; the one he wore around his neck on a lanyard made from silver dragon's pelt. Maldar touched the place where his precious gift was supposed to be and found it gone.

"I simply thought of it in my hand, and it was there and now it's back where it belongs." And indeed, the stone was back round his neck even before she finished the sentence. Maldar noticed that Aliedori had not really answered his question, and he was about to say so when she spoke.

"I don't know what to tell you, Maldar. I have magic; for me it's like breathing. For you, well for you it would be like having to carry Keidrop, instead of her carrying you." She laughed. It was a nice sound but she sobered quickly. "And one day soon I will have to prove I am worthy of the magic." It was as if she was reading his thoughts and they were both silent for a while, then she smiled at him.

"I know magic, and you know dragons," she said simply. Aliedori was right, he did know dragons; dragons were in his blood in the same way magic was in hers, and not just because he was a dragon knight.

Chapter 7

As regent of a Realm you are not destined to lead, you are free to choose your own path. He became dragon knight not because he had been round dragons his entire life. Not because his father was supreme leader of dragon knights, it was because of something else. He was given a golden dragon for a reason, he was destined to find out, he knew that, and when he did he would be whole for the first time. Aliedori was right, well, partly right.

At first he was drawn to Dragon's Rest in the hope of finding clues to his birth, but later, so much later, he returned to Dragon's Rest for an entirely different set of reasons. For example, and he surprised himself for somehow gaining and retaining this information, he knew that dragons had two skins, one above the other, the outer scaly skin protecting the dragon. Between the outer skin and layers of fat was the soft hide. He had never seen the second skin except when they were made into clothes, but it was there and he knew it. He also knew that the second skin was a purer version of the outer layer. Keidrop was a golden dragon, and her second skin would be of the purest golden colour. Velvet traders had been known to make deals with knights for the specific colour of their dragon. They would pay handsomely for the right hide and many knights from poorer families knew that deeding their dragon was a good legacy to leave to the next generation. Maldar had been approached by many traders each with even more elaborate offers for Keidrop's velvet. Maldar didn't like to think of Keidrop being traded for her velvet even after her passing. He refused all offers; Keidrop would outlive him by many generations, but his golden dragon's velvet was the most sought after prize of them all, and he liked to think that one day his children would inherit Keidrop and that upon his death, Keidrop might choose to form a bond with his offspring. If there were no offspring then Keidrop would belong to no one and would choose to fly with the wild dragons to find a mate. One dragon could stay with the same family for hundreds of years passing from one offspring to the other until the bond was severed for whatever reason.

But why was he thinking of Keidrop's passing? The dragon was a mere infant. He wondered further if Aliedori had placed the thought in his head. It was not beyond her abilities, and perhaps it was her way of getting him to begin to understand that death was coming. But Maldar couldn't help thinking about their beginnings, his and Keidrop's. She had just hatched because her shell was still in the hollow where they were found by a handmaiden to the young Intendant. Though, strictly speaking, that wasn't true, they were found by the toddling Aliedori who came upon him asleep with his dragon resting against him and his little arm wrapped around it. Maldar had been told that Aliedori had begged and pleaded with her mother and anyone who was close by. When her pleas went largely unnoticed for most of the morning, Aliedori threw the mother of all magical tantrums. But the palace was preparing for the classification and registration of several young mages and naturalists, so no one was available to take her. It was only when her mother received a report that Aliedori was readying a dragon that she gave instructions to one of the handmaidens to go with her to Dragon's Rest. Once the dragon had landed, Aliedori was said to have gone to the exact spot where she had found them in a bed of reeds in a hollowed out old tree. Maldar could not help but wonder sometimes whether, if Aliedori had been allowed to go to Dragon's Rest when she'd first asked, things might have been different.

For instance, they might have found out who put him there and why. He would know his origins and the Realm of his birth and would not be left wondering. He had been brought into the halls of the Grand Naturalist of the Southern Realm, along with his dragon and became son and brother. That was where he remained. Maldar wondered if the person that placed him there would one day return to the Dragon's Rest in the slim hope of finding out what had become of the child of Dragon's Rest.

Of course, in recent times Dragon's Rest had taken on a new meaning, Maldar couldn't help but smile at the new memories. He had no idea where he came from or who had left them in that hollowed out tree. Now it did not matter at all who he had been; he knew who he was now and was happy with who he was becoming. All Maldar knew for sure was that whoever had placed him there had not returned. His mother had placed a watch charm on the spot but no one had come. The magical watch had remained in place for weeks, much longer than was necessary, and a decree was sent all over the Realm and still no one came forward. In the end there was only one conclusion drawn, his parents and close kin were not of the Southern Realm. He often told his friends and fellow knights for fun that Aliedori was his older sister but in truth, there could only be a few months between their ages either way.

Aliedori always appeared older, though, due to her magical powers and her insistence on taking on the role of tutor to instruct him in magic.

The two had quickly bonded and, once bonded, they were inseparable. Maldar had wonderful memories of them causing chaos around the palace. As they were growing up, it was the two of them against their parents and their parents always lost. Maldar thought of his beloved Waifyn and wondered if children were part of their future. If so, then they would have to give some serious thought as to how this was going to come about. Maldar also knew he was thinking about love, new beginning, loss and death, because they were about to venture into the unknown. Aliedori always made him think beyond his own immediate needs and wants even when they were young. Her constant wonder and fascination with what lay beyond the surface pushed her to explore everything. And if Aliedori was *exploring,* then Maldar was dragged kicking and screaming along with her.

Aliedori found it fascinating that The Realm had once been unified; but Maldar just thought of all the extra work the dragon knights would have to do. The enormous densely packed forest of the Tree of Souls stood in the centre. It guarded the fire, ice, and wind cave at its heart, from where all life sprung.

Aliedori had dragged him there to see the heart and discovered it could not be found and then dragged him back home again. She called it their pilgrimage; he called it a massive interference to his time with his friends.

So it went on, and to his surprise, he found that there was no one else he would rather spend his free time with. No one else was as brave, fearless, funny, unpredictable, spontaneous and wonderful as she was. The chroniclers said that the Realms would be whole again and Aliedori wanted to find out how. What she hadn't expected was that she might be the one to reunite the Realms.

"Do you trust me?" she asked.

Maldar was surprised at the question, not only because it was a question that needed no answer, but because he thought that she had fallen asleep. She had sat for so long and so quietly resting against Keidrop that he thought she had drifted off. He should have known better; he did not respond as he knew that she was not expecting him to. Instead, he asked, his voice heavy with weariness, "So after we visit the other settlements we go into the West?"

Aliedori shook her head. "Possibly towards the Northern Realm, but in truth I do not have the answers." She pushed herself up onto her feet and stood, beginning to move around gathering wood for the fire. She did not have to do that but she needed to move. After a while Maldar pushed himself onto his feet and joined her in her task. A person who could conjure a fire from nothing did not need to gather firewood; she could make the firewood come to her. Gathering firewood was a lesson, but Maldar did not yet know what it signified. It was Aliedori's way of digesting the fact that Maldar had just told her that he would follow her wherever she led him.

"Is that where you think the settlers are?"

Aliedori dropped the pile of firewood by the fire and said with a sigh, "I have been trying to find them."

"Perhaps they are gone from this life," Maldar replied.

"No, not gone." She insisted. "Just changed. They are alive, but I am not able to find them and they cannot find the way without help."

"How many are there and what changed them?" Maldar asked.

"I am not able to tell you that either. All I can tell you is that there is Fear," came the reply. It was a simple statement of fact. They sat down again side-by-side for a while in silence. Maldar threw a few logs on the fire, and watched the flames rise illuminating the darkness around them. He knew there was no foreseeable danger. While he and Keidrop could sense danger, Aliedori was attuned to the very core of the elements around them. And she was calm.

He moved from her side and sat closer to Keidrop's head, occasionally stroking the little soft spot under her chin. After a while, Maldar took out the whetstone he always carried and tended to his swords. Magic would give him a much sharper blade, but he sharpened his sword and for the same reason Aliedori gathered firewood. Aliedori settled herself more comfortably and using Keidrop as a backrest she closed her eyes.

Her senses shifted and it was as if she could now feel and see everything all at once. Then she could feel the slow crawl of the creatures beneath her feet and the swift wings of the flying ones too. She knew that if she felt deeply enough she could identify each individual creature that crawled and flew. She cast her mind out, it was something she did easily even with her eyes open.

The sky was dark and cloudless with only the moon and stars visible through the canopy. There was no one or nothing large or close enough to pose a danger to the little group. Aliedori could cast her mind out at any time, but preferred quiet; she found she could link faster and better if she did not have to filter out background noise. She was still very alert; nothing could get past her, and even if it did there was Maldar and Keidrop to contend with. Aliedori sent her mind out above the trees to see what she would encounter; she wanted aerial views. To her surprise, she found very little. A trader on a dragon returning home would be ideal but there was no one. She found various small tree-dwelling animals and birds and noisy swarming bats. The birds were settled on their nests for the night, and there were no owls to be found, either they were off hunting or already moved into the Tree of Souls, the home of many of the owls' species.

The bats, though plentiful and highly intelligent, foraged into the night sky for one reason alone, food. Bats did not have good eyesight, and she wanted good eyes to look through if she was to get what she needed. Aliedori continued to scan the skyline. She was about to give up when she found the clear, sweet minds of a small group of young dragons. The young dragons had taken to the skies to exercise and strengthen their wings. They were flying high, and Aliedori got some wonderful dragon's eye views of the Tree of Souls Forest close to the western Realm.

The dragons were playful, swooping up and over, diving at each other as only fledglings will do. Aliedori stayed with them for a while enjoying their easy freedom. If she wanted to, she could choose one of the young dragons to command, but she chose not to, it would mean going against the dragon's own will, and these dragons were wild. To force a wild dragon; or any dragon for that matter, to go against its will always led to madness in the creature. As much as she wanted to see the Realm beyond the veil of trees, she would not send a dragon into certain madness to do so. She did not have the time to play with the dragons or get one to freely submit, so she continued to scan the landscape. Aliedori was not sure she would be able to see the Realm beyond the veil.

Surely, the veil would extend higher than a dragon could safely fly. What was she looking for anyway and would she even know if she found it?

Reluctantly she withdrew her mind from the dragons and moved on. As she did so, she caught the mind of a large bird-like creature. It was closer to the borders and below the dragons, and to her surprise she could make out the bright pinpricks of the lights of a settlement or town close to the city walls. However, it turned out to be outside the walls. Aliedori jumped from the flying creatures into the mind of a young woman. She caught the mind busy making preparation for a late evening meal. The young woman was speaking in a tongue that Aliedori didn't recognise. Aliedori knew many languages and understood many traders using the port at Fengardia, but this one she could not make out. Aliedori was sure that the young woman must be a trader from the Northern Realm.

There were about fifty or so traders in the encampment, and she was part of the cooking retinue. She didn't like it; she wanted to be home, but most of all she wanted not to be cooking. The traders were camped in a very dense wall of trees; they were happy, chatting and laughing, perhaps they had traded well or they were just happy that their journey from the north had not been in vain. Someone was talking to her, and the young woman looked up from what she was doing. Aliedori sensed the girl's pleasure at seeing the boy. She took something from the pouch on her belt and handed it to the boy, who became very excited, throwing his arms around the young woman's waist before running off waving the gift.

The young woman laughed and looked around the encampment before returning to her cooking. Aliedori could see tree trunks where sleeping hammocks were hanging, but very little else. The trees were too tightly packed together to see anything beyond the hammocks.

Aliedori wondered whether the tree trunks she was looking at formed part of the city walls or part of the dense forest of the Tree of Souls. The young woman picked up several items and a large black cooking pot from the fire and carried it to a vast table set out in the middle of the encampment. There was no way of telling where exactly the traders were, and Aliedori had to contend with jumping from one mind to the other to get a better perspective.

But it was not possible to tell the position of the camp and it remained a mystery. Whilst in the mind of other people or animals she saw whatever the observers were seeing. If the observer's eyesight was good, then she had clear views and good details of everything around.

The young woman had very good eyesight, but it was too dark and the trees were too densely packed together. The sconces attached to the trees provided limited illumination and all Aliedori observed were the others in the cooking party. At one point, Aliedori jumped into the mind of a young man who had just finished bathing. He climbed out of the water and stood on the bank drying himself by torchlight. He was whistling when the tune froze on his lips, and Aliedori felt the young man's heart begin to race.

The young man looked around but saw nothing; he pulled the torch from the sconce and raised it slightly above his head. The illumination caught his reflection on the water, and it danced back at him. He raised the torch higher and held it at arm's length, and Aliedori could see the flames flicker in the young man's eyes. His heartbeat settled but not completely. Aliedori was still finding it difficult to understand human emotions when experienced through a mind cast.

It was different with animals, even those with magical qualities as their senses were almost always the same hues – fear, pain, hunger.

Humankind hues were too delicately mixed, and she was not versed enough to unravel the overlay of differing emotions. For instance, Aliedori could not tell if the bathing man was afraid or simply startled by some unknown sound. From his initial reaction, she would assume he would hurry back to the encampment, but he did not and simply dress himself at a leisurely pace.

Aliedori noticed that he did not dry himself nor did he return to his tuneless whistling.

Disappointed that she could not get any information from the traders she withdrew her mind.

Chapter 8

The clear vision blurred again, and the world around her became soft focus without form for a second or two. Then she was back sitting on the ground with Maldar, who she knew was watching her keenly; even with her eyes closed she felt his gaze. She smiled and opened her eyes to meet his.

"Where did you go?" Maldar wanted to know.

"Tree of Souls Western Realm, but I am not sure how close to the knotted trees I was." Aliedori was distracted for a while but then quickly refocused.

"Anything?" Maldar waited for the reply, poking the fire with a stick.

"Lots of magic, but that's not unusual; they are surrounded by the Tree of Souls. But there are also uncertain feelings amongst the weary traders. That could be because they are a long way from home. Maldar, go to sleep, the last stars will soon leave the sky."

With that, a blanket appeared around them and Aliedori watched as her brother fell asleep before she succumbed herself.

****

Keidrop had been flying nonstop for almost two hours when the faintest of sunrays appeared over the horizon. Aliedori had risen and woken Maldar before dawn's early light; the stars had only just left the sky when they mounted Keidrop. Below them, and still a little distance away, was the settlement of Stornvale, nestled at the foot of Broken Hills. The hills were so called because they looked as if a giant had simply snapped their tops off and left the broken remains. Stornvale was a beautiful place and it was where the servants spent time when they were not in the service of the lady and lord of Fengardia.

The forest around Stornvale was the place where Wulfgar had been born and had once lived. As children, both Aliedori and Maldar had spent many happy hours in the dwelling of Wulfgar's parents. Stornvale was a place of happy memories for both of them; however, they had not visited for many cycles.

Maldar directed Keidrop to land far enough away from the settlement so as not to startle the dwellers. This was also because Aliedori wanted to reacquaint herself with the settlement before meeting its settlers. Keidrop landed in a clearing on the far side of the settlement so Aliedori and Maldar could enter on foot. Unlike Skellglade, there were no high walls or mages, but the settlement was enclosed.

On one side was the start of the sacred Tree of Souls Forest and on the other were the Broken Hills and all round was their mother's protection. The protection was made all the more powerful by the magic of the forest. Beyond Broken Hills, and in only a few hours of dragon's flight, were the great walls of the Western Realm.

The only thing between the Broken Hills and the wall was a large expanse of water that fed both Realms. The forest of the Southern Realm surrounded the other two sides of the settlement. The two travellers discovered a trail beneath their feet; a pathway of grey stone, quarried from the Broken Hills, and above their heads were tree canopies. The trees were in full bloom and the large pink and white flowers stood out against the flat, dark green leaves. Their perfume was intoxicating and brought back fond childhood memories for both of them. To their right the trail ended abruptly in a field of wheat and barley. The path in that direction remained unfinished. It must have been laid for a reason but it had been inexplicably abandoned when whoever had started it lost interest. Aliedori could sense no danger as they followed the path into the settlement, but something was bothering her. They were almost upon the settlement when her interest was sharpened. There was a bend in the pathway, just large enough to conceal settlers travelling in the opposite direction.

They were unable to see each other until one or the other came round the bend. By the time Maldar had picked up the sound the of drac's hooves on the stone path, Aliedori had long sensed that the settlers were near. She was waiting for them to round the bend, which they appeared to be doing at a very leisurely pace. On sensing the settlers, Aliedori asked Keidrop to close her wings and flatten her spinal barbs. She was now walking close behind them, head down and ears flattened like a docile drac. The small group of farmers rounded the corner and stopped in their tracks, surprise showing clearly on their faces as the last things they were expecting were two strangers and a huge golden dragon.

Aliedori noted with interest that, despite the surprise, it did not take the farmers long to draw their weapons. They carried an astonishing assortment of traditional and metal swords and a pitchfork or two. Aliedori and Maldar stood still, their hands clearly visible to the farmers at all times. The farmers quickly sheathed their swords and inclined their heads in respect when they recognised the three travellers.

"Forgive us Intendant, Sire, did you send word you were coming?" The farmer who spoke was at the forefront of the little group.

"It was a spur of the moment thing, we were not sure we were coming until late last night," Maldar ventured. There was surprise on the faces of the farmers once again.

"You travelled from Fengardia in one night?"

This question was directed at Aliedori but it was Maldar who replied, "No, we travelled from Skellglade."

"You are here about the dragon raiders?"

Aliedori nodded.

The lead farmer continued.

"Living so close to the border with the West there are always problems with incursions, but usually with Westerners crossing the border into the settlement."

"And now?" Maldar asked. He glanced towards his sister and when she said very little he repeated the question.

"At the start of the season dragon raiders began appearing in the sky. At first we thought they were after those who had crossed over, but when they were gone we never discovered what the raiders wanted."

"Are there any settlers taken?" It was urgent that she discovered this.

"No Intendant, they cannot break The Lady's incantation." It was good to know that her worries were ill founded.

The lead farmer turned round and walked with Aliedori and Maldar back to the settlement, whilst the others continued on to perform their early morning tasks.

Keidrop had become bored and wandered off to find somewhere comfortable, so the three entered the settlement, approaching it from somewhere towards the east side. Many of the settlement buildings were made from the local stone and it looked very different from Skellglade. Its open aspect had flowers lining the pathways, displays of water fountains and ornamental ponds full of orange fish. Stornvale was coming alive with the new day but there were very few settlers about. Smoke was beginning to rise from almost every chimney as fires were started in preparation for the first meal of the day. The settlement was much larger than either Aliedori or Maldar remembered and there were now even dwellings on the ridges of Broken Hills.

"This way Intendant, the Appointee dwelling is over there." They followed the farmer as he led the way towards the centre of the square. Outside the dwelling was a large statue of her mother carved from wood, no doubt out of a tree taken from the sacred forest, Aliedori thought. As she walked past she reached out and touched the carving, it was warm to the touch confirming her thought. The door of the dwelling opened, and the Appointee stepped out to greet Aliedori and Maldar in the customary way.

"Thank you for coming, Intendant," he said with another small inclination of his head. "There has been no word from Outer Stornvale for a few days. I sent Gems but there has been no message in reply, I am on my way there now."

"There is an Outer Stornvale and how many live there?" Maldar asked, looking at Aliedori. She had not moved from the statue and her hand was still resting on the gown.

It occurred to Maldar that she had said nothing since they arrived and very little since this morning. He didn't like that; if she said nothing then he knew that something wasn't right. She only became this quiet when something was wrong, but what could it be? Maldar didn't know much of anything about Outer Stornvale and neither did Aliedori, but he wondered if she was sensing some danger or perhaps not sensing anything at all.

He could not remember ever knowing or hearing of the existence of Outer Stornvale as a visiting child. He was a little way in front of Aliedori and went back to stand by her side. She looked up at him but he was unable to read her face. She must have seen the question in his eyes because she gave her head a little shake. Maldar did not quite understand what the shake of the head meant but took comfort in it all the same. Then Maldar realised that the Appointee was answering his question on Outer Stornvale and turned his attention back to him.

"Outer Stornvale is where many foresters and charcoal burners settled out by the large turquoise lagoon". The Appointee said "Foresters began thinning the dense woodland few cycles ago and rice farmers and families moved there to take advantage of the flood plain" he finished. Outer Stornvale was at the far side of Broken Hills. Farmers and a few traders had moved there some years ago to take advantage of the fertile lands.

Though Outer Stornvale was still a very small settlement there were now over two hundred families living out there. Maldar remembered the turquoise lagoon in the woods as a place where he and Aliedori had spent many happy days swimming when they visited Stornvale as children.

Aliedori spoke quietly now, looking directly at the Appointee.

"You have a naturalist here; in fact I believe you have more than one." Aliedori strode purposefully towards a small dwelling at the far end of the settlement. Whoever lived there had not yet risen, as it was one of the few dwellings that had no smoke curling from its chimney. Aliedori had made a simple statement of fact and now Maldar understood why she had been so quiet. The Appointee opened his mouth and closed it several times before the words would come. He could not understand why Aliedori would have said such a thing.

"Intendant, I believe you are mistaken," he said following in the wake of her footsteps. He caught up with her halfway to the dwelling and matched her pace. Aliedori smiled at him, touching him in reassurance and for some reason he had an instant feeling of wellbeing.

"No mistake, Hellaire." She stopped abruptly, forcing him to stop as well but two paces ahead of her. He turned as she pointed.

"One there and the other over there," she said indicating the small dwelling and a bakery.

"Intendant, you have identified two dwellings of those who have come from the Western Realm seeking sanctuary." Hellaire appeared troubled, but continued softly, "The younglings of these dwellings are barely beyond infancy and they have a strange custom. They believe it is bad luck to introduce their children into the community until the cycles have past. This is also when they have their Name Day. The name day for the youngling at the bakery was only a few days ago."

Aliedori thought for a while then asked, "Were they born here?"

Hellaire shook his head, "They came together almost three cycles ago."

When she had decided to come to Stornvale, she hadn't known what she would encounter, but she certainly had not expected this. Not families from the Western Realm and most certainly not naturalists; there was strong magic here, and she had felt it the moment Keidrop landed.

At first, she thought it was because the settlement was so close to the Tree of Souls and the residual magic around the area. However, as she came into the settlement she realised that it was not residual magic but something far stronger. There was something else too. Hellaire believed that the naturalists were children, "younglings" as he referred to them, but Aliedori knew that this was not true. Only one of the naturalists was a child and not a young child either. One was a girl, almost a woman and the other was a woman somewhere in her thirtieth cycle. She was the mother of the child whose Name Day had been just a few days ago. Aliedori knew why Hellaire thought the naturalists were children but spoke no more on the subject.

Instead she said, "Tell me, Hellaire; are there any families from the Western Realm living in Outer Stornvale?"

"I believe a needlewoman and her daughters are living out there." Hellaire inclined his rather large head.

"I would like to meet them; we will be back by sunset."

Keidrop suddenly appeared from round the corner, startling them all except Aliedori and Maldar.

"Hellaire, your new families are settlers of the Southern Realms, and now they will need classification and registration." Hellaire looked worried, and explained that he could not understand them, and they could not understand him.

Aliedori laughed, "Do not be fooled by that. They understand you well enough and now you will understand them too."

Maldar mounted and sat waiting for his sister. When she was ready, he offered her his hand. She took it and mounted Keidrop also, swinging her leg over the other side and settling into the saddle.

"Oh, and Hellaire, please continue to be nice to them. They are very frightened people."

Urged by Maldar, Keidrop took off before Hellaire could reply.

Chapter 9

It was clear that magic had been used to grow the trees surrounding the small dwelling. The trees were not straight up and down as in normal growth; each trunk was intertwined, overlapped, underlapped and crisscrossed so that it was impossible to say where one tree started and the other ended. Aliedori didn't know if it was to keep small livestock in or unwanted visitors out. The trees' enclosure was almost fortified and the dwelling they had spotted at the end of the pathway provided a good lookout perched on a small hillock above the other dwellings.

Aliedori and Maldar had arrived only a few minutes before. Again, they landed Keidrop in a clearing in the woods and arrived on foot, passing the turquoise lagoon on their left. The lagoon sparkled and flashed its promises in the early morning light and beckoned all as the new day danced on its surface. All who were near enough to hear its promises were unable to resist the invitation. They dove into its unbroken surface, shattering the promises to wash away the night fears. Aliedori's instinct was correct; all around them Aliedori noticed signs of the naturalist in the small settlement. She felt the presence and saw the residue of past incantations and charms, but there was also fear. The protective incantation that was in place was not her mother's; she knew her mother's colours and these were not hers. They were a good copy, and the naturalist was able to capture the essence and colours but not the subtleties. The needlewoman and her daughter were protecting their home, as the baker and the other dwellers protected Stornvale. Three naturalists in such a relatively small settlement and so close to the sacred forest meant the area was well protected or at least it should be. But Aliedori knew that the raiders had been at work, she could feel their attempts to break the protective incantation here as well as in Stornvale. Most people of the settlement were already going about their daily business and, spotting the little dwelling on the hillock, she and Maldar headed towards it leaving Keidrop to wander off to please herself. All the flying about, though enjoyable, became tedious when commanded to do so.

They got as far as the gate when a girl of about seventeen cycles appeared. She had a small, round face with large brown eyes and a stocky body. She was carrying a rattan basket filled with several items of clothing in her left hand, and in her right she carried a coin purse that should have been attached to her belt.

"Venna, is your mother home?" Aliedori asked. She already knew the answer but asked the question anyway. The girl did not seem surprised that Aliedori knew her name; she simply inclined her head towards the dwelling, opened the gate and allowed Aliedori and Maldar to pass through. Venna waited until Aliedori and Maldar were standing on the right side of the gate before she went through it herself to the other side and closed it before calling out.

The needlewoman appeared in the small patch of yard that could be seen from the gate. The gravel path, which led the visitors up to the dwelling, was lined with cypress trees. Their sturdy little feet were planted firmly in the ground and their narrow bodies swayed to the music of the morning. The sun was still low enough in the sky to cast shadows, but as the sun rose to reach its full zenith it carried with it the welcoming fingers of the cypresses to cross the path and touch the feet of their sisters.

Though on opposite sides, for a few hours or so they would join in unity. Then they would return to their lonely sentry duty to wait in anticipation for their slow journey to unity to begin once more. Aliedori and Maldar followed the path where the cypresses led into an open vista.

The needlewoman did not move but watched with care as the two approached. She wiped her hands on the white apron around her waist in anticipation. The woman stood in the midst of several small fowl as they pecked at the ground here and there with their chicks. The needlewomen suddenly shouted in alarm and ran towards the fowl, shooing them as she passed. Venna was already gone from sight and chose not to hear the shout, while Aliedori and Maldar watched as the needlewoman tried to make her way down the path in haste and avoid stepping on the fowl and their chicks. But Aliedori and Maldar were already in the yard, and the needlewoman came to a sudden halt. She dropped to one knee instantly before Aliedori could stop her. Aliedori caught the woman's shoulder and helped her up back on her feet. She was very much like her daughter Venna in the face. But where Venna was short and stocky the needlewoman was short and thin. Aliedori looked beyond the needlewoman to the younger daughter who had just appeared from the side of the dwelling carry an armful of herbs. The young woman stopped on the spot, dropping the herbs but managed to save them before they reached the ground.

The herbs hovered for a second in mid-air before they were scooped back into her arms, which were now wrapped safely around the precious cargo. She stood watching her mother with a look of horror as the realisation dawned on her; she had cast a charm in front of strangers. Her mother tried without success to cover it up by almost dragging Aliedori and Maldar in the direction of the dwelling. As Aliedori came closer she realised that the look of horror had very little to do with the incantation but with something else entirely.

"Skylar we are not here to harm you, we simply wanted to meet you," Aliedori offered. Skylar visibly relaxed, she looked from Maldar to Aliedori her cheeks colouring but then draining suddenly. The girl lowered her eyes and refused to look up even after her mother called her name.

Aliedori knew what was coming, so when Amana invited her to breakfast with them she gladly accepted.

At the back of the stone-built dwelling was a veranda resting on six large wooden stakes buried deep in the ground. The veranda reminded Aliedori of her home, but instead of overlooking the lakes this veranda overlooked ripening rice paddies. Mixed fruit orchards and the Tree of Souls lay beyond. How beautiful to be able to see the Tree of Souls every day, Maldar found himself thinking. The news of their arrival had reached the ears of the other settlers and several had already made their way up the little hillock to meet them.

Amana had allowed this to happen. She needed the distraction and the other settlers willingly participated. It was not until after they had eaten that Aliedori reminded Amana of the purpose of her journey. Amana reluctantly, but steadfastly, led her fellow settlers out and firmly shut the gate behind them. It was clear to Aliedori then who was the unofficial Appointee of this small place. Venna returned as the settlers left, and Maldar felt somewhat outnumbered and surrounded. He rested against a veranda post and observed from under half-closed eyes. The three Westerner's interest was not with him but with Aliedori, but once in a while they cast worried glances in his direction. Maldar noticed that while they appeared naturally curious and talkative, it was not out of deference to the two of them. They would wait until they were invited to talk, answering questions or giving opinions when Aliedori invited them to. The women's deference was more than just the fact that Aliedori was the Intendant and next Grand Nationalist of the Southern Realm. It was something more. They were afraid; at times their fears were almost palpable. He felt it so keenly that a feeling of dread crept over him. Maldar glanced over at his sister then turned away, but he felt impelled to look again and when he did she had turned slightly as she listened to Amana.

She raised her hand and all three women flinched in unison scattering waves of fear across the view.

"There are no reasons to fear us, we are not here to harm you. You came out of the Western Realm; I simply want to know why and more importantly how?"

The three women exchanged glances and were silent for a while. Those looks meant something but the meaning was lost on Maldar. Skylar and Venna busied themselves clearing away the meal things, while Aliedori and Maldar waited; finally Amana spoke.

"We came and were offered a home. We can't say how we came to be here." She stopped as her children came to join them again. Venna sat down again beside her mother but Skylar placed herself against one of the posts, her arms folded. It seemed like a casual gesture, but she was tense and afraid, although her pride would not let it show. Aliedori stood, pushing the seat back until she was free of the table. She was patient and could wait, for a little while at least.

"Did you use magic to cross into this Realm?" Aliedori asked.

"You are mistaken I... we have no magic."

Aliedori looked at Skylar, but Skylar's eyes were on Maldar and now she understood why these women were so fearful. There was magic, Aliedori could feel it, she knew which woman had it and what classification she was. They hid it well with a confusing charm that would fool only a lesser naturalist. When the Intendant travelled across the Realm to see someone they had no choice but to welcome her.

That was what they did, welcomed their Intendant and gave her the hospitality she deserved. Aliedori knew that she could do nothing more to alleviate their fears, it was all these women had ever known, and it would take some time for them to feel safe.

"We are not what you think we are. Skylar, you said that you have no magic and so we are satisfied with what you have said." Aliedori walked towards Skylar, inclined her head and turned to take her leave. Maldar followed and the walk down the hill was fast. Maldar tried to talk to Aliedori but she shook her head. She picked up the pace and her long stride took them into the woods and they stood under the dappled shadows whilst waiting for Keidrop to return. Aliedori finally spoke.

"They are too afraid to say anything, but I have learnt a great deal."

Maldar was not certain that there was much to learn other than that the women were liars and very afraid.

"What now, a return to Stornvale?"

"We could return but I do not think that we will learn any more than we already know."

"Aliedori we have learned nothing at all." Maldar waved his hand signalling Keidrop to come to them.

"Not true, we have learnt that there are at least three new naturalists in the Realm, and we have learnt that there is a crossing point somewhere between the two Realms.

"A place so terrifying that they have used magic to rid themselves of the memories but somehow still live with the fear. I have also learnt that they are still trying to hide, not from me but from those they escaped from." Aliedori mounted Keidrop followed by Maldar. "We need to find this place Maldar."

"I got the same image from their minds as I did from the trackers," she said into his back as the golden dragon took to the sky.

"What else?" he spoke into the wind, and when she did not reply he assumed that she did not hear. It was nightfall before Keidrop did as instructed and landed in a small clearing close to a charcoal burner's hut. After Keidrop landed, Aliedori found some Gems close to the hut. It was a good place to make their nest as there were always small animals and charcoal readily available. The little green and brown dragon was only too willing to help and Aliedori sent a message to Hellaire to explain that they would not be returning to the settlement and advising him of the three naturalists.

"We are in the neutral forest close to the border so I can *scan* for any breaches and perhaps I will find the place."

"Are we going to go into the Northern Realm?" Maldar was not relishing the journey into the cold lands of the North.

They were utilising the empty charcoal burner's hut and Aliedori sat on a stool by the unlit fire and was busy placing dry twigs amongst the charcoal in the hearth.

Maldar went out to the nearby spring to get fresh water and returned with a full gourd; he also carried fresh fruit he had liberated from the trees. Once the hearth was piled with enough twigs and kindle, Aliedori used magic to light the fire. The single blue flame danced across the hearth until the centre of the fire was aglow with bright yellow fingers. That was the only magic she used, the rest they did manually: pouring water, placing the pan over the heat and making mead tea. Eyes closed and legs up on a stool, Maldar sipped the hot sweet liquid.

Aliedori joined him at the table with her tea and took up the same stance. She had strung together meat and root vegetables wrapped in green leaves and skewered them on a large metal rod. The food store at the back of the little hut was well stocked, and the charcoal pit was burning. This would suggest that the charcoal burners would be back in the morning to check on progress. With dragon raiders stealing settlers, it was not safe to be away from a settlement. Outside Keidrop could be heard rooting for coke stones.

Dragon's favourite foods were coke stones, small animals, fruit, and root vegetables as well as the occasional tree stump and hard bark. However, not all dragons' diets consisted of mainly vegetables. The dragons of the North Land had evolved to be mainly meat eaters, but even they were known to eat a few vegetables.

Aliedori relaxed and sank deeper into the seat, her head almost touching the back. She had a good view of the pyramid roof and concentrated on the very point, though she did not see it for long. Aliedori was in the mind of a bird and had a bird's eye view and was studying the fortress. But the trouble with the bird's eye view was that it was a binocular vision and while it functioned well for the bird's purpose, it was no good for Aliedori to see through. It also meant that due to the position of the bird's eyes, Aliedori saw two different visions at the same time, making it impossible to see properly. But from what she could make out there was a settlement near a wall and it was clearly a garrison town to protect the city. There were high lookout platforms in the wall and one platform looked out over high towers.

She was unable to make out the purpose of the towers as the bird was circling away from the wall and towards the sacred forest. Aliedori could see a large gateway, firmly closed against the night; there were lights in the gatehouse that flanked the gate. As the birds flew over she saw campers, perhaps the same campers she had seen the night before. There were also other, more permanent settlements, outside the gate and along one of the walls. The bird creature landed in a nest full of squawking babies, and Aliedori was treated to a close up view of the young chick's open gullet.

Her mind's eye left the bird to tend to her young and moved on. She was close to the border and wondered if she could *jump* into the mind of the residents. It was something that she found was becoming increasingly easy with each attempt, but she needed to be able to *see* the person before she could make the *jump*. It took her some time to find a mind that was open, which would suggest that mind shields were in use, or that the general protectiveness of the fortress Realm protected all those close to it. When she found one it was the mind of some domesticated small animal she didn't recognise. It was hunting in the settlements outside the wall.

She had tried several times to enter into the minds of the warriors in the watchtower but could not find a way in. The animal's mind was a cloud of pain tainted with hunger, but its hearing was still keen. The creature was wandering the dark alleys near residential dwellings. Strange tongues assaulted her all at once from behind closed doors. It was still early, yet all the doors were closed to the night, even the taverns. Aliedori wondered why she could not understand the language; she was in the mind of a creature from the Realm.

She listened for a short while longer but still could not make sense of the language. Aliedori knew that she could not listen to them all, so she tried a new tack. Slowly, very slowly, using another part of her mind, she began to 'turn off' the multiple voices until there was just the mind of the animal. Aliedori grinned; this was something else she was discovering she could do. However, now was not the time to be distracted; she needed her full concentration. She could explore her newfound ability at a later time; right now she needed to concentrate on the animal. The animal looked to its right then to its left, it appeared something had spooked it. Now hunger and pain were joined by fear. Aliedori could see nothing through the animal's eyes, but if it was afraid then it had good reason, night hunters had more to fear than just starvation. This animal was not a true hunter; it was simply scavenging. It darted in and out of gardens in search of food, stopping here and there. Finally, it darted through a hedge and out into an opening that looked like a small square.

As it did so, Aliedori caught sight of a seated form somewhere in the middle distance. The animal moved towards the figure, its keen sense of smell drawing it to the figure, in the hope of some little morsel. The animal's instincts were right and as it approached the figure he threw something into the middle distance between himself and the animal. The reward for its night's scavenging was a good-sized piece of meat of some kind. The animal grabbed the meat between its teeth and ran off to devour it later.

The last sensation Aliedori experienced just before she *jumped* into the young man's mind was pleasure tinged with fear. Aliedori watched the animal run off through the young man's eyes; it was scraggy thing, its body around thirty-eight to forty centimetres long. The creature was about the same shape and size as a small Gem but instead of wings Aliedori saw a large bushy tail sweeping the ground disappearing round a corner.

Chapter 10

The young man's thoughts were ordered, and she understood them. It was difficult to know what she was going to get when she jumped into a mind. Aliedori's intention was to use his eyes but not search his mind. But once inside a mind, she found that she was able to pick up on the person's immediate and on-going thoughts. This mind was clear and uncluttered compared to that of the poor animal.

There were thoughts of many things, but his clearest thought was of his approaching coming of age ceremony. Soon he would be a man, and a public celebration meant that he could no longer hide behind childish behaviour. He had done so for far too long, but in a few days' time he would be a man and would have to start taking his duties seriously. There would be no more running off with friends, losing themselves in the...?

Aliedori did not know the word; it was a word she had never heard before. She couldn't find an equivalent word in her tongue no matter how hard she tried, so she stored the word carefully away to come back to later. Whatever the word was, it stood for simple pleasure. Aliedori felt the joy the word conjured for the young man. Then her 'vision' was gone and Aliedori found that she had *jumped* into the mind of someone about to fall asleep. The young man's mind went blank and she felt his body relaxing, eyes closing and his breathing steady.

With a sudden start the young man's eyes snapped open again, his vision blurred for a second, then cleared. He looked around with clear, sharp vision and mind. The young man smiled as a thought was beginning to formulate, then stopped. From where he was sitting, he could see the square clearly, directly in front of him was a street lamp. The strong, solid, metal base was topped by six lamps, which cast a bright glow across the square. Goods and chattels could clearly be seen, he was in a market place. The market may have been bustling during the day but it was now quiet, closed down.

Traders had secured their wares for the night to begin trading again in the morning. There was so much to do before his coming of age... the young man's thought process was interrupted as his attention was caught by an approaching figure. Aliedori was sure that the thought about coming of age was to hide the original thought process. He tried to hide it, but the pleasure that the germ of a thought had started remained with the young man. The thought filled him with a secret sense of well being as he watched the figure. Aliedori smiled as she recognised so well the approaching man. Her grin spread as she recalled the times when she and Maldar were small and their mother had often told them stories about this figure. One such story that her mother often told was of sneaking out at night to do the rounds with one of the local dousers. The douser approached the young man, his job momentarily forgotten. He inclined his head, palms together as a sign of greeting. The young man brought his palms together and inclined his head also, a deeper bow as a sign of respect to his elder. The douser had been doing the job for a very long time; he knew the young man and his family of drac breeders.

"The hour is late Sorin, even you should be weary of being found out after lights are extinguished." The young man smiled up at the douser and leant back resting his elbows on the stone steps behind, throwing his head back to look at the night sky. He appeared relaxed, but his casual stance hit an expectant tension.

He brought his head forward and caught the eyes of the douser. The hood of the grey cape the douser wore was hiding his face so the only things visible were lines and shadows. But Sorin fancied that he had caught the douser's eyes and smiled in a lazy manner.

"I fancy a moonlight walk and who better to do that with but my good friend the douser," Sorin mused.

The douser said nothing for a while, as if he was thinking over the offer, and when he spoke, his voice was full of unexpected merriment.

"Walk with me, then we shall tackle the hunter's moon together and we will hunt after dark."

Sorin sighed and treated himself to the glorious view of the silver moon as he stood up reluctantly. He didn't really want company but once the lights were extinguished only fools and thieves chose to walk the streets alone.

"If you have another of those, our moonlight stroll will merely be seen as work and no one will know differently."

He winked at the douser and chuckled at his own small joke,

accepting the douser he was offered by the master of illumination. The lights of the six lamps in the square were quickly put out rendering almost total darkness. Sorin waits for his eyes to adjust to the darkness the lights at the other end of the market place suddenly seemed very far away.

There were many bandits in the settlements and they had been known to cut a man's throat the instant the lights were extinguished. Sorin swallowed because, despite his bravado, he was a little afraid.

Aliedori felt Sorin's fear, palpable, unknown, faceless and nameless but nevertheless very real fear. Sorin was experiencing a mixture of joy and fear, deep bright colours and dull grey hues tumbled through his emotions in equal measure, Aliedori had no trouble recognising these emotions; it felt as if Sorin had discovered something new and tantalizing. The discovery brought joy and fear in equal measure, both emotions vying to be the dominant one. Suddenly Sorin stopped. He had been looking at the moon and smiling to himself, thinking that it appeared to be so close. He could almost reach out and touch it and he was about to stretch out his hand when he froze. Sorin didn't move until douser grabbed him and pulled him forward, almost off his feet. The douser had removed his hood, and Sorin was looking into the calm face of an olive-skinned man. Soft brown eyes showed slight concern for the young man. Sorin moved quickly, he was a fool to have stayed out so late, but he had become lost in his own thoughts of the upcoming ceremony, and he had not noticed the dark creeping in. What kind of man would he make if he were frightened of the dark?

He had been born close to the settlement by the wall and had spent almost his entire life there. Everything he knew about the Realms he had learnt whilst there, and yet... and yet. Aliedori wanted to find out more, but the young man's thoughts were now unclear, jumbled and full of imagined and unimaginable fears. Aliedori caught small glimpses of features but somehow she felt that this was more about what Sorin had imagined rather than what he had seen. Aliedori wondered if she should probe Sorin's mind to find out more, but she knew that she had no right to any of his thoughts. They were his thoughts and fears, and she had no right to any of them, not without his permission anyway. She could not find a justifiable reason to search his mind, so she concentrated on what she was there for. She had simply wanted to use his eyes to gather information on the city outside the wall.

When she had cast her mind out she hadn't expected to find set-tlers, nor did she expect to enter his mind so easily and freely; it was strange, but she would have to think about that one later as well. The douser and Sorin had reached the last lamps on the Square and before he put them out douser drew out a torch, held it against a lamp, and lit it. With the lamps out, the entire square was plunged into total darkness. The market was for day traders and there were no residents about. Once trading for the day was over there was no need for illumination and the small market was plunged into darkness.

Sorin was out with an old man whose only experience of the world was to bring illumination to others. The younger man turned and looked behind him, he was sure he had heard something out there in the darkness, something large and unfathomable. He felt something touch him and almost cried out until he realised that it was douser's hand on his arm.

"I find it is always best to look forward, sire, head up, shoulders back... best way, sire," he said. "We will walk to your dwelling."

"And you?" Sorin enquired.

"Don't you worry about me young sire, I have been walking these paths before you were born. Besides I am not a wealthy man, I have nothing of worth. Bandits want gold coins, and I have none, I am simply not worth the effort."

The douser was lost in thought for a moment, perhaps thinking of his coinless life, or perhaps the welcoming sign of a tavern. Sorin handed the dousing implement back so that he could draw his sword. He did not believe that his sword would be of any use, or that he would get the chance to use it if something was there in the darkness. He was a good a swordsman and liked to think he was getting better, but he was always a disappointment to his trainer, the master swordsman. It was a comfort to feel the weight of the sword in his hand, though, and what a triumph it would be to single-handedly take down some of the settlement's bandits. Sorin and the douser moved forward together as one, and Sorin noticed that the douser also had a large club in his hand. Perhaps not single-handedly then... the thought began.

Then there was nothing, Aliedori could no longer sense him, Sorin was gone. He had disappeared into the darkness, the connection was severed so suddenly that when Aliedori found herself staring at the distant moon she did not realise for some time that it was through the window of the hut. She pulled herself up from her comfortable position and tried again to re-establish a link. But nothing. Sorin was gone. Aliedori continued to search for Sorin but was unable to find him again. Now she knew where to *look* she would continue with her search. Once she had a link to something she could always find it again, and Sorin was a dweller in the settlement by the wall. Aliedori had no doubt that the settler called Sorin would be just as easy if not easier next time; they were the same species with the same traits and a similar mind map, it would not be hard. Her main concern was for his safety but at the moment there was nothing she could do. She searched the streets and alleys for another human but was not surprised that she could find no one. Even the douser was gone. It must be some kind of mind shield, and there was nothing she could do now but wait. There were a few nocturnal creatures in the trees and the sky but nothing she could use to help in her search for Sorin and the douser. What sort of place was the Western Realm that its dwellers appeared afraid to be out after dark? It took Aliedori some time to realise that perhaps the time just after sunset in the Southern Realm might be much later in the Western Realm.

Perhaps the street did indeed belong to thieves and bandits, but what leader would allow that to happen? Were the settlements outside the wall not subject to the same protection as those within? She smiled a tight little smile at the proof, as she had thought that the Realm would be protected and it was. The entire Realm was shielded. When Aliedori pulled herself back up to a sitting position she found Maldar watching her. He had not taken his eyes off her at all. She looked sad but was smiling and before he could ask her what she had seen she spoke, still not looking at him.

"Okay time's up, you have done enough watching for tonight... yes you out there," and with a gentle turn of her head she shifted her vision. Maldar turned in surprise as the door pushed open and a male came into the hut to join them.

"You too," Aliedori continued. The male paused as a female joined him; together they came into the light of the sphere Aliedori had illuminated in the small hut.

"Such a good watch dragon Kei turns out to be," Maldar chided

Keidrop, who could still be heard crunching on something. The dragon heard and simply flicked her small golden ears in response and continued in search of her supper.

"Don't blame Keidrop. She knew they were there also, she saw them just before we landed, and you are the one who is a poor lookout brother."

Maldar ignored the chide and asked instead, "You did something new, found a new ability and you kept on laughing?"

There was a slight shake of Aliedori's head, he understood and said nothing more and he turned his attention to the newcomers. They sat down on a bench against one wall. Maldar was surprised as he realised that the newcomers were nymphs. All nymphs shared similar traits whether they were from the deep forest, the low glens, or the cascading waterfalls of Bryn-le-Fenir. Although nymphs had long ago lost their ability to fly, they retained their translucent glow and the hard bonelike forms between the shoulder blades and the spinal column. Maldar always had the impression that, any moment now, Waifyn would sprout wings and fly away. Also, they had never lost their golden translucent glow or their ability to be light footed. They were private people, guarding their way of life and continuing the traditions of medicinal magic. They had cared for nature, woods, forests, glens, streams, meadows and all the creatures within, for centuries. They made their homes in the densest and most beautiful of woodlands and glades and the purest of rivers and they sustained and maintained them. They were guardians of all the forests in all the Realms. Nymphs were masters of the bow, their only weapon, and they were second to none.

"I am Ali " But she was cut short.

"We know who you are, Aliedori and Maldar," the male said, "and the honour is ours, daughter and son of the Realm." Aliedori blinked, she was beginning to feel uncomfortable.

"You are possibly the naturalist who will being life back to the Petrified Forest, and you," he said, turning to Maldar, "are the Dragon Knight and the magnificent creature outside is the golden dragon, rarest of all dragons, Keidrop."

"I am afraid you have us at a disadvantage," Aliedori said. She did not like where this was going. She held up her hand to stop them both before they spoke again, as she knew what they were going say and she was having none of it.

"I am able, but I would never do such a thing, it is one thing to use another's eyes and ears, it is altogether a different thing to take information from the minds of others without their knowledge."

"I am sorry Intendant; I did not mean to cause offence. My name is Elowyn and this is my pair bond Sywyn."

"No offence caused, I saw you both sometime ago when I first came, but *sensed* you both long before." Aliedori was aware Elowyn had called her 'Intendant'. She had no idea that the nymphs used the same term also.

"I am not the Intendant of the Nymphs, just of my mother's Realm." She scratched behind her right ear feeling more than a little bit uncomfortable. Nymphs did not recognise humankind societies; they shared the Realms or the spaces in-between but did not involve themselves in the complexities of them.

"There was no sign that you saw us," Sywyn said softly, as with all nymphs her speaking voice was almost as beautiful as her singing one.

Maldar leaned forward, "You are pair bonded?" he asked, surprised and pleased as he noticed their arm jewellery.

Chapter 11

Maldar had never heard of nymphs pair bonding at such a young age. Not that he knew a great deal about Nymph society, but he was beginning to learn. Nymphs lived for a very long time and it was unusual for pair bonding to take place much before the sixtieth cycles. Aliedori knew why the news pleased Maldar so much and could not help but smile; she had never seen her brother so happy.

Sywyn confirmed that pair bonding at their age was uncommon but not unknown. She held Elowyn's hand as she spoke and they were clearly so happy in their love that they glowed and shimmered. They knew that Maldar was the Dragon Knight who wished to be pair bonded with one of their kind. With a smile, Elowyn looked at Maldar, his eye as sparkling and clear as the brooks in the glen.

"You are braver than you realise. There are now tales being told and poems being written of your daring entrance into the royal chambers." Elowyn turned to Aliedori and saw surprise on her face. He studied her for a few seconds, liking what he saw. Almond-shaped, emerald green eyes set wide apart, a fine but somewhat small nose and a generous, wide mouth with full lips. These were set off by a flawless skin stretched tightly over high cheekbones and framed by hair almost as black as the night itself.

Humankind had never interested him, they co-existed within the Realms, and some were of more interest than others. She was one of the interesting ones. This humankind girl held the answer to reuniting the Realms, and that was how it should be as it was the human Realm that was fractured.

It was his turn to be surprised. He had heard talk amongst his people of the expectation and she was held in some regard by Nymph society, but he had not expected her to appeal to him. Nor did he, in fact, expect to find her beautiful at all, and he liked also that he saw colour blazing in her cheeks. Elowyn cast another look at her before he turned back to Maldar and tried to see why the prince of the nymphs, Waifyn, loved this human male so. Elowyn decided that love and attraction were strange and unfathomable and continued with his story.

"This Dragon Knight swooped down on the rarest of dragons carrying the rarest of plants and laid them at the feet of Donri, the mother, and Elbin, the father, and asked for the hand of Waifyn. Keidrop carried him away before they could give their answer. It was just as well the King and Queen were in one of the high terraces."

Aliedori watched Maldar. He was uncomfortable and, needing to do something, he busied himself with retrieving the now cooked food from the fire. Finally he spoke.

"It was not quite as magnificent as that. I was awkward and bumbling, and I was almost certain I would be dropped from the tallest of the dragon towers and knew that Keidrop would not be there to catch me." Maldar smiled, he did not remember his action as heroic, he simply remembered it as being the scariest moment of his life, and he never wanted to go through it again. He would rather face his most dangerous foe than face those two again. Now Elowyn was talking about scholars writing tales and poems about it. Of course, it wasn't true but he would go through it again a thousand times over if he won Waifyn forever. Sensing Maldar's discomfort and wishing to cause no offence, Elowyn said softly, "You are some way from home."

He thought that perhaps he could guess the reason for the journey but asked anyway. Aliedori offered the fellow travellers a share of the provision of meat, bread, cheese, fresh and dried fruit and waited for them to start eating before answering, "We are heading towards the Western End of the neutral forest, but I believe you already guessed that, so what can you tell us about it? Are your people concerned, have they noticed anything?"

Elowyn nodded and there was a sharp intake of breath from Sywyn as she exchanged looks with her pair bond, but she said nothing. Aliedori sensed the nymph's unease at mention of the place.

"We all know the stories coming from the West," Elowyn said finally. "It would appear that a veil has been drawn even more tightly over the whole Realm and even dragons are beginning to avoid that part of the Realm again."

"Yes, but nymphs still move across the Realms, they have never recognised the split." Aliedori stood and began pacing, her usual stance when she was thinking deeply.

"Yes it's true the fortress means nothing to my people, but..."

"But nothing," Aliedori said a little too harshly. Then more calmly, "Well, they have taken settlers from within the Southern Realm and I... we intend to find out why." Aliedori looked at Maldar.

Elowyn hung his head and spoke softly, "There are stories of dragon riders flying out nightly only to return with settlers, but we have never concerned ourselves with the goings on of humankind." Elowyn's voice had lost its musical quality and became a little leaden, "I have never seen this, but we hear these stories whenever we are near a humankind settlement."

"And do you not think it only a matter of time before nymphs are affected?" Aliedori continued to pace, fighting and losing the battle to keep the anger out of her voice.

Maldar pulled up his legs and sat forward, his elbows on the table, and his chin resting in his right hand. Aliedori did not lose her temper often; these two nymphs were behaving as if what happened in the human world did not affect their kind. Aliedori stopped pacing the moment she saw her brother change his stance. She knew the signs, it was a seemingly relaxed pose but at the first sign of trouble, he could spring up, unsheathing his sword in one fluid movement. She had seen him practise this pose since he was given his first sword as a boy. Not that he would draw his sword without severe provocation; the stance was merely in readiness.

"Grand Naturalist..." Aliedori stopped Elowyn; she knew what he was doing.

"I am not a grand anything, I am an Intendant," and she swung round to face them.

"It is the title that many of my people refer to you by," Sywyn said.

"Still... it's a title reserved for the lady of the Southern Realm and I have yet to earn that title." Aliedori said no more, they understood well enough. The nymphs saw themselves as being above the pettiness of humankind, she had seen look in Sywyn's eyes as she appraised her. Whatever she saw in her surprised her, she coloured not through embarrassment but in anger.

The discussion was over and there was no point in continuing. Aliedori offered to share their hut, and she was thanked for her kind offer, but the nymphs said they had to go and bade them goodnight.

"Where are you going?" Aliedori asked in a kinder voice.

Elowyn smiled, "Home to Bryn-le-Fenir to receive the blessing on our pair-bonding from the high King and Queen. All nymphs must make the journey at least once; many choose to do so when they are pair-bonded," he glanced pointedly at Maldar.

Aliedori watched as the nymphs scaled a tree with ease and disappeared into the canopy. They were as comfortable walking amongst the treetops as they were walking on the ground.

"There is something else we haven't thought of," Aliedori said, closing the door and turning, her voice trailing off. Maldar moved backwards with a look of abject terror on his face. He could not go any farther as his back was against the far cabin wall, and it failed to yield. He was saying one word over and over again until it became nonsense, "Bryn-le-Fenir..." Aliedori smiled to herself.

"Don't worry, I will be there," she said offering him her hand but when he did not move she beckoned him.

"Come, take my hand." Maldar relaxed and walked towards her taking her outstretched hand. They stood looking up at each other as they started swinging hands as they had done when they were children.

"I've always wanted to go to Bryn-le-Fenir and wild dragons could not drag me away." This seemed to offer some comfort as Maldar started to look less terrified. Maldar released her hand and sat down in an instant but immediately he was up again, all the smooth, fluid movements so diligently practised temporarily abandoning him. He almost knocked over the seat then moved about in a circle until he was facing the door with his back to Aliedori.

"To reach Bryn-le-Fenir from here is what... at least what... Aliedori do you know?" but the pacing started again.

"Maldar stop, calm yourself, we have more urgent matters at hand." Maldar stopped moving and glanced sideways. Aliedori was still standing by the window but now she was staring out into the darkness. Her eyesight was no better than his, but she could see so much more than he ever could.

"So," he said coming to a stop beside her, whether it was a command or not it seemed to work. "You know what else is a long way away from Skellglade, about four weeks hard flying in fact, the Western borders."

"So they will need resting places in the neutral forest," Aliedori said, finishing off the sentence for him.

Maldar grinned, "That's why we work so well together."

"I think that I may have found it. There is something out there, I *found* it earlier but it's… it's…"

Aliedori could not find the words. She had come across something earlier when she sent her mind out, a powerful sense of strange minds, or she thought she had, about one and a half week's flight from where the hut was. This would make sense since the trackers had said that the dragon riders disappeared somewhere around there. The raiders would need a place for the dragons to rest; the place of 'nothingness' might just be that resting place. It was close to the borders of the Southern Realms, and the place was well hidden.

Therefore, it stood to reason that it would also be well fortified and protected, either by magic, guards, or both. Aliedori searched her mind and feelings to try to find a suitable word to identify what she *felt*, but all she could think of was "nothingness, the absence of something."

Maldar stared at her open-mouthed. What his sister said made no sense at all; there was either something or nothing, there could not be both at the same time, but then he had seen the images that she had drawn from the minds of the trackers. Aliedori rested her hand on his arm; she could not explain what she had found. All she knew was that they had to go to the place and find out for themselves. She intended to start at first light.

Aliedori's face was calm, but her mind was racing as she watched the shadows; there was no immediate danger and she relaxed a little. She could still feel the vibration of Sorin's mind; the link had been severed so savagely and so strangely, it was nothing like she had experienced before, and it left her nerves jangling. She strained her eyes, staring through the night and allowed her mind to drift. She caught the minds of the hunting animals, including Keidrop's and small birds, a few dragons, but nothing larger than Gems. But she could find no life around the strange place she had *found*. The moonlight stopped short of the treetops and only the light coming from the hut windows illuminated the ground. She continued to stare into the night long after Maldar had curled up on one of the bunks and fallen asleep. Tomorrow they would start their search early and within a week or so they would hopefully find out what was there. Aliedori had no fear for herself, only for those that were taken and for their families. Tomorrow morning she would start a venture into that place of 'nothingness', and she was taking Maldar with her.

The journey started well, despite the trepidation Aliedori had felt the night before. With the sun up, the gloom that clouded her mind seemed to clear. They awoke with the rising of the sun and Keidrop was happy after a night of hunting as she had found bits of charcoal, a happy replacement for coke stone. She had spent most of the night eating the charcoal that would aid ignition of her fire. By the morning, she was bloated, contented and happy to comply with whatever was asked of her.

However, the mood changed over the next few days and the closer they got to the location the more subdued the small party became. When they reached what Aliedori thought was their destination she got Keidrop to circle several times over the place. They could see nothing from the air; dense trees blocked all views below their branches. From above the treetops, all seemed fine, the sun was shining and it was a clear, bright day. Keidrop circled again flying lower and slower each time.

"What now?" Maldar asked.

"We go," she replied.

The wind had started up and the breeze caught the twisted mis-shapen trees close by and they whistled violently. Swirling, grey, smoky clouds overhead seemed to draw life out of the forest as the breeze swept across the ground. Blackened toadstools and charred brackens fed the bitterness in the atmosphere and exuded an eerie chill. Fingers of light coiled with wisps of fog and dragged it through the undergrowth and the blackened willows. Branches drooped down under the weight of thick, black sap that dripped into the ground adding to the dankness of the area. Aliedori stood in the middle of it all, listening; she had brought her hand up and placed a finger against her lips stopping Maldar in his tracts.

Aliedori was sure she could hear soft footsteps accompanied by heavy breathing or growling, but was unable to make out whether it was in the distance or coming from beneath their feet. Wherever the sound was coming from it caused the undergrowth to tremble. Aliedori knelt and placed her ear to the ground as droplets of water dripping from the withered branches above their heads splashed on her neck sending cold chills down her spine. She shivered as she continued to listen to the strange noise coming from the silent place. The sound was coming from under her feet.

On reflection, she thought it had perhaps been a mistake to force Keidrop to remain where they had landed. Under Aliedori's instruction, they had abandoned Keidrop on the perimeter some time ago. The dragon was not happy and had refused to obey Aliedori's command. Only when Maldar reprimanded her did Keidrop settle and obey the command with some unease and take to the skies. Keidrop did not like the idea of leaving her young charge and his sister alone to face danger.

Maldar had watched the struggle between the naturalist and the dragon for some time until it had became a sort of a game before he intervened. Aliedori would command the dragon; she would appear to accept the command but the moment they turned their backs to walk deeper into the 'nothingness' the dragon would follow. Finally Maldar had to take Keidrop's reins, pull the huge golden face down to his level and looking into the large golden eyes said, "My dear friend you have heard but you have not listened, if we are lost then who will raise the alarm."

Maldar tugged at a horn and patted his dragon's head as the eyes flared with understanding. Keidrop butted Maldar gently, pushing him off balance and it was Aliedori's outstretched hand that saved him from falling. Keidrop turned her head, looked at Aliedori, spread her wings and was gone.

Since then they had been alone, walking towards a part of the forest that appeared to have had all the life sucked out of it. Everything was grey and there seemed to be no natural light reaching the ground; everywhere was dull and colourless. Maldar had drawn his sword as his sister stood up again and wiped her hands on her clothes.

He expected her to say, "You do not need that" or "That will be of no use" but instead she enchanted his sword before she unsheathed her own seax, the sword she wore in a scabbard attached to the belt round her waist. Aliedori's action frightened Maldar more than he thought possible and for the first time since entering this place he felt real fear.

Chapter 12

"There is something moving underground, it appears to be in great pain, or very big," she said.

The growl came again, a fraction after Aliedori had spoken and begun to walk, indicating for Maldar to do the same. They both stopped. This time Maldar had heard the growl and seen the dull unnatural grey light that accompanied the sound. It came from a short distance away in the direction they were going and with each growl the ground seemed to heave and sigh. Maldar felt it all about him and through his body. There were four growls, followed by four flashes of the grey light, and he wondered at the significance.

Aliedori's eyes were fixed on a spot up ahead but Maldar could see nothing, only more dying or dead vegetation. Greying tentacles of fog bled around them. Aliedori moved off again, her brother at her left, sword at the ready, prepared to meet unknown foes.

High above their heads Keidrop, circled, thirty-five feet of claws, sinew, muscle and fire. To the right lay a deeper gloom of trees and shrubs preventing her from seeing beyond. But forward? Her eyes continued to search, trying to figure out what was ahead. Immediately in front of them there was a simple patch of bare ground and something else. Aliedori felt that if she reached out she would be able to touch it, but touch what? Touch the unknown. She sent her mind out and realised she could no longer reach Keidrop. She was still able to sense her, but there was a barrier of some kind and Keidrop would not able to penetrate it. She was clearly frustrated at being unable to make an aerial assault or even reach them should something go wrong. Aliedori sent Keidrop feelings of her physical discomfort as a warning, but also to let her know that while there was discomfort they were safe for the moment. She hoped the message would get through. There was no rain but there was the eternal dampness and dripping sap or water. Aliedori was uncertain what was causing the mist and the fog but she didn't like it, it was in one area only.

The fine morning mist they had encountered when they awoke had quickly burned away soon after sunrise. But here, the thin mist had become something more the closer they got to this place. For almost two hours she and Maldar had travelled on foot undisturbed. They had followed tracks made by animals going to the stream to drink, and when they had passed a substantial stream some time before, they had stopped to drink the refreshing water then continued. Aliedori and Maldar finally halted after she heard the growling four times; the same strange grey light followed the growl. But she glimpsed neither beast nor man and even her keen hearing revealed nothing in the swirling dense mist. Everything she had ever done in her life had been play-acting. She was not a seasoned traveller, nor was she a seasoned fighter. She was not even an official naturalist. Yes, she had magical powers beyond other naturalists' abilities, including her mother, but what did that really mean? Nothing, not when she had never done anything of worth in her whole stupid life. All being said and done, she was just a daughter of the Southern Realm who oversaw classification ceremonies. What good was that when she was in a grey, dark place, wet and lifeless?

Except it wasn't lifeless? There were things making strange noises and flashing grey lights and… and… everything! Aliedori almost stamped her feet. Everywhere she went her mother's people pandered to her, telling her that she had the greatest power ever seen in the Realms for many dynasties.

This was a power so great that she could unite the Realms again, but it was not magic that fractured the Realms it was humankind's greed, pure and simple. Aliedori had never really had a chance to demonstrate her full magical powers and she was not even sure that she was as powerful as they made her out to be, or whether she could fulfill any dynasty at all. She had let the idea that she was destined for great things go to her head. Look where that had got her, in trouble with grey flashing lights and grey sounds, things making grey noises. What was she doing here in this unknown place, what was she taking on? How dared she think that she could save her mother's people and return them home in triumph? What was she thinking? When she had heard of the settlers being taken, she should have simply returned to the city, talked to their parents and left it to them to raise the dragon knights. Maldar would have gone with them. That was what he was trained for; he was a Dragon Lord and commanded his own legion. Now she stood in the darkest place she had ever known with no clue what to do. Maldar was beside her, trusting her, alert and ready to face the unknown.

"You quite finished?" he asked, as despite Aliedori saying nothing he knew what had happened. She nodded her head. "Good, because I think it's here."

The greyness of the dying day was sucking the last of the little light out of the clearing. The ground trembled, and Aliedori sensed that something had changed, but it was not possible to say what it was. The strange growling followed by the greyish light was accompanied by a foul, rancid smell, and she sensed the movement of their attackers rather than saw them. They were caught in her peripheral vision, and as she raised her arm a flare of pure, incandescent light burst into life, illuminating the area. All at once Aliedori saw four shapes moving towards them, dark and sleek, hoods covering their heads and red eyes glowing from beneath. Aliedori tried a binding spell but it missed, only glancing the first attacker, throwing them off to her right. The second attacker easily eluded the spell and charged.

Maldar moved forward, his sword raised, then brought it down in a slashing movement so powerful that it almost took the arm off above the elbow of the second attacker. Aliedori had been expecting something, but it was still a shock when she saw the gaunt figures of their attackers moving at speed towards her. The hood of the closest assailant fell back as he charged; revealing shrunken features, a hook-like nose, red glazed eyes and grey skin. Startled, Aliedori froze, then leapt into action at the last second, bringing the seax up to stop the grey thing from lashing out at her head.

It swayed, veering away to her left as she spun, and as she lashed out again the grey thing leapt a low bush and escaped the blade. It turned again to charge at her but this time she was ready. Grasping the weapon in both hands, with the blade pointing backwards, she moved to meet the attacker full on. To her right, she caught Maldar's swift movements and then heard clash of steel against rock; no, not rock, something else.

Aliedori steadied herself, swallowing hard, both feet planted firmly on the ground, slightly apart in line with her shoulders. She took a deep cleansing breath to remain calm; then she emptied her mind of all distractions except her training, the moves, attack, counter attack and defence. As she saw the grey-taloned hand lash out towards her face, she bent back from the waist, and the talon missed the intended target, catching and ripping her tunic instead. Aliedori closed her eyes for a second and when she opened them again she was ready.

Speed was of the essence. She brought her right arm up and across her body, bringing the seax with it. Aliedori lashed out, the sharpened point of the bone blade reached its target, slashing the grey's chest, and opening a wound. Dark viscous fluid escaped the grey shrieked and staggered back a few paces then lunged.

Aliedori twisted out of the way to find firm footing, steadied herself, and brought the seax up again into the soft underbelly of the grey creature. She pushed the seax home grasping the hilt with both hands, slicing through soft tissues, spilling the grey's guts and fluid over her arm. The warm liquid soaked her palms making them sticky yet slippery.

She pulled the sword out with some difficulty, and the grey fell to its knees then collapsed at her feet; she had no time to think about her actions.

Another grey was upon her as she lashed out with the seax, again trying to cut into the soft underbelly. She missed, but her action brought the grey down and as it lay twisting and convulsing Aliedori was sure the thing cried out in a plea for help. She stopped, the seax raised above her head in a double-hand clasp ready to end the grey creature's life. Could this creature speak with a voice? Unsure of herself she glanced towards Maldar for some reassurance, but he was busy, caught up in his own battle. As Aliedori dropped her hands, lowering her sword, the grey creature lying on the ground caught her left ankle. It gripped her with such force that she began to fall backwards, her arms flailing as she struggled to remain upright.

She lost the battle and fell onto the damp hard ground. Her sword flew from her grip, and she lay winded for a second or two, breathing deeply to catch her breath and clear her head before she began pulling herself back up. The movement caused slight dizziness and she reached up to touch the back of her head. She brought her hand towards her face and sighed in relief to see that there was no blood on her fingers.

For a second, Aliedori had forgotten what caused her to fall then she became aware of a burning sensation on her ankle as the grey's grip tightened. Bringing her right leg up Aliedori kicked out again and again, but it only served to tighten its grip. She turned her head looking for her sword and saw it far off to one side where it had skidded to a halt up against a tree trunk. It was too far to reach.

Aliedori twisted her body as far as she could but her sword was still out of reach. She said a quick incantation and the seax slid into her outstretched, open palm. Pleased that she was still thinking clearly, she gripped the sword and brought it up and then down severing the grey's arm above the elbow. Aliedori pulled herself into a sitting position bringing her left leg up, the severed arm still firmly attached to her ankle. She pried the talon off and looked closely at the hand. It was a human hand, horrendously disfigured, but human none the less. She shivered at the knowledge. As she examined it, the talon turned into a normal, male hand. A sob caught in Aliedori's throat as the hand slipped from her fingers. She dragged her eyes away from the severed hand and looked up as she heard a grey shriek and Maldar calling her name. Then she was showered in black viscous liquid as he dragged her, twisting her out of the way. A grey thing fell to the exact spot where she had been sitting moments before. Aliedori allowed herself to be pulled onto her feet. She was trembling, tears threatening to engulf her, and she was unable to stop herself from shaking.

She looked at Maldar, around the area, then down at her feet; the human hand was still there. The illumination still blazed brightly, and she was able to see the devastation around them.

"Have they all passed?" Maldar had asked a similar question some time ago, or so it seemed. Maldar nodded, and she moved away from him, still shaking, trying to remember her duty as an Intendant, her duty on the battlefield, a duty she had never performed before and had hoped that she never would. "They are humankind," she said as a sob escaped her and tears spilled down her dirty cheeks. Aliedori bent down and tenderly touched the grey at her feet; now that it had passed it was not a threat. Rather the grey creature looked sad and pathetic; she could not distinguish whether it was male or female or even its true age. She knelt by the corpse. "You were once of nature and back to nature you will return."

"What... who... who are humankind?" Maldar looked around him, it did not make sense; surely she must be mistaken. Aliedori did not answer and instead she moved to another grey and repeated the words. After this, she came back and stood by Maldar, looking up at him.

"I think that the grey creatures are some of the settlers. So we bless their way home and we bury them."

Maldar recoiled for a second or two; he thought that was what she had said. He slipped his arm around her shoulders and nodded in agreement, seeing that she needed his comfort, his reassurance. They had come to find the settlers but he had not expected this.

He gasped, and Aliedori looked to see what had caused it. She followed his gaze down and saw a young man lying at her feet. His features were almost human again, but he was still a shade of grey and she bent down again to examine him more closely.

"My magic did not work, if I could have bound them..." her voice trailed off as she looked up at Maldar, then at the fallen.

"And what would you have done once you had bound them. You did not know what was beneath or that you would have found these settlers," Maldar replied. He knew that she meant if her binding spell had worked then there would not have been any death. But what would she have been left with, several strange grey creatures instead of just one?

He pointed to the grey bound to a large tree trunk and looked back at her when she did not respond; her face was a mask of pain, sadness, confusion and doubt.

It was not the expression Maldar was used to seeing. Aliedori's face always carried a look of serenity, calm and wisdom beyond her years, except of course when she was up to mischief. It was clear that she was not listening; she had not heard what he had said. The black tarlike fluid that had been spilt out of the grey things over her had stained her hair and clothes. She looked a fright and smelled even worse. Maldar pulled her into his arms, and she accepted the comfort of her brother's embrace.

Her hair and clothes were still sticky and when she pushed herself away from Maldar his cheeks and clothes were dirty and smeared. Aliedori felt neither strong nor wise but she had a job to do, so she gathered her wits about her and took a deep cleansing breath to steady the shaking.

With a heavy sigh, she said again, "We bless their path and we return them to whence they came. The ancestors will welcome them." Maldar knew that it was not as cold as it sounded. They stood close together as Aliedori cast an incantation. Two things happened to the bodies; firstly, the greyness detached itself, it was a solid featureless mass the same size and shape as the settlers. It was made of grey clay and mud and as it left their bodies and met the air, it dissolved, fell back to the ground and disappeared into the dirt. With the clay and mud gone, Aliedori was able to see the settlers clearly.

As they regained their true forms the earth beneath two of the fallen became soft and the bodies sank into the hole created and refilled the open grave again. For the third fallen a pyre appeared and ignited into flames, the cloaks of the fallen had become swaddling cloths. One of the two remaining graves was piled high with stones while the other only had soil. All three went on their way to meet their ancestors as the traditions of their community dictated.

All three had a rune at their feet with the names of their ancestors. Then she remembered what was nagging at her.

"There were four," she said, drawing the seax and looking around her. Maldar pointed, and she turned and looked. The binding spell she had cast had worked better than she had expected. The grey had become fused to the tree and was struggling against its bonds, the red eyes glowing dully. The taloned fingers tried to claw the air as Aliedori spoke an incantation to detach the grey from the tree but keep it bound. The grey withered, its mouth open in a scream of agony, and for an instant, she saw the true female image, then it was gone. Aliedori called the elements again, but she could not separate the female from her golem. As she turned to gather the elements again the thing spoke. The voice was cold, a growl, its humanity almost lost but not quite.

"I was Sibley, from the Eastern province of Ouran and I was pair bonded with Yarlyn; we have two children – a girl Synne and a boy Tamar. We were happy, go to them please, tell them… tell them." Sibley screamed and the grey thing took control again. Her breath was ragged and a growl emanated from deep within her. Sibley looked directly at Aliedori who could see the struggle going on between the two halves. Sibley won through again.

"Send me home, bless my path, send me home to my ancestors." It was a plea, her only plea.

"Your kind will not go easily," Maldar replied.

"I can help you with that," Sibley said looking at Maldar but talking to Aliedori.

Aliedori shook her head as tears welled up in her eyes again.

"Sibley, you cannot ask me to do such a thing."

Sibley growled again, a long pitiful sound echoing around the woods. She tried to lash out but the tree bound her arms so only her wrists and talons moved.

"Others like me; many, many others, and they are coming, and when they do I will be lost again, send me home. Please bless my path, and send me home."

Aliedori shook her head again. She was being asked to take a life; she could not do it, no matter how pitiful the life was. She could not do it, as she had already unwillingly taken a life in self-defence and fatally wounded another. She could not do what Sibley asked of her. Aliedori turned back to Sibley.

"I will give you my blessing, but I will not send you home; you are strong so fight, fight this grey thing." Aliedori's eyes were fixed on the ground, partly to hide her tears.

Sibley screamed.

"Listen, Sibley, there is another who will be able to help you; he will find a way to reverse this."

Maldar was doubtful of how they were going to control Sibley in her present state. But he knew that Aliedori was right. If there was a way to save Sibley, even a very slim chance, then they must take it. The question was how were they going to transport her back to the city, as it was the only place that could provide the help Sibley needed. Stornvale was closest and there were three mages there, but Maldar was sure that bringing Sibley to any of them could cause greater harm than good for all concerned.

Chapter 13

"Aliedori do what you need to do, because we need to go. I don't want to spend the night here and I am sure you don't either. If Sibley is right there are more of those things coming."

Maldar looked around him, since the attack he had noticed the eerie silence of the place and he was beginning to understand what Aliedori meant by *nothingness*.

He placed an arm on her shoulder and gave it a quick squeeze as she cast a brief incantation. Sibley fell forward and Maldar was quick enough to catch her before she hit the ground.

Aliedori cast another incantation, and the area around the three graves spouted fortresses of plants and flowers, even the burning pyre. Maldar threw Sibley over his shoulder, and they were off, running as the sound of numerous growls could be heard coming from the earth. On Maldar's shoulder, Sibley struggled, but he did not know if her struggle was in desperation or whether she wanted to join them. Whatever it was, her struggle was making it almost impossible for him to keep hold of her and move at a good pace.

Aliedori said, "Be still now, calm yourself," and Sibley slumped as she tried again to remove the golem. But she could not; however, the stark greyness was lifted somewhat, and Sibley's humankind features were now more apparent. Maldar could hear the continuous growls followed by the eerie grey flashes of light, and he hurried Aliedori along.

"How many?" Aliedori asked, not taking her eyes off Sibley.

"Too many," came the reply.

Out of the darkness where the illumination did not reach, came shadow after shadow with glowing red eyes. Aliedori and Maldar paused in a little clearing long enough to look back when they realised that the Greys were trying to charge, but had been prevented by the illumination barrier that Aliedori had created. They stared in fascination.

It was incredible to see rows of red eyes glowing at them as the Greys fought to get over each other. They were unable to move beyond the gaps between the two large trees where the illumination had been placed. Aliedori turned back and raced towards the red glowing eyes, ignoring Maldar's cry of alarm. She stopped in front of the glowing red eyes and reached out her hand, pressing against the invisible barrier. It shimmered beneath her palm and became opaque to the touch, sending tiny sparks racing out across the surface. The grey creatures could see and hear her but they could not move. Aliedori noticed too that while they were close to the barrier they were not touching it. She ran her hand over the invisible veil, and with each touch the barrier undulated, sending wave after gentle wave of shimmering sparks through its surface. Aliedori moved slowly around the barrier, the red eyes following her. Their growls and snarls bounced through the barrier and reverberated round the area. She could feel the tingle of the magic through her fingers and palms and up to her wrists. She tried to push through the barrier. It gave a little but sprung back as she eased the pressure off. She walked around the barrier but there was nothing out of the ordinary just a simple slit, a darker patch against a dark area of the forest. She backed away slowly until she was standing by Maldar again. They watched as the red glows began to disappear; each and every light dimmed and vanished from sight. Aliedori continued to watch and listen for some time after the last red eyes disappeared.

The growls could still be heard but the sound was receding deeper underground, and almost before she realised it the sounds had died away and the small dank area was completely silent again. After a while all Aliedori could hear were Keidrop's beating wings as she landed beside them in the clearing. Something had changed, and Keidrop had managed to land where she could not penetrate before.

"You did something with the light, Aliedori.

That's why the Greys can't move beyond the barrier."

She did not take her gaze from the illumination before them.

"I didn't do anything; all I was thinking about at the time was making the place as bright as possible. I thought that if I could keep the attackers in one area we stood a better chance," she said. "But I didn't do anything else, at least I don't think so."

"Do you think that Skellglade could also have something to do with it? It's the blessing you bestowed on Skellglade, the settlers must use these woods." Maldar indicated around the area.

"I did say your blessing would have far reaching consequences," he continued with a smile as he hefted Sibley farther up on his shoulder.

"This has nothing to do with the blessing but at least we have to find out how the new settlers cross into these Realms." Aliedori plucked a broad leaf from the nearest shrub and rubbed her hair and clothes down. "Also, why they were so afraid causing them to use magic to wipe their memories of the crossing?" By saying a little cleansing enchantment she managed to get rid of most of the fluid, but the stain and smell remained clinging to them. The scent incantation had very little effect on the smell so she gave up. Looking down at her clothes in disgust, she threw the leaf away and said, "Take Sibley to Fengardia and give her to Wulfgar. Tell him what we need and talk to our parents; tell them what has happened and see if Kastillion made it to the city. If he didn't, perhaps you can try and find out why not."

Aliedori issued the order as she pulled the seax from the scabbard, moving to the barrier again.

"Oh, and bring me back a change of clothes, these are ruined." Then she was off, headed back the way they had just come.

"N-now see here, Dori," Maldar managed to stutter. It had finally happened, he had turned into his father. It actually caused Aliedori to hesitate and glance over her shoulder before continuing her progress. He was about to follow, then remembered that Sibley was still on his shoulder; he placed her gently on the ground and ran after Aliedori. He grabbed her arm and pulled her back before she could step into the illumination between the two trees.

"If you think I am going back to Fengardia without you, you better think again."

"Sibley needs Wulfgar," she said.

"And how long do you think I will live when I return home without you."

"They will understand, Fengardia needs to be aware of this development... besides I can take care of myself."

Maldar let out a long sigh and tightened his grip on Aliedori's arm.

"That is beside the point, you can't do this alone Aliedori; I won't let you. If we go, we go together, either into the unknown or home to Fengardia, but we are not separating."

Maldar's voice was firm and final; he waited for a reaction knowing only too well that he could not leave her here. No matter how powerful her magic was she was not ready to face such creatures alone.

When her reply came, it came with a small nod of the head. It was not the one he was expecting, she had conceded without a fight; she did not argue, she did not use magic; she simply nodded her head in agreement. He looked at her long and hard unable to believe that she had given in so easily.

She nodded again and pledged softly, "Honesty, truth and above all loyalty," she said to confirm her words. Maldar relaxed the grip on her arm a little, he knew once she made the pledge she would not break her bond, "And besides I need time to learn about Sibley's condition," she added.

"We go together, to Fengardia?" he asked after a short pause. Aliedori was still staring at the place between the two trees as she cast an incantation.

"But I am not finished here so I will come back," she said firmly.

"And I will be with you," Maldar replied.

"My only worry is that I may have blocked the only escape route for those wishing to cross into this Realm," Aliedori sighed. She did not like the idea at all and Maldar could hear the concerns in his sister's voice. He placed an arm round her shoulders and they both turned to look at each other and back again to the newly discovered 'gateway'. Both were resigned to the fact that there was nothing they could do for those people on the other side for the moment.

"You said that you would never go wandering far without me and yet... here you are." The voice was deep and mellow and rippled with promises yet to keep. Aliedori turned and saw a nymph bending over Sibley. Hair hid his face and he was reaching as if to touch her, his arm hanging in mid-decision for a moment. He changed his mind and withdrew his hand as he looked up smiling and caught Aliedori's gaze.

Then his eyes slid from hers and came to rest on Maldar. The nymph stood slowly, not taking his eyes off Maldar. The smile on his face became wider and wider. He was not as wide in the shoulders or as muscular as Maldar. He stood a hand span shorter too, his skin glowing like the gleaming sun and accentuating his pecan-shaped golden eyes. The nymph brought much needed warmth and brightness into the gloom of the dying day. The long, straight locks of flaxen hair hung loose down his back, perfectly offsetting his small, slightly pointed ears; his perfect clear skin held eyes that were like the finest crystal, set in an angular face.

Waifyn was tall and lean, his shirt clinging to his gently muscled torso, his movements lithe and mature, daunting and captivating at the same time. Maldar glanced away for a moment or two as if it hurt to gaze too long on his beloved, and when he looked back he caught the expression on his face. It was one of wonder, compassion, puzzlement and deep joy. The wide grin and glint in his eyes were the first things Maldar noticed.

In an instant, he was beside the nymph drawing him into an embrace and they kissed deeply. Aliedori waited, then cleared her throat when the kiss continued to linger. The lovers moved slowly apart, grinning at each other, and it seemed that the odd smell and sticky fluid Maldar had all over his clothes went unnoticed by Waifyn. Aliedori studied her feet as if they were the most interesting things she had ever seen.

"Waifyn, meet my sister Aliedori. Aliedori meet Waifyn," Maldar said rather sheepishly before his attention was drawn back to the nymph.

Aliedori simply smiled, her arms folded across her chest, losing interest in her feet.

"So this is your nymph." The wink was lost on Maldar.

He returned with a grin, his pride lifting his shoulders. "Yes," he said, "this is my Nymph."

Aliedori had the feeling nymph was said with a capital N.

As Waifyn put his palms together, his head inclined, he aped the customary greeting of the West. Few people in the Southern Realm put palms together in greetings anymore. Aliedori inclined her head slightly, her attention drawn again by the gateway.

"How did you know we were here?" Maldar asked, still standing close to his lover.

"Elowyn and Sywyn," Aliedori said, and as she turned the pyre rose up higher and shot tongues of flame towards the treetops.

Waifyn glanced skyward with a little shake of his head to the flames. Aliedori caught the gesture and the flames shrank a little.

"Yes," Waifyn said. "Elowyn sent a message when she met you in the hut."

Aliedori had forgotten that all nymphs could communicate no matter how far the distance. Something she was just learning to do but only if those she was mind *speaking* to were close by.

"I have placed sentries around the area. It is a kind of barrier, and it keeps the grey creatures close to the gateway," Aliedori said for the benefit of Waifyn. "Three resting places for the fallen and one to fool those controlling the Greys." She turned back to the lovers dragging her gaze from the gateway as if she was finding it difficult to leave and wanted to linger. Keidrop snorted in disgust as she was approached; she was back with her master and they were safe and unharmed. She was happy and could even put up with the odd smell hanging about them and the even odder creature.

"Now we get Sibley to the city and to Wulfgar."

"Keidrop can carry us all but we will have to ensure that she gets regular rest," Maldar said.

"Don't worry about me, I may not be able to go as fast as a dragon but I will be close behind," Waifyn said.

"We leave together or not at all," Aliedori said.

Waifyn stood with his hand on the hilt of his knife; his bow lay across one shoulder, hanging along his back with a quiver full of arrows. Like Aliedori's seax, the knife he was carrying was not made of steel. It was a traditional one, the serrated third horn of a drac, used long before metal forge weapons. The serrated horn of the drac was the weapon many used and it was still used today. Many naturalists, mages, and other people with magic still preferred to use a drac's horn. Aliedori preferred the drac's horn to the metal sword but used both with ease and comfort; Maldar had always preferred the metal sword, though he had never used a drac's horn. Aliedori doubted that he had ever picked one up.

They were both looking at Aliedori.

"We all leave or we all stay," Maldar wanted to have the final word.

"If we all stay… what then?" Waifyn did not want to be the one to ask the question but it needed asking. Aliedori was looking from the still burning pyre to the gateway and back to the two young men. Maldar was sure that even though she had sworn an oath it looked as if she was about to break it. He called her name and in response she grabbed the slumped form of Sibley to hoist her up. By the time Waifyn had formulated a thought about Aliedori's size to her strength, Keidrop and her rider had disappeared over the treetops and away to the South with everyone on board.

Chapter 14

After many weeks of travelling, resting for very short periods and only rousing Sibley long enough to feed her, the scruffy, smelly, tired and very dirty band of travellers arrived in the city. Dragon riders visiting the city and seeing it for the first time saw it from the air were spellbound by the majesty and size of the capital. Fengardia lay on the mouth of several large freshwater crystal blue ocean-lakes. They were fed by rivers winding from the snow-capped mountains of Ferran-Gar and springs coming from as far away as Stornvale on the distant side of Broken Hills. The city was flanked on one side by the vast Southern forest and on the other three sides by the fresh waters of the ocean-lakes.

The water was as blue as the sky and stretched out as far as the eyes could see. It disappeared over the horizon and appeared to merge with the skies just before it dropped off the end of the Realm. Boats, commercial and private, large and small, lined the wharf and docks. Their sails were a multitude of colours catching the breeze and dancing their bellowing riot of hues across the bay. The clatter of traders was carried up to them in the air as gifts and offerings for their safe return. Of all the entrances into the city this was a sight Aliedori loved the most, but it was the one she saw the least. This entrance showed Fengardia off at its best. The ocean-lakes sustained the vast and rich metropolis with fresh water, commerce and fishing. The trading ports bustled with traders and beyond the port the sandstone and slate roofed buildings of the main city stretched out away from the crystal blue waters to the right and into the green of the forest. Bridges and walkways connected the mainland to an island in the centre of the largest ocean-lake and to the Temple Gardens, a place of worship and pilgrimage for many of the Realmers. A shard of an ancient mountain remained in the centre of the island; sharp, jagged bare rocks on one side while the other side had slopes covered with an abundance of fruit trees, shrubs, plants and wild flowers.

At the base of the slope stood the Temple Gardens and an ancient ruined temple palace said to go back in the mists of time. The temple was once the site of the original palace and home to the first Grand Naturalist, Anterian. The rest of the island disappeared when distant melted water had swelled the lakes, breaking the banks of the individual lakes and they became one large expanse of water to be known as the ocean-lakes. All that had remained on the island was the old palace and temple as a new palace was already established on the knoll overlooking the bay. After the swell, centuries before, all that remained on the island was the temple to the ancestors.

Closer to the forest and land was a turquoise lagoon where the remains of a mountain range jutted out above the water providing a perfect place for swimming. Several peaks had bathing temples and steps cut into the rock to provide access to the lagoon. While others were covered in dense shrubbery and only dragons and dracs traversed them. On land, a bridge linked the main section and oldest part of the town to the palace. The bridge was ornately decorated, carved out of one solid block of white marble to span the narrow inlet. The highly decorative swirls and curves of the solid structure mimicked the ebb, flow and gentle ripple of the ocean-lakes. Each side of the wide bridge was planted with palms and flowers, but the many coloured plants did not distract from the bridge but instead enhanced the purity of the white marble. Above the heads of the people were suspended walkways connecting the main land to the island and the temple gardens.

On the ground, equally ornate roadways made from red and yellow baked bricks, linked all the outer settlements with the city. High above the city were the dragons' towers reaching into the sky. Structures of steel, bricks, entangled with vines and trees; the leaders' magic was used especially to grow the vines and plants that clung to and bound all the towers. They were commercial towers owned by the city merchants and used for dragons and their riders from all across the Realms as trading posts. All across the city, dragon towers housed stables, dwellings for travellers and places to dine, play and even gamble. Many traders came to the city without ever landing on the ground and chose only to see the city from the towers. The central windows in all dragon towers housed the dragon masters and the keepers whose lifelong devotion was tending to the needs of dragons only.

Aliedori never grew tired of seeing her home from the dragon's eye view. But morning she barely noticed the city below her that still had not risen from its slumber. The palace was built on a large sweeping curve of the bay in the ocean-lakes; on the south side was a spectacular view of the town. Between the palace and lower town lay a lush shallow ravine and the palace, which, like the other buildings in the city, had been built from sand stone and coloured slates.

The main residential area stood closest to the lakes and extended over the water on stilts of living trees, making that part of the palace look like it had grown out of the tree trunks. There had been many, many times when she and Maldar would dive straight from her window or veranda into the crystal blue lake. It was a race to see who could touch the roots first; she was never allowed to cheat by using magic. Maldar always beat her, bobbing back up through the water first, fist raised in triumph and a grin so wide it threatened to blot out the sun. The structure over the water was wooden framed with a wooden floor interspersed with ornately carved blue wooden tiles from the blue wood of the Amelia tree. The walls and beams were also ornately carved with flying dragons, galloping dracs and plant life. The entrance from the water was large enough for guests of the palace arriving by water to moor. On the other side of the palace in the wall of the lower level lay another entrance to the grand hall and garden from the town.

The large scrolled gate was set in a gateway of an ornate arch overrun with ivy, vines and other climbing plants and flowers. Within the walls was an enormous lawn surrounded by fruit trees, herbs, shrubs and edible plants. Beyond the garden was the main building, which consisted of four domed roofs. The domes were covered in green slate interspersed with blue tiles inspired by the natural surroundings of forest and water.

From the dome spires, symmetrical turrets reached up into the sky, gleaming with warmth and magic sparkling from every surface. It was a beautiful place, but it was a fortress all the same; every wall, every stone, every brightly coloured tile was impregnated with magic – but a defence against what? Aliedori had never questioned why the palace, indeed every building needed to have a magical protection. On the far right of the wall close to the forest was the dragon tower that served the palace. The building contained the stables for the dragons and was home to the dragon knights, riders, and the palace's personal guards.

Wulfgar's dwelling and apothecary was not part of the main palace but was built in the canopy of several very large and sturdy trees and connected to the palace by walkways to upper and lower levels. The ground was reached by a spiral stairwell carved out of the trunk of an even older tree, which allowed him and his apprentices direct access to their beloved forest to collect herbs and plants. The very ground floor was where sometimes he, but mostly his apprentices, worked in the apothecary freeing him up to see customers. The nearest access to Wulfgar for a dragon rider were the upper terraces and it was into these that Keidrop and her riders landed close to dawn.

The viscous fluid from the Grey had ripened and though Aliedori had managed to rid herself and Maldar of the worst of it by casting and incantation, the smell and stain still clung to them and had even transferred to Waifyn's clothes and hair. It did not help that Sibley emitted the smell from every pore of her clay-like skin. She remained docile though she had continued to beg for release throughout the long journey. She was taken from Keidrop's saddle and was carried between Maldar and Waifyn to the physician's door. The first knock summoned an apprentice, who appeared so quickly it was as if he had been behind the door waiting for just such a summons. He jumped back crying out in fright at the sight of Sibley, almost shutting the door again in their faces. Only Aliedori's quick reaction prevented the door from slamming. She calmed the apprentice as best she could and instructed him to go and get the physician. In his fright the apprentice forgot all his manners and protocol to rush from the hall and disappear behind a curtained off area. He returned a few seconds later to deposit the basket of herbs and other medicinal paraphernalia on the long waist-high cabinet against one wall and disappeared again. Still flustered, he returned a second time and invited the weary travellers in but kept a close eye on Sibley as he closed the door behind them and disappeared behind the curtains again.

Light footsteps could be heard, then voices, and in a few moments, the physician appeared on the upper level, looking over into the hall. He made an exclamation of surprise and, gripping the rail, vaulted over with feline grace to land perfectly balanced in front of the visitors. Middle age had not robbed the physician of his agility and grace; despite herself, Aliedori smiled as he showed off his skills.

"Intendant... Maldar... Waifyn..." Wulfgar exclaimed, bringing his palms together and inclining his head. He knew Waifyn very well and there was no mistaking his sister's youngest child. With his head still inclined, Wulfgar said, "Who or what have you brought me at this hour of the morning, children?"

Wulfgar was used to Aliedori and Maldar bringing all kind of strays and the sick to be healed, but this was something new. He had attended Aliedori's birth and attended Maldar when he was first brought to the palace and had even attended Waifyn as a child. They were young people he had known and loved all their lives, but now his eyes were firmly fixed on Sibley. He would talk to his nephew later; there was much to be said, especially if the rumours were true. He was handfasted to a humankind and it would appear that his nephew intended to do the same.

"What manner of creature is this?" he asked, raising his eyes to the three young people standing before him. Wulfgar was once a great warrior nymph, skilled with the bow as well as the sword. He had chosen to leave his beloved forest home and spent his formative years as a soldier. He had fought in border skirmishes with the Western Realm in defence of the liberty of the Eastern Realm.

Chapter 15

Wulfgar, like all nymphs, carried medicinal magic in his very being and developed his talent further by collecting the right herbs to help the wounded on the battlefield. He had started with the battlefield and his fellow warriors and the battle dracs, healing wounds that ordinary medicinal magic failed to heal. He realised that he would rather bring life than take it and had worked tirelessly, but only after he saved the life of the Lady Minoria. She had been a young Intendant then, and she was fighting in the same border skirmish.

Minoria was thrown from a drac after it was wounded and was taken to the medical tent by another warrior; she was hardly breathing, with a broken leg and internal bleeding. When he was offered the apprenticeship with the palace's ancient physician, he had accepted it with great humility and honour. The ancient physician had told Wulfgar that he would be happy to teach him what he knew, but he knew that Wulfgar already knew more than he did, as he would not have been able to save the young Intendant's life had he been in the same position. Wulfgar listened as Aliedori quickly explained how and where they found Sibley and asked him if he could find a way to reverse the spell. He asked if Aliedori had tried, and when she did not reply, he agreed to try.

"I cannot promise you success Intendant, but I will do my best," he said, "and she is, or rather *was*, a settler from the Eastern Realm you said?"

Aliedori nodded her weary head, bringing her hands to her temple and using her fingers to massage there before she spoke again. Her voice was weary as she said, "Wulfgar, she is someone's mother and someone's mate… please…" she did not finish the sentence, in fact she was not even sure what she was going to say. He clapped his hands summoning his apprentices and asked them to take Sibley and make her as comfortable as possible. Wulfgar discreetly wrinkled his nose as Sibley was taken past him, then he turned back to the small group.

"Who is she, *was* she, before?" He waved his hand in Sibley's direction, still not sure that he had heard correctly.

"Sibley," Aliedori said slowly, partly through tiredness but not entirely. "She is from the East, hand fast to Yarlyn with two children Synne and Tamar."

"Then who made her... turned her into that?"

"That is what I... we were hoping you could find out."

"I will do my best Intendant," Wulfgar said again.

"Thank you, you always do."

As they turned to leave, Aliedori said, "I know that I don't need to ask but please tell your apprentices to be discreet, and report your findings as soon as you have them please."

"What is it you want me to do, Intendant?"

"Save her if you can."

"And if I can't?"

Aliedori was quiet for a while; she looked towards Maldar and Waifyn who were standing close, Waifyn leaning into Maldar, united. They were both gazing at her, their faces in the shadows, yet she felt alone in the early morning light. She rubbed her palms over her face still unable to see Maldar and Waifyn's faces clearly. She knew their thoughts as well as she knew her own and, her face unreadable, she turned back to Wulfgar.

"Do your very best for her but find out all you can about the 'Greys' how they are made and attached, and what incantation, if any, can remove it."

"And if I can't?" Wulfgar asked again watching her keenly.

"Then bless her path and send her home so the ancestors will welcome her, but not before you find out all you can. Sibley may be our only hope of finding a way to stop more Greys being made. Magic alone may not work so we have to find out what else will. But remember we only got Sibley here because she submitted her will to me".

She moved closer to Wulfgar. It took all his strength of will but after all, he was an old soldier, not to back away from her, so strong was the stench emitting from her clothes.

"I have tried to remove the golem and as you can see I was not successful. Our clothes are covered in the fluid that runs through Sibley; I think it is corroding her from inside but if you can change the fluid back to blood she may live." She looked down at herself. "I will send an article of clothing to you, it may of some use. See what the fluid is, perhaps it can be drawn off and be replaced by blood."

"You mean for me to bleed her?" Wulfgar sounded none too pleased.

"No Wulfgar, you know that I do not mean that, I mean draw off the fluid from one arm while replacing it with blood in the other arm." Aliedori walked towards the door, Maldar opened it for her and she walked through.

"You may want to keep it open for a while," she called over her shoulder. Wulfgar stood, his hand on the handle, and decided to take the young Intendant's advice; leaving the door open he walked behind the curtains. Deogol, one of the apprentices, had put Sibley in a cage, which had been furnished with a bunk. The bars of the cage were reinforced with magic, to prevent little dragons burning their way out.

The baby dragon had been one of Aliedori and Maldar's first finds; she found the wild infant dragon and brought him home to fix his broken wings. It was she; aged five, who had reinforced the bars after the dragon had burned his way through the first time. Now the cage housed another of their rescued creatures and this time it wasn't just broken wings, it was a whole broken person. If Aliedori was right then all the Realms were in danger not just theirs. She was not a young person taken to flights of fancy; in fact, he had always thought her far too serious for her age. Thanks to the ancestors she had always had Maldar, and now Waifyn. Wulfgar walked around the cage, studying Sibley as she lay on the bunk, panting. The binding spell had been removed and replaced with a simple calming incantation.

He turned to Acca, who had just walked in, "Go to the Intendant's bathhouse, wait and bring back the clothes she leaves by the door."

The young apprentice ran off to do her errand without question, but not before she gazed open-mouthed at the cage. Wulfgar turned his attention to Sibley again. How was it possible to have made something like this and what was to be done? He thought, steepling his fingers. Perhaps we can start by stripping back the layer, he mused to himself. He placed his hands behind his back and continued to pace, still in deep thought. Or perhaps I can try Aliedori's idea and bleed off the strange fluid and replace it with blood, but whose?

"Come Deogol we have work to do," he said to the young apprentice. "We may also be in need of blood." The apprentice looked a little worried and a frown furrowed the young man's brow.

"Don't worry Deogol I would never ask you to do a thing like that; it's a good thing I know many who will be happy to help out an old apothecia."

He gave the apprentice a smile before shooing him into action.

Aliedori leant against the wall; she was so tired she could hardly keep awake. She watched one of Wulfgar's apprentices dash past them and disappear through a side door into the palace. The last of the night had drained away and the glow of a brand new day was upon them.

"I am going to my bathhouse; I need to get out of these things and get some rest." She smiled at them as she turned and walked away. She was sure there would be very little sleep for those two. As Aliedori walked away, Waifyn turned as if to follow when Maldar stopped him with a hand on his shoulder.

"We go that way; my private quarters are accessed through the archway on the right." He pointed just in case Waifyn had a problem with directions. "Let her be. Anyway, the whole place will be awake soon and I need to clean up and so do you."

Waifyn wasn't about to protest. As fascinating as he found Alie-dori, he wasn't about to pass up spending time in a hot steamy bath alone with Maldar.

"We'll see to Keidrop, raid the breakfast then clean up and sleep or not," Maldar said smiling; sleep was the last thing on his mind. Alie-dori entered her private bathhouse and was surprised to find the bath already running, until she saw the young apprentice. She pulled her tunic up over her head and handed it to Acca asking her to take it directly to Wulfgar and thanking her for the bath. Alone, Aliedori sat on the side of the large oval bath and watched the water run out of the open mouth of a copper dragon. The water was hot with herbs and petals floating on the surface. Steam rose filling the bathhouse, and heady scents filled her nostrils. She quickly undressed, pulling off the stained and smelly garments and dropping them in a pile as far away from the bath as possible, then stepped into the inviting water.

Sliding under until she was totally immersed, she soaked the goo and smell from her hair and skin. They had travelled almost nonstop, pausing only to allow Keidrop to rest and now she was tired to the bone. They had discussed stopping at either Stornvale or Skellglade or any of the other settlements, but had felt that delaying would cause Sibley undue pain.

Now all she wanted to do was sleep but there was so much to think about, and every time she closed her eyes, she saw the death of the Grey. Aliedori lay under the water, not thinking, just allowing the heat to cleanse her skin and wash her mind clean. All that she had learnt, and all that was to come, was beyond belief. She pushed herself up, running her open palms up over her face and head until her hair was brushed back from her forehead and warm water trickled down her face. She brushed the water away. What did it all mean? Was someone amassing an army of human golems? At this moment all she wanted to look forward to was Maldar and Waifyn's hand- fast ceremony, having fun and stress in equal measure and watching their parents arguing as to where it was to be held: at their home in Fengardia or at the home of Waifyn deep in the forest. She would also enjoy her brother's abject fear of the upcoming handfasting. Not because of the ceremony but because the closer the ceremony came the closer he was to going to be to Bryn-Le-Fenir.

Chapter 16

Suddenly she *found* Sorin; she had been *searching* for him on and off since he dropped out of *sight.* Now as she touched his mind again, she smiled happily because he was safe and unharmed. Aliedori found that she was looking towards towers; they could be the towers she had glimpsed before. It seemed like it was many, many months ago but was really it had been only just a few short weeks before. She was still unable to tell what kind of towers they were; she knew that in some settlements, especially in the dryer regions in the Eastern Realm, water was stored in towers to sustain the settlers in the dry seasons.

She had never seen a water tower; the only towers she knew were the dragon towers of the Southern Realm. But they did not look like dragon towers, they were not high enough and the tops were all enclosed in a half dome. Sorin was looking directly at the towers, without reaction. They were clearly something he saw daily and he no longer registered them. The towers were simply part of the landscape, as the dragon towers were to her. He was happy; it was the same feeling he had when she last *left* him and she felt his emotions like a warm glow. To his left was a pretty olive- skinned girl who looked as happy as Sorin felt riding beside her. He was surrounded by his friends; Aliedori saw that others were riding racing dracs, and he was somewhere in the midst of them. Sorin and his friends were enjoying their early morning ride and somehow Aliedori had the feeling that he had allowed her to *find* him.

He and the other riders turned away from the towers and headed out across a flat plain of gorse grass and shrubs. In the distance, a vast green forest spread out before them, a sea of trees known by all as the Tree of Souls. It didn't matter what it was called, it was the place where all life started and where the ancestors lived on after they were called home.

Aliedori liked the dense forest or Tree of Souls because of the mythology and magic that lay within it. The forest covered all the Realms in equal measure, even the Eastern Realm where all other trees were lost in the last magical war with the Western Realm. Aliedori felt Sorin's pulse quicken at the sight of the trees and his fear and excitement heightened in equal measure. A shout went up at the sight of the trees and the dracs began to race. The girl who had been riding by Sorin's side raced off, laughing, and he gave chase. Aliedori did not like the feelings she was having. They were odd feelings of something not quite right but she could not place them. She knew that they were heading to the Tree of Souls and they were in high spirits; it was part of Sorin's coming of age celebration. She had heard stories of initiations, of people walking with the ancestors into the fire cave. The first dragons came out of the caves deep in the centre of the Tree of Souls. The dragons were formed in the ice caves, given shape by winds from the wind caves and fire by the breath of the fire caves. The centre of the Tree of Souls and the three caves was the most sacred place of all the Realms. Aliedori was happy that Sorin appeared to be safe and was enjoying his coming of age celebration. She withdrew her mind and was left with a feeling of unease but was unsure why; finishing her bath she then dressed and left her chambers.

It was still early but the palace staffs members were now awake and busy with their duties; the new day had started in earnest. Leaving the grand halls behind, Aliedori climbed a stairwell leading to the message tower and found Berefel there. Berefel was the master of all bearers; he had low-level magic, which allowed him to ensure that the bearer got the message to the right person. He was a nervous, jumpy man, small in stature and fine of bone. He had spent so many years with animals that he had taken on their appearance, his nose twitched frequently and his arms flapped about so much that he looked like a bird or a Gem dragon about to fly off.

"Has there been any message brought by Kastillion, a tawny owl, in the last few weeks?"

Berefel, surprised at the Intendant's sudden appearance, dropped his breakfast.

"Oh dear, I am so sorry, I didn't mean to startle you," Aliedori said as she stepped into the room.

She stooped down to retrieve the bowl and, placing the spoilt food on the table, she apologised again.

"I receive many messages daily and over the week I have received several hawks, black birds, Gems and Cobs all out of the forest from settlements from all over the Realm." He paused, looking at his spoilt breakfast before he spoke again, "A tawny owl did come, but no message was received."

Berefel had regained some of his dignity and he took up the bowl from the table then placed it down again looking longingly at his breakfast.

Feeling a little guilty, Aliedori cast an incantation and cleaned the breakfast cereal whilst adding fresh fruits. Berefel smiled, picked out a purple berry from the bowl and popped it in his mouth. He then picked up his bowl and moved to a seat before the silly child knocked it over and he lost his breakfast again. Berefel regarded Aliedori suspiciously before holding the bowl close to his chest. He relaxed a little when he saw that Aliedori had moved to the other end of the long table in the middle of the room. Along the back of the room were a series of slots and small boxes engraved with the name of the person for whom the message was intended. Aliedori looked along the shelves and saw that there were several messages in Maldar's box and even one or two in Waifyn's but there were none in hers. That would suggest that all her correspondence was Realm's business and were dealt with by the appropriate staff.

"So you have not received any messages from Skellglade?"

"None, Intendant. Two bearers came in from Skellglade, and an owl came in some weeks ago, late in the evening. The owl bore no message, and like the others it was simply exhausted."

"Did you not think it odd that the bearers came without messages? Aliedori asked stroking the head of a small cob dragon. "Stornvale has three mages there you know."

Berefel said nothing; he simply looked at Aliedori as if she was mad. He really didn't like people coming into his tower disturbing his breakfast, upsetting his bearers, not even the Intendant.

"What do you think happened to the messengers?" Aliedori asked.

"I have no ideas, Intendant…" he said staring at Aliedori. "My job is to care for the bearers not wonder what happened to messages."

Aliedori stared open-mouthed. Berefel really did not like people.

"But are you not curious as to why the bearers are arriving exhausted and without messages?"

She was used to the old fool but she was in no mood for his

quirkiness not after the weeks she had just had.

"I have been trying to get information from the bearers," he said finally, before putting a spoonful of what Aliedori thought looked like bird food in his mouth.

"And did you get anything?" Aliedori wanted to know.

Berefel shook his head and pointed vaguely towards the back; it was about time the child left.

"The owl is that way, through that door and in the rest area Intendant. He was quite unwell when he arrived, but he is well now." Berefel made his point; he turned back to his breakfast.

Aliedori thanked him and left him with his breakfast. It was clear that someone was intercepting and extracting the messages before the bearers could reach their destination.

But why release them afterwards? It would only be a matter of time before it was discovered, so allowing them to continue on their way had to be significant, perhaps the interceptors were sending another kind of message. She had not been able to detect anything during their return; no magic, no incantations, but the Realm was big and the bearers could be taken anywhere. She had sent her mind out time and time again, searching for something that would explain the reason why bearers were not reaching their destination intact. The Realm was as it should be apart from the *Greys*.

If messengers were unable to fly safely between the capital and the outlying settlements, the Realm could not be safe. If something was not done, and done soon, then all communications between Realms would be affected. Deep in thought, Aliedori stepped through the door and into the darkened rest area. There were several Cobs and Gems from distance settlements, but most of the bearers were blackbirds and rooks.

Kastillion was on a bed of fresh straw, wings drawn up and head down. Aliedori turned to go but was stopped as her mind received a clear thought from Kastillion's mind.

"I am not asleep, Intendant."

"Then rest, we will talk later. Come and find me, I know that your kind like the dusk best."

"Yes, Intendant, it is true, but I am well rested now. We do usually hunt at night and rest during the day but this is not usual, Intendant, I am at your disposal; I have tried to remember but I cannot. I need to fly soon as I have been away from my home for too long already." The Owl still sounded exhausted simply remembering his ordeal.

"Thank you for staying until our return," Aliedori said. "What do you remember? What is the last thing you remember before you arrived here?"

Kastillion thought for a moment or two. "I flew until the sun was almost up. I was tired, then I stopped for a rest, the moon was low and I had a good view of the surroundings…" the voice trailed off.

Aliedori thought for a while then said, "You mate for life, you have a pair bond and possible younglings, and you stopped to tell them of your journey?"

Kastillion's large round head turned slowly as he thought and Aliedori gazed at his facial discs and black, round eyes. It was rather a plain face but the large black eyes were very expressive giving him a rather humankind quality.

"I stopped at the nesting tree with food for the younglings and I flew off again towards Fengardia."

Kastillion paused for a while then continued, "The nesting tree is on the edge of the woods where the vegetation had begun to blacken and the younglings were not ready to leave the nest so we were unable to leave."

"I know to where you are referring. I have been there; your mate and younglings are safe and you may return to them when you are ready."

"Thank you, Intendant." Kastillion said no more, ruffled his rich brown plumage and settled back down on the perch.

Aliedori left the aviary and climbed higher into the tower. Below her the city was beginning to come awake, and beyond the city was the great forest of the Realm. High above some of the trees were the busy dragon towers and Aliedori cast a search, find, disable and a keep safe incantation with a sweep of her arm. It was one of those catch them all incantations that would play havoc with hunters' and trappers' devices, but that could not be helped.

Every day dragons arrived and left the city and no one reported seeing anything, but that was no surprise. After they had got Sibley and mounted Keidrop, the dragon flew over the area several times again. But they had not been able to see anything even with the illuminated gateway.

Aliedori descended the stairs and made her way to the breakfast room. Maldar and Waifyn were coming in the opposite direction; they had both bathed and changed their clothes but their hair was still wet.

"What have you found out?" It was Waifyn who asked the question. He had bathed and was in clean clothes, as was Maldar, no doubt.

"It would appear that all carriers are reaching their intended destination. But all messages are removed from their minds, Kastillion cannot remember anything."

"Does he remember where he was last?" Waifyn quizzed. The clothes were a tad too big for him making him look slightly at odds with them.

"Yes, it was near the Gateway. He has his mate and younglings there," Aliedori replied

"You should know that I have sent message to our parents that we are home." Maldar's voice was shaking slightly with nerves.

"They are in their private chambers?" Aliedori caught his eye and winked at him.

"No, over at the Garden Temple, they went to pay their respects to the ancestors and give tributes for our safe return. Apparently, the palace has been in uproar every day since we did not return on schedule. They will be back soon." There was nothing he could do; they would be back soon. Maldar sighed, accepting his fate.

"Good, it will give me time to speak to one of the masters of the dragon towers," Aliedori said as they entered the breakfast hall.

"Oh and Waifyn how does that feel, you look better?" Waifyn looked down and saw that the slightly over-large clothes now fitted perfectly. He thanked Aliedori with a dazzling smile.

Breakfast was ready and laid out, and the serving staff were lined up and at the ready. Aliedori ignored the place settings and waved the staff away as they started to approach.

She grabbed fruit, cheese and bread, telling them where she was going and giving them instructions to inform her the moment her parents returned. As she turned to go Maldar grabbed her and hugged her hard.

"I am coming with you," he said.

"No, you two get some sleep. I won't be long; I will be back before their return."

He saw uncertainty and fear etched in her features and he dropped his hand, watching as she slipped quietly out of the hall. There was no need for him to say more; he glanced towards Waifyn before turning to the breakfast table.

The visit to the dragon towers yielded very little and the way up was grindingly slow. She stood on the platform and watched the worker dracs and wrenches as she worked her way up. The counter balances worked together to raise the platform slowly. Aliedori decided that she would take the stairs through the different levels next time. When she finally arrived at the top she got nothing. Yes, there were traders who traded in the West but none had ever gone farther than the traders outside the wall.

Chapter 17

The hard ground came up to meet her with a thud and wetness enveloped her like a warm embrace. The warmth caressed her and she began to relax in the viscous fluid as it moulded itself around her. In a panic, she snapped her eyes open, and the dark viscous fluid was dragging her down into darkness covering her head and face.

She tried to pull herself up, but instead she found herself lying on her back on the floor in an unknown bathhouse. Aliedori turned slowly until she could now see the thick liquid floating in the bath. She was fully dressed, and as the end of her robe melted into the fluid and as she pulled at the hem trying to separate herself from the swirling dark mass. Strange sounds filled the bathhouse.

The haunting melody of the song drifted in on the breeze filling her head with pain and prickling her skin like sharp claws. As she listened, the realisation dawned on her that it was not bird song she was hearing but the screams of baby dragons.

Aliedori tried to stand but was unable to do so; she turned her head the other way to look through the door out beyond the bathhouse. There were high windows above her head and as she looked through them, she saw a strange craggy landscape in the distance. Atop the craggy hillock stood a lone tree, its frozen, branches stark against the steel grey sky. The leaves were caught by the winds; stiff and frozen they twisted in agony. As they screamed they became thousands of baby dragons mewling. From behind and above her head, movement caught Aliedori's ears; the roof of the bathhouse was coming alive.

There were dragons and dracs untangling themselves from the delicate latticework intertwined with coke stone and vines. Ten dragons and a single pure white drac moved before her. Why was there a white drac when the temple bathhouse was carved from black marble?

The black flowers and fretwork liquefied and dripped down, covering the floor and every surface with blood red stains. At the entrance to the bathhouse, a woman stood, framed by the doorway. She had her back to Aliedori and she was pointing at something that was out of sight. The woman called as fear vibrated through her body, but all

Aliedori could see was the sunlit courtyard.

The sun was bouncing off the pale cobbled stone and scattering its light into even the darkest corners of the courtyard. The sound of movements came from the roof again as the dragons began to unfurl and climb down. Aliedori reached over to draw her seax from the scabbard at her side as she tried to ease herself back in the bath and out of the way of the dragons. An unpleasant smell drifted through the bathhouse and caught in her nostrils and throat causing her to gag and choke. She coughed and swallowed to clear her mouth of the acrid taste. Unable to move, she remained still and watched as the seax turned into a single pure white Amaldia flower. She held up her hand, offering the flower as a tribute as she dropped it into the fluid. The hot viscous liquid that had made it impossible for her to move now yielded and she freed her hands, once again holding the seax.

Outside the window on the far away tree, the baby dragons had ceased their mewling, and her senses heightened as the air thickened with Amaldia scent. She caught her breath and her lungs burned for a second or two before she could breathe more easily. As the black dragons moved out of the latticework their breath intensified and it began to burn the air in the bathhouse, but Aliedori found that with each breath from the dragon she could breathe easier.

A high-pitched, terrible sound of agony and despair came from the woman as she suddenly gave birth. The woman wrapped and placed the newborn baby in Aliedori's arms. The child's arms reached upwards as they became a tree trunk and the fingers became branches. They grew tall and strong and pierced the shadows moving above the black dragon. A sigh, a sound of sheer agonising pleasure, came trembling out of the infant as hot viscous liquid poured down from the bathhouse roof. The bathhouse floor began to steam, and the dragons fell to the floor, their life's blood pouring from the gashes in their underbellies. Aliedori, now free from the goo, began to rise, and she floated above the bath. She struggled to keep hold of the infant, but the infant pushed her up and away from itself as its feet buried themselves in the floor of the bathhouse. The bath emptied itself and the viscous liquid floated up and above her then fell like rain, soaking her again but never reaching the floor.

Aliedori had absorbed all the liquid and she sank back down until her feet touched the floor. At her feet were the dying black dragons, their blood pooling around her feet, flowing up and over her body until it was over her head.

She closed her mouth but soon her lungs were burning, and she gasped for breath, the fluid filling her mouth. As she absorbed the dragon's blood, her body became limp and she could no longer stand. She dropped onto her knees then fell flat on her stomach onto the now cooled marble tiles.

As she lay prone on the floor, the dragon tree shook, the craggy hillside trembled, the leaves shook, and the baby dragons took to the skies. Their fluttering wings cracked the base of the tree. Aliedori lay on her stomach facing the window that was far too high for her to see out. Still, she saw it all and watched the tree crack as tiny new shoots grew from the centre of the old dead trunk. The new shoots spread fast covering the craggy hillside in a blanket of green. Aliedori pulled the seax close to her bringing it into view, and used it to push herself up onto her feet. The seax was the third horn of the drac, and its serrated edge dripped with dew, splashing on the floor then arcing out. When the dew reached the dragons, it pooled around them, tentacles of dew crawling up and seeping into the dead bodies. The dragons began to stir then one by one they flew out of the high window.

The sun began to blaze through the tears left by their claws as they ripped the steel grey sky apart. The sky became the lakes of Garan Fell and the dragons plunged in, taking the babies and sealing the water around them. Aliedori found herself on the floor again but this time on her back and she lay there on the cool tiles watching the ceiling grow roots. The roots sprung out everywhere trying to find purchase as saplings and vines fought for space among the trunks of the ancient's trees and roots.

Aliedori gripped the seax tightly and used it to pull herself up on to her knees, then push herself up and stand in a fighting stance. Instead of enemies, Aliedori found emeralds and golden Gems eggs at her feet. Opening the pouch on her belt, she stooped to pick up the eggs. Before she could reach them, the eggs grew feet and sprang into the pouch as she felt their warmth spreading out from her hips around her body. She ran from the bathhouse through the arched doorway into the cobbled courtyard and then into the Tree of Souls. She stopped, frozen in mid-stride, as an eerie silence filled the world. She cried out, but her voice was lost in the silence and drawn back into the earth, rippling unheard through the Realms. The trees began calling her name in one voice. They whispered it, and she tried to answer but her voice was still rippling through the ground calling out to all who would not hear.

The trees continued to call out her name, and Aliedori tried to turn to catch the direction that the sound was coming from. But each time she turned the sound would come from somewhere else. Dizzied, she tumbled forward falling face down and was caught face-to-face by the woman who had given birth to the baby tree in the bathhouse. The woman transformed into the Grand Naturalist, Anterian. She put her fingers to her lips to hush the trees, and the fingers disappeared into the darkness of her face. Aliedori was still unable to see the woman's face, but she knew that it was Anterian.

She watched as Anterian pointed, her sweeping gesture taking in all directions at once. Yet her hand did not move and the leaves on the trees shook out Aliedori's name again. Aliedori reached out for Anterian, but she dissolved into nothingness. She reached out again and this time touched someone solid and warm. She opened her eyes and sunlight was streaming in through her window. She sat up and looked around her own bedchamber, her dream all but forgotten.

"You said to wake you, Intendant," said Elyann, her handmaiden, "when the lord and lady return."

"Thank you," her voice was hoarse.

"I think you were dreaming."

"Was I? I don't remember." Yet the essence of the dream lingered, though she could not recall its content.

"You kept saying, "The time is here… the time is now…""

"The time is now?" Aliedori asked.

"I don't know, Intendant, you kept saying the 'the time is here'. The Lord and Lady of Fengard have returned."

"You have already said that, thank you anyway."

"Is there anything you need, Intendant?"

"No, thank you."

"A dragon boat race is about to start and I believe that the masters of the kitchens have ensured that refreshments will be served on one of the high balconies overlooking the ocean-lake," Elyann said. She busied herself tidying away non-existent mess; folding and refolding a cape several times before Aliedori took it away from her.

"What is the matter, Elyann?"

"Nothing Intendant."

"Elyann, you and I know each other well enough for me to know when you are worried."

Elyann sighed; Aliedori was as close to her as her own children would be, had she any.

"There are rumours of a strange creature that you brought back with you from Skellglade."

"Ah," Aliedori breathed.

"Is that all you have to say to me, child? You and your need to collect the strange and the broken and now you have found some strange human-golem hybrids that could put the Realm in danger, and all you can say is 'ah'?"

Aliedori finished pulling her boots on and smoothed down her clothes; she really would have to talk to Wulfgar about his apprentices. She knew that Wulfgar would never disclose what he was asked not to, not even to Elyann.

"Elyann, the poor creature is called Sibley, and she was once like you and I, it's simply that some dark mage has changed her. We need to find out how and why. It is the only possible way of saving her life."

"But you brought it here Intendant, it could be diseased, it could be dangerous, it could be anything."

"What would you suggest that I left her in that dead place? She poses no danger." Aliedori said, but thought *at least I don't think she poses a danger.*

Minoria was looking out over the ocean-lakes, watching the myriad of dragon sailing boats. The race master was trying to impose some order before the start of the races and was fighting a losing battle. The ocean-lakes were as calm as the millponds amongst wheat fields, and the flotilla of small boats milling around the dragon boats made the referee's job even more difficult. A rhythmic drum beat a signal and it was time to start the race; the boats were of all the colours of the rainbow and colours that were not. Wulfgar the Warrior apothecia had strolled in looking glum, and joined Minoria at the railings to watch the boats. The pair was quickly joined by Berefel who was nervous and twitching as he stood by Minoria. Maldar and Waifyn were in their own secret world that only the newly in love knew how to find and they missed the start of the race.

Minoria regarded the young nymph with approval. She had liked him as soon as she met him and he was as handsome as the gossipers had said. She had met with Wulfgar when she first heard that her son was wooing the apothecia's nephew. Minoria knew of her son's reputation around the city and was very pleased when the nymph's name was linked with Maldar. Almost overnight Maldar's wild ways had ceased. His trips to the dragon towers with the other dragon warriors were exchanged for solitary trips into the forest. On their return to the palace, the young nymph had first greeted her in the tradition of his people then with the greeting of Fengard. Minoria was pleased with her son's choice; Waifyn had calmed her son's behaviour when no other could. Maldar had fallen in love with a nymph and intended to be handfasted, the Amaldia stunt was proof of that. Warian had pulled a similar stunt with her parents, presenting them with Purple Dragon's Claw, a delicate aquatic plant that only grew at the deepest parts of Jurong and could only survive in water collected at the same spot as the plant and at the same time. A nymph in the family would certainly be interesting and could unite the two Nations, humankind with the magical kind. Minoria could not be happier; Maldar was in love and that was all that mattered. She had known for some time that her son had been wooing the nymph, but she had been waiting for Maldar to come to her. Of course her son did not come to her or his father; instead, he went to Aliedori as she had known all along that he would.

It wasn't wise for parents to let their children know that they know more about their lives than they wanted them to. She had even known when he went off into the centre of the Tree of Souls, to collect the Amaldia tree shoot. She was happy for her son, she could not have chosen better for him. Maldar was happy, and she could feel the love and happiness vibrating through them both; in the same way she could feel their sorrow, pain and loss. Minoria bent and kissed the top of her son's head, not the act of a leader but the act of a mother. Maldar caught her hand and squeezed it.

As for her daughter, well that was more difficult; Aliedori was to become Lady of Fengard. Whomever her heart chose must be strong enough to rule with her but not as her equal. Minoria knew that her daughter was far more powerful than she was and that's how it had always been. Aliedori's great-grandmother had little or no magical powers beyond that of medicinal magic. But that's how it had always been, sometimes the ancestors bestowed and sometimes they did not. And on very rare occasions the ancestors gave in abundance but never more than the receiver could handle. Minoria knew that her daughter had been given these powers for a reason and in a very short time all would be made clear. Minoria wondered again if her daughter would be as lucky as she was to find Warian, a man with absolutely no magic but with the biggest and bravest heart of anyone she had ever known. Aliedori had her father's heart, and so did Maldar for that matter and her heart filled with pride each time she saw her children.

Aliedori was the last to arrive to join the party and she greeted the lord and Lady of Fengard first with a formal greeting. She then greeted her family with hugs and kisses. Aliedori looked out across the ocean-lake taking in the spectacle, then she turned away. As she did so her face became set, unreadable yet calm, her expression telling nothing of her inner feelings. *The mark of a true ruler*, Minoria thought with pride. Her only sign of nervousness was brushing non-existent hair from her eyes several times before she composed herself. When she was composed, her voice was clear and she realised that she had to show caution, not because of undue fear, but because she knew that already Sibley's presence was causing unease amongst the palace staff and it would only be a matter of time before rumours reached the people. Many of the palace staff did not reside within the palace walls and gossip, like petals falling from a tree, always reached the ground. She knew that she also had to protect the Realms, and she did not want to spread fear and panic, so she asked them to open their minds to her.

Chapter 18

I believe there is trouble coming to the Realms and it may already be here in Fengardia. Dark magic is at work. This is clearly evident in the neutral forest near the border with the Western Realm; a gateway was opened between the two Realms.

I believe that I may have closed the gate but I cannot be sure that 'they' did not close it after Maldar and I sent those creatures home.

We have taken it for granted that Fengard would always be safe, and it has been for a thousand cycles. We concentrated on developing our people's minds and prosperity, our places of learning.

In our years of peace, we forgot that there are those who do not believe in harmony. I was brooding on the puzzles of the 'Greys' while on the return journey, and I have come to the realisation that while the risk to the Southern Realm appears very small the consequences are great. If a mage is developing human-golems to attack the Eastern Realm then it is only a matter of time before the Southern Realm comes under the same threats. At present, all I have is supposition that there is a very great danger looming for us all. I believe… no, I know… that the attack from those grey creatures and the gateway is only the start.

The gateway is in neutral forest, it is sealed and sentries are posted, but before long the mage or naturalist who turned Sibley and others into Greys will learn how to break the incantation and reopen the gate. Bearers from the outlying settlements who try to report on activities are being intercepted. Traders and dragons crossing the neutral forest saw nothing unsettling, which would suggest that the mage who cast the incantation is very powerful indeed. Settlers have been taken from this and other Realms; Sibley and the fallen are proof that the Realms are under attack. If we were not caught in that binding charm we would be none the wiser.

Therefore, our leaders and the people would have been unprepared as the Realms were plunged into darkness. I believe that action must be taken accordingly to ensure that our line of defence is strengthened against this unknown enemy. For if the enemy is advancing on this Realm then it will be advancing on the others too. The Realms must be *protected and the people defended. The good, strong stockade we have erected around our Realms must not be breached again. Our city, our Realm, is a peaceful Realm and so are the Eastern and Northern Realms and I am sure they have no desire to have that changed, but we have to prepare to defend what is right and decent not if, but **when**, the time comes.*

****

Having spoken, she withdrew from the others' minds and became silent, feeling a little lost for a second or two. Aliedori looked all around the conference table; of all the people there, her parents' minds were the most difficult to *access* but she felt their warmth, their pride and most of all their expectations. She had never accessed her parents' minds before and she knew that she never would again. She felt sad at the sudden loss of *connection*.

Aliedori felt a hand on her arm; it was her mother; Minoria gave Aliedori's arm a quick squeeze then withdrew her hand and placed it on her lap. After making sure that everyone around the table, including Kastillion, was able to understand her mind speak, Aliedori sat back and waited. The trick with mind speak was to make sure that the other parts of your mind were shut off. The speaker could not afford emotions to cloud the conversation or to let a secret part of themselves be revealed. Aliedori sat quietly waiting for the others to digest the information.

"How certain are you of the danger?" Minoria asked. She was seated close to her daughter and was experiencing some of her emotions, not just from the direct mind link contact.

Maldar stood with his back to the rails, his head sunk in his chest. The drums of the dragon boat race beat out the tempo of his heart as his mind raced. Aliedori had been inside their heads leaving tiny footprints across their minds, and he did not like the feelings. He reached for a glass of fruit wine; most of the refreshment had not been touched. He sipped it without tasting it, his mind on other things.

He had seen the Greys, he had fought them and they were not creatures he wanted to experience again. If Aliedori was right, he knew that it was only a matter of time before they encountered the Greys and perhaps something worse. Maldar did not like that idea either.

"Very certain, my Lady, and what Aliedori fails to say is that the threat appears to be coming from the West." It was Maldar who spoke.

Aliedori opened her mouth, but closed it after a moment without saying anything. She rose, joining her brother and in the distance across the ocean-lakes the dragon boats were turning. The flotillas of small boats skipped along the surface of the lakes, carried in the wake of the larger dragon boats. She wondered if the Realms would be like those small boats, caught up in the wash of something bigger. She turned her back on the vision and the dragon race and rested her back against the warm wood.

"Did you learn anything from your trip to one of the dragon towers, and what did you see when you sent your mind out? Her mother asked softly.

Minoria was calm; in fact, the entire table was calm including Berefel, who had suddenly stopped his nervous twitching and was very still.

Maldar found that unnerving most of all and he rested his elbows on the rails, his legs sticking out in a relaxed stance not indicative of his true feelings.

"Nothing from the dragon tower and shadows, everything is veiled."

Aliedori could be a young woman of few words, and sometimes each word carried such weight and dread that Maldar was afraid even to think of the connotations of the word 'shadows'. He had seen the Greys; he had even fought and killed two of them. Someone had created the Greys by dark magic, but he knew that there was no such thing as dark magic. Just selfish, greedy people with evil thoughts who simply wanted to serve their own self-interests and would stop at nothing to get what they wanted.

They used magic to achieve their own goals and it was the user who made magic evil. Over the centuries, magic used for the self-interest of individuals became known as 'dark magic', though strictly speaking magic had no hues. Someone whose only interest was to do evil had created the Greys. They were mindless golems bred for evil and to be someone's personal army of death. But beneath the clay and dust they were once humankind like Sibley.

Berefel cleared his throat. He had listened with care to everything Aliedori said and it had made him even more nervous. That was his natural state anyway, but it bore out his own misgivings. He had spent too many years with animals not to understand their fear. He had seen fear in the exhausted bearers, an unknown fear that the bearers were unable to remember who or what had caused it.

"It is not unusual for messengers to go astray, or even lose their messages, especially in adverse weather conditions. But the weather has been very good of late."

The conference all nodded in agreement and waited. Berefel started to twitch again, as he continued,

"However, of late many bearers have lost messages, even Kastillion here has lost one from the Intendant, and it was only over a short distance".

Kastillion was perched on the railing; Berefel had brought him along to the meeting as requested. The owl could not remember any more other than what he had already told Aliedori but he needed to be at the conference.

"I have tried to glean even the smallest bit of information but as you can see I have not been successful. I have tried with the Gems sent from Skellglade but again no luck."

"What about the Cobs?" Minoria asked, "Cob dragons come mainly from the East do they not?"

"There is no evidence that the Cobs have suffered the same fate my Lady. But then we get so very few messengers from the settlements near the Western borders. Their colouring indicates where they come from," Berefel answered. "All Cobs, including those from the outlying settlements, have arrived intact."

"Can you be sure Berefel?" Minoria asked.

"No my Lady, I can only surmise." Berefel exploded in a series of ticks and shakes as his discomfort increased under the direct gaze of her ladyship. Sensing the little man's unease Minoria turned away, redirecting her gaze on a small, distant boat.

"So," she said calmly, "there have been cobs from the West, all messages intact but none requested aid or carried reports of missing settlers. Clever, very clever indeed; whoever is taking the settlers wants to make sure that the East appears guilty."

Minoria smiled. She shared her idea with the group. "They have used 'black' dragons and they appear to have left the settlements close to the Eastern border alone. Their intention is for their actions to be blamed on the Eastern Realm." Minoria lapsed into a thoughtful silence then continued after a while, "I do not think that the messages are intact, I believe they are far from intact. I think that they have been changed. Bere," Minoria's voice was even gentler, "go and talk to the Cobs from the East. I bet they will all have a tale to tell." The old master of the bearer scrambled from the table, gave a little bow then nodded towards the owl. The wise old owl, never one to pass up a free ride, spread its wings and took off, only to land on the top of Berefel's inclined head. The two of them disappeared into the interior as the group watched them in bemused silence. Wulfgar broke the silence; he did not want to but it had to be done.

"I have a little better news; I think I may be able to remove the golem, but it is complex, and I am trying to keep the poor young woman alive," he said.

"What have you found out?" Aliedori asked.

"The blood idea did not work, she could not tolerate blood. It caused her skin to blister and burn." Wulfgar shook his head slowly. "The golem is killing Sibley's humanity, and I think when her humanity goes the golem 'lives' on."

"Is there nothing you can do to change that? Will the poor child be lost if something is not done? Minoria asked.

Wulfgar shook his head, but before he could answer, Maldar spoke up, a crestfallen frown clouding his usual cheerful countenance.

"The golem did not live on when Alie and I sent three home to the ancestors in the forest. The golem's hold was severed after death and that is how we came to realise that they were human kind."

Wulfgar was equally crestfallen. He was very good with medicinal magic and an even better apothecia but he knew that he would not be able to save Sibley's humanity.

"Then things have changed," he replied simply.

There was silence once more; everyone knew the real meaning. Golems were creatures of magic and only the most powerful magic could stop them. They all turned to look at Aliedori; she raised her hands as if in defence and surrender all at the same time. "I have tried and I will try again but I think that it is magic that is beyond me." She brushed that non-existent hair from her eyes again. "It is beyond my abilities at this juncture, but I think that I could reverse it if I learnt more about the Greys."

Wulfgar looked at her for a short while before turning to watch the returning boats. What was a golem if not a clump of clay and dirt given life to be commanded by its creators? They were created for their owner's needs whether that was good or bad. In the distance past many, had used golems to do work that was too dangerous for settlers because once life was breathed into them they were all but indestructible. Only those who created the golem could take the life force from it and turned it back to dust. But, as with many living thing, golems began to develop their own sense of individuality. While it was on a simple level, they nonetheless gave themselves names. The four Realms drew up an agreement to release all the golems and not to create any more. No one even knew whether golems still existed as it had been centuries since any had been seen. Was the knowledge needed to create them still in existence? It would seem that it was. The Western Realm was turning captured settlers into a new race of golems; they were making their very own warrior tribe.

"How are they created, and how were their life forces taken?" Minoria asked.

Maldar shrugged, "All I know is that Dori enchanted my sword." Maldar found that his hand had somehow strayed without his knowledge. It was now caressing the nape of Waifyn's neck. He took his hand back and folded it firmly across his chest and hoped that it did not stray again.

Wulfgar shifted his gaze to Aliedori then round to the others one by one until his gaze was resting on Minoria again.

"I don't know and neither do I know how to remove it without sending Sibley to the ancestors." Wulfgar admitted he was helpless.

"Aliedori removed the golem from the others and from Sibley also," Maldar said his hands still firmly crossed.

"And that may be the only reason I can do my work, whatever it was that Aliedori did preserved Sibley's humanity. But for how much longer it's difficult to say. I believe Sibley wants to be with her ancestors…," Wulfgar's voice trailed off.

"This creature that was brought back, originally named Sibley, came from a settlement in the East?"

The Lord of the Southern Realm had spoken for the first time, his voice gravelly and warm. Aliedori loved her father's voice.

Aliedori nodded, "Yes, Ouran Province."

"Then that is where you must start Aliedori." When she did not respond her father continued, "You made a promise to her and a promise you must keep."

"I had intended to return to Stornvale then onto the gateway as soon as I collected my travelling pack and a dragon from the stables," Aliedori replied, her head lowered, gazing on her hands clasped in front of her.

No one was surprised that she was packed and ready; Waifyn rose and stood the other side of Aliedori leaving no one in doubt of his intentions.

"There are also three young mages from the West settled in Stornvale; they came through the now blocked gateway along with scores of other escaping from the forts Realm." Aliedori's face was set as she glanced at her father waiting for his response.

"I will send dragon knights to the outlying settlements and your mother will deal with the classification of mages," Warian said his words final. Aliedori sighed but said nothing further.

"You leave in the morning for the East on the Dawn Mist and before you leave go to the Garden Temple and ask for guidance from the ancestors."

This was an instruction from their mother. Waifyn was about to protest when Minoria spoke again, "It would appear that you intend to go with my two children rather than return home. Send word to your family and travel with Aliedori and Maldar, it is only a matter of ceremony to make the handfasting official. Waifyn you will also go to the Garden Temple and pay tribute to the ancestors."

That being done, Warian pulled the chair back and stood. His daughter was very much like him, a person of very few words.

"Walk with me Kits." It was what he had called Aliedori and Maldar when they were young. He still used the term to this day; they were his children, his babies, and they would never be too old to be called 'Kits'. "You too Waifyn, we need to talk of your duty on this journey. Come, come, Minoria needs to call her council of mages and naturalists," and with that he strode off at a pace causing the three younger ones to chase after him.

Chapter 19

Warian was not the simple mate to the Lady of Fengard as he would often make out; he was a Dragon Lord. He was the master and commander of all dragon fighters and a fierce warrior. He had fought in the last border war as a young man, defended the black dragon gate and helped save the lives of thousands from the Eastern Realm.

While he was no longer as young as he once was, he had lost none of his skills. The peaceful haven of Fengard and the Southern Realm had not made him soft. He led a full official life and still participated in warrior training daily. He was commander of the elite Dragon Knights and he could not be soft except with his children.

The palace dragon stables and knights were under his command, including his own son. The dragon stable was part of a long building; the ground floor comprising of stables for the dracs. The knaves looked after the dracs and all dragon knights started off as knaves, including Maldar. They all had to master the art of fighting on dracs before they could apply to become a dragon knight. Above the dracs' stables was the dragon tower, the accommodation for knaves and knights and the dragon stable reached high into the air. It was from the high tower that Aliedori found herself watching Keidrop and the knave attending her. She was looking through one of the large windows as her father talked. She had stopped listening some time ago; something was running through her mind, it concerned Sorin but she could not place it. Her father, seeing her face, misread the signs, stopped his general chat and spoke directly to her.

"Aliedori, are you listening to me?" Aliedori turned to her father, her face blank. "As I was saying, you have Maldar and no doubt Waifyn, but this is your journey too. It is the start of who you are and who you will become."

Aliedori looked at her father's kindly but strong face; she reached out and placed her palm against his cheek. He held his daughter's hand there, her face clouded with doubt.

"How do you know that this is my journey? Why is it not Maldar's?"

Her mind was struggling to absorb what she was learning about the possible dangers posed by the Western Realm. She was coping with the knowledge of her own powers and other's expectations of her. And Sorin, what was it about the stranger that she could not leave alone? She did not need to 'have a journey'; she tried to withdraw her hand but her father held on to it.

"I know, I know," her father said, patting her hand. "You do not want this or feel ready. Maldar and Waifyn will be with you, but it is more yours than theirs, Aliedori, you know it is."

"But mother is the Lady of Fengard, I am just the Intendant."

Warian stared off into the middle distance for a long while, and still holding on to his daughter's hand he brought the palm to his mouth and pressed his lips to it.

"Do you think that your mother did not say the same thing when she discovered that she had to lead your grandmother's warriors into battle?"

"Mother never talks about it and neither do you, but I know my mother almost passed," she said wishing her father would release her hand.

Warian understood his daughter's feelings all too well, he gave a long sigh and looked around him.

"If it wasn't for Wulfgar she may very well have passed, but you are different Aliedori, you can self heal. I have seen you demonstrate it countless times for Maldar." When she said nothing Warian asked, "Tell me what you see."

Without hesitation, Aliedori replied, "Darkness, sorrow, loss, pain, and it's all around us, but there is something else that I cannot see."

Warian smiled sadly, "What if it is not *something* else but *some-one* else?" he said looking down at the beautiful landscape that was his home. He had asked his daughter what she saw and she understood clearly that he was not referring to the scenery. The Border War of the Eastern Realm and the taking of the Dragon Gate had been his test. Minoria leading her warriors into battle was her mother's test and all young ones must be tested. That was how they could take their rightful place in the realm. However, he did not want the same test for his children, he had always known that his children were destined for something more. He could not in all good faith hold them back; the ancestors had blessed him and Minoria with these two children for a reason. He just did not think that it would be so soon; neither of them had reached their coming of age cycle yet. Aliedori was his child, the precious newborn he had held in his arms for the first time just a few short cycles ago.

The precious newborn who could cause a jungle of flowers to grow in her nursery when she was happy or a chamber full of thorns and prickly plants when she was not. Now she was almost grown, and she must find her own 'Black Dragon Gate' and Maldar and Waifyn must forge their own path also and in accompanying her they would. The Western Realm had never been a threat to the Southern Realm but they wanted to extend their borders. They had always chosen the Eastern Realm as their target, but that did not mean that the Southern Realm would not be there next. There had been many attempts and the other Realms had always come to the aid of the Eastern Empire, but in the last attempt the Southern Realm had been at the forefront in defence of the borders. He and Minoria and their dragon fighters had helped sweep the enemy away from the Dragon Gate. Warian had never been in any doubt then that the Western Realm would try again, but he had hoped that it would not be in his lifetime. Now they were taking dwellers from the Southern Realm and Warian was troubled. He was not a young man anymore and the trouble with war is that it does not remain isolated it spreads and affects everyone. He knew that when the call came his children would be the ones to answer that call. He looked from his daughter to his son and knew that they were ready for whatever there was to come.

Perhaps there would not be another battle; perhaps the journey that his children had started today would be enough to stop the battle before it began. But he was not ready to allow his 'Kits' to take part in any conflict. He knew that Aliedori had doubts about who she was and her abilities and she would be tested many times before she came to accept her true identity and realise what she was capable of.

"The child of the Eastern Realm… Sibley and the others at the gateway are the first. If you are sincere in what you say then you need to discover more about what is happening in the Realms. The East is a good place to start; the more you learn the more knowledge you gain. The more knowledge you gain the better your understanding, therefore the better you will be in dealing with this threat," Warian said softly.

Aliedori nodded, she was thinking along the same lines as her father, but she had intended to go in a different direction. Whoever or whatever the 'Greys' were they were once men and women. They were people with mates, families and lives to live; they were taken away from all that to become golems for the Western Realm.

"Are we making assumptions about the Western Realm?" Aliedori asked thoughtfully.

Warian was equally thoughtful with his reply, "The threat came from them before and all indications suggest that the threat is from them again." Warian's hands were behind his back; it was a trait that Aliedori had picked up from him.

The first attack on the Eastern Realm was to destroy all magical creatures of the Realm. The second was wiping out their forest and destroying the magic of the Realm. When they could not, the Western Mage, Azorean, froze the forest in a dark spell for thousands of years. The magic of the Realm was greatly reduced and shaken, but it was not lost and they did not fall. But they did not know that pockets of green would be left where the dragons fell. After the second all-out attack failed also and the West withdrew and closed their borders, Azorean threw up a forest of trees that was impenetrable from either side and started to plot his next move.

"What will we achieve going to the Eastern Realm?" Aliedori asked the question but they all wanted to know. "Surely if I… we are to learn about the Greys we are better off returning to the gateway."

"Have you listened to nothing I have said to you Kit? Going to the gateway will teach you nothing but how to send the Greys home. Going to the East may teach you how to preserve essences. Besides you made a promise to Sibley, and her family need to know," Warian reinstated.

"And after that?" Aliedori insisted.

"You go where you go," Warian replied.

She shook her head slowly. "What does that even mean?" she asked crossly. "You go where you go; what if I go to the West?"

Her father did not reply. If there was more, she knew that she would not get it from her father. He would tell her nothing whatsoever of what was out there. She would have to find out for herself. Her mother was calling her council and assembling her mages whilst her father would instruct the dragon knights. They would be sending them out to the borders and settlements close to the borders. What was she doing taking a message to the East when she should be going back to the gateway?

"I do not think that this is the time to leave the Realm, Father. If the threat comes from the West then I would… we will be best served by returning to the Stornvale and the gateway," Aliedori said again.

"You said that there were three new powerful mages in the district and the charm you placed around the area will serve. As I have said before I will dispatch dragon knights to the borders and your mother will dispatch mages to Skellglade and other settlements. Your mother's blessing will go with them and I do not think we are in immediate danger from the Western Realm. You made a promise and you must keep that promise Aliedori," Warian said.

Aliedori started to protest, "But, Father, I can send a messenger to the family…"

Her father's gaze stopped her and she lowered her eyes. "…We sail to the East tomorrow," there was nothing more to be said.

Neither Maldar nor Waifyn had spoken; they had simply watched the battle between father and daughter. Maldar was rather pleased that it wasn't him under his father's steady gaze, because he had never won an argument yet, and that look was enough to put the fear of the ancestors into anyone.

Maldar knew that it was the intention for him and Waifyn to travel with Aliedori and he would never let her go alone, but there was just the most obvious question and he was about to speak when.

"Forgive me, Lord Warian, this may not be the time to speak but I feel that I must. You wish Maldar and I to travel with Aliedori to protect her, but do you not think, sire, that it will be the other way round?" Waifyn was looking from one face to the other. Warian smiled and placed his arm round Waifyn's shoulder. He gave it a squeeze before walking off, hands behind his back as, with a gentle shake of his head, he disappeared into the dragon stable. Waifyn shrugged. Whatever happened it would be an adventure, he thought, as he wandered off too, slightly bemused.

"Where are you going?" Maldar enquired.

Without turning, Waifyn said with laughter in his voice, "Come with me and find out."

Maldar was only too happy to comply.

Chapter 20

Wulfgar was deep in thought when Aliedori caught up with him, walking through the garden leading back to his home and work. He had chosen to walk along the rough ground rather than along the pathways through the trees. Walking up amongst the trees seemed too carefree for a moment like this. He paused and watched as she approached, her walk was purposeful, her face set and unreadable, and he wondered when she had become so grown up and how he had not noticed. He had delivered her not so long ago, and now she was almost of age with magical powers beyond rival.

Wulfgar took a certain pleasure in thinking of Aliedori and her brother and all the others that he had brought into this Realm as his children. He did not have children of his own, as he and his mate Elyann had not been blessed. But they had their apprentices who came to them at a very young age and he took great pleasure in watching them grow and achieve. He had taken even greater pleasure in watching the children he had helped into this Realm grow up and achieve. He could not be prouder of this young woman had he been her father. She came straight to the point.

"What did you not say when we were all together?" Aliedori asked.

Wulfgar gave her a wry smile; she had asked him to tell her only what, if anything, he had discovered about Sibley and he had agreed to do so.

"The golem absorbs humanity," Wulfgar replied.

"You already said that."

"Yes, I know, but, Aliedori, 'our' Sibley is only a blueprint. According to what she is saying there may be another ten perhaps twenty other Sibleys out there." Wulfgar was not happy.

"Is this the *true* Sibley, I mean the one that was from her home?" Aliedori felt sick at the thought of how so many Sibleys came to be.

"I believe that she could be the *true* Sibley," Wulfgar replied "I don't know a great deal about the magic that fractures essences, but I do know that only the 'original' retains all memories of their time before.

Aliedori stared at him horrified.

"You know about that kind of magic?" She couldn't believe it.

"I don't know about it, Intendant," he said, making it as clear as possible. "I have heard of it but I have never seen it done, in fact Sibley is my first encounter with a fractured essence."

"If this Sibley goes home to the ancestors then the others will also." It was a statement of fact not a question. Aliedori leaned against a tree, crestfallen. The implication was clear.

"It would appear to be so, Intendant; if the original dies the individual essence can be severed."

"And if we get all the other parts of her essence we could make her whole again?" she wanted to know.

"That could be possible, you said yourself that you did not know that they were humankind until they passed." Wulfgar did not like where this conversation was going.

"Can you keep her alive?" Aliedori asked.

"Not for very much longer, and I think it's what Sibley wants. She may *take* the others with her if it's not too late."

"I see, but she may not, whoever created these golems will know how to make them separate entities. Especially after what happened in the forest," Aliedori said and heaved a long drawn out sigh.

There was silence for a while; in order to create many out of one then the essence must be shattered into pieces. Aliedori shuddered and pushed herself off the tree and then began to pace slowly as the full force of Sibley's revelation hit them. That was why they were using humans, fracturing the human essence to make a hundred golems was a lot faster than the conventional ways of making those creatures. Aliedori stopped pacing and leaned against a tree again.

"The gateway."

"Gateways," Wulfgar corrected.

"How many?"

"Sibley is unable to say. She said the others were taken underground and then she was begging to be sent home." Wulfgar sighed and continued, "But however many there are, Aliedori, you will need to do something about them, close them if you can or I think the Eastern Realm will be lost."

"I am not sure how I did it in the first place or if I did it."

Wulfgar placed a hand on Aliedori's shoulder to still her just in case she started pacing again, but she remained still.

"Does Sibley know where she was taken or where the gates are? Do any of them pose a danger to Fengardia and the Southern Realm?" Aliedori wanted to know.

"Sibley doesn't know that either, but she thinks that when you and Maldar send those three golems home they' may have lost as many as a hundred."

After a short silence, Wulfgar said, "But of course all this does is serve to provide more question and answers."

"I know… I was thinking the same thing and whether it was I who *locked* the gate or whether they did." Aliedori sighed.

"You may not have *locked* the gate, but the charm you placed made sure they cannot move from that area and that is good enough for me."

They were talking in the lush, green, colourful and peaceful area. There were settlers all around them and children playing in the garden. Aliedori shuddered as she thought of the gateways and what lay behind them. Sibley said that there were other gateways; the question was where they were and why they had not been noticed. Even with magic, dwellers would notice the change in their surroundings. They would report it or at least avoid the area and tell others to do the same. Rumours were always quick to spread, but that had not happened.

"What is most important; is Fengard safe?" Aliedori was watching a family as they strolled by.

Wulfgar did not reply; he was not expected to give an answer. Aliedori appeared to have reached a decision and turned to him.

"I need to return to the gateway, learn as much as I can about it." Aliedori walked off in the direction of Wulfgar's home, and he followed, talking as they walked.

"The Lady is sending a mage accompanied by dragon knights to study the gateway. The Southern Realm is safe for the time being and my guess is that the gateways will be somewhere near the Eastern borders."

Wulfgar kept pace with her. They reached his door and he opened it for her to enter, following her in. The door opened onto the area where the apothecary received patients, not the private area she and her brother had used earlier. The room was large and light flooded in from the glass windows close to the ceiling. There was a large table running the length of the room and it was covered in berries and flowers of all colours. Leaves, tree bark and other paraphernalia needed for medicinal magic were plentiful and two of Wulfgar's apprentices were busy at the table. One was mixing and grinding ingredients with a pestle and mortar while the other carefully and delicately combined small amounts of different coloured powders in a glass beaker over a gentle blue flame. As the powder mixed with the clear fluid in the jar it sparked into the colours of the rainbow before it became clear again. The apprentices paused only long enough to acknowledge the master apothecary and the Intendant before returning to their individual tasks.

The room that Sibley was kept in was small, the windows were shuttered, and there was a small dull light hanging from the ceiling. Aliedori waited for her eyes to adjust to the semi-darkness before moving towards the cage that held the cot. Sitting by Sibley's cot was Wulfgar's third apprentice who sprang to her feet as Aliedori came close.

"I don't think she likes to be alone, so we take it in turns to sit with her," said Acca.

"Please remain seated. How is she?" Aliedori waved the girl to sit down again and she did.

"Ready to go home I think, but she also wants to do whatever she can to help." Acca sounded sad; her voice was small, just above a whisper. Aliedori stooped down by the cot and Sibley turned her head towards her. Aliedori was pleased to see some semblance of humanity still remained in the pale creature. She reached through the bars and stroked Sibley's head and the touch had an instant effect as Sibley visibly relaxed. Her breathing became less of a pant as she stopped struggling for breath and her breathing evened out into a rhythmic, restful sound. Soon Sibley was curled up, arms and legs pulled up as she fell asleep. Aliedori pulled the blanket up and covered the sleeping woman.

"You can leave her now Acca, attend to your other duties, Sibley will sleep for a while yet." Wulfgar instructed his apprentice.

Aliedori stood and Acca slipped out quietly, glad to leave the darkened room and the strange creature behind. Aliedori turned to follow her out but Wulfgar stopped her. He had tried everything in his knowledge to calm Sibley, to make her life easier and enable her to sleep, but nothing had worked, at least not for very long or successfully. Whatever he had tried, Sibley simply remained fretful and her sleep was fraught with dreams and nightmares and the sounds she made were frightful.

The sound made the apprentices afraid even to enter the room alone. He had to give them a calming draft before his young apprentices were any help to him or Sibley. All Aliedori had to do was place a palm on Sibley's fevered brow and the creature had fallen into a restful sleep. Wulfgar smiled, the proud smile of a father and led Aliedori out into the late afternoon sun through a small side door that she had not known existed. Once out in the sunshine Wulfgar was surprised to see tears stain Aliedori's cheeks. He said nothing but continued to hold on to her elbow and he did not release it until they reached a gate in the palace wall. There he left her to her own devices and returned to the conference to update The Lady Minoria on Sibley's progress.

Aliedori did not return to her quarters immediately but instead spent some time with the messengers, the Cob dragons from the Eastern settlements and Kastillion, who wanted to return to his family but not before he had said goodbye to Aliedori. Aliedori cast a protective incantation; she had enlisted the help of a trader who had agreed to take Kastillion into the West.

Finally, she tried to reach the mind of Sorin but could not; there was not even the smallest sense of him. Aliedori wondered why that was, because once she made a link the essence of that link remained, it was like an invisible thread that she could easily pick up again to make future connection easier. Perhaps it did not work that way with dwellers that lived outside the Southern Realm borders. She had made several links, one with Athelstan of Skellglade and an ex-student of Wulfgar in Stornvale.

Sorin was a stranger, and maybe she could only link with him if he chose to, but what if Sorin was 'hiding' from her? This would mean that he was aware of the link, but he had shown no indication that he was aware that she was 'using' his eyes. The only other explanation, and the most logical, was that the West had a mental 'shield'. Aliedori shuddered at the thought. Was it possible that Sorin was not the 'ordinary young man' about to celebrate his coming of age, but a skilled mage? She had linked with several animals since returning to Fengardia in or around the Western Realm, but picked up very little sense of anything as the Realm was very well guarded by powerful magic. Aliedori went to the palace depository still pondering the idea that Sorin could be a mage. She found the tome she was looking for and spent the rest of the afternoon and evening reading about the fracturing of humankind essence. By the time she had finished and gone to bed, she was unable to sleep so she went in search of her mother, finding her where she had left her earlier but now alone. It was late into the night before tiredness overtook them both and they went off to bed. It still took some time for Aliedori to succumb to sleep, only for her to dream of Sorin and the creatures from the gateways.

Chapter 21

The Dawn Mist was fully laden and ready to sail. Three dracs were tethered towards the stern and the coxswain was already at his post when Aliedori, Maldar and Waifyn boarded. The coxswain greeted them and from the hessian bag slung across his shoulders he drew a large glass sphere, which he offered to Aliedori. She took the sphere in both hands and looked deep into the glowing, dancing yellow and blue light inside the sphere. She closed her eyes for a second then opened them again as the lights bloomed bright and filled the sphere. Then they died back into tentacles of light that danced across the inner surface.

Just below the wheel was a set of astronomical housing for the sphere. Aliedori laid the sphere in the central arc and closed the small door, encasing the sphere. Boats were once sailed by golems' strength; a golem would have been placed in the wheelhouse and an incantation placed on the light essence that was then put in the chest instructing the golem to move the boat. Later, when the golems had all but disappeared, dragons were used. They were harnessed to the boat and would fly low over the water dragging boats behind them.

Aliedori knew that some traders still used dragons to assist sailing but they were mainly from the Western Realm and did not venture this far south. After the small party boarded, minus Elyann, who had to be removed by one of her father's dragon riders, they departed without ceremony as Aliedori gave the order and the anchor was drawn up. They left Elyann's protests scattered in the early morning breeze of the breaking dawn.

Dawn Mist left port to make the short crossing to the temple garden where the entire crew disembarked. In the inner sanctum of the ancestors' garden, Aliedori and her crew honoured their ancestors and left tributes and runes bearing their names, so that the ancestors could begin preparing a place for them should they not return home from their journey.

Each member of the crew spoke to their ancestor, asking their own private blessing for a safe passage into the unknown and to return from danger. They returned to the *Dawn Mist*, each deep in their own thoughts, and set sail as the journey began in earnest. Maldar and Waifyn secured their cabin and remained there for the rest of the morning. Sometime during the late morning Waifyn climbed naked from the bed and sat cross-legged on the floor, watched by Maldar through half-closed sleepy eyes. Maldar thought of his parents; before Waifyn there had been no one whom he loved as much as he loved them, with the exception of Aliedori. Maldar did not realise he had dozed off until he opened his eyes and found himself staring at the ceiling of the cabin; he returned his sleepy gaze to Waifyn, who was still cross-legged on the floor with his head down, chin resting on his chest. It was a simple way to communicate amongst nymphs; all nymphs had a telepathic link with family. Since all nymphs shared a common ancestry, they all shared that ability to communicate with each other telepathically. The only humans who had the ability to communicate telepathically were naturalists and mages.

Very few were like his sister, who had the ability to communicate with all of nature. Waifyn raised his head and opened his eyes to grin broadly at Maldar as he raised the cover. Waifyn slipped back into bed to be greeted by the solid form of his lover who pulled the sheet over their heads.

"Your family?" Maldar quizzed stilling his busy hands for a second or two.

Waifyn stopped his busy hands also and let out a gentle sigh, then busied his hands again.

"My dear, you may not have noticed, and I am sincerely hoping that I am not mistaken, but this is not the time to be asking about my family."

"I have noticed," Maldar said, also catching his breath, "believe me I have noticed."

"Good, I hate to think that all my efforts have gone unnoticed."

Maldar did not respond, he could not even if he had wanted to. With nothing to do but wait, Aliedori spent the first part of the morning in quiet contemplation and meditation. The later part of the morning she was occupied with sword practice and exercising her mind and body with the crew. Each exercise was designed to make her body and mind sharper and more supple. She cast her mind out, concentrating on reaching as far as she could, soaring out over the water. She could reach her mother, but her mother's mind was *closed* and so was her father's so she reached high up in the air and deep below under the water.

As she balanced on her right leg, arms at her side, she inhaled deeply as she brought her arms up slowly and out at each side. As she brought her arms around and out in front of her, she exhaled through her mouth. Aliedori's breathing synchronised perfectly with the movement as she pushed her arms out, palms open, facing out and expelling air from her lungs. She reversed the movement as she inhaled and repeated the exercise, changing legs and accomplishing it with ease and grace.

The final movement was to uncurl herself from the sitting position, standing up in one fluid motion. She stood looking towards the dracs and saw that they were becoming uneasy. She glanced around her; the ocean-lake was clear except for a few trade boats sailing towards the port. Then she glanced skyward. There were dragons, about six of them, far out over the water in the direction in which the *Dawn Mist* was heading. She saw them only as a distant speck on the horizon, but she noted with interest that riders so far out must have been trying to hide from detection. Aliedori thought that there must a vessel out there large enough to accommodate at least six dragons and she *sent* a mental "pat" to the dracs necks in turn and said, "Well done."

As creatures of magic, the dracs had a spurious link with other creatures of magic and they had sensed something that made them uneasy. Aliedori knew that the dragon riders could cause trouble for them; this journey may not be as easy as she would have liked.

'Pirates/bandits' was the clear message from the minds of the dracs. Aliedori watched the horizon to see if the riders would turn towards shore, but they kept going until they disappeared. She warned the crew of the *Dawn Mist* to stick close to the natural curve of the land, as she was reluctant to leave the land behind for the moment.

Aliedori cast her mind out but was unable to reach the dragons or their riders. Both riders and dragons were shielded or perhaps they were something else. The barrier they were using was solid and noisy and Aliedori knew that it was not a natural shield. She tried to break through to their minds but failed. The dragons were also shielded, perhaps in the same way that the Greys were made. Even though she could not reach the minds of the dragons, she could sense that they were alive. They were not like the Greys, which had layers of nonlife entwined with natural life, creating something entirely different and new. Aliedori knew that bandits and pirates had shields, as did most traders. People with low-level magic were especially in demand by sailors who hired them to outwit bandits and pirates. With an adept on board, cargos and passengers would reach their destination intact. Aliedori watched the sky; if she could reach their mother and father and Wulfgar then she could reach others. She had spoken to them all before the boat left and they had promised to rip the Realm apart if they did not return safely. Aliedori had no doubt that they would be as good as their word and was glad that the dragon riders did not turn.

Wulfgar had been packed and ready to sail with them but Aliedori had sent the apothecia back to his work, reminding him that he was needed at home to unravel the secrets of Sibley. Wulfgar had asked with some sorrow, "What if you do not return?"

"Then you come and find me warrior; besides, your nephew is always linked to you."

With two great warriors watching them and awaiting their return, she almost felt sorry for anyone who dared to attack them. She paid the dragon riders no more attention, but they did not leave her mind. The *Dawn Mist* clung to the shore line for three days and on the fourth it sailed into open water, slicing through the water at cruise speed, the crew busy at their posts and Maldar and Waifyn otherwise engaged. Aliedori took the time alone to continue with her sword training and exercise. She practised her moves, defence and attack, until she was interrupted.

"Good, but remember to use your whole body, your body is a weapon too. I know that you have magic and you may never need to use swords... but all the same."

Maldar and Waifyn had finally emerged from their cabin and stood watching her. Aliedori winked at them and saw the colour rise in Waifyn's handsome features. She smiled at him. Maldar showed no such coyness and continued with his instructions, his left hand beckoning while his right hand held his sword in readiness. Aliedori was a force to be reckoned with even if she was still learning. She swung the seax while moving forward, and Maldar easily deflected her, or so he thought, until he felt the slight pressure under his ribcage.

"Okay, so you are good, but not as good as me."

Maldar twisted out of the way, and Aliedori found the blade pressing against her throat and that she was being held in an arm lock. Maldar pushed her away from him and showed her again. This time she did as instructed. The power of the attack threw Maldar off balance and the hooked horn of the drac was pressed against his throat before he could regain composure.

Aliedori stepped back, and Maldar attacked, which she blocked. Waifyn did the same from the other side and Aliedori deflected him, proving that her left arm was as strong as her right. Their sparring kept them supple and focused; they sparred, defended and deflected, using all of the deck, only stopping when the meal bell sounded. Waifyn agreed to instruct them both in using a bow.

"Anything out there?" Waifyn asked.

Aliedori wiped her arm across her forehead. "Apart from the dragon riders you mean, of four days ago. Yes something is out there, not sure what it is, but it's there."

Chapter 22

"We are still within the Southern Realm's protection, we are not in natural water yet," Maldar said. Aliedori was wearing her hair loose down her back and stray strands of hair stuck to her neck sending a sudden shiver up her spine. Something on the distant horizon caught her interest and she watched. Her breathing was steady and after all the exercise she had hardly broken into a sweat.

She turned from the horizon and headed towards the gallery but Waifyn stopped her before she entered. His arm was on her shoulder and she turned to him, her brow arching questioningly. He led her away from the entrance, to the front the boat.

"We have not been able to talk. I have spoken at length to your parents before we left… but you…" Waifyn paused as bearers approached with food and wine for them both. Aliedori took hers and sat with her legs dangling over the side of the boat. She placed the plate on her lap and the goblet of fruit wine on the deck.

"You want to know what I think of your companionship?" Aliedori was direct and to the point, which surprised Waifyn.

"Why do you need me to approve of you; is it not enough that all the parents do?"

"Maldar speaks of you as he does no one else, there were even times when I think I was jealous of his love for you," Waifyn said as a way of explanation.

Aliedori's hair hid her face from Waifyn; she put a piece of meat into her mouth and chewed slowly. Under the circumstances Waifyn should have felt uncomfortable but to his surprise he found that he wasn't fighting down the urge to fill the silence. His instinct told him not to push her for a verbal reply; he allowed her silence to envelop him until he was drawn into her calmness. Waifyn smiled as he felt the sudden spark of his telepathy, less than a second then it was gone, and he felt warmth spread though him.

"Have you two finished yet? Maldar asked, hating to be left out.

Waifyn looked at his lover as Maldar sat down; Aliedori got up, taking the empty plate and still full goblet with her.

"Thank you." Maldar gave his sister's hand a quick squeeze as she walked away. Waifyn looked confused but Maldar laughed.

"She approved. Believe me, I can feel the residue, she approved."

Waifyn knew that Maldar was fiercely loyal to his sister and managed to look as if he believed Maldar.

"She said nothing, but the simple truth is that she didn't reject me."

Maldar kissed Waifyn. "Better?" he asked, pulling away. Waifyn pulled him back and kissed him more deeply as they lingered in each other arms and then slowly pulled apart. The boat jerked as it changed direction, suddenly swinging towards land and bringing a sharp end to the young men's lingering gaze.

"We have company, and they're coming fast," Aliedori said. The 'something' that she had sensed earlier was now moving towards them very quickly indeed. The sky was clear and so was the horizon; not even the coastline of Fengardia or the temple garden could be seen. All around them was the open water of the great ocean-lakes. The boat had made good time and the day had not yet turned to dusk, there was still plenty of light to see the clear horizons. Maldar looked at his sister knowing that her instincts were never wrong.

He was about to turn away when he saw the small dot approaching fast. Within a few minutes, the dot was recognisable. It was a dragon boat, black and red and low in the water, indicating that it was heavily laden or full of bandits. Maldar looked at Aliedori questioningly.

"It's the *Ironclad*, a metal boat, and it appears to be full," was Waifyn's simple reply. His eyesight was better than Maldar and Aliedori's.

Maldar and Waifyn grabbed their scabbard and bow respectively and a bearer brought Waifyn's quiver to him. Aliedori was ready. In one hand was the serrated edged drac sword and in the other she held the hooked horn. The three stood together. Behind them, the crew, all experienced warriors on land and water, were also armed and ready.

"I can't use magic on them; they are shielded, so we have to fight. They don't take the boat," was the command and she sent a boat wide blessing. Everyone knew that if raiders took the boat the crew were already dead or broken and she was not going to allow that.

"How many?"

"I can't tell because of the shield, they could be ten, they could be forty. But I believe they are many because she is riding low in the water," said the coxswain.

"It could be full from successful raids." Aliedori was uncertain of who had voiced her thought. Most of the crew had low-level magic; it was a basic requirement when you were a member of the crew of the Dawn Mist. The boat was close enough to the Dawn Mist for its passengers to make out the markings among the red and black. The insignia bore the name *Y'onrand*. The name meant nothing to Aliedori or the others, but she knew their intention.

"We may be outnumbered," someone said.

"We are outnumbered, but not outmatched," Aliedori replied.

"Friends of the dragon riders of earlier?" Maldar asked.

"No doubt, and I bet they were told exactly where to find us."

"So we are still in Southern waters?" Waifyn looked towards the shore as if in some vain hope they were not be in open water and somehow Fengard would appear.

"No, sire, just before we sat down to eat we sailed into neutral waters," said the coxswain.

"Good, so we can sail back into Southern waters before they reach us," Waifyn suggested with hope in his voice.

"When we breakfasted, sire," the coxswain corrected.

"So any bright ideas, Aliedori?" Maldar wanted to know.

"One, possibly two."

"Are they going to ram us?" the voice was small and frightened. Aliedori located the speaker; it was a cabin boy. While part of his training was with the sword, he was not expected to face bandits.

"No they won't ram us, they can't risk damaging the boat, go below Yrre." The cabin boy stood his ground for a few seconds more then followed the instruction of his Intendant.

"Defend the boat but not with your lives, I will try to find a way to break the shield," Aliedori instructed. "And remember, alive we have hope, pass, we only have tributes."

The metal boat was almost upon them as its wash rocked the Dawn Mist, but the humans were steady. The *Y'onrand* began to slow and turn port side. The bandits were clearly visible, about twenty of them; their captain flanked by ten on each side.

"Surrender your vessel and yourselves, and you will not be harmed," he said, his voice full of glee at the rich pickings, a fancy boat with a bunch of children. There must be at least another twenty to thirty below, Aliedori thought quickly.

The *Y'onrand* was large enough to carry at least fifty crew members. Aliedori counted the portholes, but she was still unable to find a way to penetrate their shield. She tried scanning the metal boat again; magic wasn't going to work, not on the boat or its crew. She sent another blessing to her crew and boat, the incantation penetrating everything and everyone on board.

Even the golem on board steering the *Y'onrand* was shielded, but if she had had time, she would have tried her newfound ability. However, she knew that this was not the time to attempt something new; the lives of her crew were at stake. The boat was too well shielded and Aliedori knew that this was no ordinary bandit's boat. This boat had come for them specifically. She would have laughed but there was little humour in this situation, someone knew that they were responsible for the deaths of the golems.

"I love a good old fashioned close quarter combat, none of this long distance magical nonsense," she said, assuming the stance.

"Surrender your boat, and your lives will be spared," the captain said again.

"Turn away and your life will be spared, captain," Aliedori said.

"Board her," came the reply.

"If you or your men come on board this boat captain, you will die and so will some of your men."

The captain laughed. This was going to be good, at least she was feisty. He had been paid to get her and that was what he was going to do. A fight just made it more interesting.

"My men love a good fight girlie, what a pity we are not going to get one."

Aliedori stood her ground, ready to defend her people, but she gave it one last try. "We are under the protectorate of the Lady of Fengard of the Southern Realm." This just provoked laughter from the crew of the *Y'onrand*.

"Ready, Waifyn?" She received a slight nod but he did not take his eyes off the bandits. The *Dawn Mist* shuddered as several gangplanks hit her deck. The first bandit didn't make it across; neither did the second, third or fourth as Waifyn's arrows rang out, each one hitting its target. Neither did the fifth; he fell from the gangplanks taking two others into the water and they disappeared below the surface.

Waifyn almost single-handedly send the first wave of bandits home, until all his arrows were spent. Then they came one after the other hitting the deck and Aliedori sprang into action. She moved at speed, kicking out and knocking a bandit overboard, hitting his head against the metal boat. She blocked to her left and attacked to her right. As they came towards her, she turned and brought her arm up and out, the drac hook slashing and tearing the flesh across a bandit's throat.

A barbed hook attached to a silken rope flew towards her face and she caught it in her peripheral vision. She flipped backwards, landing firmly on both feet as the rope missed her and caught a bandit in the face. He screamed as the hook ripped the flesh from his face. The bandits were everywhere all at once and she lashed out, opening up a gash on the bandit's chest. The barbed hook in her left hand stopped him moving and his legs were unable to take his weight as he crumpled and crashed to his knees, before falling face down on the deck.

Chapter 23

Before she had time to think, two more bandits appeared. Aliedori struck at everything that moved with the drac horn. She turned, shoved, bent, jumped, swiped, swung and slashed out, catching some, missing others, but never allowing herself to be caught by the bandits or their weapons. She could not tell how many bandits were on board, but she knew that her crew would soon be overwhelmed.

A high-pitched scream halted her, and in that instant Aliedori turned and a steel sword was thrust under her chin. Forcing her head back she moved her own weapon casually and tapped it against the inside of the captain's thigh, pressing gently but firmly.

"They say that a death strike is as certain as a death grip, and I am willing to find out. Are you?" She pressed her point home, and the captain's eyes widened slightly.

"Get off my boat now; you are not going to save face but you may still save your own life." She was as firm as her weapon.

"You and your people are outnumbered; I can kill you all and still make a tidy profit on the boat."

Aliedori smiled, or rather the corners of her mouth turned up but the smile did not touch her eyes. She glanced at the metal boat; there were at least thirty crewmen still on board.

"Get your men off my boat, or you may be meeting the ancestors sooner that you would like, captain," she said again.

The blue eyes of the captain were equally cold; he had bellowed and frightened and sent a good few home to the ancestors, but he had never left a raid empty handed, and he wasn't going to do so now. He looked again at the female. She was not what he would call a woman; she was a pretty little girl. But this pretty little girl had personally butchered three of his men.

What a pity she was a special request. He would have enjoyed selling her or perhaps keeping her until he broke her will. Still, he could take the long way back home, who was to know? She was wanted for sure, but no one had said unharmed. He was looking forward to sharing a cabin with her for a few weeks. The men no, boys, would fetch a few pretty coins too; there was always a calling for two beauties like those. There were no instructions about her fellow travellers; it was a simple case of "get her and bring her to me."

"You have lost many of your men to my crew, look around you, captain, I still have all mine intact."

The captain followed her gaze. It was true, her crew were still breathing while his men were cast out, sent on their journey home.

"Send that one home," Y'onrand pointed to a female at random.

It would be a shame because she was a pretty young one, and the people he knew would pay handsomely for a handmaiden. Aliedori knew that if they were captured they would all be sent home to the ancestors or worse, be sold to the highest bidder. Perhaps they would become Greys. Aliedori knew that she would not let the crew of the *Dawn Mist* be sold. The crew were subdued as Captain Y'onrand stood proudly on her boat, smiling broadly, and Aliedori returned the smile, "If your man harms Racene, I will end you. I ask once again, get off my boat," she said.

"Or what, little girl? You cannot use your magic against me or my crew." He was pleased with himself.

"Yes, but I can use magic on so many other things. Would you like to know what else I can use my magic on" she said.

The Captain's smile disappeared from his face. Aliedori's voice was hard and cold. She did not ask a question, she made a clear statement of fact.

Maldar saw his sister's back stiffen, the captain had called her a little girl, and silence fell across the deck crew and bandits alike. When she spoke again her voice was like steel and everyone heard it, yet she barely spoke above a whisper.

"Release my crew, and get off my boat, captain, or you will you will be sent to the ancestors."

The captain did not move; instead, he pressed his sword into her flesh against her neck, not quite breaking the skin. The words were clear, the voice calm and the *Y'onrand* rocked slightly as if caught by a wave. The boat began to float out of the water and into the air. Tentacles followed the boat and one caught the captain round his legs, swinging him out over the water, hanging upside down, arms flaying. His sword fell from his hand and he screamed in terror. It was too late, there was no return; what was done could not be undone. The captain knew that his life was over, unless… the crew of the Y'onrand dropped their weapons in fear as tentacle after tentacle came up out of the water gripping the boat.

Collecting those who had passed, one tentacle gripped an orb on top of the boat, squeezing it until it splintered into tiny fragments. Suddenly, the fearful minds of the bandits were open to Aliedori, and she ordered them off her boat but not before they had cleaned the decks of the Dawn Mist. Tentacles searched the deck until all the departed were found and collected.

Waifyn spoke. He was standing beside her, his crossbow slung across his shoulders.

"It's done. All weapons seized and secured below deck and the bandits are disembarking," he spoke quietly.

The captain was still hanging upside down, although he had now stopped screaming and was bargaining with the ancestors, asking them to guide his path home. Everyone knew that the Rakan would not return to its watery home without an appeasement for being disturbed; the captain had sealed his fate.

"Bless their path and send your crew home, captain," Aliedori said sadly to Y'onrand. Her eyes filled with tears and she blinked them away as the captain began to scream again. She had managed to get to the age where she was a respected Intendant, never taking lives, and now in the last few days she had taken so many.

"Release him, Rakan, you have enough, you do not need another, the spell has been broken, take the departed and return home."

The tentacles released the captain and he fell upon the deck of his boat with a thud. His pride was broken, but his life was intact.

Aliedori scraped her fingers through her hair and pulled air into her lungs before she spoke. Her voice was tight, it did not sound like her at all and she shivered a little.

"Return the people to their families and homes, you have no right to them," she commanded the captain and his crew. Then in a gentler voice, "Take us away from this place coxswain, we have a long way still to go." She kept her eyes down, refusing to look up.

She did not see when the Rakan sunk back under the water taking the departed with it, nor did she see the Y'onrand sail away, but as it set sail, she heard the mournful song for the departed ring out and felt the gentle current left by the Rakan.

The *Dawn Mist* slipped its anchors and sailed away. One or two of the crew were badly, but not fatally, hurt. There were enough crew on board with medicinal magic abilities, including Waifyn. They would ensure that their crewmates recovered quickly, but the younger ones were shaken, and Aliedori offered them comfort and reassurance. She realised that even after the mind shield had been removed she had learnt very little from the bandits or their captain, except that they had been sent to get her. She had not *discovered* who had sent the captain.

Bandits often traded with the highest bidder or stole on demand for specific customers, one of which was the Western Realm. All that Aliedori had been able to find out from the captain's mind was that she was the intended target. Who had put the price on her head was another matter; the captain was either too afraid or too well disciplined to reveal that particular gem of information. The clear image that came from the crew's minds, but suspiciously not the captain's mind, was that they were all afraid of the shadowy figures in the towers. Sibley had not mentioned towers as she had been kept underground, and therefore figures in towers were a new thing. However, there were no indications of which towers they meant or where the towers could be found.

There was no indication that the captain was operating under the orders of a Western master. Were they dragon towers or the towers she had seen through Sorin's eyes? Were these shadowy figures Greys, or were they their creators? Aliedori could not tell and with each passing day, she had more questions than answers. She wrestled with the idea of invading Sorin's mind for more information then decided against it. There was no indication that Sorin would know of the Greys and, besides, Sorin was difficult to find and searching his mind would leave too big a footprint.

Chapter 24

Alone on deck, Aliedori removed her boots and outer garments and dived overboard. She needed to wash the stench of blood and death from her body and only the open water of the ocean-lakes could do that. The crew were asking questions about why she had let the bandit's crew and captain go. Maldar and Waifyn answered most of them for her but she knew that they had questions too.

She had not told them that the captain was after her alone, but she would have to and soon. Despite this knowledge, she could not take his life, and neither could she take him prisoner. Aliedori had cast a charm that would ensure that his bandit days were over but there were always others to take his place. Whoever was after her would not give up so easily; they would send others, which would put the lives of the crew in danger.

With nothing to do for the remainder of the day, Maldar and Waifyn retired to their cabin again where they passed the time making love and planning their future. The giving and receiving of pleasure left the two young men spent and they lay entwined in each other's arms and legs. The porthole on the far side of their cabin was open, and moonlight streamed in sending rays of golden light.

They lay listening to the pleasant sound of water lapping against the boat and the lilt of a crew member playing a sitar. Maldar heard the voices of Aliedori and Yaran and he listened while Waifyn slept.

"Beautiful evening, Intendant," the coxswain said.

"Is it? I have not taken much notice of the evening."

There was silence, then, "Did you learn much from the bandit's mind which could prove helpful?"

"Nothing more than I've already told the crew; they trade humankind with the Western Realm. They are bandits who trade for the highest reward."

"You let them go to continue with their trade in human…" Yaran began.

"Perhaps, perhaps not. Besides, what do you suggest I should have done with them?"

"I would have set them against each other," came the reply.

"Would you?. It was a simple question. Yaran was quiet as if in contemplation but did not make a reply. There was a long, significant pause, finally broken by Aliedori.

"Yaran, is there something else on your mind?" she asked.

"The young wood nymph, Intendant, does his people know where he is?"

"I believe so," she sighed. "Waifyn and Maldar are life companions now; they will be handfasted one day."

Yaran laughed, "I believe there are many young males and females across the entire Realm with broken hearts." Aliedori laughed too.

"Well, he was a little, perhaps more than a little, wild at heart," Aliedori said, her voice full of glee.

"The Nymph is good for him," Yaran said after a short pause.

"They are good for each other," Aliedori countered. Yaran remained silent.

"Yes they are," he conceded after a while.

Yaran laughed but sobered suddenly. "They said that some naturalists could see things, things that can happen in the future. Do you see something in their future that makes you afraid?"

"I cannot see the future. I just get feelings, and their future is all I hope it will be. Long lives, full, never boring, many children and grandchildren and great happiness before they go home to the ancestors." She spoke with a calm assuredness that not even the ancestors would have dared to question. Yet Yaran could not help but noticed that her voice carried a touch of something he was sure was fear.

Yaran thought for a while, wry smile curled his mouth up, how two males would produce children without the help of a female. He grinned at the young Intendant; she was looking at him, waiting for him to say something, a bemused expression on her face.

"But before any of that can happen I have to travel to the Eastern Realm to deliver a message." She was cross, and she didn't lose her temper easily.

"And you Intendant, do you believe it is your time?"

Ignoring the question, she said, "We… I have to go the Eastern Realm to find Sibley's family and keep my promise to her." She was more than a little angry, "This is my time."

"I think it is."

Aliedori made a sort of snorting noise that was not befitting an Intendant.

"Hear me out," the coxswain pleaded. "Lady Minoria has the Southern Realm; Lord Warian is master and commander of his dragon warriors and knights. Maldar has Waifyn. Intendant, his future is bright. Their names are known across the Realm. What about you, Intendant? Who do you have?" Yaran was insistent.

Aliedori thought for a while before responding, "I have friends… I have… I have my bro…" but her voice trailed off and was washed away by the noise of the water against the boat.

"What are your names?" It was an unexpected question and it hung there between them, waiting.

"Don't let me beat you with my seax. You know I could." She started to laugh, but not used to her jokes, he did not join in. She sobered. The boat whipped the water into foam bubbles and they chased one another across the surface to find the distant shore. She snatched the question from the air before it could be repeated.

"My name is Aliedori Minoria Raesrian."

"I know your many, many names, Intendant, but how many others do, including those on this boat, and what do your people call you?" Yaran asked gently.

Aliedori replied instantly, "Intendant," equally quietly. "People always call me Intendant, and they are not my people they are my mother's peop…" Her voice trailed off again; there was no more to be said.

There was an uncomfortable silence that pushed the words back before they could escape the speakers' mouths. It filled the space between them and spread its clawing tentacles until it found its way into the cabin and filled that space too.

"I believe that your father wants you to go on a journey and not just to deliver a message. He wants you to find something that belongs to you and you alone. Intendant, you need to find your place and you need to claim your place in the Realm and let your name be known."

There was a long pause from outside. Waifyn was curled against Maldar still sleeping. Long after Aliedori and Yaran had moved away, Maldar lay awake in the quiet cabin thinking. He lay listening to the gentle lapping of the water against the side of the boat and the wind in the sails. The comforting sounds he had spent the last week falling asleep to were no comfort at all now.

Chapter 25

The main commercial port of Memgalah was smaller than the main port of Fengardia. The *Dawn Mist* made her way cautiously around the commercial port until it found a place to dock. The green swathes of trees that rushed down to greet travellers to the Southern port were absent from Memgalah. The landscape appeared sad and dead, the little greenery being vines that twisted themselves around the trunks and never quite reached the branches of the petrified trees.

The landscape as far as the eye could see was frozen trees. There was supposed to be a dragon's backbone but none could be seen from the port.

The trees' branches were like withered fingers clutching at dead leaves and reaching for the sky. The supposedly charming and mystical Petrified Forest was lost on Waifyn; he could see nothing enchanting about the place.

The stories he had heard travellers tell about the wonders of the Petrified Forest were not true for him. His life, his home, the world that he came from was so very different from this one that he could not imagine anywhere beyond it. Waifyn found the forest before him eerie and full of foreboding. He shuddered as he thought that the forest appeared unusually silent. In reality, it had stood this way for over a thousand cycles. Generation after generation had grown tired of waiting for the forest to wake up, to spread its shade once more over the ground, to bear fruit and give life again and spread its natural magic across the Realm. For some unknown reason, the forest remained petrified. For many, many centuries, the trees and bushes had stretched out across the Realm creating an enchanting darkness that held the secrets of magic. It was said that the Petrified Forest held its secrets in a veil of magic that could only be released when the secrets could be deciphered.

For thousands of cycles, the forest remained alive, every leaf as green as the day they were first frozen. Brand new shoots, buds, flowers, and branches were simply holding their breath waiting to be set free from the dark hues that encased them. The ancient woods people could then return, and the branch walkers claim their homes again. Waifyn found the loneliness of the forest was beyond imagination.

The forest had been a place of magic for thousands of cycles but birds and animals no longer visited it and even the forest people avoided the area. It was too much for him to bear and Waifyn turned away from the forest in despair. He saw Aliedori watching him, her face carrying a look of understanding and empathy. She had been even more private since the conversation on the boat with the coxswain. She was always alone and lost in thought. Waifyn went and stood beside her and she put an arm around his shoulders as if to protect him from the loneliness and stillness of the forest. Her action served to swear a friendship forever. Maldar came into view, emerging from the cabin, Waifyn's eyes washed over him. The sight of his lover sent a different kind of shiver through him. Maldar joined them and stared out at the forest; it was beginning to become a habit, the three of them side by side. Aliedori, like the rest of them, had worn very little whilst on the boat but now she was bathed and dressed in more appropriate clothing. Her black hair was encased in a golden net, which hung down the back of her neck. The top of the headdress ended across the crown of her head, which was secured in place by a thin, gold, emerald-encrusted headband. Around her neck, she wore her mother's symbolic gold choker with the emerald green eye.

A clean shirt and leggings of the palest yellow over a green leather skirt and soft leather boots, her cape was held in place by an emerald eye brooch on her left shoulder. The tail was thrown over her right shoulder as was customary in the Ouran Province. Around waist the belt hold a scabbard with her drac horn seax; she looked every bit the visiting Intendant of the Southern Realm.

What she really wanted to do was to find the Ouran Province to deliver her news and be on her way back to the gateway. However, protocol dictated that she could not visit the Realm without first presenting herself to the Elders.

When they first arrived in Memgalah, Aliedori had sent a message to the Elders of the Sun Palace informing them of their arrival. Now they waited, pacing the deck like caged animals, partly because of nerves but mainly because they wanted to be on their way. It had taken them almost thirty days of hard sailing to reach the Memgalah, the main city of the Eastern Realm. After their encounter with the water bandits the remainder of the journey had been uneventful. The *Dawn Mist* had been able to drop anchor on a small, uninhabited island and take on fresh provisions of fruit and water. Maldar and Waifyn had wandered off with Yaran and returned with freshly hunted Gimles. They spent a night on the island, where Aliedori was happy to show off her magical skills. When they left the island, the *Dawn Mist* was restocked with fresh meat, fish, fruit and water. It was Aliedori's concern for the dracs on board that made her stop on the island to allow them to have exercise.

They were getting none on board and about half-way through the journey; they sailed close to a small island. Aliedori moored the boat, allowing the dracs to run free while the crew refreshed themselves and paid tribute to the ancestors. Now that they had moored, Aliedori was busy giving instructions to Diera about the dracs' exercise when someone touched her shoulder.

She turned slowly in a half circle to find that Maldar was indicating with his head towards the harbour. Aliedori turned away from the young woman, following Maldar's gaze. There were three large gilded covered seats each carried by four bearers. They in turn were flanked by what appeared to be the entire palace guard. Aliedori slapped her forehead with the heel of her palm in exasperation and rolled her eyes.

"In the name of all the ancestors!" she exclaimed.

Maldar laughed, "They don't do anything by halves do they?"

"It is not every day they have the honour of welcoming the children of the man who held back the enemies at the dragon gate, saving thousands of lives," Waifyn teased gently.

Aliedori gave Waifyn a cross look as he slipped between the two of them and placed his arms around their shoulders. He kissed Maldar's cheek, clearly choosing to ignore Aliedori's look. The messenger, having failed in his task of asking the Elders for discretion, greeted his Intendant a little shamefacedly and with head bowed.

"I tried to stop them, but it would seem that word had reached them of our impending arrival," he said, head still lowered.

"Thank you Yrre; it's not your fault."

The man who approached Aliedori was no more than a metre and a half tall; he was slender and dressed from head to toe in bright orange with a flowing red cape. The cape was tossed casually over his shoulder and it caught the breeze and bellowed out behind as he walked.

As he approached the three standing on the deck, he fell to his knees, his arms raised above his head. Palms facing out, he lowered his torso until his forehead touched the deck, his palms flat on the deck also. The cape settled over him so that all the three saw as they stood there was what appeared to be a bundle of clothes with arms.

Beyond him, the greeting party assumed the same position. Mystified, Aliedori exchanged glances with the others, then stooped and helped the bundle to his feet.

"Daughter and son of the great Warian, you have arrived at the most inopportune time, or perhaps you have not," he said rising to his feet. He was looking out beyond Aliedori and a confused expression crept slowly over his fine features.

"Where are your warriors? Out in deeper waters?"

Aliedori was about to speak when the emissary spoke again. "You are awaiting your dragon knights, even better if the attacks are by air not by water."

The man was becoming more agitated. Aliedori realised that he was going to say no more, but he continued to be agitated as he waited for a reply.

"It is just my brother and Waifyn, son of Don and Elbin of the tree people." Aliedori stopped the emissary from tripping over his own cape as he paced and continued to look for the armada.

"We have received no entreaty to come to the aid of the Eastern Realm; we are here on a private visit."

The emissary looked as if he would burst into tears as he surveyed the small group. Maldar and the others were looking towards the walled city; it all appeared calm in the afternoon light. The port was busy with traders but there were very few other visitors. She saw no boats carrying the insignia of the Southern Realm. Port workers were going about their business loading and unloading dragon boats. Upon closer inspection, though, beyond the docks, here and there scorches and burns were evident. It was dragon fire, but there should have been more damage; dragon fire could even turn stone to cinders.

"We asked for a contingency of dragon warriors," the emissary said.

"I am sorry, but we never received such a request. As I have said we are here on a private matter." The emissary grew crestfallen.

"So, no dragon knights and no warriors?" he asked again just to be certain.

Aliedori shook her head in reply and her action almost brought tears to the emissary's eyes.

"What about the black dragons, they are the sworn defenders of this Realm?" Maldar asked.

"Without the black dragons we would have sunk below the water already and our people would have starved. They can only come one, perhaps two, at a time and we are under siege almost every night by more and more dragon riders; we are without respite."

No one spoke for a while, and the crew all remembered the dragon riders a week into their journey. The emissary suddenly remembered his honoured guests and his duty to welcome them. He started the official welcome speech but it was soon given over to a cry of despair. The emissary looked towards her pleadingly, "Can you do nothing to help?" he asked. "Our defences cannot hold out much longer."

Aliedori looked from Maldar to Waifyn then back to the emissary. A decision needed to be made. They had asked for help and if she gave them the help they wanted, she would be drawn into a conflict far away from home. This was not her fight, yet she remembered what Yaran had said to her. Perhaps this was her time to show that she was capable of much more than just being the Intendant.

Chapter 26

There were so many things to consider – could she draw Maldar and Waifyn into a dragon fight? Fighting bandits to save their lives and the lives of their fellow crew was different. She could not ask them again, but if she did nothing to help then the Realm could be destroyed and its people turned into Greys. If the Eastern Realm was consumed it would only be a matter of time before the Western Realm used their newly acquired might to move against her homeland.

The Realm was supposed to have lost its magic when it lost most of the forest, and subsequent battles had apparently been fought and won without much magic. Aliedori knew that this was not true; there was magic here and she looked to her brother and Waifyn for their council. She could not make a decision like this on her own, not when their lives would also be at stake.

"I'm with you sister whatever you decide," was all Maldar said.

"Me too, sister-in-pairbond," Waifyn grinned as if he had just volunteered for diving duties.

"We are supposed to call a council to discuss options and make a decision," she said.

"You are not Mother, you are Aliedori, and besides you have already made your decision. You know that, I know that, and so does Waifyn. So be Aliedori." Maldar placed a reassuring hand in the centre of her back and she nodded. A decision had been reached and the emissary seemed immediately relieved.

"Okay, Maldar you take Keidrop and scout the area from above; Waifyn take a drac and do the same area from the ground; Drefan and Leof will go with you. The dracs could do with the exercise. I will go and speak to the Elders; the rest will stay on the boat".

Maldar was about to remind Aliedori that Keidrop was still in Fengardia when a golden head rose up out of the water. Keidrop took to the sky, showering the deck and its occupants, before swooping down to hover just above the deck.

"What are we looking for?" Waifyn suddenly possessed his bow and quiver and was busy arming himself.

"I do not know." She shrugged. "But Father always says know the lay of the land." Maldar intoned too, remembering their father's words.

Maldar climbed onto Keidrop's bare back and chided her for soaking them, but his words were lost in the sudden beat of her wings. They were gone, flying high in the sky, before he could even finish the sentence. Aliedori was marching off the boat; she was almost to the end of the gangplank when she realised that the emissary had not moved. She turned back and led him off the boat by the hand. As soon as Aliedori's feet touched the ground, she felt the sudden surge of magic even through the soles of her boots. She refused the bearers' offer to carry her to the Sun Palace, preferring to walk. If warriors needed to know the lie of the land then she needed to know the lie of the magic.

"Lead the way, Chin Ya." The emissary paused in surprise that she knew his name and the correct way to use it. The dracs were happy to be off the boat and on solid ground again as they thundered past him, causing him to jump. He hurried after Aliedori. *That young lady's legs are far too long. She doesn't know how to take small steps,* he thought as he struggled to keep up with her.

Keidrop took Maldar over the walled city at a gentle pace; the only thing outside the walled city was the port. Those arriving by boat entered the city through the dragon gate his father had so gallantly defended. They could, like his sister, walk, or ride, as Waifyn was doing or sail in on smaller boats through the waterways and into the heart of the city. But everyone arriving at the port had to enter the city through the huge dragon gates set in the wall.

Maldar banked Keidrop to the right, and saw there was more evidence of a city under aerial bombardment. To the right and beyond the walled city was the mysterious Petrified Forest. Maldar thought it beautiful; it was very different from the forests at home, but magnificent all the same. He had seen many paintings of the forest, all of which attempted to capture the surreal beauty but failing miserably. A large painting of the Petrified Forest hung in the ceremonial hall of his home. It was of the black dragon's gate and represented the view his father would have seen on that fateful day.

Maldar had always liked the painting and now he saw why. The frozen trees reached out beyond the horizon and across time and engraved themselves into the very essence of all who saw them. Maldar circled back to have a closer look at the towers that lined the bay and crisscrossed the walled city.

The towers had drawn Aliedori's interest the moment the boat had rounded the bay and the walled city had come into view. She had not been able to take her eyes off them, had tried and failed in her attempt to pretend that they were of no interest. She had emerged from the cabin to join Waifyn, who was already on deck. He had seen her watching; her eyes flickered from the towers to Waifyn then back to the towers. Her gaze had just rest on Waifyn for a second when he shivered at the sight of the frozen trees.

It was Aliedori who Waifyn had reached out to, taking her attention from the towers in an instant. To his surprise, Maldar had felt a bite of jealousy, especially after the look he saw in Waifyn's eyes. He had to use a lot of self-control not to drag Waifyn back to their cabin. Aliedori was distracted too. She focused on Waifyn, the towers filed away but not forgotten. Maldar and Keidrop circled another tower for a closer look; the tower was very much like the dragon towers back home. They were not as big as they were not for leisure, these were fire and arrow towers. There were even towers using a strange kind of static charge, and some towers were built into the walls, while others were free standing and reached only by walkways and stairs.

Maldar wanted to land Keidrop in one of the towers, but he thought better of it; they were certainly big enough for large dragons but he did not want to alarm the warriors. There were many Cob dragons sited around each tower and in times of siege the Cob were needed to pass messages between towers and commanders. It struck Maldar as he and Keidrop flew close to another tower, that the warriors did not react. They did not send fire arrows shooting into the skies.

Instead the approaching golden dragon and rider were an excuse to stop what they were doing and gaze in wonder at the sight. Maldar circled one last time then urged Keidrop upwards, the city spreading out below them, the gleaming azure waters of the Eastern Realm to one side and the jagged dark mountain peaks to the other. Nestled in the middle was the walled city; while Fengardia's roofs were of greens and blues, Memgalah's were of reds, yellows and gold. Their bright colours and the strange curved angle of each roof were defiance against all those who dared challenge them. Maldar felt for Waifyn, he was used to the green lushness of the Southern forest. He would miss the beauty of his home and the abundance of life and that shimmer from every leaf and petal. This would be too much for Waifyn to bear, even for this short time. Maldar could not avoid looking directly at the forest even if he wanted to. He felt the stillness and silence dragging him in to some deep, dark, secret place. Perhaps it was his encounter with the Grey in that silent, dead place that allowed him to make the distinction.

That place where they had encountered the Greys was green, but the stench of death had clung to every leaf. This was different; this place was brown and brittle but it was on the brink of life, you could almost feel the vibration. Whatever the reasons for him feeling that way, he had nothing but empathy for the people of the Realm, for they had lived like this for so long, feeling the vibrations of life and waiting for that one moment. It showed their strength, determination and their will to survive, because they knew what was to come and it would be worth waiting for. Maldar could not help but admire them.

Sunlight had glinted off an object in the distance, drawing Maldar's attention, and he realised that it was some kind of mountain settlement. The settlement was in the forest and he would not have been able to see it had the trees not been so still. Maldar turned Keidrop back along the ridge and stopped, startled, for despite their size, black dragons had appeared silently from nowhere.

They were perched, if dragons of their size could perch, around him on the rock face overlooking the distant city. Maldar took a long, calming breath and urged Keidrop on, noting that she showed no sign of fear. He relaxed a little as Keidrop flew towards the ancient guardians. Maldar lowered his head as a mark of respect as his dragon stopped before the ancient ones. Maldar bade Keidrop to land and she obeyed him. She swooped down and Maldar dismounted and stood looking at the guardians.

He was standing on a craggy outcrop of rock overlooking the city. From this distance, the city gleamed in the sunlight. The Sun Palace was on the highest ground surrounded by an inner wall and in the grounds of the palace walls were temples and dwellings, stables and armouries, serving the Elders. Beyond the inner wall were the general population, watchtowers, and the greenery of the fields that supplied food to the settlers. The green fields were a welcoming sight and Maldar lingered on them, hoping that Waifyn would discover them and find them comforting. The guardians regarded them in silence as he took in the rest of the view. Some way up ahead of him along the ridge was an opening in the rock face and he moved towards it.

Chapter 27

The drac riders galloped off the boat led by Waifyn, his bow and quiver swung across his shoulders. They came in through the gate and into the capital and stopped to admire the beauty of the waterways around which the city was built. Everyone talked about the Petrified Forest but no one talked about Memgalah and its waterways and channels. The city was a series of islands with channels of water separating each island connected by stone or wooden bridges. No one talked of the greenery within the wall or the peacefulness of the trickling water over stones.

Off to his left as Waifyn rode was the Sun Palace with its long, sweeping stairs from a black gateway leading from the central canal up to the palace entrance through a red gateway. Waifyn knew that the wall had been built after the loss of the forest to help protect the people. It was evident that many outlying settlers had abandoned their homes to move within the walled city. Over the years, many settlers had returned to their settlements and continued with their lives, but the city was still very overcrowded.

Waifyn's mind was swamped with odd images and the feelings of dread threatened to engulf him. He used the reins to get the drac moving again and he almost laughed as he identified the feeling that had crept over him since arriving in port. It was homesickness; he missed his home! Waifyn could not help but laugh out loud. He had always prided himself in being a seasoned traveller, then he realised that he had never travelled beyond the Realm. While few settlers remained in their settlements, a great many came to live within the sight of the new wall. An outer wall was built around the settlements causing the wall to reach down to the waterfront. There was a stark contrast between the greenery within the wall and the landscape outside its confines. Fruit and vegetable trees and vines were growing over the wall adding small amounts of green foliage to extend into the forest closer to the wall.

Waifyn and the other riders reached the first inner wall and stopped as they had found themselves in a thriving settlement. It was full of noise and the laughter of children playing. He issued instructions to the other two riders and he then separated from them, sending them through the settlement and to the left. Waifyn turned the drac and took it along the wall to his right away from the crowded square and towards one of the towers. The panting animal came to a halt before one of the bridges in the centre of the isles on the highest level.

There stood a construction that Waifyn had not seen before. He understood the arrow and the fire towers dotted around the isles, but this was new to him. Waifyn could only assume that it was a weapon of some sort; it was set on a solid square base on small stone wheels wrapped in twine which allowed it to move on a round flat stone surface. Two people could wind the handle and coming out of the base were two huge columns.

Attached to the ends of the columns was a counterpoise and at one end of the counterpoise sat a spoon shape. Waifyn dismounted the drac to have a closer look at the machine and he felt the tingle of magic through his boots. Someone had cast an incantation that allowed magic to be drawn out of the ground and which infused all the weapons. Few were powerful enough to do that kind of magic. Aliedori was said to be one of them, though he had never seen her do it.

He watched two operators both of whom were turning handles manipulating the machine. The top of the machine rotated on the base in the direction of the oncoming dragon riders. The two operators secured the long arm of the counterbalance and large rocks were placed in the spoon. It was an impressive weapon but Waifyn wondered if there wasn't a better way to use the limited magic. He watched the machine operators and wondered what chance it had against the might of a dragon.

He did not have to wonder for long, as he saw the evidence for himself. This was, as the emissary had said, a city under siege. Dragon riders came nightly and yet apart from a few scorch marks the city was intact. Their mages had used their magic wisely and held out so far and with Aliedori's help, they might hold out a bit longer. He remounted and geed the drac up and moved on; he knew that there were hundreds more of these weapons all over the city. Like the arrows and fire towers, these strange weapons appeared to have had more than a modicum of success defending the city. Waifyn realised something else too. This was not the poor defenceless Realm of his imagination; this city was full of magic.

It crackled and seeped up from the ground and into his very bones. He shivered; magic was part of the fabric of his realm but in his realm, it came from the trees. Here there were no green trees but there were living roots for the trees to store their magic in, waiting for it to be harnessed.

Waifyn could not help but smile; he sent a message to Aliedori and her reply was simple, *keep holding on.* Waifyn stopped before the trebuchet and spoke to the operators before he rejoined the other riders. Whoever was responsible for these attacks was winning slowly, but the battle engine imbued with the ability to draw a little magic from the earth was helping to stave off the dragon riders.

The Elders were gallantly defending their people, but for how much longer? Waifyn turned, heading back to town as some young children came towards him pulling a small food wagon. As they passed, they giggled shyly; even the children, Waifyn thought, were doing their bit. The people in the towers also noticed the food bearers and cheered at the welcome sight. There was no mistaking that the Realm was under siege as the once mighty kingdom was reduced to putting its children to work. As he went farther he noticed the green had been replaced by charred stone and ground. The trees were gone, frozen on top, but the living roots remained. The evil mage who cursed the Realm for thousands of years had not foreseen that. When the trees were first frozen many of its people dispersed across the Realms in fear. Those that stayed started to build the great wall and those who had dispersed returned to help to fortify and extend their city, but without the tree's magic the task, though not impossible, remained restricted.

Every few years pirates and villains with ambitions of lordship wishing to expand their wealth would lay siege the Realm. There were those who believed that the reduction of magic was a loss of the Realm's right to free existence. Waifyn cast his gaze towards the sky and caught sight of black dragons perched high on the distant peaks above the walled city. The golden dragon was hovering in front of them and Maldar was a mere speck, too far away to be seen clearly. Waifyn turned the drac and headed back to the Elder's temple as the black dragons took flight.

****

The walk to the inner temple of the Elders would have been a much slower one if Aliedori had allowed herself to be distracted. The people wanted to touch, talk and thank her; the Southern Realm has come to their aid again and they wanted to show their gratitude. They would be disappointed when they discovered there were no armada, no dragon warriors, just three young people and their crew on a private visit.

By the time Aliedori reached the grand stairwell to the central temple palace she must have stopped thirty times. It was the emissary who finally demanded that Aliedori allowed the bearers to take her the rest of the way. There were several guards by the lower gate and on reaching them she bowed as she passed through. Stretching up above her was the stairway to the Sun Palace and she reached the inner temple palace with fewer incidents. There were five huge dragons in the court-yard of cobbled, pale yellow stones.

Something flickered in Aliedori's memory, but it was gone as quickly as it came. However, it left a strange feeling in the pit of her stomach. She signalled for the bearer to stop and put the sedan to rest, and then she climbed from it and stood surrounded. Maldar was already in the courtyard of the temple and Keidrop was perched on the high wall. The hooves of the dracs could be heard as the riders returned, and Alie-dori took it all in. They had not been defeated in battle and the city had not fallen. There was still confidence and pride in its people and leaders, which was made more real by the presence of the Intendant. Down the steps, coming towards her were five of the Elders. Some had their hair elaborately styled while others wore their hair long and partly loose. Aliedori dropped to her knees, observing the custom as demonstrated by the emissary earlier, the others following suit. Someone tugged at her arm. "Intendant, get up!"

Aliedori rose slowly to her feet and the others rose also; the vast courtyard was quickly filling with people, all coming to see the Inten-dant. Aliedori and her party were quickly ushered up the stairs to join the Elders in the main hall. Aliedori got straight to the point.

"You have dragon raiders each night and it is not by pure chance that the city is not more damaged."

"We have our own ways of defending our people, Intendant."

Aliedori raised her eyes to the speaker, "You have magic, I

know, the city crackles with it." Aliedori cast her eyes towards the tree-less hills; the questions were obvious.

"I know, with our trees gone, so should our magic have gone, but it did not. It changes the way we get and use magic.

Aliedori smiled, "You can draw magic from the ground, the roots of the trees, as well as from other elements, but that was not my question. I simply wanted to know why you did not send for help when you are clearly struggling to defend your people." She was careful not to make it sound as if she was accusing them.

"We are, were doing well, it took us some time to build our defences but our magic was all around us and we just had to learn new ways to collect and channel it." The Elders all inclined their heads slightly, but Aliedori couldn't detect any magic from them. She looked back down at the court and at the five black dragons. She arched her eyebrows and was about to speak again but was interrupted before she could begin.

"We do not have time to explain, Intendant. The attacks always start soon after dusk, so our nights are spent defending the Realm and our days in preparation for the nights."

Aliedori glanced behind her; the courtyard was full and everyone appeared to be busy in preparation for another night of attacks.

"You are right though, child, we are the embodiment or the human forms of the black dragons. We are separate but linked; it is the price we must pay; if one feels we all feel, the black dragon's heart is inside us all."

Aliedori turned and looked at the hand of the speaker; she already knew what he had just said was true. These four were not mages. The five dragons were shape-shifters who were linked through their commitment to the Realm. Ten were needed, but there were only five, so they shared their hearts and five became ten. She noted that the tenth was not there. She wanted to know more, but this was not the time.

"How many come at dusk?" she asked

"More and more each night," came the reply. "They never attack during the day."

"And they ride what appear to be black dragons."

"How did you know?" one of the Elders asked. He had long flowing hair and a face that was ancient and youthful at the same time.

It was a face full of wisdom, pain and sorrow and as she looked into the eyes of the ancient, she saw his pain.

Into Aliedori's being, came a bolt of mental and physical charge, an invisible force emanating from the black dragons. The force wrapped itself around her and exploded into her very core as she shuddered. So strong were the images that her feet almost gave way beneath her, but she recovered quickly. She felt Maldar and Waifyn's reassuring hands at each elbow and took strength from their presence. Fragmented images embedded themselves into her conscious mind then faded, leaving only traces.

With her protectors at her side, Aliedori, now fully recovered, stood silently waiting for the feelings to pass. The joyous cheers that had greeted them would soon turn to shouts of command and instruction as the city prepared for the nightly attack. She could not fall apart now.

If she could not help them, she would try to be useful in some way, but what could she do? She was not a strategist like her mother. She did not command a band of dragon warriors and she had not fought in a battle. All she had done in the way of fighting was to kill a few bad men and a grey creature. Dragon riders were coming and the people were looking to her to provide them with aid. The Realm had made a request for dragon warriors, mages and naturalists and what did they get, they got her. The battle cry would soon be heard and the Elders and their people were all looking to her to provide something more than just platitudes.

She had no real plan of action, no battle strategies, just magic, a golden dragon, Maldar, Waifyn and the crew of a luxury dragon boat. Stones, arrows and static power were being used against dragons but somehow it was working. The ancient ones had learnt to harness magic in a new way and use it in defence against the dragon riders. The people looked to the Elders to defend them and they were doing so gallantly, but how long could they continue to do so under the nightly bombardment of dragon bandits. Her magic would help them greatly, she knew that, but more was needed. She called to the ancestors for guidance and she only hoped that they would hear her.

Chapter 28

They needed to bring the fight to the dragon riders, whoever they were; it should be a plan of attack not defence. Above the walled city were the ten peaks that the black dragons emerged from a century before when they first shape- shifted. It was the birth of the black dragons that caused the lands of the Eastern Realm to form, the peaks stood now as a constant reminder.

Even before the thought could be formed in Aliedori's mind the Elders' forms shimmered and they transformed into their true selves. The 'Elders' stood before them now and one of them did not appear to be much older than the visiting party.

"We find that we are better accepted as Elders' if we appear as such."

Aliedori did not speak for a moment; she simply looked out at the dragons still in the courtyard before turning to Senn Ju. Forgetting herself for a moment she gazed at him until he brought his hand up and his fingers traced the wound across his forehead to his left cheek.

"A battle between me and a mage from the West," he said softly.

Aliedori's eyes lowered as Maldar touched her arm and she turned her green-eyed gaze on him. He shook his head slightly. She cleared her throat and was back to the business at hand. It was obvious that they did not see what she saw; the wound was still fresh.

"Do you have dragon warriors? Or do you and the others intend to ride?" she asked Senn Ju.

"We are the riders of the black dragons," Senn Ju replied as Aliedori spoke again quietly. Maldar moved from her side and stood beside his lover who leant into him questioningly.

"She likes him?"

Maldar shook his head, he never really knew his sister's taste; her name had never been linked to anyone for very long.

"She may do, but there is something else, I think it's to do with the mark Senn Ju carries on the side of his face."

"What does the mark mean?" Waifyn asked.

Maldar shook his head again, "I don't think it means anything, I think it's more what she sees."

"Still, it's rude to stare."

Maldar chuckled quietly, "This from the nymph who has not stopped staring," Maldar replied.

"Well, he is rather delicious and he is a shape changer too. Well, that's taking riding to a whole new level."

Maldar looked at his lover with his hands on the hilt of his sword, and they exploded into silent laughter. From where Aliedori was standing looking over Senn Ju's shoulder, all she saw were the shaking shoulders of the two young men. She allowed herself a few moments of distraction before turning her attention back to Senn Ju, who was in the middle of explaining why so many dragons kept away from the Eastern Realm. While Senn Ju turned to address the other group giving instructions to each in turn, Aliedori took the opportunity to talk to the small crew of the *Dawn Mist*.

"The Elders are preparing their dragons, so Yaran, Yrre, return to the boat and get the cache of weapons we took from the water bandits; I think they can be made use of. Waifyn, find the armoury please and see if you can find some extra arrows, as many as your quiver can hold. There are some very skilled craftsmen and women here so use their talent, get their advice and let's see if we can be of any help. Oh, and see if they have a spare crossbow and bolts, you may need them." She issued instructions and commands and watched as her people rushed to their tasks, clearly glad to be of help. Turning to Maldar, she put her hand on his arm and was about to scold him like a naughty child.

"What's with the scar?" Maldar asked softly.

"You saw the mark of an old wound, I saw a fresh wound," she replied.

"So he sustained an injury from the raiders, Aliedori. It is par for the course."

She shook her head, "It is a wound sustained when the forest was frozen." She wrapped her arms around herself, and her body appeared to sag for a moment.

Maldar stood open mouthed for a while, then wiped a hand over his face and rallied himself, "Are you sure? Of course you are sure, what am I asking? How long will it be? As soon as this battle starts and what will that mean?"

"No, not that soon but soon," her shoulders came up slightly, too slightly to be called a shrug.

"You like him, you are drawn to him." Maldar tilted his head, watching her through half-closed eyes.

Aliedori did not reply at once, she could not give clear voice to her thoughts, so instead she said, "We have work to do Maldar and this is where my true skills as a naturalist will be tested."

"But you can do something, something to help him I mean." He leaned towards her, forcing her to make eye contact, if only for a moment.

Maldar gave her shoulder a reassuring squeeze and she patted his hand in thanks and said, "Your golden dragon awaits; brave dragon warrior. To your dragon and… and… and go get them!"

Aliedori threw her hands up in defeat, it was not quite what she was hoping for and she joined Maldar in laughter. He patted her shoulder again. "At least it started off well," he said.

Maldar's long legs took him down the stairs two at a time, she watched him go and thought; *it's not the start I am worried about; it's the ending!*

Once orders were issued, they all went off and the square began to empty, only to start filling up again with the very young and the very old.

Aliedori stood alone as she realised that she had not been given anything to do. Was that because she was an Intendant, or was it because she was seen as a magical vessel and had no other skills to offer? She sagged and was surprised that her body language had showed no outward sign of the dread she felt inside. Her legs felt weak and she was sure she would fall to the ground if she tried to move them. She stood still a little while longer but knew that she needed to be busy, so she steadied herself. She took a deep breath before walking down the stairs into the square and into the throng of children.

Her father and mother had fought many years ago at the battle to hold the dragon gate at the Western end of the city. Her father had held the enemy back; saving the lives of thousands, and his bravery was inscribed on the wall of faith, which was set in the garden of remembrance at home for all to see and to remember. She did not sink to the ground when she moved but was relieved when she navigated the stairs and reached the people with her back straight and her head held high. She sat on the grass surrounded by the very young and the very old. She was deep in thought and feeling the tremors in her arms and body, she was glad to be finally sitting.

Her father had done so much to prove his courage and leadership and to win the heart of the Intendant. Her mother also led her warriors against the invaders of the Western Realm when they had tried to encroach on the borders joining the two realms. Now this could be her turn to prove her worth, to prove that she was deserving of the title Lady of Fengard. Instead she was sitting on a clump of grass playing in the dirt like a child because she was too afraid to stand.

Aliedori had come to the Eastern Realm to keep a promise made to Sibley, not to be involved in a battle and not to get her brother and his beloved hurt, not to mention the crew. Even Yrre was making himself useful, so what was she doing sitting in the dirt. She busied herself, reassuring and comforting those who gathered around her. She eased pain, dried tears, served meals and helped settle some of the smaller ones in makeshift beds.

When Aliedori made her way back up the stairs she felt a little better knowing that she could offer some comfort and support. She found a seat and sat down, looking towards the sky. It was still bright but the sun was low. She sent her mind and searched the sky but found nothing, not even the 'noisy' shield she had encountered with the dragon riders. She had come to a stop in front of a large table that was displaying a scale model of the Eastern Realm in all its splendour. It was a beautiful Realm nestled between the azure blue water and the ten peaks of the Kuok mountain range and the settlements beyond. There were magnificent temples and the most magnificent of all was the Temple Palace, a palace of black, red and gold. It was the place of homage to the black dragons and the home of the Elders who were the guardians of the people; though the Elders and the dragons were one and the same thing. The temple was a two-storey structure, and the second storey was at right angles to the lower one. At the point of each roof was the carving of a black dragon and at the top of the palace was Senn Ju, the first guardian to change and emerge from the Kuok Mountain.

Aliedori admired the miniature trees surrounding the palace and was not surprised to find that they were real trees. The waterways ran freely and there were tiny stone bridges to cross them; all that were missing were the people. All the dwellings were built on a series of knolls surrounded by waterways that ran on a grid pattern feeding every single dwelling with fresh clean water. Aliedori placed her palms on the glass tabletop and took a deep, steadying breath. An image of Senn Ju, the black dragon, bleeding at her feet suddenly snapped into her mind. She did not need a reminder, Aliedori was well aware of what was to come; she turned to the sound of approaching feet.

"Intendant." Senn Ju bowed, "It is clear that I cannot hide from your eyes what I can hide from the others."

"It is not as hidden as you may think, your people know that something is wrong." She rounded on him with an anger she had not known she felt.

"I was content with what was to come, I have lived a long and full life; I have served my people well and am ready."

"To give up on your people when they need you most?"

"Perhaps," he replied, "I can reclaim my heart, remain in this shape and do my duty to my people." He was resigned to his fate.

"It is not your time yet, but…" her voice trailed off not allowing herself to finish the sentence.

He finished it for her, "But I chose and I had chosen for it to be soon. It has been a long time to live with a wound like this. Whatever dark magic was used it is beyond me, my brothers and sisters and the Realm's apothecary." He reached out and took her by the hand and Aliedori consented to be led into one of the inner chambers.

Senn Ju lifted Aliedori's chin and lowered his head as if to claim a kiss before she could protest. He then chose not to, and she moved back, the expression on her face unchanged.

"I know that you chose this," she said softly. "You asked for the dragon heart to be taken from you and you are giving your abilities over to the others."

"I have served my people faithfully; those that I loved are long gone. But I continue, I wish to live even if it is just for one day as myself again," Senn Ju remained steadfast.

Aliedori nodded her head, she understood. "When the forest and magic were frozen there was enough for the five mages to become ten dragons, in order to ensure that the Realm was protected for as long as necessary, am I correct?"

Senn Ju watched her through the dragon's eye, not speaking. Aliedori placed her palm on his arm but before she could speak again Maldar and Waifyn walked in. Maldar wondered if something profound had taken place and if they had intruded on an intimate moment. He moved to stop Waifyn but Aliedori stepped back and beckoned them. Senn Ju turned away and Maldar questioned her with his eyes, but she said nothing.

Waifyn joined them standing on the opposite side and Senn Ju turned back to face them, his eye colours flickering. He gasped, almost doubling over as she withdrew her arm. He caught himself in time and as he regained his composure looked at Aliedori and the others before moving past them.

"There is work to be done and we do not have much time," he said as he passed them. He was in full command of himself again.

"What just happened?" Waifyn asked quietly.

"Senn Ju wishes to give up his dragon self," came the reply.

"Can he do that and live?" Waifyn asked.

Maldar shrugged; he didn't know, he doubted that very much, but this was not the time to discuss the intricacies of human dragon hybrids.

"He can live but not for very long, not as he is now anyway." It was Aliedori; she continued to watch Senn Ju's disappearing back.

"We have done all we can in preparation Intendant, all we can do now is wait," Maldar said, using her formal title. He had secretly entwined his fingers with hers. Aliedori was thankful for her brother's closeness and took strength from him.

"Yes, that is all fine," Waifyn said. "But what did you do just now, he almost collapsed."

"I removed the dark charm that was keeping the wound from healing."

Waifyn grinned, "You are very good," he said. "Now Senn Ju has a choice." His grin widened, "I like that." Maldar looked at him but said nothing.

The Elders had gathered as they always did on nights like these to give their final briefing and Aliedori listened. The Elders outlined their defence plan, and she took note, wherever possible offering her opinion to be considered. Encouraged by Maldar and Waifyn, she left so that they could speak a little freer; she and Maldar had learnt a great deal from their father over the cycles. It was not really her opinion she was offering, it was her father's, and one of the things her father always said during their training was that sometimes the best form of defence was attack. Now it was time to see whether her father's tactics had any validity in reality. Senn Ju had taken his place with the rest of the Elders who were still assuming human form. They would not change back to dragons until the time was near. Senn Ju knew that Aliedori had done something to him but he did not know what, he just felt different. He knew that when he chose to relinquish the dragon self to be a human mage again his time would be short and filled with pain. He knew that, but it would mean that his brothers and sisters would be pain free. He would not only save his fellow guardians from further pain they would also receive his abilities. He had chosen to remain human and he had all but severed his links with the other guardians freeing them, but once again the connection between himself and the others was clear, sharp and without pain. He had endured the pain for so long that he could not remember ever being pain free. His brother and sister mages had all suffered with him and they endured because it was the only way to defend the Realm.

To be pain free once more was beyond all hope and yet here he was without pain. His fellow guardians felt his renewed vigour and his clear pain-free mind. Their questions bombarded his mind and he had to *shout* them down to he *heard*. It was good to be whole again; the separation from his other selves was too keen to bear for long.

Chapter 29

"You will be fine you know," Maldar said softly. He had found his sister leaning against the floor to ceiling door looking out onto the square with her arms folded across her chest displaying a calmness he was sure she did not feel. The brushing of the invisible 'thing' or sweeping her hair from her face was a good indication and she was doing it now. He stopped the constantly moving hand by placing his palm over it, and she unfolded her arms, but not knowing what to do with them she folded them again.

The room behind them was quiet now, *the calm before the storm,* Maldar thought. He had watched her slip out about halfway through the briefing and he had excused himself sometime later and followed her. She did not need to be in the room, she was not part of the attack, but she felt even more useless standing on the sidelines.

"Can you communicate with the black dragons?" Maldar asked, his eyes resting on Waifyn who was talking to one of the Elders across the room. Aliedori turned following Maldar's gaze and she smiled as she saw the person he was watching. She knew that Maldar was worried about Waifyn for he was not a warrior and she squeezed his arm in comfort.

"Are you okay?" he asked.

"Which question do you want me to answer first?" she asked smiling.

Maldar reluctantly dragged his eyes from Waifyn and looked at his sister.

"I am not okay, Maldar, I am out of my depth," she said. She was about to say more when she paused and looked to the sky.

"They are coming and they are early, it is still daylight," she said and moved away from the door. There was no haste in her stride just a purposeful walk, her long steps taking her across the room. Maldar moved with her and Waifyn came to join them as they walked through into the great hall. Maldar signalled to the dragon warriors and a few moments later the alarm bells rang out across the city. The Warriors, who were gathered in the hall and they fell in behind Maldar. He knew that as a Dragon Lord he would prove his worth, even though he had never been into battle before. After all, he was his father's son.

Aliedori needed him; he must assume command of himself in order for her to start her journey to becoming the naturalist she was born to be. Besides he had trained all his life for this moment and for every moment that was to come. Aliedori dropped back two paces, allowing Maldar to pass her, and as they emerged into the courtyard Maldar was in the lead. The dragons were saddled and waiting and Maldar signalled for his warriors to mount. Senn Ju bowed low in Aliedori's direction then mounted along with the others. He signalled and the dragons and their riders took off one at a time, their wings hardly stirring the dust.

Maldar's eyes rested on Waifyn and they travelled slowly up until their eyes met and locked for a few moments, an understanding passing between them. Waifyn was the first to break the look with a slight incline of his head before turning his attention to his own charge. Aliedori had suggested that they took the fight to the raiders using the mountains. The raiders would not be expecting it; the city had always acted in defence. They were to use the mountains to hide the dragons and wait until the dragon are close and used the mountain as the line of attack. The raiders were not to pass beyond the mountain peaks. They watched as black specks became dragons in flight and the first wave of riders appeared in the distance. Aliedori had cast an incantation to ensure that all weapons reached their intended target. It was all she could do for now, her next job was to make sure that the city and its people were safe and help the warriors anyway she could.

The riders advanced in waves but Maldar sent a signal for the defence to wait, he breathed slowly and deeply. He was linked to all he commanded through Aliedori. The link was easy enough but they were not his warriors and they only had a very short time to work out attack strategies. If there were spies in the city then the element of surprise would be lost and so to be certain that no information got out, Aliedori had placed a dampening incantation across the city.

Maldar's eyes did not stray from the horizon as the dragon flyers came closer and he shuddered. Aliedori closed her eyes for a second or two and drew a deep breath, the space around her crackling with magic. The Elders had used their earth magic to protect and defend the city and the Realm but they could not use it in the air. In order to use earth magic the mages needed to be touching the ground. It was up to Aliedori to do what she could to help the warriors, so she climbed into one of the arrow towers and used a dragon's eyes to see the faces of the dragon riders. They were the creatures she had named the 'Greys', golems made into flesh.

Aliedori was reminded of her task and why she had made the journey to the Eastern Realm. Sibley had asked her to seek out her family; she had been turned into one of those creatures. Maldar could sense Aliedori's mind as she allowed him, and no doubt the other warriors, to share the image. She was calm and unafraid and this helped Maldar to concentrate on the task ahead. There was a feeling of dread as the image reached the minds of his fellow riders. They had no idea who or what they had been defending the city against. This was their first sight of the creatures that attacked the city night after night. Maldar could understand their fear but with Aliedori's help Maldar sent a calming message.

"Stay calm, they can be killed. Aliedori will help and she has enchanted our weapons. They come, be ready!" The battle was swift, and Maldar was prepared; the attackers came in waves and the defenders on the black dragons rose up to meet them, their rider's crossbows primed and crackling with a surge of magical energy. Maldar raised his hand ready to signal and glimpsed Waifyn standing astride a green dragon, feet hooked into the footrest, crossbow primed and ready. His trusted bow and quiver were still slung across his back should he need them. As the first wave came, Maldar dropped his hand and the dragons rose to meet the incoming Greys. The impetus gained by the surprise attack was not lost; it remained with Maldar and his warriors.

They flew swiftly, using the mountain's peaks as a shield. At the signal, the golden dragon led the others low, allowing the riders to fly over so that the enemy was trapped between the phalanx of dragons and the mountains. Maldar instructed them not to get between the raiders and the mountain as a hail of heated rocks and stones were fired from the catapults on the ground. Keidrop banked to the left and Maldar released his long sword from its place on his back.

"Aim for the area under the Greys' right breasts with your lances," said Maldar. Fire arrows rose up through the air reaching their targets every time. Maldar urged Keidrop on as she folded her wings close to her body and came up under one of the Grey's dragons and tipped it off course. As the Grey fell, Maldar brought his sword up and through the heart of the Grey. The Grey fell and Aliedori took command of the dragon, freeing its mind from the shield. With the fall of each rider, she was able to command the dragons and use some of them against the other Greys and their dragons.

Senn Ju commanded the left flank, coming around in a sweeping motion to counter attack. His riders came from off to the left and swept out towards Maldar cutting off all escape routes. The Grey riders were trapped between the dragon warriors and arrow towers. With their path cut off they had no choice; they had to go forward into the path of the oncoming volley of enchanted arrows. Each arrow reached its target, piercing the thickened armour-like skin and into their heart, stopping it instantly. Maldar's sword rang out as it made contact with the skull of a Grey trying to turn, catching it off guard. The head snapped back, but the Grey remained in command of its dragon. The raider's dragon shot flames towards Maldar and Keidrop sprang back almost vertically. With her wings spread wide she rode the updraft and appeared motionless for a second or two then swooped down and caught the other dragon by its tail. The contact was so powerful that the wounded Grey fell, and with her free talon Keidrop was poised to strike the Grey's dragon. *Keidrop, no, do not harm him;* she retracted her claw, releasing the dragon. The request came from Aliedori who took command and guided the dragon to land. Maldar patted Keidrop's neck in a quick gesture of thanks, as another raider came towards them. The Grey twisted in the saddle, raised his crossbow and took aim but before it could release the trigger a bolt exploded through its skull.

The bolts came in volleys one after the other in such quick succession that Maldar could hardly believe his eyes. The Grey slumped forward and into view came Waifyn, standing up in the saddle as his mottled green dragon glided past. The large bow he carried was already rearmed and ready to fire; he winked as he passed by.

Maldar could see that already Waifyn and the dragon were working as one. Waifyn was not a warrior but his skill as an archer more than made up for his lack of fighting knowledge. Maldar was a skilled dragon warrior and that allowed him to manoeuvre close to the enemy and use his sword to great effect. Waifyn was skilled with the bow and combined with his agility, balance, true aim and speed, this made him almost as skilled as his lover in the art of attack. Zhang, the mottled green dragon Waifyn was riding, slowly raised his wings close to his side as he glided the thermals.

The warm up-current allowed him to float on the air as he skimmed the mountain peaks. Waifyn was using a crossbow with great ease as expected, even though the longbow slung across his back was his weapon of choice. A crossbow on the back of a dragon in flight was an easier weapon to load and as the crossbow rung out six more raiders fell. With the riders disposed of by Waifyn's crossbow, Aliedori was able to command the dragons to attack and the dragons turned against their own as fire erupted from their depths, burning and turning the Greys to dust. The few enemies that were not sent home to the ancestors began to fall back. But even so there was no escape as Senn Ju and the other black dragon and mage were at their flank. None survived, and for the first time in a long time the Mage felt that they had the upper hand and that they would send a message.

Senn Ju and the other black dragon riders gave chase and cut down those who had not already been dragged from their saddles.

For the first time in weeks, he had a sense that, while they had not won the battle, they had made some gains and they were not only defending the city but they had defeated the raiders too. A shadow fell across him and he raised his head, as above him a dark dragon was descending at speed. He looked to the right and left of him but there were more grey creatures on dragons; he was trapped.

There was an incantation to protect all the Realm's warriors against dragon fire and weapon strike, but he did not know how it would stand up against three dragon fires at once and he had no magic. He and the others either never learnt or had the abilities to draw power from the air. Perhaps if he had spent less time thinking about victory and kept his mind on the fight he would not be in this mess. There was only one possible escape route, back the way he came; he glanced behind him.

It would be tricky as the gap was being closed fast by a fourth dragon. Senn Ju sat back in the saddle and gripped his lance with both hands. He glanced round him again, which one was nearest? It was the one from above, but he did not want to have to kill a fellow creature. He sent a clear message to the dragon he was riding: *I am trapped and all dragons must be unharmed.* Senn Ju felt the dragon beneath him jerk

– *hold on* – he just had time to grab the reins before the city came into view, then he was upside down.

His dragon's claws were now extended as he rose up to meet another oncoming dragon. Senn Ju was thrown violently in the saddle almost losing his lance – *be ready*. Though he was still not the right way up he was at least vertical, he brought his body close to his dragon's neck and was almost lying flat. Senn Ju brought the lance up too; the black dragon, Kyra Lin, was a larger and more powerful species than the Grey's dragon. Kyra caught the Grey's dragon by the neck and shook the smaller creature bringing the rider into view. Senn Ju took aim and released the lance. The lance reached its target, and Kyra swung the smaller dragon over as Senn Ju found himself the right way up in the saddle again. In that instant Kyra released the Grey's dragon and it flew through the air like a missile. It caught the other two dragons and Greys off guard and Senn Ju and Kyra filled the space left. She spread her vast wings creating a sudden and powerful draught of wind then belched a stream of fire into the path of the oncoming dragons.

There was a sudden howl then nothing as breath and sinews, fluid and clay were incinerated. The oncoming dragons dived to avoid the flames and were free from the mind control. Senn Ju felt pressure on his back as the hair on his arm began to singe and smoke. Kyra dropped fast and the sudden action lifted him out of the saddle. As suddenly as she had dived, she was rising again, and she came up under the smaller dragon's neck as Senn Ju twisted round in his saddle and reached for his lance.

Then he remembered that it was still embedded in one of the Greys, so he released his seax from its scabbard. He brought up the serrated-edged drac's horn and thrust it down again. The seax vibrated sending tiny shooting pains up his arm as it connected with the dragon's well-armoured body. Senn Ju turned and saw the creature for the first time; it was unharmed save for the talon-like fingers. He lowered the sword and then brought his hand up again and the grey creature swayed. With an unnerving slowness, it unhooked the harness and threw itself from its charge. Senn Ju watched helplessly as the creature fell.

Chapter 30

The city showed very little visible sign of attack but several of the towers had suffered damage resulting in some casualties.

There were a few scorch marks and smouldering dwellings were evident despite the protective incantation that had been placed over the city. Aliedori walked among the dwellers, pausing here and there to offering help wherever she could. Some of the dwellers were still busy putting out the few flames that still burned. However, many of the newer buildings were made of stone and bricks that showed no sign of damage.

Above her head, an arrow tower was alight but it soon fizzled and died to the sound of cheers. The water that had been pumped from the canal below cast a dazzling rainbow arc over the arrow tower. Whatever she could do to help reduce the settlers' anxiety, Aliedori did. She worked with the apothecary to tend to the bodies of the Greys. Aliedori was sad to see that none of the Grey's had survived and there were cries of woe when death returned the Greys to their true selves again.

She stooped down and gently touched the face of the Grey at her feet; it looked to Aliedori that it had found peace. "We bless their journey home," she said. The young men paused in their task of loading the body of the Grey onto a cart. They looked at the Intendant questioningly.

Aliedori stood slowly and spoke in a quiet voice, "It is the way it should be," answering the unasked question. The young men nodded and continued to put the body on the cart, before moving past her to the next body. The air was still a little smoky and the smoke swirled like soft mist above her head and filled her nostrils with the strange smell of burning incense. Maldar had lost one of his warriors when she was knocked from her charge. It was too far a fall to survive and the incantation had only been against dragon fire and weapon strike. Another two warriors had also fallen and were so badly hurt that they were not expected to survive the fall either.

Waifyn and the apothecary's medicinal magic did very little except ease their agonies on their journey home. Aliedori found the warriors and their families at the back of the apothecary. She stood in the doorway; behind her were floor to ceiling shelves stacked with drawers and glass and ceramic bottles of all sizes. In front of her was a small, well-lit room containing three bunks, two of which were occupied. Aliedori waited to be noticed, when she was not she turned to go but then changed her mind.

If she could be of any help to these poor warriors and their families then she must try. Not wishing to intrude, she cleared her throat.

"If I can be of any help," she inquired. The apothecary turned to Aliedori.

"All help will be gracefully accepted, young lady," she replied and beckoned Aliedori in. She walked between the bunks and knelt down; the floor tiles were cool and the energy was welcoming. She rubbed her palms together as if to warm them before placing them over the two warriors. Her open palms were close to the chest area but she did not touch it. She had used magic to heal animals and small wounds, but she had never used magic this way on a human except Sibley. Now it was time to find out if she was as good as they all said she was. She rubbed her hands together again and placed them back over the warrior's chest area.

Closing her eyes she whispered a little chant and cast the incantation; there was a sharp intake of breath. Aliedori opened her eyes and looked around her as if she had forgotten what she was doing, then down at the two warriors on the bunks. At first, she could not see any change as the first warrior began to sit up. Then she saw that the gaping wound caused by the fall had gone; all that was left was a scar running across the left side of his chest. She stood and stepped back out of the way as the other warrior began to stir. He also sat up.

She slipped quietly out before they realised she was gone. Outside the moon shed her silver light onto the space where Aliedori stood at the back of the apothecary. She sighed, pulling the moonlit air into her lungs to fill them with silver light and feel the rejuvenating air travelling through her veins, giving her strength. She brought her palms up to rub her face and stopped suddenly.

There before her, a hooded figure stood in the half-light of the moon and the shadow of the city wall. They should not be there. The thought was only half formulated before the dark figure turned and disappeared through a gap in the fence. Aliedori followed, pushing through the gap until she found herself standing on a bare patch of ground under a large tree. Ahead of her, the hooded figure ran. Without thinking, Aliedori gave chase. She swayed out of the path of a flaming arrow as it whizzed past her, missing her head by inches. She clenched her fist; a glowing yellow fireball spun as she released it.

A staff came into view, splintering the sphere and sending tiny sparks of light dancing to their death. Then the figure was coming at her, staff held out in front and Aliedori felt the full force of the blast. Her back impacted with the trunk of a tree winding her; dizzy, she blinked, the hooded figure was upon her again. She twisted out of the way and cast a binding spell. Vines encased the figure but they were cut down in an instant. Without a pause, the dark figure continued to advance; Aliedori felt the air drain from her lungs, forced out by the staff's stranglehold. She panicked, her hands flailing, all thought gone from her mind except that she was going to die. Her hands fell to her sides and all she could think of was Maldar. He would be alone again and in danger. Her hand fell onto her seax and she gripped the handle. With the seax in her hand, her mind began to clear and her breathing settled. She was unsure of her abilities but her seax was true. She gripped the weapon with both hands and instantly felt its power. She held the sword in both hands across her body and severed the tentacles of light. Air filled her lungs and she spluttered and gasped, still bent over, waiting for the dark figure's next move. It came fast, flaming bolts of fire blazed a trail but she blocked them, parried and slashed and defended as she evaded instant death. She held the sword low in her right hand, slightly away from her body, using her left hand with palm open to block the razor tooth.

Bringing the seax up, she gripped it with her left hand and sweeping it down she severed the razor tooth's head from its body. She brought the sword up again and away from her body and caught the fire stream. The impact forced her backwards and she allowed the momentum of the force to flip her backwards as she twisted and landed on her feet. She glimpsed the serpent and brought the seax up just in time; the head of the fire serpent fell at her feet in a silent hiss.

The dark figure stood in the clearing up ahead, staff charging. Aliedori leaped onto a tree trunk, then another. She charged at the hooded figure and raised the seax over her head and down on the head of the staff. With the full force of her body, she split the staff down the centre shattering the crystal. The serpent hissed, its fangs dripping with venom; then it dissolved into mist and was carried away by the breeze. The dark figure fired a lightning bolt at Aliedori then turned and ran. The bolt hit her with full force in the chest and she catapulting her into the air, landing a little way off; as her body surrendered to the full impact she uttered one command.

Chapter 31

"Who is she?" Senn Ju's voice was a hoarse whisper.

"I do not know." Aliedori's voice was equally hoarse. "But this is hers." She handed the guardian the two pieces of the staff and all the crystal she had gathered. "She is a level two naturalist, the crystal in the staff helps to harness her powers."

Aliedori turned to walk away; she was not hurt, not now anyway and when she woke in pain, she simply drew healing energy from the ground. By the time she got to her feet and reached the dark figure all her pain had melted away.

"Intendant *you* will have to release her, I don't think that we can." Senn Ju spoke again. There was nothing that he could see holding the naturalist suspended in mid-stride, but neither he nor his fellow guardians could release her from whatever Aliedori had caught her with.

"She is free." The naturalist fell; Senn Ju turned to thank Aliedori but she was already too far away to hear.

She was making her way across the courtyard when she encountered the young men still at their duty. She had been able to save the lives of the two warriors and catch a spy but there was no such help for the Greys. She felt the loss of the grey creatures far more acutely because they had not asked to be changed and set against the Realm.

"We will ensure that the departed are buried according to the customs," the young men said again as they took the reins of the drac and led the animal away. Aliedori still needed to find Maldar, she was aware of his sadness at losing his charge, but at that moment she needed a little time on her own to pay tribute to the fallen, to clear her mind and be presentable.

Maldar would understand, besides he was with his warriors and she would talk to him and Waifyn later in private. The guardians now had a prisoner that the people could never know about, or they may suspect that there were spies living amongst them. They must never learn the truth about the one the guardians were secreting away in the Temple Palace. The moon was a large silver ball hanging low over the city in a sea of blazing stars; Aliedori completed what she had started and pulled silver lit air into her lungs.

It was almost impossible to believe that a battle had taken place only minutes earlier. Aliedori had won her first magical battle but only just, she won simply because the naturalist needed to replenish her powers. She, like the dwellers, could not celebrate; there were no shouts of joy, just the quiet tributes paid to the ancestors. She had watched the city dwellers file into the temples to pay their own private tributes just like she was doing on top of an arrow tower. That was where Maldar and Waifyn found her; they stood together in companionable silence. Waifyn's hand still gripped the crossbow and he was resting his weight slightly on the hilt while the other end rested on the ground. Maldar stood with his hands behind his back; it was the same stance their father took when he was trying to be strong.

They turned in unison to watch the people file out of the temple onto the nest knoll. They saw pain and relief etched on their faces in equal measure. It was Waifyn who spoke first.

"I think the citizens recognise some of the Greys as their own people"

"I know, I have spoken to a few of them and they were pleased to have their family members back, even in death." Aliedori was also subdued.

"Does it strike you as odd that the Greys died so easily?" Maldar asked.

"Their creators were not expecting a fight, they were dragon riders, but you are right. They were different, maybe those were earlier attempts…" Aliedori did not finish the sentence; she did not need to.

"I have seen the families of the fallen; fortunately there were not many. But unfortunately not even Waifyn's medicinal magic could help some of the wounded," Maldar said, unable to keep the pain out of his voice.

"The wounded are now fine, I saw to them earlier," Aliedori explained.

"How?" Waifyn asked.

Aliedori smiled, she was still thinking of the Greys.

"The Greys are fallen too and we bless their paths and send them home. Now I think I should return to the *Dawn Mist*," Aliedori said.

"What about Senn Ju?" Maldar suddenly remembered the intimate moment he had witnessed earlier; it all seemed like a lifetime ago.

"I believe he is with the other guardians. The dragon riders will continue to come and they must be ready. Senn Ju has a duty to his fellow guardians and the people of the Realm. He will do what is right and…" she ran out of words so she said nothing more.

"He is a shape changer and he can't change that can he?" Waifyn asked wearily.

"No, but he can choose what form he remains in. He told me that the dragon heart was given to him, but that is not true. It was he who gave part of his dragon heart to another."

"Do you know who shares his heart?" Maldar was still watching the sky, there were far too many stars for another attack, he thought.

"Not yet, but I believe the garden holds the answers," Aliedori replied.

"Garden, what garden?" Waifyn and Maldar asked in unison.

Aliedori's head snapped up in surprise and she glanced from Waifyn to Maldar before taking a pace or two back. None of them spoke for a while and Aliedori realised that neither Maldar nor Waifyn could seen the garden that was in plain view from inside the Sun Palace.

The magic used to protect the garden was very powerful indeed. Aliedori stepped back farther, then turned around and walked down the steps. Waifyn looked at his lover, eyebrows raised. Maldar shrugged his shoulders; the garden was a puzzle to him too. They followed in Aliedori's footsteps and caught up with her at the bottom of the tower where she explained the secret of the garden as they walk.

Chapter 32

The next morning, the dawn found Aliedori in the stable with the two dozen or so dragons that had submitted to her will the night before. There were no black dragons, but ones of all hues. Magic had been used to place black over the original hues with very convincing effect. The black effect was created in the same way that the golem had been placed over Sibley's human form. Aliedori was standing with the dragons when two dragon keepers walked in and watched her as she worked. She had created a new dragon stable out of the old ruined one she had found at the back of the Temple Palace.

The true black dragons had never needed stabling because they took their human form, when they were not guarding the people. When they were in dragon form they used the caves on the mountain, their place of birth. She stood among the now docile dragons slowly removing the final remaining body and mind control. She stripped away the black shades at the same time as untangling and removing the deep charm. As with the clay from the Greys, when the 'layers of darkness' were removed, they dissolved in the air and were carried away with the breeze. The young dragons were happy to be free, and they curled about her feet without the need for a calming incantation.

The new self-appointed keepers watched her work, and they exchanged a glance as if they both knew the significance of what she was doing, even if she didn't; Aliedori was controlling over two-dozen juvenile dragons at the same time. The dragons, free in body and mind, could choose to form alliances with the citizens or return to the wild. These dragons were not wild, but neither were they tamed.

It was the bond formed with their owner or owners that had allowed their minds to be captured. Aliedori hoped that they would choose to stay but she would understand if they did not. These dragons had very good reason not to trust humankind but she hoped that with her freeing their minds they might remain in the Realm. The Eastern Realm was a Realm in desperate need of dragons larger than the Cobs that remained when their larger counterparts were killed. Earlier Aliedori had woken with the light streaming into the cabin or rather she was woken up by the rising sun shining on her face and noise coming from the next cabin. She had heard that danger can act as an aphrodisiac and Maldar and Waifyn were living proof.

They had returned to the *Dawn Mist* together after she had settled the dragons and went straight to their cabin. Aliedori frowned and pulled the cover over her head and tried to get back to sleep, but sleep eluded her. She finally gave up when she realised that the intimate noises were not going to stop any time soon. She yawned, stretched, and sat up, washed and dressed then went on deck. She would have to get them to move their bunk back to the other side of the cabin. There was no one about so she went to see to the dragons to finish the work she had started the night before. When she returned, many of the crew were already up and relaxing on deck. Being in the harbour they had very little to do except enjoy the hospitality. The first meal of the day was served within minutes of her coming on deck and she sat in the early morning sun enjoying fresh fruits and hot honeyed tea.

Aliedori was on her second glass of tea when Maldar and his lover joined her. Waifyn yawned in an attempt to hide his shyness, and Aliedori pretended not to notice and continued to sip her tea.

"Today we join the people in sending their departed home, then we continue on our journey," Aliedori said sipping her tea.

A shadow fell across the deck and Maldar and Waifyn both looked up as Aliedori continued to sip her tea.

"He came by about an hour after you all went to bed," Yaran said. "He flew off, circled and returned."

The dragon landed on the highest point of one of the outer walls and folded his wings close to his body. He was speckled with hues of blue, green and yellow and not yet fully grown. He was the dragon Aliedori had stopped Keidrop from hurting. In fact none of the dragons that had been freed were fully grown; it was much easier to control the minds of young dragons. The speckled dragon was much younger than Keidrop being less than a cycle old. He had large, gentle nut-brown eyes, a wide wingspan, narrow face and head that ended in graceful pointed horns. His tiny pointed ears flickered and twitched at the slightest sound and his tail was long and powerful, tapering into a sharp point.

He was the first dragon Aliedori had released from the enchantment the previous night. She had woken up with the sound of him in her head and at first; she had thought it was Senn Ju and the other black dragons that had posted themselves as sentries on the mountain peaks around the city.

Aliedori had sent the dragon back to the stable when he first appeared at her cabin window but he soon returned. She was trying to ignore the speckled creature perched on the wall but it was proving difficult.

She had been wondering why she was allowing the dragon into her head when Maldar and Waifyn joined her. She stood up and the dragon did too, spreading his wings ready to follow her.

"Well, he seems to have chosen," Waifyn said watching the young dragon.

"I believe he has," Aliedori replied.

"What are you going to do about it?"

"There is nothing to be done, he has chosen," she replied softly.

The ten chairs were placed in a semi-circle and the ten Elders were there but had not yet taken their seats. With the coming of the morning the mage shape changers were humankind again. They all acknowledged Aliedori, Maldar and Waifyn with a small incline of their heads as they walked into the hall. They were all still having their breakfast when their presence was requested. Senn Ju, who had been standing alone, stepped forward and Maldar took the lead and reached out and took Senn Ju by the hand.

Maldar could see in an instant that Senn Ju looked different and knew why; Maldar leaned in and spoke in a quiet voice. He was straight to the point, to avoid any misunderstanding later.

"We cannot stay; we will do what we can to help your people and the new dragons work together, but we cannot stay. When the training is over we will continue our journey."

"Where is your journey's end?" Senn Ju asked.

"Ouran Providence," Maldar replied.

"The hill people?" Senn Ju asked.

"Aliedori has a promise to keep."

"Ouran Providence is another four or five days sailing, farther around the coast," Senn Ju said. "What promise could be so important that you need to go into the wilderness?"

"I will not discuss this, we are here to bless the path of the dead and send them home." Aliedori looked from Senn Ju to Maldar.

Senn Ju shook his head; his hand reached up to the wound on his face. In a very short time the open wound was healing very fast and it was almost a scar now. The bells announced that the funerals were about to start and Senn Ju excused himself to officiate the burials. Aliedori and the others joined him and led the blessing to send the dead home. Aliedori did not use magic; she simply provided one of the blessings. The burial took place just beyond the city walls overlooking the Petrified Forest. The 'once golems now humankind in death' were buried in their family plots so that they could be honoured. After the funerals, Senn Ju asked the three of them to accompany him. The room they were shown into was not a room at all but a large formal water garden. Large pale pink and white lilies, leaves and flowers opened to receive the sun through a huge glass roof.

Below the surface Aliedori glimpsed fish calmly swimming but she was more interested in the ancient trees. She realised that the garden beyond the water was crammed with all the trees that were once found in the forest. Like the model that was on display at the entrance of the Temple, this garden was holding the living trees that were now frozen in the Petrified Forest.

"When we realised that we would lose the forest we commanded the people to take saplings and planted them here. This garden and the display took a great deal of our magic, but it gives the people hope," Senn Ju explained.

"In the same way that the model of the city contains real trees, this is an exact replica of the city," Aliedori observed.

Aliedori sat on a low stone bench and the others sat with her. Her town protectors flanked her and she felt, as always, happy to have them near.

"Aliedori what are we doing?" Maldar asked quietly.

"Waiting."

The garden was beautiful and peaceful but not enough of a reason to delay their onward journey. There must be some purpose in prolonging their stay and he chose to be patient. They did not have to wait long, the inner door opened and a woman walked in. She was elegantly dressed and her hair was elaborately styled and of pure silver set off by a delicate peony of the palest pink. She was about Senn Ju's age. Senn

Ju bowed and Aliedori indicated to Maldar and Waifyn to do the same; they all stood and bowed. When they raised their heads again the woman was sitting on the dais, and Senn Ju was by her side.

"Who is she?" Waifyn whispered.

"The real reason why Senn Ju wished to retain his humanity," Maldar whispered back.

Waifyn glanced at Aliedori who nodded and he received a jab in his side from his lover for his trouble. The woman on the dais was Chin Yah, one of the ancient people who had helped save the garden. When it had become clear that the Realm would be broken and the trees were to be lost, Chin Yah and Senn Ju, along with the others, had built the models in the golden hall and the garden. They had been unable to save the forest around them but they saved what they could in the model and the garden. It was a last desperate act of the guardians to save their people and to hold on to some of their magic.

Ten mages sacrificed their humanity to be reborn as ten black dragons, while the others swore to guard and protect the dragons and the people until the ancestors called them home. The garden of Amphora, so called as it held not only the magic of the trees but also because it held the lives of the remaining guardians, became their home and the black dragons became the guardians of the forest and the people. Chin Yah and Senn Ju were to be handfasted. The bonding ceremony was arranged but the ceremony never took place. Now Chin Yah was almost ready to start her journey home to the ancestors. Aliedori sat down again with her head bowed; she had worn her hair loose and when she bowed her hair had fallen, hiding her face. Her face remained hidden, and she appeared to be deep in thought.

Chapter 33

After a while, she raised her head slowly to see that the Elders were all in the garden. Then she stood and looked directly at Senn Ju as he spoke, "Thank you for saving the lives of our warriors," he said.

Neither Maldar nor Waifyn knew what had happened, she had said nothing to them. Now she was aware of their eyes on her; she had intended to tell them at breakfast but the summons had come to attend the funerals. Aliedori did not respond to Senn Ju, instead, she addressed the gathering of the Elders.

"You and the other guardians defended your people not us, and you cannot lay your lives down for Chin Yah; your job is not done. The Amphora will take her as it has done with the others in order to preserve the remaining magic," she said sadly, looking from Senn Ju to Chin Yah. She turned back to the other guardians.

"You, all of you, will have to let the garden take her. Have you not worked out why you have been attacked so frequently? Your enemies cannot allow you to be reborn," Aliedori said as snatches of her dream crawled into her consciousness, but always remained just out of reach. Beyond where they stood on the opposite side were the grounds surrounded by water. She stood by the beautiful and intricately carved topiaries that were of humankind, each carrying in their hands sacred texts. Despite living in the garden Chin Yah had suddenly started to age; the aging process had been slowed but it showed in her silver hair. While Chin Yah aged, Senn Ju remained young, as young as he was at his rebirth.

The garden was the clue, and the texts held vital information of the rebirth of the Realm. Aliedori didn't know how she knew that, all she knew was that Chin Yah had to allow the garden to take her. There was a place in the garden for her, as there were only nine topiaries, but Aliedori knew that Chin Yah would not go willingly, if at all. There was something about Chin Yah that Aliedori could not figure out.

The garden not only held the trees of the Realms it also held the secret to the rebirth of the forest. Aliedori knew that she would play a role but she did not know when and how, all she knew was that it was not today.

"What is the significance of Chin Yah and the garden?" Waifyn asked suddenly.

"There is no significance," Senn Ju said.

Aliedori shook her head slowly before answering, "The garden may hold the secret to the return of the forest."

"But you do not know that for sure." Ling Yow, one of the Elders, spoke for the first time.

Aliedori gave her head another slow shake.

"I cannot be sure but I think I have worked out the significance. The tree in the middle of the garden was taken from the deepest part of the Tree of Souls. It's where the magic is most powerful, which has helped to preserve and nourish the remaining magic. The trouble is, someone else has worked it out also and that is why the Realm is under attack."

Ling Yow stepped forward, separating himself from the rest of the guardians. He was a tall and handsome Wood Nymph and carried himself with the elegance and grace of all Wood Nymphs.

"How do you know this?" he asked.

"Because that is when settlers began to go missing and strange sightings and even stranger tales began," Waifyn said. He had noticed Wood Nymphs amongst the city dwellers and was pleased that Ling Yow carried a black dragon heart inside him, but he wondered how Wood Nymphs could live in a place without trees, even as dragons. The two men flanked Aliedori and as she stood up, they stood with her. "What I think will happen is that your Realm will be lost if you do not allow Chin Yah to be taken by the garden."

Maldar and Waifyn remained with the Elders while Aliedori crossed the small stone bridge to go into the centre of the Amphora garden. After a while Maldar stood and followed her. As they walked their feet were surrounded by dragon's breath, so called because of the tiny, delicate flame-like orange, red and yellow flowers and leaves. Aliedori bent and scooped up a handful of the plants and brought them to her nose. The smell was pungent; it was an herb used to flavour food but also to ward off evil. Some said that dragon's breath grew where the first dragons trod, others said it was where they breathed their first fire. Wherever the herbs came from they were closely linked to dragons and hence to all that was good. Aliedori placed the crushed leaves and flowers in the pouch she wore on her belt.

"You can't possibly know these things. How can you know these things?" Maldar was by her side.

He watched as she placed the dragon's breath in the pouch and pulled the drawstrings to secure it.

He was standing before her but she gave all her attention to tying the string on the pouch before looking up.

"Some of it comes all at once from nowhere and sometimes it comes through touch and sometimes…" Maldar took an involuntary step back and instantly regretted it, but it was too late, the damage was already done. She turned away and concentrated on readjusting the pouch on her belt to hide the hurt. A feeling of unease crept around the garden contaminating everything it touched as it grew and spread. She stood alone against them, against her brother. Tears came, filling her eyes and spilling out over her lids and down her cheeks. She wiped them away before turning from the garden; she did not look at Maldar, she couldn't. She surveyed the Guardians with care, unsure of herself and her instincts, as small fragments of the dream came back to her. There were no details that made any sense, and the more she tried to hold on to it the faster the images slipped away. After a while she stopped trying, this garden held the secrets to the return of the trees but she could not find them. Each time she thought she had worked something out something else would spring up and jumble her thoughts. She touched the nearest topiary in the hope of getting a hint but nothing came; no clear images and no answers, only more puzzles.

Perhaps they had been topiaries for too long and the centuries had wiped away all possibilities. Frustrated, Aliedori crossed the bridge and tried to pass by but Waifyn took up his position in front of her.

"He doesn't understand, he does not have magic, I will talk to him," he said. "Aliedori stop, stay." He caught her by the arm and shot Maldar a look that froze him to the spot.

"I can't give you answers because I don't have any to give," Aliedori said, "and I don't think it is up to me to provide them. All I know is that the garden needs to take Chin Yah."

"When?" Senn Ju asked.

Aliedori knew that until she could convince the Elders to let the garden take Chin Yah nothing would change. But how was she going to do that, it would take some convincing to let Chin Yah go. The other Elders would also have to agree that the garden needed to take the last original guardian. Going into the garden would be like going into the Tree of Souls and allowing the ancient magic to change them. If they would not let Chin Yah go then Aliedori would make sure that the Elders were better equipped to deal with the raiders, but she and her companions could not stay.

"Intendant," Aliedori turned towards the voice. Yaran was standing at the entrance to the garden, his mouth gaping open in awe of the sight before him. It took a clearing of Aliedori's throat to get him to remember the reason for the intrusion.

"A Gem with a message from Fengard," he finished.

"From our Lady?" It was Maldar who asked the question as he walked towards Yaran.

"No sire, from Wulfgar," he replied.

"Please excuse us we need to attend to this and remember the cloud people are your people also."

Aliedori turned away from the Elders and she and Waifyn followed Yaran and Maldar out into the courtyard. Aliedori did not need the message of the dragon to know that Sibley would soon be with the ancestors now, but the small brown and blue Gem dragon with clear, intelligent blue eyes had further news. She was on a perch in the yard and Maldar noticed for the first time that the courtyard was paved with golden stones. He wondered why he had not noticed it before and if it was significant, but the thought was dismissed as quickly as it came. Aliedori and Waifyn joined them and the Gem began to speak, her voice small but clear.

"Master said that the one called Sibley is strong, but the ancestors will call her home soon."

While this wasn't news to Aliedori, it was to the others and she allowed the Gem to speak without interruption. What she wanted to know was what else had been discovered about the Greys. Wulfgar would not have sent the Gem with news that Aliedori already knew.

"What more has Wulfgar discovered, anything that will help us?" Maldar asked.

"Very dark magic, very strong and very puzzling but not unbreakable."

"And that will cause Sibley's death?" Maldar asked.

"No, but my master said that his attempts would contribute to Sibley's death and the death charm that comes with the golem will almost certainly do the rest." Aliedori was not happy to hear this.

"So the news is that even if the golem is removed the person still dies?" Waifyn was not happy either.

"I was hoping for some good news, no matter how slight," Maldar said.

Waifyn gave him a comforting pat on his shoulder, but they still needed to talk.

"Why would Sibley's creator place a death charm on her?"

"Insurance. A captured Grey will not be able to *talk* with a death charm placed on them," Aliedori said. She could not bring herself to look at him; she was still too sad and angry. Maldar shifted, feeling slightly uncomfortable. He hated it when it was like this between them; sometimes he forgot that he was supposed to be on her side no matter what.

The small dragon continued: "The Lady and Lord of the knights send news also, the gate you have found is still secure, but the Lady Minoria can confirm that they have found other…" The news was not good and she would have to return home as soon as possible so the quicker they got to Sibley's people the sooner they could start for home.

"The Lady Minoria asks that you travel north and formally seek the support of the Northern Realms." Aliedori said nothing for a while then asked Yaran to take the Gem back to the boat.

"I have given the Gem a message to take back to Fengard, make sure that he is fed and rested."

Despite protestation from Senn Ju and the other Elders, the *Dawn Mist* and her crew set sail almost five days after they had arrived. Maldar and Waifyn had worked with the dragon riders on defence and attack and trained them to be competent with the long and cross bows whilst flying. Aliedori had worked with the elders on harnessing and improving their magic from the air as effectively as possible.

She had also worked with the riders to develop strong bonds with their new dragons by securing a mild telepathic link; a link which served to increase trust and understanding between riders and dragons. When Senn Ju realised that Aliedori would not stay he reluctantly gave them directions on how to reach the mountain people of Ouran Province. Senn Ju had offered them the use of dragons, saying they would reach the mountain more quickly. Aliedori thanked him but said that she would rather use the *Dawn Mist* as the mountain people were no longer used to large dragons. She did not want to offend or frighten them by arriving on dragons.

Chapter 34

The Dawn Mist sailed for four days close to the shore until they found the small jetty Senn Ju had told them about. The days on the boat started awkwardly as Aliedori and Maldar were still not on speaking terms, despite Maldar's attempts to apologise and Waifyn acting as mediator. By the end of the second day Maldar cornered Aliedori in her cabin.

"You don't understand," he said, "it was nothing to do with you. Waifyn and I… you have no idea… you reached to touch me, and I couldn't… I couldn't let you. You would know more about me and Waifyn than a sister should, please forgive me." Maldar allowed himself to slide down the door until he was sitting with his head in his hands. There was silence and he waited, comforted by the gentle movement of the boat as it glided over the water.

"You do realise that you know things that you shouldn't, and you blurt them out instead of keeping them to yourself."

He continued to wait, then finally Aliedori responded, "I think it would be a good idea to move the bunk back to its original position. You are right; I already know enough, have heard enough."

The colour in Maldar's face rose with him as he pushed himself back into a standing position. With nothing more to be said, he slipped out closing the cabin door behind him.

The stone jetty protruded out into the water from a beach of wide golden sands and the same petrified trees beyond the shore. There were several tracks leading from the beach into the forest, evidence that the mountain people made the trek to ocean-lakes to fish or perhaps to trade with the city. Even though there was only a small jetty it was large enough to moor the *Dawn Mist*.

When they dropped anchor it was late into the evening and the crew of the *Dawn Mist* were glad to be on land again. They all stood on deck wishing that they had moored at the large private marina at the palace rather than the small dock at the edge of the Petrified Forest. There was no sign of any other boats or evidence that the jetty was in frequent usage. They were suddenly showered with water as two large shadows appeared. Aliedori was sure that the two dragons secretly enjoyed dousing them all with water and as they flew overhead, circled and dived back in the water again, Aliedori thought perhaps the joy was not so secret after all. They were coming back for another flyover until she stopped them.

Dragons were excellent swimmers and almost as comfortable in water as they were in the air. Keidrop and Tao had swum and frolicked alongside the *Dawn Mist* for the past four days. The dragons strode from the water and onto the beach shaking the water from their wings, covering humankind and nymph alike.

"We will have to go from here on foot and dracs to reach the Cloud people, the dragons stay here." Aliedori looked at them.

"Is that wise Intendant, you do not know what is in the forest?" Yaran asked.

Aliedori had already given in to pressure in allowing her brother and his lover to accompany her. She was not going to give in and allow the dragons to make the journey too.

"Yes I am sure, besides you heard what Senn Ju said, the mountain people have taken a stance against all dragons larger than Cobs. What do you think would happen if we turned up with dragons the size of those two? Waifyn was studying Aliedori; the last few weeks at close quarters had given him plenty of opportunity to do so. He was discovering that she did not make rash decisions or take rash actions. The traditions and beliefs of others were paramount to her and she always showed respect.

She behaved with dignity at all times; she was representing not just her parents, but the Lady and Lord of the Southern Realm. Maldar had seen glimpses of the strength contained in his sister's slight frame, not only in her ability to fight with swords but in using her magical powers with such care.

Yet there was something about her that he could not quite put his finger on, sometimes it was there in her eyes. Aliedori's magic was pure, unlike most humankind's magic that was more like alchemy. Not even the fabled guardians of the Realm had pure magic; that too was alchemy, very powerful alchemy, but alchemy all the same. The power to change one thing to another; that was alchemy, and used in its purest form it was very powerful indeed. Maldar still did not understand his true purpose but Warian knew and so did Waifyn and that was why they had been asked to travel with her.

Aliedori's powers could make Realms shake; she had taken centuries of pain from Senn Ju and had healed two warriors as if it was nothing but a simple task of healing a small blade injury. Waifyn knew for sure that the warriors had been on their way to the ancestors when he last saw them. He knew that every time she used her power in that way her magic strengthened and deepened at a rapid pace. Waifyn trembled at the thought and for a moment he could not look directly at her, so he glanced instead at the dragons before facing her again. He realised that he had grown to love her almost as deeply as he loved her brother in such a short time. Maldar was her gauge and now so was he. Aliedori had become more than the sister of his beloved, she was the hope that his people were clinging to, for if humankind fell under the might of the great mage then it would only be a matter of time before his own people came under threat. If it happened to the Elves then it could happen to the Nymphs too.

Waifyn became aware that Aliedori was looking at him, reading him and there was concern etched on her face. He deliberately avoided looking directly at her but neither could he look at the forest before them. He turned back instead, the way they had come, concentrating on the large expanse of water. He watched the dragon boats in the distance as they headed towards the horizon. Perhaps they were heading home after a day's trade in the capital or perhaps they were just at the start of their journey.

The Wood Nymphs of the Eastern Realm had learnt centuries ago to live without their beloved forest. They had moved into the Tree to Souls while still maintaining their care of the forest. Waifyn knew that the Nymphs lived amongst the 'dead trees' and that it was partly through their care that the tree roots retained so much magic. Still, he was not sure if he was capable of living like that. Aliedori argued that the trees were not dead but simply sleeping while they waited to be awoken. The people of the Realm made their homes as green as possible by growing vines and tall grasses. Waifyn could not bear the thought of even travelling through the Petrified Forest much less living in it. He had fought side by side with two other Nymphs, one a black dragon, the other a warrior and he would continue to do what was asked of him, and that was to travel with Aliedori and fight by her side if necessary.

The *Dawn Mist* had arrived at the time in the evening when the bright light of the day was being drawn out of the sky. The dying day added to the gloom of the frozen trees, and the whole Petrified Forest marked the dark and brooding spectre of the entire Realm. Straggly thorns and vines around the edges of the trees. No matter where one looked, there were the same 'dead' trees and the entire forest was sad to the core. Many of the animals were gone because the eco system had broken down. The occasional wolf could be heard as it roamed amongst the unnaturally silent, frozen trees.

The only other noise was the sound of the few night birds and Cob dragons that still built their nests amongst the branches. Already the light had drained out of the forest and Waifyn, who had spent all his life in the vibrant greenery of the Southern forest, felt a shiver run through him. Aliedori could sense Waifyn's unease and sadness as if it was her own but said nothing.

"We spend the night here and start afresh in the morning; Yrre please let the dracs have some exercise."

Maldar, who had been watching his lover and sister from a distance, knew of Waifyn's struggle to deal with the Petrified Forest. They shared the same bed and it would have been impossible not to know what his lover was feeling. Later when Waifyn was sitting on the bed stripped to the waist, Maldar rested on his knees behind him, his fingers dancing across Waifyn's shoulders. Wherever the fingers paused, they pressed down into flesh, massaging the lumps out of Waifyn's neck and shoulders. Waifyn sighed as he enjoyed his lover's touch and the pleasure of the closeness and feeling of Maldar's warm breath against his skin. Waifyn manoeuvred himself until he faced Maldar.

"I won't be able to massage your neck," Maldar said.

"My neck is fine now; I need to be massaged elsewhere, like here," Waifyn lay back and pointed to the spot. Maldar's fingers danced across the spot.

"And there," Waifyn whispered.

Maldar proved that he could follow instructions implicitly and his fingers danced there too.

"There, with your lips," Maldar's lips understood instructions also.

"Here with your mouth." Warmth enveloped Waifyn; starting at his toes and spreading through his entire body. Each touch increased Waifyn's pleasure and enhanced the sensation coursing through his body. Maldar massaged Waifyn with his fingers, tongue and lips and the most pleasurable level of touches continued long after Waifyn was capable of giving instructions. The *Dawn Mist* rocked gently and the sound of the wash drew the lovers down into sleep.

Maldar woke, not with a start, he simply opened his eyes and lay listening. Something or someone had woken him. He blinked at the brightness of the moonlight in the cabin. He was encased in Waifyn's arms and legs, but Maldar knew where to touch to get Waifyn to release him; and he touched his lover there. Waifyn groaned softly and released Maldar without waking. Maldar slipped out of the bed. The moon shone in through the window lighting the cabin and he found his cape, wrapped it around his waist and left the cabin.

Chapter 35

He climbed the stairs onto the deck then went down onto the jetty. There was a fire lit farther down the beach, some distance away from the boat and the two dragons were lying next to it. Maldar scanned the beach, but other than the dragons it was empty. He tried to see into the forest but the darkness was all encompassing. Maldar watched as Aliedori emerged a little way down the beach. She stretched out her muscles after sheathing her weapons. Maldar glanced back at the forest, which remained shrouded in darkness despite the full moon that lit the beach with its silver light.

Yet, it could not penetrate the tangled branches of the trees to reach the ground and the forest floor was left in an eerie darkness. Maldar walked down the jetty, hopped onto the landing bay and continued down the beach. He enjoyed the cool sand beneath his feet and between his toes as he strolled casually.

Aliedori had reached the two dragons and was sitting close to Keidrop's neck, resting against her as Maldar joined her. He towered over her and Aliedori rested her chin against her chest.

"Are you alright? Do we still need to talk about what happened in the garden?" he dropped down into the sand opposite her.

"Count dragons," she instructed him.

"Count dragons... why?"

"A hundred or so dragons, but count anyway," she laughed as Maldar began to count.

"One dragon..." and he had reached one hundred dragons when Waifyn appeared on the deck of the *Dawn Mist*. He too was wrapped in his cloak despite the warmth of the night.

"That's what I mean Aliedori, there are some things that you shouldn't know and yet you do."

"And there are some things that I just know, and they have nothing to do with magic." She looked at him pointedly. Waifyn glanced towards Maldar who suddenly smiled and leaned back, his cheeks colouring lightly.

"You and he are two sides of the same Bitt, you are lucky to have found each other"

Maldar knew that he was lucky to have found Waifyn, he knew not all would approve of the union but as long as their parents did, it didn't matter what the rest if the Realm thought.

"I don't think my face will ever appear on any currency, but if you are going to grant me that honour let it be a gold Bitt" he said with a laugh

"Listen," she said suddenly, "it's been some time since you practised your magic." Choosing not to hear his little jibe

She held out her hand and he saw that her fingers were closed around something. Maldar looked up at Waifyn who was still on the *Dawn Mist* stretching and yawning. Then he looked back down at the still extended hand and reluctantly reached out his hand, palm open. Three small, perfectly smooth round stones fell into his palm and he closed his fingers over the stones, which were warm to the touch.

"Search," Aliedori instructed, "find him."

Maldar look up at his lover, who had just climbed onto the small jetty.

"I can see him; he is there in front of me."

"Good, that will make the charm easier."

The 'Seeker Charm' was an easy incantation to cast or so Aliedori kept telling him, but he had never found it easy, in fact he had never found doing any magic easy. Waifyn had started the short walk towards them and Maldar's fist tightened over the stones as the warmth increased. He held the stone against his heart and closed his eyes for a second or two; then placing the stones on the sand with his palm covering them he whispered, "Seek."

Maldar gasped as the stones began moving, leaving a strange little trail in his mind rather than on the sand. Then it was gone, had disappeared without a trace, leaving Maldar with a strange, cold feeling inside.

"What happened?" Maldar questioned her.

"Call them back," she instructed him again.

Maldar reached out but nothing happened. He tried again and was about to say it was no good when the stones appeared on the sand in front of him. He picked them up to hand them back to her, but she shook her head.

"Keep them," Aliedori said and laughed at the look on his face. She laughed again and glanced back at the forest. The full moon hung large and low and stars sparkled like gems in the night sky. A night for lovers she thought as she watched Waifyn approaching; she should leave them alone but she did not.

Her trip into the forest was very different. There were no moon and stars to light her path or alleviate the brooding eeriness of the imprisoned trees. A roosting bird called out overhead, and the call was answered from some distance away. Others soon accompanied the cries of the night birds and the chattering became so loud it was heard across the forest. For a lesser person the sound would have sent chills down their spine but to Aliedori it was yet another proof that the forest was waiting to be green again. She moved with confidence through the pitch black deserted forest. There were no twigs cracking under her feet so each step was silent. The trick was to accomplish a walk amongst the dry twigs and leaves without making a sound, but on the edge of this forest, the dry twigs and leaves were long gone; taken by humans and animal dwellers alike. Aliedori continued her exercise with the seax and the drac's hooked horns together fighting an unseen foe.

Although practice with the blades was not necessary she nonetheless continued until beads of sweat gathered on her forehead. Aliedori finished her exercise, sheathed her swords and continued to move soundlessly through the forest. Her muscles were aching slightly from the constant swing, thrust and slicing motion of the practice, but it was a good ache. The gentle breeze caught her skin and cooled her a bit but because of the frozen leaves the gentle breeze took on an eerie undertone and whistled overhead, sounding like an animal in pain.

She could feel the breeze cooling her skin more and more and she quickened her pace. The tall trees made eerie shadows on the ground where she stood. The silhouette of swaying branches painted a picture as if hands were about to grab her from behind, yet in her mind she only saw the branches and leaves catching the gentle breeze.

For many visitors to the Realm the Petrified Forest was full of foreboding and yet exciting, inviting, repellent and eerie. Oak trees that had stood for hundreds of years haunted the edge of the ancient forest spreading their shade into the fields and creating a natural boundary between the fields and the gardens. They were frozen, waiting to be awakened. Frozen trees and bushes of all kinds lay behind the oaks, stretching for miles and miles and, like the Tree of Souls, they created their own unknown gods with their own untold events.

Even though the moon was shining on the canopy of the forest, the branches were so thick that the light could not penetrate inside. The forest was frozen even though it was the height of summer when the trees and flowers were at their most abundant. It was said that everything was frozen in one wave, even the animals, but of course that was not entirely true. While some were frozen along with the forest many more animals lost their lives due to the loss of their habitat.

For many days afterwards, dwellers would rescue birds and animals, only to discover that they did not reanimate once out of the forest. Dwellers had no choice but to return the birds and other animals deeper into the forest. Aliedori wished that she had time to go into the heart of the forest to visit the animals and their keepers, but that would not be fair to Waifyn. The chronicles recorded how dwellers had witnessed a wave of crystallising magic crashing into the first trees and reverberating through them until all in its path was frozen. Azorean was the mage responsible. The Western Realm had disagreed, not with the division but with the way in which the division was made.

Azorean had taken up the centuries old disagreement and argued that the Eastern Realm and thus the Guardians had a large share of the land that belonged to the Western Realms, and swore to take back what was rightfully theirs. Azorean set himself against the Eastern Realm and each battle had been more damaging than the last and culminated in the forest being frozen.

Chapter 36

Aliedori could not imagine the immense power of Azorean. The mage had caused such devastation in the hope of wiping out the magic of the Realm. The loss of magic could have made the Realm more vulnerable and susceptible to the will of others, but it did not happen as Azorean had hoped. The East was not lost and some magic remained. Although depleted of magic, the East fought on and kept their freedom. What Azorean did not take into consideration in his haste was that magic did not just come from above. Magic was in the air they breathed, the water, the ground and the people; it was the very Realm itself. The Realm had produced shape-changing mages; no other Realm had done that before or since.

Aliedori placed her palms against a tree trunk and then rested her forehead on it and whispered softly, "It's time… it's time…"

The trees responded with a shudder that reverberated around the forest.

After a short pause Aliedori continued to train and practice her swordplay. She did not need light for what she was doing. In fact she had her eyes closed throughout the practice. Aliedori had no need for swords, but practice with the sword was a discipline and she needed discipline. Should there be times when she could not use magic; swords were the next best thing. Besides swordplay kept her mind supple, which was always good for magic. Now she watched as Waifyn walked towards them smiling, and while his smile encompassed her, it was for her brother's benefit alone. She always felt their joy at seeing each other no matter how short their time apart. She did not need magic to see or feel their joy their happiness was infectious.

For one brief moment, she felt envy and wondered if there was anyone out there for her, someone who would look at her the way Maldar and Waifyn looked at each other. She dismissed the thought as quickly as it came into her mind. He deserved all his happiness; she knew what was to come and he may never forgive her.

Waifyn sat opposite her and close to Maldar resting a sleepy head against his shoulder and closed his eyes. Aliedori pulled her feet up and rested her chin on her knees, lowering her eyes so she did not have to look directly at the lovers.

"Keep practicing," she said.

Waifyn opened his eyes lazily and glanced down as Maldar placed the stones on the sand. Satisfied that Maldar was practicing the 'Seeker Incantation' he closed his eyes again. With his eyes closed and his head in a comfortable position, he remained there listening. Aliedori instructed, cajoled, and corrected as Maldar's stubborn brain refused to accept that he had the ability to learn simple magic. Waifyn liked their voices and realised how very similar to each other they sounded.

Aliedori had infinite patience with her brother, but Maldar had somewhat less patience with himself. Aliedori would praise even the smallest of gains, and Maldar grumbled at his lack of magical abilities. Waifyn knew that, despite Maldar's protests that he was in no way magical, he wanted to learn to prove his sister's faith in him; Waifyn felt it in every sinew of his lover's body. Waifyn didn't know if it was because he was resting against Maldar that his lover did not became tense or angry. He remained calm when Aliedori said, "Try again, you almost got it then." And Maldar would try again, with the same eagerness and belief as he had shown the first time.

Waifyn came to understand that Maldar believed in his sister's abilities without question. When Waifyn opened his eyes, Aliedori was sitting in the same position, feet drawn up, arms wrapped around her feet and her chin resting on her knees. With her eyes downcast, he did not know if she was following Maldar's tracking skills or simply resting, but she was smiling.

Waifyn pulled himself up and with a casual flick of his hand swept his hair from his face. He saw Aliedori raise her eyes momentarily before lowering them again.

"He's got it but I don't think he believes it and he is not concentrating," was all she said before moving the subject to the next day's travelling. Waifyn had the feeling that she was simply waiting for him.

"Are you sure it's wise to have the dragons accompany the boat back?" Maldar was not sure he liked the idea and voiced it.

They then passed an hour or so setting out plans for their journey through the forest. Their talk briefly touched on their travel into the Northern Realm. It was clear the real talk was of their return home but with no real plans of when that would be.

Aliedori, Maldar, and Waifyn set off on the dracs early the next morning, after first giving Yaran clear instructions that no one else should go to the settlement with them.

Yaran was not happy with this. His job was to protect the Intendant, which of course was a joke but duty was duty. His duty was easy, he was a dragon warrior, master of arms and captain of the *Dawn Mist* and his job was to follow instructions.

Aliedori warned Yaran to be on his guard at all times and not let anyone wander off. The claiming raids were still in the middle of the season, and everyone was fair game, even visitors.

Yaran was sure that Aliedori did not want to deliver fresh subjects right into the Ourans' hands. He satisfied himself with the knowledge that his Intendant knew what was best, but he did not have to like it. He had agreed with his Intendant up to a point. She had sent several Cob dragons with news as it developed. He could not easily agree with her latest instructions, but he was not about to question his Intendant's wisdom. He agreed that it was prudent to ensure the safety of the Dawn Mist and her crew until she sent new instructions or they returned. However, he could not agree with allowing the three of them to go off into the unknown. The Ouran Provinces were made up of tribal leaders who were marauders and traditional Claiming Raids were still practiced. He could not agree to let them go alone. Yaran anxiously paced the wheelhouse that also doubled as his private quarters. He could see the Dragon Knight and the Nymph Prince with Keidrop; the dragon was no doubt as outraged as he was to be left behind.

"I cannot agree to this Intendant, it…" His voice trailed off. His Intendant was leaning against the small bunk and dancing in her open palm was a ball of ice fire. The ball of ice spun slowly as white-hot flames shot from it and then it was gone, only to reappear larger and fiercer as she released it and watched as it dispersed into nothing.

He could say no more. In an instant and without words, she showed him why it was fine for them to go alone. The two dragons were also to remain on guard and before leaving Aliedori placed a safety incantation around the boat. The small party took the path up through the trees and Yaran and the crew watched them leave. Yaran wished he was going along too and waited until the small party was out of sight before calling the crew to eat.

The forest proved to be a lot less eerie in the light of the early morning sun, and the three of them made good time. They paused in the dead forest only to eat a quick meal, and to rest the dracs. Aliedori had noticed since arriving on the shores of the Western Realm that Waifyn had lost some of his essence. The journey through the forest seemed to sap all that was vital about Waifyn and he was unusually quiet. During their quick meal he said very little and remained very quiet for the rest of the journey.

They arrived late into the night in the settlements on the plateau and there were very few dwellers awake to greet them. When she left the city, Aliedori had sent a message by one of the dower Cob dragons, common in these parts of the settlement, to remind them that they were on their way. She was happy to discover that there was no welcoming party and Waifyn was very happy to leave the forest behind and make it into the plateau in the clouds.

He simply did not care where he was; it could have been into the arms of his ancestors as long as it was out of the forest. He saw very little of Sibley's home due to the lateness of their arrival, but he was very happy to be there. The three were given the Lead House to rest in and two of the settlers served them a late meal of meat, fruit, bread, and a flagon of fruit wine with water. The dracs were taken to a stable by the dwellers with an assurance that they would be fine until morning. The travellers were tired to the bone and just wanted to eat, drink and go to sleep.

In the past, Lead Houses were dwellings specifically set aside for leaders wishing to spend time amongst their people. It was customary for the tribes of the Ouran Provinces not to have Leaders living amongst their people, but instead dwelling high above in a palace carved out of the mountains above the plateau. The leaders, often their most proven and powerful warriors, lived with their companions, children and servants. Counsellors and mages would make the daily journey up and down the thousands of stairs and gateways to and from the palaces.

Visitors and servants alike would pass through gateways that became more ornate the higher they climbed. Between the lower and upper gates were gatekeepers who guarded the gateways and the palace. Food and gifts were brought to the upper gates and the edicts and commands of the leader of the tribe were sent down to the dwellers below. There was the belief that the high leader should not live with the lowly dwellers but live amongst the clouds instead, to dwell somewhere close to the ancestors and to be the intermediary of the dwellers.

The mages of the High Leaders bestowed daily blessings on the dwellers, livestock and crops below. Then on a glorious spring day High Leader Kim Suyn came to the plateau and took over the Lead House. His intention was to remain amongst his people to celebrate the end of the claiming raids and to listen to the singing of the megalith as the mages brought the giant stone to life. He was to enjoy the festival and then return to the palace high above his people, but he never left; he regarded living amongst his people as a true blessing. Instead, he set his most accomplished builders to work and commanded the building of the great Cloud Palace for himself, his companions and his children. Successions of leaders had continued to live amongst their people and Lead Houses lost their status and simply became the dwellings for all travellers.

Chapter 37

Waifyn awoke with the dawn and left the Lead House he was sharing with Aliedori and Maldar. He wandered out to greet the dawn light. The settlement was a plateau at the foot of two mountains and was set between the two most prominent ranges. To the Eastern side between the white cascading river and the lesser peak was the rolling plateau. The plateau was a place where all the trees were long gone before the time of the great magical war.

The waterfall that fed the river appeared to be falling out of the sky and it was so far above the clouds that it created its own rainbow. The dwellings were built close to the river, and beyond them were the farms. Waifyn understood now why the quay down on the ocean-lakes was so small. The settlers did not really use the quay; they were high plateau dwellers with very little need to venture beyond their homes.

They had all the fresh water and food they needed but the landscape appeared barren without its trees, and Waifyn felt the sadness of the landscape keenly. He had left his beloved forest to be with this man he loved beyond limits, but he had not imagined following him into a place like this. How could people live without trees? How could a Realm continue to exist without trees? He did not consider the petrified landscape anything other than just dead trees. Something nuzzled his hand and he looked down at a Cob dragon, it was licking his hand. Waifyn bent and straightened up again bringing the little brownish-grey dragon up as well. Laughter rippled across the settlement filling the early morning with a feeling of warmth. There were three women and some children feeding Cobs outside their roost; one of the women was Aliedori. Waifyn almost didn't recognise her; she was dressed as a native, her striking black hair hidden beneath an earthen brown cloth that was wrapped around her head several times.

She wore a shapeless underdress of the same colour that reached mid-calf and over that she had a tan tunic secured with ties on each side. They had arrived late the previous night and had been given the Lead House to rest. They had not been treated as honoured guests but simply as travellers needing a place to rest. Aliedori was not behaving as the Intendant and future Ruler of the Southern Realm; she was just a traveller.

Now she was helping to feed Cobs with the women and children of the plateau as dawn broke over the mountains. When Waifyn had woken and climbed out of the bunk he shared with Maldar, he had not noticed if Aliedori was still in her room. He had simply dressed and left the dwelling, not because he wanted to be away from the warm body of his lover, but because he had been restless all night and could no longer lay in the bed unable to sleep. For some reason Waifyn felt comfort in seeing Aliedori, and was surprised that he felt this way. It was strange that he should find comfort in seeing her, more so than he did when seeing his lover. She noticed him and waved. Leaving the Cobs and their keepers, she came to join him and they both leaned against the dwelling catching the morning sun on their faces. Aliedori's eyes were closed and a smile played around her lips.

"I hardly ever see you alone," Aliedori said as she scooped a little dragon from Waifyn's arm. She threw the Cob into the air in the same manner that one would release a bird.

"Go and feed with your brothers and sisters little one." She turned to him, "Oh, Fyn, I am so sorry, I never thought of how you would feel coming here," she indicated with a delicate toss of her head, encompassing the landscape.

Waifyn was not surprised that she had noticed, what had surprised him was the use of the familial 'Fyn'. It was the first time she had used his name directly and she had not said his name in full. Only Maldar called him Fyn; they had shortened each other's names to Mal and Fyn very soon after they became lovers. The diminutives were their terms of endearment for each other and were only used when they were alone together, yet the name felt as natural coming from Aliedori as it did from Maldar. He liked her calling him 'Fyn'. It made him feel that she had finally accepted him. Waifyn eased in and kissed Aliedori; her cheek was soft but cold against his lips. She touched the spot, closing her hand into a delicate fist as if holding something fragile and laughed.

"My first kiss from my new brother, I shall treasure it." She opened the little pouch attached to her belt and placed the kiss in it, carefully closing it again. The kiss nestled amongst the dragon's breath she had placed in there days before.

Waifyn laughed also, she was teasing him and he was enjoying the intimacy. He planted several more kisses in quick succession making her laugh even more, and Waifyn suddenly realised it was the first time he had heard her laugh. Moments of 'firsts' could come like petals in spring, and all were gifts to be treasured, secreted away and kept forever.

But none was as precious as this moment in what promised to be a day like no other; Aliedori accepted him into her heart. She did not know what that meant but he did, he saw the thread woven into the fabric of time tracing the paths she could take. He did not know her, he had met her only as the sister of his beloved but when she chose a path, he followed. The path was clear; they were caught up in what appeared to be the start of another magical war, and she would be at the forefront. The very Realms would fall or rise at her say so, and she did not know it and neither did he, fully. He saw glimpses of something else in her, something that was untamed and wild and yet to be controlled. He knew her secret, or perhaps it was truer to say that he had guessed at her secret; he had guessed because he carried the same abilities within himself. His magic was in no way as powerful but it was there all the same, and he knew when she used magic and when magic was used against her.

He understood her, he liked her more than he thought he would, and he liked her infectious laughter. It was full of humour and came from somewhere real, deep inside, and it was full of warmth; it hid her fears and uncertainties. With each first, he saw more of her, her true self, and he understood her a little better each time. The change had started before they met, and the changes continued. These changes were almost infinitesimal but he could see them. Flecks of gold would appear in her green eyes and were gone again in the next blink without her even knowing. But her laughter caught him, it made him want to laugh too and it felt good to laugh and feel the release the laughter brought. Feelings of warmth and joy exploded inside making him feel so much better. He forgot everything else except the feeling of pure joy and love, and he laughed out long and loud.

Aliedori leant in and pressed her lips against his temple, and she kept them there just long enough for him to become aware of the gentle pressure. She pulled away as her fingers brushed against his arm to further prolong their contact. He felt rather than heard the whispered incantation and as he looked out across the valley the frozen trees appeared less dead. For the first time since arriving in the Eastern Realm he could experience a little of what she and his beloved saw.

The small branches and leaves appeared to shudder in the cold morning air and did not seem so desolate. Waifyn wrapped his arms around her in a tight embrace, grateful for whatever she had done. In a moment of 'first', a sliver of life and their path intertwined and stretched out to be woven through time forever.

"Should I be worried?" It was Maldar emerging into the morning light.

He tried to make his voice carry a note of concern that he did not feel. Waifyn was truly his, of that he had no fear, and Aliedori would rather lose an arm than hurt him. She grinned in that easy style reserved only for him, and now Waifyn it would seem. Waifyn smiled too, and Maldar was pleased to see that the smile was real. He felt his heart fluttered in his chest. He shook his head trying to shake free the image that was taking shape. The other two stepped away from each other but Aliedori's palm was still resting on Waifyn's arm, they were so at ease with each other. Waifyn continued to grin, some of the tension and sadness was gone from his body, and he felt slightly light-headed. Maldar kissed his sister's cheek and stole a long, deep kiss from his lover's mouth. He felt the renewed vigour in Waifyn's supple body and longed to discover just how much vigour there was. The image that he had just shaken away, sparked up again, clear and tremulous. Waifyn returned Maldar's kiss just as deeply and with all the promise of desires to be fulfilled.

"You two really will have to stop doing that in front of me. I am starting to feel just a bit left out."

They parted but their arms stayed around each other's waists while Aliedori took in the Petrified Forest with a rueful smile on her face. Waifyn was more relaxed but she knew that she had to get him way from this place before too long.

The incantation was only light relief and would wear off soon enough; Waifyn was a nymph, and humankind charms rarely worked on nymphs, but while he seemed happy she was in a playful mood and began to tease.

"I don't mind, I will stand here quietly and wait for the tribal leader to return while you two have your pleasures," she said. "And I won't tell you that I have found Sibley's dwelling."

"The leader is not here?" Waifyn was surprised.

"They say he is on a raid with the eligible people of the settlement, they are in need of new blood," Aliedori replied.

"You think he is here, though?" Waifyn said, not missing the tone of the sentence. Aliedori nodded.

"A Claiming Raid, I like the sound of them," Maldar said excitedly. He was not really listening and was already lost in the romance of it all. It was well over eight hundred years since the Southern Realm stopped Claiming Raids. But he had only a few short weeks ago taken part in his own private Claiming Raid, when he had gone to Waifyn's parents' home on the back of Keidrop carrying that ridiculous plant.

There were still Claiming Raids of sorts taking place in squares and courtyards all across the Southern Realm, only they were accompanied by musicians and alchemy and were called Festivals of Dance. The Eastern Realm, or certainly the tribes of Ouran Provinces still freely practiced claiming their suitors.

He knew that was how Sibley had come here. Yarlyn made his claim and she acquiesced. Gifts were bestowed upon the ancestors, and a new life was started as a pair bond in a settlement amongst the clouds. This was the Realm he had heard of as a child; everywhere he looked it was as if he could reach up and touch the clouds. The clouds swept low over the mountain peaks and rolled out across the sky like one continuous blanket made of white drac's wool. A young man approached them; as he neared he paused and looked at Waifyn, who was studying the crystal clear river twisting its way down to the ocean-lakes through the Petrified Forest.

"You are a Nymph. We do not have many of your kind here, nymphs live on the borders close to the Tree of Souls," the manchild said." But we have a few close by, I have seen them when I have been in the forest."

"Synne, I asked you to invite our visitors to eat morn feast with us, not talk them to death," a man said, from the front of a dwelling across the square, beside him was a girl. Aliedori looked at the young man who was clearly still a few cycles away from coming of age. Even so, his interest in Waifyn was more than a child's curiosity. The manchild favoured his mother; he had her smoky grey eyes, high cheekbones and full lips.

"To whom do you belong?" Synne asked, his question directed at Waifyn. Maldar raised a brow at his lover and grinned.

"I belong to no one, I am my own Nymph," Waifyn grinned back at Maldar.

Synne grinned too, there was a glint in his eyes as he said, "Then your heart is free?"

"I said that I am my own Nymph, I did not say my heart was free." Waifyn was not sure what to think of the manchild but decided to humour him anyway.

"To which one does your heart belong, the male or the female?" Synne did not bother to look at either Aliedori or Maldar; if he had he would have noticed that they were both trying to hide the smirks on their faces.

"The male," Waifyn replied and there was a long pause as they all waited for the young man to speak again; Aliedori had been studying the family. Sibley had asked her to seek them out and tell them what had become of her.

"Pity, or I would have claimed you for myself, but Mother's journey on the Claiming Raid would be fruitless." He grinned again then said, "My father would like you all to join us. Our leader is away in the next settlement so it falls to my father to greet strangers." The voice was suddenly unsure, very young, and carried a hint of fear.

Synne spoke directly to Waifyn, "There are many here who will be tempted, so make sure that you wear lover's symbols at all times while you are here."

"Why is that? I do not have a symbol. Where we come from we do not have symbols until we are handfasted." Waifyn was getting bored but did not want to appear rude.

"We have always taken our bed mates and companions from outside and to keep the bloodline pure we wear the symbols," he raised his hand and on his upper arm was a twisted vine made from silver.

"This is our family symbol," he said, "my companion's symbol and mine will be incorporated to become one." Aliedori had noticed the same twisted vine on Sibley's arm; she watched Synne walk towards his father they met halfway, spoke, Synne took little sister back to the dwelling.

"We must talk," she said and took Yarlyn's forearm.

"I know, Intendant," he said softly and responding to the urgency in her voice he allowed himself to be led away. He glanced backwards once in the direction of his two children.

Chapter 38

The monolith was in the centre of the mountain settlement over-looked by the Cloud Palace. It stood between the grand stone stairway rising up to the entrance and the long house that was once the High Leader's home.

The stone rose up out of the ground as if had grown from a pebble to become the great stone it was today. The lower part of the monolith was worn smooth by the centuries of touches. Hundreds of thousands of settlers had talked to the ancestors asking for guidance, support and blessings. The shallow pit around the base of the stone was made by a century of footfalls. The pit was full of flowers and fruit and there were garlands hanging from the craggy shards higher up.

All offerings were in thanks to the ancestors for providing them with another successful Claiming Raid. Towering above even the great monolith was the magnificent square structure of the Cloud Palace. Running vines and plants traced the terraces and outlined the structure drawing lines of colours across its surface. The vines and runners overhung the balconies bringing much needed greenery to the yellow and grey stones. Vaulted stone terraces were raised one above the other resting on square pillars. The terraces were constructed of stones and asphalt, and steep stone stairs accessed the highest levels. In the highest of the terraces was the accommodation and to reach it you first had to climb up through the terraces of beautiful plants and flowers of many colours. The building was a testament to the ancestors, to thank them for all they provided daily, a gift from the tribe leaders and their people to the ancestors for the blessings bestowed on them. The lower rooms of the palace were a tribute to fertility and the good health chamber where mass-bonding ceremonies took place.

He saw her, the strange girl from the South, dressed in tradition-al clothes. He watched her palm rest on the monolith. He had heard the sound of song, the long soulful cries of the ancestors and climbed from his bed to find her. A stranger to his home was making the stone sing; no one had done that since the time before the forest. The great stone shimmered under her touch, and the sound was sharp and clear and he closed his eyes and listened to the strange song.

The song was of his people and the cry of ancestors and for a moment he thought he heard his father's voice amongst the ancestors' many voices. It had been many years since the monolith sung and it brought a feeling of dread, yet at the same time, it brought clarity and peace of mind.

She was a slight slip of a thing this Southern Intendant, he was not even sure he knew what her title meant. Did 'Intendant' mean she was a queen in waiting or a naturalist waiting to come into her powers? He stepped back into the dark, found a robe and pulled it on, wrapping it around him and securing the tie around his waist. She was not to be underestimated; he had seen what she could do just by touching the sacred stone. How did she know what to do? It usually took many years of training for a mage to make the stone sing and to draw out the voices.

The other two with her were there to guard her perhaps, but she did not need them in that way, not if what he had heard from the capital was true. One of the warriors she had saved came from this settlement. The message of their coming had been received weeks before, brought by a Gem from Fengard and another by the local Cob from the Elders in the city below. He had been expecting them. He knew that the message was for Yarlyn and that it concerned Sibley, but he had no way of knowing that the message they brought would change his life and that of those he cared for forever.

Aliedori stroked the monolith again and again and he could feel the unmistakeable tingle of magic beneath his feet. He wondered if she did not realise that it was her presence in the Realm that had awakened the magic that had lain dormant for over a century. From beyond the edge of the square Yarlyn stood alone watching her also; he needed the time to gather his wits to face his children. The girl had been kind and she had tried to explain what had happened to Sibley but he was unable to take it all in. He could not imagine how Sibley had suffered nor could he understand what had happened to her or how she had changed. Aliedori had explained it to him while the children ate their breakfast. He knew that they would have to leave soon, but if he stood there a little bit longer listening to the ancestors then he would not have to leave. If he went in and told his children what he knew; that his beloved Sibley, the mother of his children, was gone forever, then it would become all too real, so he stood and waited and watched.

The city of Fengardia was many weeks sailing from his home and his people. He knew that they must go to Sibley but instead he found that he was unable to move so he remained transfixed.

Yarlyn had not left the Realm since he was a young man on a claiming raid. His family's only journey was the annual pilgrimage to the Temple Palace gardens to pay homage and give tribute to the ancestors for the Black Dragons. When the news of the Southern visitors arrived, he had felt responsible for ensuring the visit went well, his only regret being that Sibley was not by his side to greet the Southern Intendant. She had been away for a while but that was not a worry. The only reason Sibley had gone on the Claiming Raid was because Synne had been unwell. He had caught a chill that had turned into a full-blown fever. Yarlyn had to almost tie him to the bed to stop him riding off on the raid with the other eligible people. Synne had dismissed all talk of going in the next cycle; he was ready now, ready for a companion and he would not wait another cycle. Many of those who went out on the Claiming Raids were only just returning and those who had returned early would have to wait until the end of the harvesting. That was when many handfast ceremonies would take place. The steps of the palace would be lined with new bond mates ready to start their lives together but Synne would not be one of the newly bonded, not until the next claiming season anyway, but what would that matter, his mother would not be there. The settlement was waking up and coming alive; dwellers were coming out to start the day at the sound of the singing stone.

Yarlyn hurried back to the children who were still inside. He kept the young woman in his field of vision for as long as he could, only taking his eyes off her as he reached the entrance. He cast one last, long look at her and saw that behind those kind and gentle eyes a storm was brewing. He did not wish to be anywhere near when it was unleashed as it would be unfathomable. He hurried inside to tend to his children and prepare them for the journey in more ways than one. Yarlyn ducked back into his dwelling unnoticed by all except two; one was Aliedori and the other was… he glanced up at the Cloud Palace before closing the door and then he paused again. He was about to turn away and close the door when the two young men joined her by the sacred stone. The Nymph spoke, his voice hidden behind a surprisingly delicate hand, and waited. After a while, she shook her head in reply, a small, slight move-ment that held meaning only for them. The Nymph reached out and touched her arm, giving the same small shake of his head to the other before they both walked away from her.

Aliedori had said that Sibley was brave; she had fought against the dark magic to choose her own path to the ancestors. She said that there was a dragon boat on the ocean-lake ready to take them to the Southern Realm. A message was sent to the *Dawn Mist* and the Southern Realm to inform them that they were coming. He went along with the prepara-tions to leave because he could not think of anything else to do. Yarlyn instructed his children to pack with care taking only what was necessary. This was perhaps the best time to leave the Plateau, handfasting would start shortly and they would not be amongst those celebrating a new life. Yarlyn knew that Sibley could not rest amongst the ancestors if her family did not pay the correct homage. They finished packing the few things they needed for the journey and then Yarlyn gathered Synne and Tamar to him.

"We will give tributes to the ancestors and ask them to guide our path, then we leave." He waited for his children to reply and when they did not he continued; "Now we make our offering."

They placed flowers and dried fruits on the small shrine in the cor-ner of the dwelling. They kissed the shrine of the ancestors and slipped out through the back door, following a small track down through the forest. Four people saw them leave, Aliedori, Maldar, Waifyn and Syun. Syun was standing on the uppermost stair of the Cloud Palace watching the girl when he spotted Yarlyn leave. Some settlers had gone missing at the start of the Claiming Raid but that was not unusual, it was part of the process.

Claiming Raids worked both ways, alliances were formed and dwellers only returned to the settlements to collect their belongings, but it was with the arrival of the dragon raiders that he realised that some-thing was wrong on the plateau. News had reached the plateau of the raiders taking dwellers from the city. It was no longer a problem just for those in the city but those in the provinces also. This girl with her small party from the South brought news of only one but he knew that the fate of the one was also the fate of the many. Yarlyn and his family were on their way to the Southern Realm to say goodbye if they were lucky. If they were unlucky then Yarlyn would be claiming his dead mate and the mother of his children.

Chapter 39

Without warning Aliedori raised her head and looked directly at him. Syun went still; he knew that she had seen him, and it unnerved him to know that she had been watching him also. She lowered her gaze and the stone vibrated as she removed her hand and waited.

The settlers were beginning to gather in the square to greet the newcomers from the South. Syun remained standing in the shadows for a while longer before emerging into the early morning sunshine. He swept down the elegant stone steps and stood before the girl who was about to bow. She was prevented from doing so as she was grabbed by the arm and dragged up the stairs of the Cloud Palace. Startled at the sight of Syun dragging Aliedori off, it took both Maldar and Waifyn a few seconds to realise what had happened.

"Release the Intendant at once!" Maldar commanded, catching up with them.

"Why are you here?" Syun asked, closing the large heavy doors behind them.

"To keep a promise," Aliedori replied even though she knew that Syun had been watching her ever since they arrived. He had witnessed the exchange and watched as the family left, he knew it all but still she answered the question with respect.

"To whom?"

"To the family, Sibley, Yarlyn, Synne and Tamar. Sibley was among the people who were taken by the dragon riders.

"Release the Intendant!" Maldar commanded again drawing his sword, but a small shake of Aliedori's head stopped him mid-draw. He pushed the sword back in the scabbard as Syun released her hand and stepped back until he was resting against a pillar. Aliedori rubbed her wrist to get her circulation going again.

"You have very powerful magic, the sacred stones have not sung in many a generation. No one has ever made the sacred stone sing as you have." Syun said, as if he had not just dragged the Intendant like she was a naughty child.

"I am the Intendant of the Southern Realm; my name is Aliedori, and these are my brothers Maldar and Waifyn of the Southern Nymphs."

Syun dismissed her with a wave of his hand and turned away.

"You should not have come, things will not be better for your presence here."

The entrance where they stood was high with vaulted ceilings and strong stone columns topped off with a fan effect to support the height and weight. Large, square slabs with small, highly polished crystals formed grilles in the windows to allow in light.

"You have magic," Syun suddenly said again. "It would have been better if you had stayed away." Aliedori could not see how the obvious was relevant but nodded and waited for him to continue.

"I am the High leader; the ceremony to send my father home, and the ceremony to declare me High Leader took place on the same day. That was less than half a cycle ago and now you bring more news of loss and pain."

"News you were already aware of High Leader Syun." Aliedori reply

He gripped the column and then rested his back against it as, head in hands, he said nothing more. He slid to the floor, and from that position he said again in a quieter voice, "You should not have come, Intendant."

Maldar stepped forward from his sister's side and helped Syun up from the floor where he had collapsed onto his knees.

"Tell me High Leader, why should the Intendant not have come?" The young leader stood facing Maldar as if trying to decide what to do.

Syun came to a decision and walked away, Maldar following after him. The inner sanctum was warmed by the blazing fire and was the only source of light in the room. Maldar could make out a figure on the bed, but he could not see clearly whether it was male or female.

"Your people are coming," Maldar said as he watched the procession of people cross the mountain path. He had pushed aside the heavy cloth draped across the window.

"She summoned them, using the sacred stone." Syun appeared lost for a moment then focused again on Maldar. "Your sister is here to wake the Realm and bring the land back to life again; what are you here for?"

"To protect her," Maldar replied, "and she is not here to wake the Realm, we are simply here to deliver a message.

Syun laughed at the ridiculousness of the statement and the figure on the bed stirred but did not wake.

"Protect the girl who can shake the Realms and turn them to dust. You and the beautiful nymph are here to protect her?" Syun laughed again but there was no humour in the laugh. "Yes," he said, suddenly sobering, "I can see that, I understand what you mean." He glanced towards the outer chamber. "The girl who could shake the Realm needed to be protected from herself."

"Why do you say that?" Maldar was incredulous. "And why should she not have come?" he asked again.

The High Leader studied Maldar for a moment or two.

"You are aware that there are Cobs that can do that simple task." He moved closer to Maldar and almost whispered his reply.

"It may sound strange, but our father was very clear and we were sent with her for a very good reason. But regardless of what my father said I would never have let her travel here alone."

It was a long procession as more people joined the walk across the mountain, everyone coming to see his sister. The idea was ridiculous. She was not some kind of spectre, an apparition to be gaped at. Perhaps Syun was right and she should not have come. The Provinces were too far spread for his sister to reach the tribes even if she used magic. The next nearest province would take days even weeks to reach on dracs and on foot; the settlers were not coming because Aliedori had summoned them. The High Leader was questioning why Maldar had accompanied Aliedori; he knew that it was not just because of his father's wish.

He had always assumed that his path was clear as a dragon master and commander and he would be happy to protect the Lady of Fengard. With Waifyn at his side, he would be content to be the Realm's dragon warrior. He had never questioned his father's wisdom and had spoken to his father before leaving. His father's message had not been very clear, all he had said was, "Aliedori's journey is also your journey; you need to find your own path." His path was with Waifyn, if not at Fengard then wherever they made their home, but his father had meant something different.

He had tried to pump his father for more information or at least persuade him to be clearer but he got nothing more. Aliedori was born a naturalist and possessed powers from birth, but they were becoming stronger the closer she got to her coming of age. Syun was right, but while Aliedori did not need to be protected she should not be left alone with her new powers. They were manifesting themselves very rapidly and so wherever Aliedori went he and Waifyn would go also.

"And the Nymph would not leave your side?" Syun enquired. Maldar had almost forgotten that he was there so lost was he in his thoughts.

"Something like that," Maldar replied casually, wondering if Syun had celebrated his coming of age yet. The High Leader was very young, not much more than a boy.

Maldar had moved back to the entrance of the inner chamber and shook his head at them both; he had learnt nothing. Aliedori was still where he had left her by the door; she was watching the people gather in the courtyard. Waifyn was pacing, his bow and quiver slung across one shoulder and his back. His mood had changed since the disquiet charm Aliedori had placed on him earlier and it was strange to see his lover behave in such a manner. While Waifyn took on her traits Aliedori stood calmly, her hands clasped behind her back just like their father and he joined them.

"Syun said that you have summoned the people. Why?" He stood watching the approaching crowd; already music could be heard.

"I did not summon them. They started their journey while we were still in Memgalah and Syun knows this. But if he believes that I am here to restore magic to the Realm and help in restoring the Realm itself, then the people have to be united. This cannot happen if the city remains isolated from the provinces and its people remain scattered."

"And you think the city guardians and Elders will come to the Cloud people?"

Waifyn became still and Aliedori start to pace, her head down, hands clasped behind her back.

"That is what I am hoping for Waifyn, but…" she shrugged, a small, slight up and down movement of her shoulders suggesting that she had very little hope.

Maldar had seen her pace a hundred times. A slow, deliberate stride marked her pacing, showing that she was deep in thought. Maldar knew that usually when she lifted her head she had reached a decision.

The mystery of the bed mate was resolved as Syun and a female companion came into the chamber stopping Aliedori's pacing midstride. The High Leader and his companion were both dressed in ceremonial robes.

"If you are going to unite the tribes Intendant, then we must at least look the part." Syun swept past and his companion tried to mouth words of apology but was dragged past before she could finish. She inclined her head and Aliedori smiled. How could she leave the Realm her father had fought so hard to save in his youth? But she had no place here either; she did what she could to defend them from the raiders but they had to save themselves and restore the trees and the full magic of the Realm. As much as she wanted to leave, the Realm was not finished with her. She had sent instructions with Yarlyn to send the dracs back with extra clothes and food. A simple return incantation that she had placed on the dracs would ensure that they did not stray too far. They would continue their journey as soon as the dracs returned. Keidrop and the newly acquired dragons were to return home with the boat to ensure that the crew remained safe and got to their journey's end. Keidrop would not be happy with the instructions and would no doubt make her feelings clear, but in the end, she would agree.

They watched the High Leader and his companion glide down the steps, and Aliedori threw up her hands in surrender and followed. The Cloud people streamed onto the plateau until the stream became a river and still the people continued to flow. The High Leader had called the Cloud people not for himself, but so that they could see the children of the great warrior who had defended the dragon. They came not because of Aliedori and Maldar but because they were summoned by their beloved High Leader and they answered the call.

Torches marked the way across the mountains and the plateau that connected dwellings and walkways to the Cloud Palace as the night drew in. And still they came, with music, laughter and joy to greet their High Leader and his new companions and stand by his side. At first Syun looked on with dread and disbelief, as if somehow Aliedori had indeed summoned his people. He had tried to unite the Cloud people and thought he had failed; even the ceremony to guide his father home had not been enough to bring his brothers and their people together. Syun was the youngest of three brothers. Kuok was the eldest and Koeh the middle brother. They had been with their own tribes when the youngest of the three become the High Leader of the Ouran Provinces.

Koeh was the first to be captured in a Claiming Raid; he had set out to claim a mate and return to his home on the plateau, but he was captured instead and became the mate to Anaria. Anaria was leader of a tribe famed throughout the Realm for their skills as bareback drac riders. When they were handfast in accordance with the custom of Ouran they became joint leaders. Koeh was happy and proud of his place in the Provinces, he was loved and respected by his mate's people and over time, they became his people, especially after their first child was born and though he missed his home he thought very little about Ouran. Koeh was on his way to Ouran to present his daughter to her uncle and High Leader when the news of the visitor from the South reached him. Koeh had not been able to attend his father's burial or Syun's celebration as High Leader. Anaria was close to giving birth and he did not wish to leave her side. Koeh deeply regretted the rift this had caused between himself and his younger brother.

But now, his young brother was High Leader of the Cloud people and all the Provinces and Koeh knew that he would be a great leader. Ouran was the largest and most powerful of the Cloud Provinces and the people had stayed loyal to their young leader, proof that he was worthy of the title of High Leader. They saw something in him that he did not see in himself, the ability to lead. For many cycles the people of the Realm were tribal people like those of the Provinces. Over the last few cycles trading tribes had moved to the ocean-lakes at the foot of the plateau and when Memgalah was born, Osleza was all but forgotten.

It was different for Kuok; he was not on a Claiming Raid but rather an annual pilgrimage to the Tree of Souls. He had become ill whilst there and had been taken to the far island by a fellow pilgrim from the island. Osleza was the Eastern Realm's only inhabited island and its furthest province. Whilst recovering on the island Kuok fell deeply in love, not only with the island people and a mate, but also with the greenness of the island.

No one knew why Osleza had escaped the terrible charm that had frozen most of the Eastern Realm's trees. Some said that Osleza escaped because the charm could not cross water, while others said it was all the magical creatures on the island that protected it against the charm. Whatever the reasons, the charm did not reach the island and

Kuok gave tributes to the ancestors for sparing it. He made Osleza his home and was content, but he had always vowed to return home with his mate and child to claim his place as High Leader. Their father, however, had chosen to make Syun High Leader; the message brought to him by a Cob from their father was simple: "He knows the path the Provinces must take, help him lead the way."

Kuok knew this to be true because even as children Syun had talked only of the return of the trees and the return of the magical creatures to the Realm. Syun carried this belief in his heart until it became part of his very essence, there for everyone except him to see. Syun was High Leader of the provinces now and he must lead the people along the right path.

Syun felt humbled as he accepted with great humility Aliedori's homage before the sacred monolith. He felt more than a little ashamed at the way he had treated her with such disrespect, and surprised at her for allowing herself to be treated in that manner.

Kuok and Koeh presented their companions and children to Syun, who was too happy to dismiss them as he had intended to do. Aliedori approached and bowed to all three, as did Maldar and Waifyn. As Syun sat on the stone throne, his two companions took their seats also. It was the privilege of the High Leader to choose as many companions as they so desired and in times past High Leaders had as many as ten. Syun received his brothers with the respect their status deserved and then they greeted each other with joy and love at their reunion.

Syun did not see the visitors leave. Was it when the two Black Dragons arrived or when his companion Mahh began to make the monolith sing? The people were overjoyed, as were Syun and his brother to discover that they had a mage in the Provinces again. The Black Dragons took their human shapes as Mahh rested a hand on the stone and it glowed and sang out. The Cloud people took up the song and a procession moved down the hill and into the Petrified Forest. Soon there were twinkling lights on branches setting the forest alight with life. Syun stood proud, his other companion, Isao, was by his side; the female companion he had claimed in the last raid. He had to go on a second Claiming Raid after his father reminded him that he needed to look to the future. The day he came of age was the start of the month-long Claiming Raid, and he had returned within two weeks with Mahh. The following cycle he and Mahh went on another Claiming Raid and it had taken them more than two weeks to return with Isao.

"She left a gift for us," Isao said holding out an egg. "Dragon's eggs." Isao held three large eggs in her arms.

"How did she know that we were three?" Syun asked taking one of the eggs and holding it close to his heart with his eyes closed. He opened them again smiling; he held the egg up to the light and saw that new life stirred within the shell, his rule had started in earnest.

Chapter 40

"I think we should stop there for the night," Waifyn said pointing to the low over-hanging shelf off towards their right.

"It will afford us good shelter out of this incessant rain." He was not happy he was soaked to the skin, as indeed they all were. He wiped the rain away from his eyes as he spoke. They had sneaked away from the celebrations just as the young mage touched the sacred monolith drawing the crowd's attention. Waifyn had thought the sound was excruciating, but he was nevertheless interested in listening to it at least from a distance.

"There are very few who can draw the trapped voices from solid granite stone," Waifyn had commented. The sound had followed them for some distance. "You Aliedori are one and now the young mage which means he must be very powerful."

"He is a marvel; I've heard but never seen it done before. I didn't know *you* could do it." Maldar was watching his sister as he spoke; her head was turned away from him.

"All things have a voice you just need to find it. I think it is going to rain," Aliedori said as her eyes drift skyward.

They had been travelling for two weeks since leaving Syun and his brothers, and the sun had been in her favour.

But no sooner had Aliedori spoken those words than large heavy drops of rain began to fall.

"If we don't get out of this, I think we will all drown. Are you playing with the elements Alie?" Waifyn asked. The rain was heavy, unbroken and he was already soaked to the skin.

"I cannot make it rain, I can only use the elements, there is a difference," she had replied.

The overhanging cliff with its dry stone floor was a gift from the ancestors. The shelter, though natural, looked as though it had been carved just for that purpose. To the right of the entrance was a pool fed by a small but strong waterfall, made stronger by the rain no doubt. It ran down the rock face and pooled before disappearing under some dense growth of Dragon Breath.

"It an ideal spot for traders to rest, water themselves and their animals, so let's make the most of it," Maldar said.

The prolonged heavy rain had made the ground around the entrance soft and small pools of water had gathered in indentations.

"It looks well used," Waifyn said. He jumped over the pool and onto the roughly hewn rock at the entrance as he spoke.

"It's clean and dry and there's clear evidence that it was once frequently used," he shivered.

There was a permanent fire hole with half burnt wood and some charcoal but no ashes. Aliedori said nothing but busied herself unpacking the utensils. She had followed the dracs in.

"Will you fill this please?" she asked.

She offered up the pan while surveying the shelter. Someone had driven a hooked metal stake in the rock over the fire hole creating a holder for boiling tea and cooking pots. She stooped down and began to build a fire using some chopped wood then lit it using a fire charm.

"Much better," Maldar said as the flames burst into life. He held onto the empty pan and his gaze drifted from the inviting fire to the rain.

"Well this pot is not going to fill itself!" he said reluctantly as he dived out of the cave into the rain again.

Fastened to the rock by another much smaller iron rod was a rune stone. The symbol asked for replenishment of the firewoods and a tribute to the ancestors. Aliedori pressed her palm over the rune and stood for a second or two with her eyes closed, feeling the traces of all who had used the cave.

Maldar and Waifyn were happy to take the shelter as a good omen, they were both drenched, and to find a dry, warm place to dry out was welcoming.

"You could at least manipulate rain and keep us dry," Maldar was complaining as he re-entered the cave. "I am wetter than ever if that's possible."

Aliedori did not seem to notice the rain even though she was as wet as they were and her unusual quiet left them both with a feeling of unease.

"We are all dry now," she said turning from the rune. "Everything is dry, happy now."

One second he was soaking wet and the next he was completely dry. A grin spread across his face, "How do you do that?" Maldar asked although he already knew the answer.

"Magic." She grinned back at him playfully, but then the smile faded.

She had said very little since leaving the Cloud people in Ouran Province and she seemed to have retreated into herself. Maldar didn't like that at all, but he would have to wait until she was ready to talk about what was on her mind. Aliedori continued to say nothing as she relieved the dracs of their burden and sent them off. By the time the last of the light was gone from the sky they were dry and warm and drinking hot honeyed tea and eating roasted hare.

"We are still deep in the Petrified Forest," Waifyn said gazing at Aliedori's back. The rainclouds had obliterated the moon and stars that normally brighten the night sky bringing on a premature darkness. Aliedori took her cup of honeyed tea and stood by the entrance to the cave, appearing to be watching the rain.

Maldar knew that she was not with them in the shelter. "She is out there 'searching'," Maldar explained. Waifyn, who had never seen cast her mind out in such a fashion, became concerned but kept it to himself. However, he could not fail to speak up when he later brought her some bread and sweet dates for a light supper. He had to pry the drinking vessel with the cold honeyed tea from her grip. He tossed the cold tea into rain and turn towards Maldar.

"You are not worried?" Waifyn questioned Maldar, who seemed to not have noticed.

"I want to show you something," Maldar said in a way of a reply, picking up Waifyn's bow.

"What?" Waifyn said looking down at the bow. "What do you want to show me?"

Waifyn placed the plate and drinking vessel by his feet as Maldar sighted the bow.

"Watch this." And without a second thought, Maldar released the arrow, aiming for the centre of Aliedori's back. Aliedori caught the arrow. Waifyn did not see how she did it; the arrow flew from the bow and then it was in her hand. Aliedori's hand holding the arrow was by her side and she had moved slightly to the left of where she was standing.

"That was..." Waifyn left the sentence to hang unfinished in the air.

"I use to do that all the time when we were younglings," Maldar said using the nymph's term for very small children. "No matter where she was in her head she always knew what was going on around her," he finished.

Waifyn drew in a long breath, he was not entirely comfortable but he let it go.

"So what you are saying in your very own special way is not to worry about her, she is fine."

Maldar nodded and leaned the bow against the wall of the shelter.

"I'm not sure about her being fine, but at least we are not in danger tonight."

Aliedori did not move out of her trance-like state when Maldar called the dracs in for the night and settled them down. Nor did she move when Maldar and Waifyn unrolled their bedding and climbed into it. Wrapped in Maldar's arms Waifyn continued to watch Aliedori standing guard, arrow still in her hand until sleep eventually took over.

"In answer to your question, yes, I am concerned but I just wanted you to see..." His voice tailed off like Waifyn's the night before.

Maldar left the sentence hanging; he had continued in the same vein as if they had not slept between the asking of the question and the answering of it. The feeling of dread that he had been unable to shake off since meeting the three naturalists from the Western Realm deepened. He had said nothing to either Waifyn or Aliedori, and now he felt that something else was happening but he just did not know what it was.

"She always looks after me, protects me, guides me; she was always there for me." A frown etched across his brow he continued softly, "I'm not sure that I'm always there for her, because I don't know how to help her."

Waifyn was sure that was not true and said so. "You help her every day in so many ways."

Maldar turned to stare at Waifyn then gave him a wide smile as he decided to accept the complement, letting out a deep sigh.

"Well, whatever it was that she was searching for out in the gathering darkness I hope that she doesn't find it." Maldar stood with his back against the cold stone. It made him shiver and he pushed himself away from the wall.

"Whatever or whoever it is it will be ugly and dangerous and lurking somewhere within the darkness ready to pounce."

Waifyn watched his beloved but made no attempt to reply as he could see the concern and fear in his eyes.

"I keep seeing Aliedori's face and the strange look in those green eyes of hers that quickly disappears whenever she catches me watching."

Maldar gazed out of the entrance to the shelter. Standing in the gloomy morning light he could not help feeling that phanthora was not too far away waiting to spring up against her. He pushed the thoughts to the back of his mind, but they would not go quietly, new thoughts mixed with old memories and fought for supremacy.

Chapter 41

Farther up, beyond his eye level, was the coppice, a straight line of trees with a slight curve off to his left. Maldar held his sword in his right hand, though he was not sure what use it would be and because he was not allowed to use it. The coppice above him was called the Dragon's Backbone as were all coppices including those perched on a hillside or ridge. Instead of the fast-growing small trees that grew in most coppices, this one was a real dragon backbone that quickly grew into giant trees that dominated the rocky outcrops.

Dragons' backbones grew out of the remains of slain dragons, killed by a mage of the Western Realm in his attempt to sever all ties to the ancestors, many centuries or so before the forest of the East was frozen. Trees grew where dragons fell and spurted from their backbone whilst the feet and wings became the craggy ridge or hillside. That was why, dotted throughout the Petrified Forest, pockets of greenery sprouted from the dragons' backbones and a line of trees stood protected by the powerful magic of the fallen dragons.

Maldar shook his head, *so much for magic,* he thought as he surveyed the trees paying close attention to the lower branches and the dark, cool shaded area. Then he allowed his gaze to drift upwards and took in the towering trees reaching out towards the sky to greet the sun.

"This should be easy," he said almost to himself with a grin.

There was always something very mysterious about the dragons' backbones; they held the secrets of life. Maldar could almost feel the area crackling with magical residues or perhaps it was just nervous tension. He could almost see the trees transforming once again into dragons. The dragon lifted its head, swished its tail as it shook off the incantation and took to the skies once more.

Maldar could understand that, dragons were his special connection to the ancestors. As a Dragon Knight, he had his own connection to dragons but especially to Keidrop. He wished he could take flight with the beautiful creature and escape the ridiculous dare he had set himself. Maldar paused and shifted his gaze from the line of trees to the Makka bushes closer to the ground and swallowed. The trick was to get through the Makka bushes up to the trees and return without the large thorns ripping him to shreds.

"I know this. There is a trick to it, if only I can remember. I wish I had listened to Aliedori," he said with a sigh.

"Did you say something?" someone asked.

Maldar ignored the voice behind him and concentrated instead, not on the dense thorny foliage or a transformed dragon, but on what Aliedori had told him.

"The trick, the trick is, the trick is to… try," he mumbled to himself. "How do I tame a dying dragon's last breath?"

The Makka bushes could be tamed; he knew that. There was a special way to touch the bush to make the thorny head 'sleep'. He glanced behind one last time. Kryspyn gazed up at him, one hand resting on his hips the other on his training sword. *All because I wanted to impress you*, Maldar thought *and now I am going to be shredded*. He began to turn back to the task at hand when from the corner of his eyes he glimpsed her hair streaming behind as she moved at speed towards them.

"Dori what are you do …" Before he could finish she raced past him up the hill. Aliedori placed herself between him and the makka bushes, one arm raised, palm forward, while with the other hand pushed him backwards. His anger flared.

"Go away, you don't ne …" His anger suddenly turned to fear when he saw the look on her face. It was only a quick glance as his arms went up and the sword fell from his hand. But there was no mistaking what he saw there, what was plastered across her features was abject terror.

He tried to save himself from falling backwards down the slope; and as he began the slow awkward movement he felt an arm around his waist. Kryspyn caught him before he could fall and steadied them by holding onto a tree with his free hand.

"Your sister is good; no she is more than good," Kryspyn said in awe gazing in Aliedori's direction. Maldar followed the gaze, the Razor Claw was in mid-spring and his fangs, beard and claws were all extended.

"I could have been with the ancestors by now," Maldar had troubling swallowing.

Aliedori had caught the creature in a suspension charm, which meant they were all out of danger. She turned her back on the springing animal and looked to the small group of friends. Her glance took them all in one by one and then rested on her brother and Kryspyn a fraction longer than it did on the rest before she blinked, and the trance was broken.

"Of all the stupid… fourteen centuries of the seasons have passed since… you could have… I have tried teaching…" She stopped unable to find the words, her expression a mixture of pain and fear.

"I think she may do what the Razor Claw didn't." Kryspyn laughed. Aliedori lanced him between the eyes with one of her looks and his laughter froze.

Maldar was sure that there was a certain glee in Kryspyn's voice and was pleased when it was brought to an abrupt end. He felt the stab of each of Aliedori's unfinished sentences and all of them through the heart that hurt so much that he pressed the heel of his free hand in the centre of his chest.

"Look at what could have happened." She was almost in tears; her eyes filled with water but did not quite spill over. She was grey and shaking as she dropped her hand and walked back down the slope, the Razor Claw forgotten.

At that moment Maldar heard mewling for the first time, the kittens were calling for their parents.

"I would have heard them if… if…" He didn't finish the sentence anger rising to the surface again.

"I told you it was a stupid idea," Kryspyn whispered close to his ears ensuring that the others didn't hear. He had a stupid grin on his face when Maldar glanced at him still feeling a little irate. Maldar grinned back and allowed his anger to subside, but his smile quickly disappeared as soon as he saw Aliedori's face again.

"I would have sensed the danger but I was so intent on impressing that all else was forgotten."

All his attention was focused on the pain in his sister's face and his head swam with it. His skin burned as if he had been thrown in the makka bushes and he was covered in scratches.

"The mother must be out hunting." It was a girl's voice, but Maldar did not look to see who had spoken.

By the time Aliedori reach the group the Razor Claw was back with his kits. Her voice usually steady and calm quivered with fear and relief in equal measure as she tried to admonish him again. When words continued to fail her, she pressed herself against him in a tight embrace. He felt her relief as she sagged against him for a second before releasing him. She stepped back, unable to look at either him or Kryspyn. Her head hung low as she spoke.

"Take care where you go, you never know when danger is close," was all she managed and continued her walk back down the slope. Her eyes shifted from her feet to his face for a split second, and he caught the flecks of gold in those green eyes. She swept past him and was making her way down the slope faster than she came up it. Maldar became conscious again that Kryspyn's arm was still around his waist, the grip tight and comforting, and oh, so welcoming.

"Just so you know I was prepared to be impressed," he said with a magnificent grin again.

Maldar reluctantly pried the arm from around him, turned and took the grin in exchange for a coy kiss on the corner of Kryspyn's mouth, then raced after Aliedori as she disappeared from sight.

"She never told our parents, though I suspect that they found out. It would explain why my duties in the stable increased from three to five evenings," Maldar said still caught up in the memories.

"Why that memory?" Waifyn enquired out of politeness rather than a need to know. He was not jealous, they had both known others intimately but there was something in Maldar's voice that he could not quite put his finger on. He had listened carefully to Maldar as he worked on some arrows, he pause momentarily to glance at his lover.

"Didn't you re-string your bow after the battle in Memgalah?" Maldar asked already knowing the answer.

"I like doing it. I have always found bow work to be very calming. Anyway I need new arrows and this is a good time as any to make new ones."

Waifyn sighted the bow as he spoke. The battle had left him with a strange feeling; it had been a very long time since Nymphs engaged in battles, and it had not been in his life cycle. He put the arrows aside, and picked up a new piece of wood, and began working on it.

"It was a good idea to stop on that island or you would have long ago run out of arrows."

The subject had been changed subtly, and Waifyn knew it.

"Aliedori, can do return charms you know." Maldar gave Waifyn a dazzling smile designed to throw him off.

It had the desired affect, and Waifyn averted his gaze.

"I will bear that in mind next time we are in battle." He did not know quite how Aliedori's enchantments worked, but he was sure that arrows fired from this bow would always be true.

"It won't work you know, you are trying to avoid the question so I will asked it again – 'why that memory'?" Waifyn asked.

Maldar appeared to be considering the question, or perhaps he was still back on the coppice with Kryspyn. He shook his head and with his hand he swept invisible hair from his face. Waifyn's bright, intelligent eyes flashed there was no escape from that gaze.

"Because…" Maldar knew that there was no point in delaying any further. "…It was the first time I had ever seen her so scared for me, and she had the same look as when she was talking to those women from the Western Realm," he replied.

Waifyn's hand stilled as a thousand different thoughts that ran through his head fighting to be voiced, but only one could be first.

"Are you in some kind of danger?" Waifyn's voice was pinched with fear and concern was etched across his features that he could not hide. When Maldar did not reply he asked the question again but this time his voice was more his own.

"No, no, why would you think that?"

Maldar, unable to stay still, rubbed his hands together and leant against the cold stone as casually as he could muster. It did not work; Waifyn's distress and anxiety followed him until he changed tack.

"I don't think it is immediate danger, I think it's something to do with those women's fear of me that is worrying Aliedori."

"You said…"

"Fyn, I know what I said but I also know what Aliedori said. She has seen us in one of her visions somewhere in the distant future." Waifyn visibly relaxed. His shoulders lowered and he drew in a long breath and released it slowly but the frown continued to crease his brow.

"But why should they fear you? You are not that awful." Waifyn's question was part joke but mostly serious. Why would they fear humankind they had never met before? Waifyn studied his lover for a moment or two longer waiting for the reply that never came.

"You told me that they were afraid, especially Amana, the mother, but not of Aliedori," Waifyn said refusing to leave the subject alone.

"Yes, I was concentrating on the fears of the family but I was watching my sister." Maldar's voice changed slightly causing Waifyn to reach out and offer a comforting hand.

"What do you think it could be? What do you think they saw in you?" Waifyn asked the questions he was sure that he did not want the answer to particularly if it involved Maldar coming to some harm or to be in danger.

"If Aliedori is afraid, I am sure that her fears are out of concern for real danger Maldar."

"I'm not sure Fyn and I don't want to think about it." As far as he was concerned the conversation was over.

Maldar took Waifyn's hand and brought it to his lips and kissed the palm. How quickly an act of affection from a parent to a child takes on an entirely different meaning from a lover. In one moment, all things could change, and your life took you on a journey that was not expected, like travelling across the Western Realm into the unknown. If on that fateful day he had not escaped another tedious official celebration, he would not have skipped along the treetops happy to be alone, hot and bored. If he had not climbed down undressed and placed all his fineries on the bank of a river and dived into the water. If he had not resurfaced carefree and unhindered, if he had not spotted the warrior and the golden dragon, he would have continued carefree and unhindered for a while longer.

"Do you know in that moment my parents' – well mainly Mother's life plan to find a suitable mate amongst the nymphs of Bryn le Fenir was shattered forever?"

"What moment?" Maldar was still with the memory of that day on Dragon's Backbone and the family of women.

Waifyn frowned and said nothing for a moment then Maldar's grin said it all, "Well I suppose my plans changed forever too, which goes to show that you can't predict the future."

He was trying to shake free the vivid and scorching memories that were burned into his brain.

"Aliedori can," Waifyn said.

"No she can't, she can…" Maldar caught himself but it was too late. Waifyn turned away and hid his true feelings behind concerns for Aliedori.

"Do you think that she stood sentry or do you think she had some sleep?" Waifyn looked out on the dull morning. He did not want to discuss the real concern, but he could not shake the feeling that Maldar's tale evoked.

"I don't think that she is standing sentry I think that she is *searching*, or she has *found* something," Maldar replied.

Waifyn glanced towards the entrance of their little shelter again then back towards Maldar, but did not quite look at him. His feelings were too close to the surface and Maldar would know instantly so he concentrated on his bow.

Chapter 42

"We were given clear instructions; or rather Aliedori was sent clear instructions to head north into the Northern Realm. We were to seek leaders, mages and naturalists loyal to the Southern Realm who are willing to come to our aid as the West will need allies." Waifyn ran out of breath, he filled his lungs and continued, "Well, that was the unofficial order anyway; the official order is for an Intendant grand tour."

"Is there a point to this?" Maldar asked patiently as he packed away the bedrolls. Waifyn was filling the space between them with words; Maldar prepared his face before turning round.

"Waifyn I know that we are not travelling north, I do know how to navigate using the sun by day and the stars by night."

Waifyn's first thought was that Aliedori had chosen that path to spare his feelings but as the days wore on it became increasingly obvious that she was continuing her *search*.

"Whatever she was searching for or whatever she had found it lay not in the north but somewhere in the forest."

"I know," Maldar said mildly, "if Dori has found something then it must be very important for her to disobey The Lady of Fengard's instructions."

Waifyn picked up his bow and arrow and looked down its sight before releasing the air from his lungs and sending the arrow flying.

"Which tree?" Maldar knew the routine, and was curious because he needed a distraction in the same way that Waifyn did.

"The sixth one on the right, but not the tree with the vine," Waifyn said. In the dim morning light Maldar could hardly discern the tree much less the twisting vine.

"Well, a nymph's vision is so much better than those of humankind." He watched Waifyn release the arrow and even though he could not see if it reached its intended target, he praised Waifyn's skills all the same.

"Not me, well me in part, but Aliedori's enchantment did most of it." Waifyn took a chance and glanced at Maldar, his handsome face was creased with worry but his voice appeared light.

"I don't think so; I think it's all you. Aliedori's enchantments can sometimes be task specific, once the task is over the charm wears off."

Maldar was still trying to see where the arrow had landed.

"The battle is not over. Perhaps it has just begun."

Waifyn voiced Maldar's thoughts, and Maldar reached across and cupped Waifyn's face in his palm then gave a little smile.

"I think I shall have some tea, how about you?" He finished packing the bedrolls his voice carrying a cheerfulness he did not feel.

He did not want to hear his thoughts given voice, not on such a grey morning when his thoughts were full of nothing but death and darkness. The pan over the fire was bubbling gently and the drinking vessels were all waiting to be filled with honey-spiced tea.

"At least this is evidence that she did not leave the shelter too long ago," said Waifyn. He understood a little better now, while Maldar appeared almost indifferent and remained calm; hiding his worries deep inside himself.

"You two ready for tea?" she asked as she came up the stone steps into the shelter carrying the arrow. In two or three strides of her long legs she was standing by the fire and offered the arrow up. Maldar, being closest to her, took it as she picked up the boiling pot with the other hand and began to pour the teas.

"This place has wonderful acoustics you know," she said casually filling each drinking vessel in turn. Neither Maldar nor Waifyn said anything as they exchanged a glance, it was clear that she had overheard them. If she had heard the full conversation then she would have heard Maldar talk about the family of women and recalled his little adventure. Yet she said nothing, she acted as if she had not heard it and chose to say nothing. Maldar could see that Aliedori was trying very hard to keep her true feelings from her face.

Maldar sat by his sister and stirred his tea with his index finger, flinching as hot liquid burned his skin. He withdrew his finger, blew on the honeyed tea and watched the steam float away before plunging his finger and thumb into the tea again. He pulled out the small bit of honeycomb, blew on it several times before placing it on his tongue.

Enjoying the sweetness for a second or two, he used his tongue to wedge the honeycomb between his teeth. Slurping his tea he drew the liquid through the honeycomb and savoured the warming sweet brew.

He didn't want to have to think about the implications of Alie-dori's fear. He didn't want to annoy her with his gloomy thoughts. He achieved his goal as he looked up and saw both of them giving him a look of disapproval. He grinned at them innocently until they both relented and smiled at him, oh how he loved those smiling faces.

"You do know that you are stuck with his disgusting habits forever and that's an awful long time."

Aliedori was addressing Waifyn with a grin that came from somewhere deep inside. He could not help but grin broadly as he remembered his earlier conversation with Maldar.

"I may have to re-think this whole handfast thing; that was maybe one disgusting habit too far!" Waifyn was ready to join in the distraction but it was all too short-lived.

"We are not going into the North, at least not right away are we?"

Maldar finally stopped grinning. He knew his sister well enough to sometimes know her next move, but never quite what she was thinking. She remained standing and raised the still untouched tea halfway to her lips, but then lowered the drinking vessel before taking a sip.

"We are going to the Northern Realm as the North may hold some of the answers, but we are not leaving yet."

"To what questions?"

It was Waifyn who spoke; he too had stopped grinning.

"That is the trouble brother in name; I do not know what the questions are, not yet anyway. It's the same as the makka bush. It's prickly, and I do not like thorns." She smiled at them both before draining her tea and pouring the dregs into the still burning fire.

"I don't like riddles, Aliedori, and it seems to me that you are speaking in riddles."

Waifyn wanted to grab her and shake her, but there was something in that smile that wrenched at his insides.

"It is not my intention, Waifyn, but the West trades primarily with the North…"

"And if you can't get to the primary source then you try the secondary one," Maldar said.

"The first mage to fracture humankind essence came from the Northern Realm," Aliedori said.

"And you found this out, how?" Maldar shuddered he could not hide his disgust at the thought of a fractured essence, a thought which made him shiver.

"Is there any possibility that those Grey creatures are coming out of the North?"

Aliedori massaged her brow with a finger and thumb, the other hand holding the now empty mug that rested on the hilt of her seax.

It was a sign that Maldar knew well; it meant she wasn't going to talk any more. He emptied the dregs from the bottom of their drinking vessels onto the fire.

He took Waifyn's cup along with Aliedori's and put them into a saddlebag. Waifyn watched the cooling embers and waited for Aliedori to say more but she remained quiet. They ate their sweet bread and dried fruits as they rode, following a path that was clearly a trading route.

"This was a well used route."

Waifyn was looking at the ragged tributes and blessings to the ancestors for keeping traders safe.

"The coloured clothes are old and faded, some are just ribbons attached to strings and fine poles, so what happened here?"

"Traders travel by water and dragons now," Maldar ventured. Aliedori remained silent.

The rain from the day before had left the ground soft and boggy in places but the going was good. They were making a speedy progress to a place known only to Aliedori. To Waifyn they were travelling into the unknown and they were travelling in silence most of the time, except when Aliedori was helping Maldar to practise basic charms, or when she was giving a voice to the fluttering flags.

Waifyn found this strange. "It is simple Waifyn. Each tribute represents a traveller and each traveller has a voice. Sometimes that voice needs a little help to reach the ancestors."

"You will get used to her," Maldar said in a loud whisper.

Waifyn accepted the explanation without question, partly because he liked the idea and said, "I am just getting to know you new sister and what you are capable of. Since you did that thing I have found it easier travelling though the dead forest. So who am I to question you about the voices of the travellers and their tributes to the ancestors?"

They had travelled for most of the day keeping to the path, and had met no one; it was clear that the path was no longer used. Maldar became bored with Aliedori's instructions and began to try incantations in an attempt to do tricks. He managed to retain the incantation but had very little success except with the Seeker Charm.

The sun came out sometime during the morning, but the day was still cool. Due to Aliedori's reluctance to leave the Realm, the dracs, happy to meander at their own pace, did just that. Riderless, the dracs stopped now and then to munch tasty dragon's breath and other sweet fresh plants, while the three of them walked.

Towards the late afternoon, Aliedori called the dracs and they remounted and set them into a canter.

"I take it that you have found what you have been searching for all day?"

They were looking up at the rocky outcrop as they made their way to a ridge in the distance.

Waifyn was not sure how he felt as his earlier conversation with Maldar was still on his mind, and now they were heading for a ridge he didn't like the look of.

"You want to spend the night here?"

Maldar surveyed the ridge, a bare rocky outcrop remembering the several very good places she and Waifyn had found that would have suited them better.

"What was wrong with the hunter hut Waifyn found, the one you dismissed for this ridge?"

"This ridge would have been in constant use, it forms part of the trade route. It would have been an ideal place for woodsmen and their families to camp."

"What? And you want to share the sense of history?" he asked.

They reached the ridge just as the sun was setting. It cast its light and painted the clouds red and orange, sending the last of the golden light across the landscape.

"There is an old trader's settlement down there." Aliedori pointed in the general direction of the valley.

Waifyn was standing on the edge looking down into the valley and could see nothing. He had to admit to himself that it was a good place to camp, there was enough shelter as well as clear views all around and down into the valley.

"It was not unusual to have abandoned trading settlements, but I have never known settlers taking their dwelling with them. Aliedori there is nothing down there."

"I think I saw water in the distance," Waifyn said.

There was some evidence that the old trading routes were still in use, there were one or two new tributes amongst the fluttering rags. Waifyn was joined on the edge by his beloved and they searched in the hope of finding the old settlement that Aliedori was so sure was down there.

"I am sure that's water," Waifyn said, pointing.

"Can the saddles and bags to be left on?" Aliedori asked.

Both Maldar and Waifyn had given up looking for the settlement and began to unpack the dracs' saddlebags.

"If there is a settlement down there we can spend the night down there. It will be nice to spend the night in a bunk. We all need a good night's sleep," Maldar said.

"I've thought of that," Aliedori said softly. The three of them had settled back on the ledge overlooking the valley. "But something is wrong. I have tried reaching their minds, but can't. I have been trying all day and most of last night."

Maldar and Waifyn exchanged a glance.

"And nothing?" Waifyn ventured. "If there are dwellers down there, do they have a Mage? Maybe that is why Maldar and I can't see the settlement."

"If there was a mage down there, I would sense it. I have glimpses of someone then it's gone, but there's something else too. I cannot quite put my finger on it, there could be a naturalist, but the settlement is well guarded."

"An old deserted settlement, protected by charms, what could be down there?" Maldar asked.

"Greys," Waifyn offered, "this could be another gateway."

"Greys," Maldar agreed, "and throw in a few humankind to throw us off."

"Us?"

Waifyn glanced at Aliedori, the conversation was partly for her sake, but she was not listening. There was a static storm gathering, and the once bright sunny afternoon had given over to dense dark clouds carrying ribbons of static charge.

"I hate static storms," she said, wincing against a pain that had suddenly started in her head. "There is no rain just the wind and those awful lights."

She watched arcing silver lights hit the ground and massaged her head with both hands. "The last time I drew on its energy, I could not expel it properly."

The last of the sun disappeared below the horizon to be replaced by the oncoming storm and the sky darkened further.

"The last time you did that you were only ten cycles old," Maldar said.

"And I have been afraid of them ever since."

Maldar didn't know what to say to Aliedori's admission, she was afraid of static storms. He had never known her to be afraid of anything.

"Anyway, you remember what happened the last time there was a static storm."

Maldar said nothing further and watched the rolling clouds tumble over each other for space as the wind whipped itself into a frenzy and fingers of light scraped cross the clouds.

"How can she sit there so calmly? I love that about her."

"She may look calm as if she is simply enjoying a bonfire picnic with friends, but believe me Fyn there is nothing calm about her I know she is terrified."

Chapter 43

In the simplest of terms, she was who she was, Waifyn surmised, as he watched her sit straight-backed with her chin resting on her chest. She was the child of the Southern Realm, but then, so was Maldar. She was destined to be Grand Naturalist and Ruler of that Realm. What was Maldar destined for to be handfasted and tend stables forever? But Maldar's destiny wasn't any different from Aliedori's; he would not allow it. The chroniclers said that Aliedori would govern a united Realm, but didn't say what role Maldar would play.

"Have you been able to contact your family?" Maldar's voice interrupted his thoughts.

"I haven't for a while, why?"

"Assuming that our parents are now knee deep in handfasting plans, I need you to let the Olds know we are all well," Maldar said quietly.

"The what?

"Parents."

"Oh."

"It's been some time since the last message was sent," Maldar's attention was drawn away from the sky.

Above them, a family of dragons undulated and skimmed the clouds causing electric static as they moved. They were not the usual winged dragons but very rare serpents, wingless and moustached, a reminder that the ancestors were never far away. The East more than any other Realm had been blessed with these rare creatures; that was, until the war against the magical creature of the Realm. Their movement caused the clouds to spark and tiny fingers of lightning etched the outline of the serpentine shapes as they swam through the clouds.

Waifyn tried to *speak* with his parents but it was difficult because the creatures had caused a static storm that blocked his line of communication.

"Surprisingly 'the Olds' as you call them aren't together yet," he said.

Waifyn turned his attention back to Aliedori and watched her as she sat staring at the valley below deep in thought, contemplating her next move.

Not even the rarest of dragons, the serpentine dragon, a direct link to the ancestors, could hold her attention for long. Maldar's attention was also on dragons, "That damn dragon, I wish Keidrop was here now, she would make things so much easier." Maldar was missing his dragon.

"The serpentines are a good omen; why else would they appear now?" Waifyn decided that he was spending far too much time with humankind. He was beginning to take on their superstitious beliefs, so he asked a question and hoped that they had not heard what he had said.

"Have you ever been to the Western Realm?" Waifyn asked.

Maldar stirred and dragged his gaze from the dragons and spoke. The wind was picking up so he placed his mouth to Waifyn's ears, "To the West no, but we visited the North. Aliedori and I once spent two whole seasons there. It's still very tribal, why?"

"I know the history well," Waifyn said.

"Mages and naturalists battle for supreme control over the smaller tribes who are scattered across the Realm."

"Are you attempting to teach me humankind's ways?"

"Not at all, I was simply thinking of the chronicles and their true meaning."

"Fyn, we, Dori and I, know the true meaning of the chronicles," Maldar said. "Our mother is called home, which means Dori becomes supreme ruler."

Maldar let out a long, deep sigh that was so pain-filled that Waifyn put his arm around Maldar's waist and pulled him close.

Waifyn did know the history of the frozen Realms very well; he had seen it as Aliedori saw it, first hand. The most powerful tribes are those who are ruled by either a mage or naturalist. He knew of the nomads, of how those nomadic settlers were the most valuable to mages and naturalists and who saw magic as a bargaining tool to bind the nomads to naturalists and mages.

In the Realm of Ice, magic was a commodity to be traded to the highest bidder. It was used not for the greater good of its people but to gain the most power and control.

"You and Aliedori spent two seasons in the North; it must have been difficult for her," Waifyn ventured, remembering how the wealth of ice and barren landscape overwhelmed him the first time he visited the Realm.

Maldar chuckled but it was without humour. "It was beyond difficult but we were younglings. We should have spent a full cycle there but mother had to come and get us after Aliedori threatened to raise Nyborg to the 'snow covered ground' if Grand Mage Leof continued to do nothing to stop the trade in magic."

This time the laughter was genuine, its sound warm against the chill wind.

"That must have been fun."

"Oh it was, Leof was and still is the Grand Mage and commanded the most powerful magic and the largest tribes, but still he was no match for Dori."

"And you, what did you do there while Alie threatened the Grand Mage?"

"Oh she didn't just threaten. I have never known Dori to say something she didn't mean. It was when Leof lost the west wing to the snow that he contacted our mother."

"Oh, I see," Waifyn glanced at Aliedori.

"And to answer your question, I fell in love. Before you get mad, I was thirteen cycles when I fell in love with the sheer adventure of it all."

"So why did you not stay and let Aliedori go home?"

"I was given that choice but when I thought it through I realised it was Dori who made it such an adventure, she has a way of making everything an adventure."

"And here we are on yet another of her adventures."

"Yes, but this time it's not just a disappearing west wing, this time it's the threatened disappearance of everything we hold dear."

"The Eastern Realm did not disappear when most of its magic was siphoned off to be used against them," Waifyn said but somehow he lacked the courage of his conviction.

"And you think that is my worry," Maldar asked, "the lack of magic in the Realms?"

Waifyn knew that Maldar had bigger worries than magic disappearing from the Realms.

"Did I ever tell you of my first ever memory?" Maldar asked.

"No, I don't think so."

"It's of her; my first memory is of Dori.

She is leaning over me her face is in shadow as the light is behind her. Bright, bright morning sunlight and she is speaking to me and all I hear is her voice telling me it's morning. And this thought just came into mind, not just my mind it was the total realisation," Maldar said lost in his own thoughts.

"What was the realisation?"

"So this is it, this is what it's like to be alive. It was my first conscious thought," Maldar laughed. "Her voice, not mother's, not my nursemaid, her voice, Dori's voice."

Waifyn folded his hands across his chest, wondering where it would all end.

"What does it mean, Mal? Is Aliedori expected to take a simple tale and bring it to life, to unite the Realms at the expense of her mother?"

"I don't know, Fyn. All I am doing is telling you about my first and most significant memory. It is of my sister. Why do you ask this now?"

"It stops me thinking of what's down there, because whatever is down there can't be good."

The Serpentine dragons were gone, and Maldar cursed to himself at the absence of Keidrop.

"And what... thinking about the passing of my mother is better?"

"I wasn't thinking about that at all, Mal, but I can see what you mean," Waifyn said.

"I was simply trying to make sense of some ancient text that said a young woman must choose between unification and the loss of her mother."

"One to save the many is how it's been put. So, Waifyn, stop this now. Don't you think she hasn't gone through this? Don't you think I haven't? I even followed her to the Forest of Souls."

"You went into the caves? What were they like?"

"I don't know, we arrived late into the night. We fell asleep, and when I woke, Dori was gone. Terrified, I searched for her for what seemed like hours, and when I eventually found her, she was sitting very much as she is now, but she was different somehow."

"And she has never spoken of it?"

"No, whatever or whoever she encountered she never said, but I think she dreams of it to this day."

Waifyn rubbed his palm over his face and knuckled his eyes, left then right.

"It would be worth talking to the Scribes, they are the keeper of the chronicles."

Maldar remain silent for a while; then finally said, "I think Alie-dori did and that's why we ended up in the Forest of Souls." He paused a moment longer then added.

"This isn't just about a few Greys and in the grand scheme of things they are just a few. But they are the start of what must be yet an-other attempt by the Western Realm to take control the East."

"What a sacrifice for unity. Is it worth it, Mal?" Waifyn asked.

Waifyn wasn't expecting an answer and wasn't surprised when he didn't get one.

"Have you ever asked yourself why?"

"I know why, Fyn I've seen it for myself, the trading in magic, the slave markets. The pitiful people of the North, the child labour of the East. People that are held prisoners by the very thing that should protect them, magic. A leader who thinks it's her right to send her people to be turned into those creatures," Maldar argued.

Waifyn could hear the anger in Maldar's voice. "Fey has always kept out of humankind affairs. But more and more the two Realms are colliding." He paused, then, continued. "I don't disagree with anything you say Mal, but still…" this time his voice trailed off.

The daylight had almost gone and the last of the sun streaked the sky with red, orange and gold and the silver light of the static rain con-tinued to crackle. Waifyn closed his eyes against the last of the golden light and tried to clear his head, but the thoughts refused to leave.

He understood why Aliedori would want the other Realms to share the freedom and wealth of her Realm. She sat there watching the oncoming storm, the girl whose home was a gilded cage waiting to be-come the Warrior Queen.

A child from a gilded cage was going to change the Realms and unite them all. An image flared in Waifyn's mind, and he could not shake it, but it was not of Aliedori. He gasped, pulling away from Maldar and stood shivering.

Aliedori glanced up at that moment and their eyes met for a second. And in that instant, his thoughts were confirmed. Waifyn saw her as if for the first time, the regal queen she was to become and the young woman she still was. He saw her fears, her concerns and her love in that brief moment as her gaze drifted past him to linger on Maldar for a few seconds before turning her attention back to the valley below.

Waifyn made to move towards her but she stopped him with another look.

"How old were you when you went into the Forest of Souls?" he said turning back to Maldar.

"Just before we went to the Northern Realm, so we were in our thirteenth cycle."

"What do you remember?"

"Not much. I slept through most of it and dreamt a lot; the closer we got the more vivid the dreams became. In one dream, a guardian took Dori. I tried to follow, but a phanthora blocked my way and told me to wait."

"Perhaps it wasn't a dream. What if that's how humankind experience being so close to the sacred caves?" Waifyn asked softly.

"Perhaps, I only know that when I woke she was gone," Maldar said.

"Aliedori believes that you have magic," Waifyn said. He glanced towards her as he spoke, her palm closed round the dragon's eye she wore around her neck.

"Is it relevant at this time?" Maldar asked with a shrug.

"I think it is; I think that it is more relevant than you realise," Waifyn replied. Somehow he knew that the pendent she always wore had something to do with it.

Chapter 44

Aliedori had known her fate and the fate of humankind and the Realms, and she had kept it to herself since she was only thirteen cycles. Did she know that of Maldar also, Waifyn wondered. Was that what was behind her fear? She knew Maldar's faith.

He had seen her studying Maldar in the same unreadable way she was now studying the valley. He had even come under that unreadable look and knew that there had been nothing casual about it. Not about her, not her gaze, not her action, nothing, everything she did, she did for a purpose.

What did Aliedori know about Maldar that she wasn't saying? Maldar himself had said that she was always looking out for him, protecting him, teaching him, keeping him safe, but safe from what? Waifyn knew that it wasn't as simply as a razor claw.

The wind reached its zenith, and Waifyn blanched and pulled his coat around himself. The frozen branches were being whipped into a frenzied dance, and hellish cries of agony as the wind played its merry tune. The sound was eerie and it crawled through his veins causing him to shiver once more. A myriad of silver lights shimmered across the sky and caught fire as the colour struck the earth. The settlement that had been guarded by an invisible barrier suddenly appeared as the lights hit the ground. Its rounded wall appeared first as the barrier peeled back revealing the small neatly build dwellings inside.

Light shone from some of the buildings and traders could be seen in the compound before the fortress disappeared almost as soon as it appeared. Aliedori stood; her movement interrupted Waifyn's thoughts and drew his attention back to her. His thoughts now broken, and the valley revealed, he stood as the light faded and so did the settlement below.

"So that's where they were, hiding or hidden by someone." Maldar turned away from the valley. "Keidrop, I could really do with you now, where are you?" He reached for his sword at his hips bringing it up as he pulled it from the scabbard to his belt.

"When we get down there, there are about thirty-five men, woman and children, including several yearlings." Aliedori was moving as she spoke and was about to suggest that they should prepare but they were already armed and ready. From where they camped there was a small but well used track leading into the settlement.

"What did you do?" Maldar asked.

"A simple reveal charm, I used the static storm to my advantage."

"I told you there was nothing to fear," Maldar grinned.

She returned his smile, but it didn't reach her eyes, those told a different story.

They took the path, Aliedori leading in front, followed by Waifyn and Maldar at the back leading the dracs. The sun was all but gone from the sky and was about to be replaced by the moon hanging above them. But for now, both sun and moon lit their way down the ridge. Aliedori breathed deeply, pulling in the power and strength from both and felt it course through her.

Pausing for a moment at the bottom of the ridge, she lifted her face; lights and shadows danced across her features. The veil hummed and shimmered in and out of existence, revealing its secret, and she inhaled the strange earthy smell. A mixture of charms and nature combined to create a potent fragrant, and she continued on with slow, deliberate steps.

The sounds of their feet were lost to the wind's merciless tune as shifting patterns of light hit the ground again. The ensuing fire revealed the green brown of the moss- covered logs that made up the small fortress of wood as it appeared before them. The gateway was etched in an eerie greenish light and the full height of the fortress and was sealed by charms.

The trees to the left and right of them danced as the wind captured the frozen branches in its fury. As they fought to be free from their enchanted bonds their screams could be heard echoing across the valley. The cold silver moon was now alone in the sky watching the group as they neared the edge of the settlement. They emerged, Aliedori first, from the path between some densely packed saplings and stopped before the invisible veil.

The rallying wind sliced through her hair, directing it over her left shoulder. With a turn of her head, she saw the scene change again and a breath taking view of a garden and lake stood in the near distance. Fruit trees surrounded the lake, and the sweet intoxicating smells of ripened fruits caught in the breeze. They waited. They listened. It came.

The ground beneath their feet shook as if being trodden by a thousand moving feet. The terrifying screams of the dwellers joined with the howling screams of the trees.

"There are thirty-five in there and when this is over…" Aliedori started.

"You want thirty-five to be still breathing and their bodies intact and not on their way to the ancestors," Waifyn finished the sentence for her.

Aliedori nodded and reached out, putting an enchantment on their weapons again. Then she bought her hand up as the door was revealed again. They moved as one, even the dracs, as the gateway opened up to admit them through the gaping yarn in its side. At the far end of the fortress another gateway yawn open, spilling forth its contents. Aliedori stood for a second and took in the scene before her, images clicked into her mind. Of the thirty-five people only a few were in view, the others remained hidden.

She had sent a clear message asking the dwellers to go out through the gateway, but since two gateways had opened up simultaneously it was impossible for the dwellers to choose the safe route so they chose to hide instead. She sent another message in haste asking them to follow the illumination and sent out a flaming sphere of blue white. All but a few chose to remain where they were. Aliedori turned to seek out Maldar but he had already met his first Grey. She turned instead to Waifyn as she sent out another sphere, this time filled with yellow light in the Grey's direction.

Waifyn nodded his understanding and was moving – *get them all out intact* – he glanced back but she was gone, racing towards the far gateway, seax in one hand and a sphere of magical fire in the other.

During Aliedori's first fireball attack, Maldar concentrated on his defence and let his muscles settle into the rhythm of swordplay. It was a dance he knew well, he had practised for many years and was beginning to put into play all he knew. He had to kill, but he did not relish the taking of lives, he knew that he was fighting for the lives of the dwellers. Maldar spared a thought for the Greys; it was a kindness to send them home and ask the ancestors to welcome them.

The traders who had either scattered or remained inside in fear and panic as the gateways opened, suddenly became braver. Ringing blades and the rush of arrows reached the Greys and they heard the hoarse rasp of the creatures being cut down. They exited the dwellings as Waifyn called them out, as he released a score of arrows each one reaching its intended target. Waifyn grabbed a child and slung the youngling on his hips and turned to grab another.

"Hold on," he said to the youngling as the child's hands curled around his neck. Waifyn with four arrows in the same hand as his bow, with expert care nocked an arrow and released it in one smooth action. He pushed the child farther up his hips, nocked another arrow in the same smooth action.

He slung the child round so that it now clung to his back, its tiny feet wrapped around his waist. One thought bloomed in Waifyn's mind, and he released the second arrow and found another three more pressed into his hand instantly.

Waifyn turned and picked up another youngster and ran, one child clinging to his back and another in his arms clasped around his neck.

The Grey's weapon slipped past Maldar's defence and slashed towards his throat. He twisted out of the way then slashed backward to return a blow, severing the Grey's arm. Maldar moved again and thrust his blade horizontally cutting the Grey in two. He turned away as the two halves of the Grey slid apart and hit the ground sending sprays of viscous fluid into the air. He blinked the sweat from his eyes and saw the clear green fluid pouring out of the fallen Grey. Almost at once, Maldar was attacked again; their weapons clashed catching each other in mid-air.

The sound of metal against metal rang out around the settlement, and the impact vibrated through Maldar's body.

They stood face-to-face, body-to-body; the Grey's touch adding a cold shiver to the vibration. The Grey's rank breath caught him as he breathed in and almost choked Maldar, he spluttered and gasped. He felt unsteady for a moment and blinked again turning his head away. The weight of the Grey pushed him back. Maldar stumbled and fell and the Grey was immediately on him his sword poised.

Maldar twisted out of the way. The Grey's sword came at him slicing the air just inches from his face. The Grey was stronger. Maldar used his sword to block and kicked out at the same time. The Grey staggered back but did not fall. The creature charged at him again but this time Maldar was on his feet. He sidestepped again missing the swing of the sword but moving into the path of the Grey's talons.

Maldar flung his head back, stumbling; he felt wetness against his face and reached up feeling dazed for a second. When he looked at his hand it was covered with blood.

The gash at his temple stung, and he wiped the blood from his face. The Grey charged at Maldar its sword high above its head. Maldar sliced through the air in an arc. The Grey shuddered then continued its charge. Suddenly it fell, the sword embedded in its side. Maldar caught his breath, wrenched his sword free and quickly turned away to face another oncoming Grey. Dark green goo exploded into the back of his head and shoulders and a Grey fell at his feet.

Waifyn didn't see the Grey fall as he was already racing away with two younglings clinging to him. His bow nocked, ready to release, as he dashed for the gateway beyond the veil. Waifyn placed both youngsers in the arms of a settler before rushing back into the settlement.

"Don't you think that you should move?"

Waifyn grabbed the young man's wrist and swung him out of the way of an oncoming Grey. He spun on the ball of his right foot dragging the boy with him, his free hand holding his knife. The Grey's thick skin stopped the knife at its hilt and as Waifyn withdrew it, the Grey collapsed. Waifyn and the boy were through the gateway before the Grey hit the ground.

The Greys from the forest had unthinkable speed and incredible strength; their talon like hands was used for slicing through flesh. But these new Greys were also equipped with swords and battle-axes, and while slower they were nonetheless just as deadly. A fire sphere of white-hot heat appeared in Aliedori's palm and with a quick glance she surveyed the settlement. All the traders were out of immediate danger so she released the sphere and called out to Maldar and Waifyn. The killing blow struck the ground and exploded in the centre of the Greys coming through the far gateway.

The eruption sent fingers of white-hot heat off in all directions, catching every Grey in its grip. The captured Greys exploded and showered the ground in dry, hard clay. The shattered broken lumps of clay did not return to flesh but turned to dirt and disappeared into the ground.

"Now you run and take them with you." Aliedori indicated to the traders at the entrance.

"You are not staying here alone there are too many of them and you have the safety of the traders to think of."

Maldar was beside her. She did not speak directly to either Maldar or Waifyn but they got her meaning.

They were through the gateway and out into the frozen forest again. Aliedori sent a sealing charm to *lock* the gate; the green outline of the gateway turned red as it was sealed.

"It will slow them down but I do not think that it will stop them."

A Grey who had fallen by the gateway transformed to human-kind as the veil went up again. A gasp of surprise came from the settlers behind her but she ignored them as she mumbled a quick incantation and the body disappeared as the earth closed over it.

"Which way, back the way we came?" Waifyn enquired having accomplished his task and now free of settlers. But his bow was still nocked and ready, the thirty-five essences were intact but they were not out of danger yet.

"We can go back the way we came, but the choice is not ours it's theirs."

She turned to face the settlers who were already moving in the opposite direction.

"I believe the people want to go a different way," she said, with a quick jerk of her head.

"Let's try their way," Waifyn said moving in the general direction that led away from the gateway.

"You and Maldar keep going until you find a safe place for these traders. I will come and find you, but first the gateways need to be made more secure."

Aliedori began pacing around the entrance examining it; it was secure for the moment, but for how long she could not say.

"Remember the rule, we all stay or we all go," Maldar said.

Chapter 45

"That was easy," Maldar said to no one in particular, more of an assurance that he didn't have to fight Aliedori as well.

The three dracs carried the youngest in the two empty saddlebags, which were just large enough to hold the youngsters. There were two on each drac's back bound to the animals for their own safety as dracs can move at great speed if necessary. The other two saddlebags contained some food and water and a few personal items that the traders had the presence of mind to collect as they waited.

"Stay together, look after each other," Aliedori commanded. The charm would ensure that they stay together instead of scattering across the forest floor. She did not want them separating, alone they could be picked off one by one by the pursuing Greys.

"Mal take the lead, Fyn, you take the back and I will stay behind." She rested a finger against Maldar's temple for a second. The burning sensation ceased and so did the splitting pain across his forehead. He was fully clear-headed again. He gave Aliedori one of their father's looks; she lowered her eyes with a slight incline of her head.

"I am not arguing, I know what that look means; it means that I am not staying behind by myself… but…"

"I won't allow it."

The expected challenge did not come and the look on her face told the truth, she was terrified.

"I suppose you are right we do have the traders' safety to think about."

She hid her hands behind her back to conceal the fact that she was shaking from the others. Growls reached their ears as the Greys' cried out in frustration at being trapped. The sound vibrated through the veil, and the ground trembled.

"Run!" Aliedori commanded again, and footfalls of fear and panic hit the ground adding to the tremor.

As the settlers moved, Aliedori moved with them, the scene became a blur of silver and dark. The lighted sphere carried by Maldar bled into the surroundings only to be dark again in seconds. Aliedori ran with the traders experiencing their fear and panic causing her to choke and become breathless.

With each growl, the settlers cried out; the sounds of anger, frustration, fear and pain mingled and became one. What was she doing, the traders were in more danger now than when they were locked in the gateway? Her breath was coming in short pants and she breathed deeply trying to fill her lungs with oxygen. She could not knowingly kill all those Greys. She knew what they were; they were not lumps of clay they were living breathing settlers. But somehow she had to stop them. If she failed then the traders were doomed to an instant death or to becoming a Grey.

Aliedori paused and glanced back, then commanded, "Faster!"

The Greys were not halted for long; the barrier she erected was quickly torn down.

"I think they are free," Waifyn said.

"I hope you are not developing the gift for stating the obvious," Aliedori said catching her breath as she spoke.

Waifyn nocked an arrow but kept running, his feet barely touching the ground. Aliedori swivelled on the balls of her feet quickly picking up speed as she released another charm.

A mage, she thought, as the charm dissolved into nothing, *there has to be a mage somewhere.* No, she came to realised it were no mages. The Greys were protected by a dark charm; they were expecting her or they were prepared for a magical battle.

"They no longer appear to carry the Death Charm," Waifyn regretted the words the moment he uttered them.

"Yes, but charms and incantations don't work only on direct weapon contact." She unsheathed her seax. "I wonder why."

"Because some place like the Southern Realm relies heavily on conventional weapons and not swords and arrows," Waifyn replied.

She glanced over her shoulder again and saw the glowing red eyes and mouths open like maws. She didn't have time to think on Waifyn's reply, the Greys were blurry shadows, but the lines of red glowing eyes were getting closer, they were gaining on them.

"The traders cannot outrun them, a few perhaps," she turned back to the traders up ahead of them.

"They are exhausted, and the battle of survival or surrender to the Greys has already begun," Waifyn said.

He was right. If she was fighting so hard to keep that thought out of her head, what must they be thinking.

"I can stop them; I just have to figure out how without sending them home." She wasn't being bold.

"How? There are too many! We can't stop them all, and I certainly don't have enough arrows."

Beyond the first few were the oncoming force. She hung her head studying her feet but they told her nothing.

"Then what do I do?" She was afraid; she was swallowed up by the fear. All thoughts dripped from her mind forming a pool around her feet tripping her up at each turn, and she wanted to cry.

"You are the one with the Realms, full of charm; you are the only one who knows how to end them."

He released an arrow, then another and another, each one reaching their targets but it only served to slow them a little. He reached for another but they were all gone. He threw out his hands in surrender, and Aliedori placed her hand on the quiver. When it was withdrawn the quiver was full again, so Waifyn nocked the newly returned arrow. Something appeared; solid then it shimmered and faded; only the Grey colliding into it proved that it was still there.

"A wall?" Waifyn enquired with some amusement, "Well at least it's effective."

"It is not a wall."

She turned on her heel and set off as the howls of frustration came at them.

"Don't you think we need something a little more permanent than a wall?"

"It is not a wall," she said again.

She reached up with her left hand, palm open, while her right hand gripped the seax. The clouds began to broil as lightning arced down disappearing behind the 'wall'. Waifyn caught up with her as the howls became more agonising and wisps of smoke rose into the air.

"Enough!" Waifyn caught her arm.

"You wanted me to do something."

Shaking Waifyn's hand from her arm she moved away from him, as tears cleaned a path down her cheeks. She placed her hand over her ears to block out all sounds but the cries of agony she had caused echoed relentlessly around her head.

"We should catch up with the others; the Greys carry a dark charm which means they will keep coming no matter what. They may break through soon so the more distance between us and them the better."

Waifyn did not want to think of the implications. "Golems could only be destroyed by their creator, but we can kill them. Aliedori, what's happening?"

"I do not understand what is happening, but I do not think that there was ever a death charm placed on the Greys."

"I think you may be right," Waifyn said.

"Whoever is doing this is… is… it is like alchemy… they are experimenting… trying to find the right ingredient," Aliedori said her breath coming under control.

She turned on her heels and ran. Waifyn gave chase, catching up with her and urging her on.

He wanted to put as much distance as possible between himself and those awful sounds. They rounded the corner and saw the group up ahead, the illumination bouncing off their surroundings urging them on.

Waifyn and Aliedori caught up with the main group and took the lead, joining Maldar.

"We have to stop soon. Even the dracs are tiring." Maldar gasped for breath as he spoke.

He had one of the youngsters from the drac and another youngster was now riding. Aliedori did not know how far or how long the traders had been running but she knew that Maldar was right.

There was a terrifying sound; all the Greys' voices came in one blood-curdling howl of triumph that shook the ground. The tree around them quivered and the darkness was illuminated so brightly that everyone was blinded for a second or two. Aliedori blinked, sparks danced in front of her eyes before her vision cleared.

"The Greys are free again." She could hear their footfall even above the pants and sobs of the traders. Why could she not stop them? She had closed the gateway on the edge of the Southern Realm, what sort of enchantment were they under? Aliedori did not like the conclusion she was rapidly coming to, but she could not expect the traders to outrun the Greys for much longer.

They were gasping with effort and she could hear the trader's sobs and cries of desperation. She knew, like her, they were trying to ignore the burning sensation in their legs. They could run but if they do what chance did they have?

"Keep moving," she ordered. She was not going to lose anyone else to the Greys. She paused just long enough to set a series of charms.

As they set off again in their desperate race, Aliedori could feel their lungs burning as they struggled for breath.

One voice cried out above the others, desperate and fearful, "You are a mage why don't you stop those creatures?"

What was the point of all this power if she couldn't cast a simple charm to stop them for good.

She wanted to say, *"Because I don't know how to without sending them home to the ancestors,"* but instead, she sought out the speaker.

"They were created for death and whoever created them must want them to die." It was the boy Waifyn had dragged away from the golem in the settlement.

There was some logic in the argument she could not deny that, but they had not been created for a purpose they had chosen.

"There has to be another way," she argued.

She would have liked to argue further but her lungs were on fire now with the effort of running. Talking was becoming impossible, she needed to conserve her energy; it was bad enough that she already felt as though she was breathing in hot air. Suddenly, her feet hit the ground and sunk beneath it, she drew herself to a full stop.

The traders collided into her knocking her off her feet; she splashed face first into the cool water swallowing a mouthful. She pulled herself out of the water and stood bent over coughing, choking on the water and bits of debris. Maldar caught her, steadying her as those at the back push the front few, threatening to knock her headfirst into the water again. She urged them on, waving them past between coughs. They went farther into the boggy ground until they were almost knee deep in the black water.

"Find them some hillock, some dry place, get them out of the water," she said to Maldar and Waifyn as she straightened up.

Aliedori shook the water from her and started back the way they came.

"If I am right, and as you know Maldar I am never wrong, we are on the edge of the wetlands of Jurong Fell." She tried to insert a bit of levity but failed.

Maldar frowned and made to stop her but Waifyn stopped him with a slight shake of his head.

"We do as she asks and get these younglings to somewhere safe." He corrected himself, "Somewhere dry at least."

"She can't…" Maldar faltered.

"She can and you must let her, of all of us she is the only one equipped to stop them."

An understanding passed between them, Maldar didn't like that Aliedori was going off alone but he understood. He watched her go, passing out of sight as he and Waifyn pushed on through the swamp. Their progress became more and more difficult; already the water was above the waist of the shortest person. Maldar could not stop thinking that he was leaving his sister alone to face hordes of Greys. But there was nothing he could do to help her now. His priority was to get the traders out of the water. He could not lose an essence, not after she was sacrificing so much to ensure their safety.

"Look we don't know how much deeper this will get," Waifyn said. "Let me take two and scout ahead."

"Good idea. Take the drac, they have a nose for dry land." Maldar released the reins of the drac into Waifyn's hand. With a slight nod of his head, Maldar turned and picked up a youngster and hoisted her onto his shoulders. By the time he straightened up, Waifyn's light was a dim glow and only the distorted shadows could be seen dancing on the water.

"Stay in the light," he ordered the small band of weary traders as they began to move at a slower pace. There were thirty-five essences still intact so she could not complain, she'd wanted thirty-five, and she got them all. Maldar divided his attention between looking out for Alie-dori, Waifyn's return and the settlers. Someone touched his arm; it was an old settler who was pointing into the distance. Maldar spotted Waifyn and the drac returning and waded out to meet him. The others followed

"There is a hillock not far ahead that is more than large enough," Waifyn said taking the youngling off Maldar's shoulders and placing her on the back of the nearest drac.

Maldar placed two more younglings on the drac and offered the second one to the old trader.

"It is part of the old trade route. The water gets deeper but not by much, come," Waifyn spoke loud enough for all to hear.

He led them back the way he had come and after a short wade through the dark water they saw the burning fire. The hillock was far enough away from the main-land to offer some comfort to the settlers but not to Maldar or Waifyn. It was surrounded by papyrus and other aquatic grass. A cheer went up for the little sanctuary as the settlers climbed out of the water.

"The huts are not too bad, and the root garden is ready to harvest," said one of the men who had accompanied Waifyn in the scouting party.

"They are only basic, but they were never meant to be anything more. They are big enough for all and your mage can use an incantation to make them safe," a young woman said waiting for acknowledgement.

Maldar realised this and made a sound as an indication of a reply.

Waifyn stood by one of the oblong entrances; inside was very basic but there were several bunks and a fire pit. The conical roof of papyrus and aquatic grass was open at the very top, letting in the moon and starlight.

"We keep these poor unfortunates safe and we wait for her."

Waifyn's attention was seemingly taken up by the examination of the hut. Maldar showed no sign that he had heard Waifyn but began to use his long knife to dig out some root vegetables. The illumination charm that Aliedori had cast earlier was still bright. The traders had used some of the embers to light fires, which welcomed the traders. With the fires lit and the youngsters, exhausted by the evening's event, they fell fast asleep where they were placed.

"While we wait we can make ourselves useful and catch Jurong stripes to go with the Dragontails," a trader offered.

"Good," Maldar replied, still distracted by his work, "and take him with you." Using his knife, he indicated Waifyn.

Another trader set to work beside Maldar, digging up large tubers, which were sliced and roasted along with the stripes.

"You have not eaten," said a young trader who had served them earlier.

Both Maldar's and Waifyn's hot food had made scorch marks on the shiny broad leaves but was now cold. Once they had been served, they discovered that they were unable to eat, and neither of them took their eyes away from the direction they had just come.

Chapter 46

"I always meant to ask," Aliedori was squatting at the water's edge by an old stump looking into the purple water. Her voice was matter-of-fact, as if she was bored and trying to pass the time.

The papyrus and dragontails rattled in the gentle breeze. She pulled up a handful of the highly scented plants and buried her face in them. No one had seen her return. Waifyn and Maldar had been watching out for her, but she had managed to sneak back without anyone seeing her.

"I always meant to ask," she said again.

Her voice no longer matter-of-fact, bored; now it was the most important question in all the Realms. "Your parents, how do they feel about you being handfasted to a Dragon Knight and a humankind?"

The question struck Waifyn as odd; he wondered how long she had been back. He had walked this way once already leaving the cold food and watching out for her. Aliedori's top half was caked in mud and her hair was plastered to her head; the green headband she had been wearing was gone. She looked a fright from what he could see of her, but she had never looked more beautiful.

"The people are right at home with their surroundings and they have fed themselves on dragontails and tried to feed us. There is enough food and water but nothing to cook in so everything was baked."

He was babbling about nothing, but it filled the space around them. He made to move towards her, but she put up a hand, stopping him in his tracks. He folded his arms as he watched and waited.

"Good, as long as they are well fed and watered what does it matter?"

She dismissed him with a wave of her hand and he sat on the stump and braced himself. He didn't know what she had done to stop the Greys, but he knew that it couldn't have been easy. The silence closed around them, freezing them in a bond of pain and loss, but he couldn't offer any comfort. It threatened to consume them both as it tore at her insides for escape. She wrapped her arms across her stomach and rocked back and forth.

"Your question," he said softly, "I have been thinking about it."
She jumped, startled, as if she wasn't expecting him to still be there.

She waited for Waifyn to continue while she concentrated on the black water of Jurong Fell's wetland.

"Of course the water is not really black it is a deep purple, but the moon and starlight was not enough to illuminate the water so it appears black." The sudden change in the conversation caused her to stop rocking. She raised her head and half turned but changed her mind and kept her back to him so he tried the old tack.

"Oh, and I am still thinking about your question."

She didn't respond but at least the rocking had stopped and she appeared to be listening. He had to draw her out of herself to stop her going to that dark place where she was clearly heading.

"You could be magnificent, but all I see is mediocrity; flashes of brilliance, yes, but the rest, most of it… well mediocre."

Her body stiffened, and she raised her head again but continued to stare at the dark water.

He continued, "Of course I…"

"Of course, of course, of course…" Anger made her usual gentle voice hard.

She cut him off as she turned slowly, getting to her feet. It was one graceful, fluid movement but so full of anger, he had achieved his objective.

By the time she was standing up the dirt and mud that had caked her clothes and hair was gone. From the gasp of the traders so had the wet and dirt from their clothes, the space around the campfire was bathed in illumination.

"Is that brilliant enough for you," she swept passed him.

"As I said, needs improvement, but much better." He smiled as his own clothes were now clean and dry. He wasn't sure that she heard him as she was already gone, swallowed up by the darkness inside a hut at the edge of the light.

Bellowing cries and howls could be heard during the night, intermittently shattering the silence, but nothing happened beyond that. The night was uneventful and the traders all managed to rest adequately. None of the group of three slept, however.

"I will take the first watch," Aliedori insisted.

"I'll keep you company," Maldar was equally insistent, and when Aliedori did not reply Maldar took it that she was fine with it.

"So we are all keeping watch at the same time then," Waifyn said. "Good, real good planning."

He smiled to himself; he was developing a trait for stating the obvious. They all dozed a little during the night, jumping awake when alerted by the slightest sound.

The morning sun ripped the darkness from the sky without warning and stood guard against the horrors of the night. The sun sent its light over the wetland of Jurong Fell and offered up its secrets in all its glory. The wetland stretched out around the small island as far as the eye could see; an expanse of brilliant purple.

"Wow, it's beautiful," Maldar said to no one in particular.

Papyrus, aquatic grass and purple dragontails grew in dense thickets around the water's edge and broad leaves of water dragons glided slowly over the surface with open flowers of purple and blue drinking in the sun.

"It is beautiful," said a young trader standing close by, "and it can also be the most terrifying place." Maldar didn't remember asking for a commentary but knew he was going to get one anyway.

"The living organisms feeding on the nectar give the water its deep purple colour. Which in turn colours the flowers. Even the dark green broad leaves are tinged with purple. In Memgalah lilies are pink or white, but here they are always blue," the young trader said proudly.

"The problem is the plant life covers every metre of water. They break off and become floating islands you see, it is glorious, but for all its beauty it can be deadly. If you don't know the water and how to navigate, you can get lost forever because of shifting vegetation."

"And do you know how to navigate the fell?" Maldar asked, there was no harm in finding out.

"They created new networks of waterways. Can you see the island over there drifting? You could be lost forever if you don't know the water?" The manchild continued as if he didn't hear Maldar's question.

His knowledge imparted, the manchild walked away, and Maldar watched him go. Then he turned his attention back to the floating island. Whether the fell was difficult to navigate or not Maldar didn't care he simply wanted to enjoy the beauty of the morning and the purple water was part of that beauty.

Most of the Jurong was beautiful, and the settlers lived on isolated pockets of islands and used watercrafts to travel around the wetland. Something was missing, and Maldar suddenly realised what it was – watercrafts – where were the watercraft? Wherever there were clumps of islands there were settlers and also their boats, canoes, watercrafts of all kinds, including dragon boats. Where were the setters now, they couldn't live and trade on the water without owning even the smallest of watercrafts?

"Where are their watercrafts?" Maldar asked.

Aliedori was facing the water with her back turned against the night, her seax gripped firmly in readiness. Her brother had voiced the question she had been asking herself since she had been knocked into the water. But her attention was now focused on the slow movement of the water, the gentle lap against the shore. The sudden wash, despite its gentleness, suggested that there were more than just pretty flowers floating by. There was definitely more going on beneath the water than there was on the surface. The sleek silver-scaled serpent forms glided under the mass of shiny dark green leaves, and she counted three before they sank deeper into the purple depth. She watched a small pod of Cyons, *water dragons,* as the mother and father swam close to the surface protecting their baby.

There was a squeal of delight, or was it fear? Someone else had seen the sleek beautiful water dragons. Aliedori was glad they were not disturbed during the night by a frantic crossing or there would not be thirty-eight this morning. The gentle wash became a ripple against the shore, but she was reluctant to face the other challenges of the day so she kept on watching the water. Even with her capacity for limitless charms and incantations, she could not ensure a safe passage.

Satisfied that the Cyons were gone she replied to Maldar's inquiry. "I have been asking myself the same question," she said almost to herself

The way back was blocked, not only by what might have come out of the gateway or the dead and dying golems, but by the secure prism to redirect the lightning to destroy any other Greys that might follow.

She didn't know how long it would take the creators of the golems or a mage to tear down the prism. The traders were safe as long as the prism held, and it was to be in place for the next six days. She needed time to think and to get the traders to safety by getting them home.

Yet she was not sure if home was any safer than being out here. It was only a gut feeling, and her feelings were never wrong, she just had to figure out what her gut was trying to tell her.

"Our watercrafts have all gone. How long have we been here?" The voice came from somewhere to her right interrupting her train of thoughts.

"Is it usual to bring youngsters of less than a cycle on such a journey, could a parent not of have stayed behind?" She kept her eyes on the ripples.

"Our children travel with us wherever we go," came the response.

"Did you not think it strange you set off to trade but find yourselves prisoners?"

"You don't understand we were not aware we were held captive. We have always used the compound. We have always used this place before we go into the West. Children and anyone else who want to remain stay in the compound until traders return." There was a pause significant enough for Aliedori to know what was coming.

"Whatever those things are they are like nothing I have ever seen before." There was a tremor in the voice.

And even though Aliedori hadn't wished to be drawn into a conversation, she found herself giving the manchild more than a cursory glance.

"We are not sure what they are, but we have named them 'Greys'."

The manchild remained standing where he was, his hands behind his back. It was a thoughtful stance as he thought over what she had just said.

She spoke over her shoulder. "So you always sealed entrances with magic?" she asked.

"I didn't use magic," he told Aliedori's back and stormed off.

The young trader gave Maldar angry glares as he rushed past; it was the same manchild who had spoken to him.

"Did you notice that he didn't say 'I can't or don't use magic' but he didn't know about the gateway or the sealed entrance." Maldar spoke to his sister's back also.

The traders were huddled around the campfire having their first meal of the day. Aliedori had used a simple incantation to multiply their own drinking vessels, so each trader could have their own. The traders had woken to find not only the drinking vessels but matching pewter plates with wavy edges to reflect the water on which they lived. The gifts didn't elicit any response of thanks and instead they remained in their own little groups watching the three of them with caution.

"They are afraid of us, Dori, and your little gifts didn't quite have the appropriate response."

Maldar paused a little distance away from her, "Here drink this whilst it hot."

The morning sun cast a long shadow on Maldar including the hot steaming tea; she reached for it without saying a word. She sipped the tea while he sipped his, both contemplating the scene before them.

"Jurong Fell is a place I've always intended to visit," he said between sips. "To share the hot springs of the dragon's pool with Fyn, with you even."

The corners of her mouth turned up fractionally to produce a smile but only for a second before the water captured her interest once again.

"I didn't dream that my first experience of the Fell would be like this, running from monsters."

"Sometimes we have no say in how the journey ends, Mal and, for that I am sorry."

"Don't be sorry. It's not your fault," Maldar said, but somehow he felt that she was apologising for something else.

So far, she had refused to speak of what happened when she went back. When she turned her face was full of sympathy for him, but it was gone in the blink of an eye to be replaced by an unreadable expression before she turned her back on him again.

The noise of their little enclave heightened; the inevitable couldn't be put off any longer. Aliedori heaved a sigh and stole a secret glance at her brother; he was fine he was not suffering from any ill effect of the Grey's talon. She sheathed her sword; she must help the traders of the Fell to get back to their people. She stole another glance at Maldar before she cast her gaze at the manchild who had spoken to her and said, "I must be more tired than I first realised."

"They are testing you... us... just like they did with the phan-thorans, to see what you can do."

Maldar only realised that he had drawn his sword after handing Aliedori her tea when he started to sheathe it. She paused in mid-step, squeezed his arm then continued towards the three old canoes lying against a hut.

"I know what's happening," she said. "*They* are not the ances-tors, so the question is *who*? Who is testing us Maldar?"

She spoke the words as she passed. Maldar followed her with his eyes, "I wish I knew, Dori someone out there is doing this."

Only then did he notice that Waifyn was also standing with an arrow nocked in readiness. It was amazing how quickly they'd learned to work so well together and how quickly they had learnt to take their lead from Aliedori. She stood by the canoes; they were old and worn but easily repairable. He watched as she worked her magic. The incantation lifted the canoe into the air, spun it before placing in on the water.

This journey was taking her on a different path, a path that she had to travel alone. This could not be what their father meant when he said that she was *ready*.

"She makes incantations look so simple," Waifyn said in awe.

"Yeah, she does, but that's not what I'm worried about, it's the other sort of incantations that worrying me," Maldar replied almost to himself.

"What do you mean? Waifyn went from awe to confuse.

"Aliedori has always used magic, its second nature to her. She has always used her magic to heal, but now, it's used against everything she stands for – the ancestors – and it's taking its toll."

Their father said she was ready, how could she be ready to send humankind home to the Ancestors? Even those creatures. He knew his sister, and he knew that she would not be ready to kill even those crea-tures. This journey was simply bringing into sharp painful focus the in-evitable, that Aliedori would one day be ruler of the Realm. She needed to start her journey now whether she was ready or not. It was a cruel twist of fate that she had to start it by sending so many of them home.

"She is doing what needs to be done," Waifyn said.

"And you think I don't know that."

Maldar followed her to the hut, when she did not acknowledge him, he cleared his throat.

"I know you expect more from me, but you have to talk, tell me what I can do. I didn't let you face the Greys alone; you know that, don't you?"

His words tumbled out rushing to be heard and leaving him breathless with anger and frustration.

She did not even look in his direction, her hand busy in a gesture of drawing on the elements. Her voice was a hoarse whisper as she strained to stay in control.

"Go away; it's not about… you… go aw… I can… not yet… go, go see to the people."

There was a subtle change in her tone. She shifted her gaze from the old canoes but not on to him.

"I need to think, Maldar, I need to find a way forward. I am sorry I need to do this alone. I need to find a way to undo what has been done to those poor creatures, to change them back."

"They are poor creatures, but so are the traders and they didn't ask to be here. And Dori, you don't need to do it alone."

The fingers of her right hand curled into a fist; the left hand gripped the hilt of her seax. She held the elements in her palm in readiness for an incantation or a charm. Maldar studied the fist carefully. It was an ordinary fist, slim wrist and slender fingers curled into a tight ball. It was what the fist contained that could be a cause for concern; that ordinary fist could do extraordinary things.

"Neither did those poor creatures," she said.

"Dori, those grey things just kept coming. Someone is sending them to hunt us – to hunt you."

He paused long enough for her to look in his direction. He didn't like what he saw. Waifyn mouthed "Go easy" as he walked away but this wasn't the time to go easy.

"Dori, if we have any hope of keeping these people safe and unharmed. We… you… must learn to stop thinking of the Greys as they once were. You had to choose Aliedori, the life of these people or the life of those things and you made the right choice. Now that you… we have taken responsibility for them we have to finish the job."

He paused watching her and trying to gauge her mood; her fist was still tightly closed.

"To take a life goes against everything you stand for," he continued softly, "but what choice did you have?"

"Is that what I am… what I am becoming… am I *death,* Maldar?"

She looked down, her hand still curled into a fist, and Maldar was sure that she did not see it.

"No, Dori, you will never be *death*… don't ever think of yourself as that!"

He was angry but not at her. He was angry at himself for not seeing what she was really going through. He thought it was a simple choice and should have known that it would never be that simple. Somehow, he had to make her see.

"I made a choice, didn't I?"

Maldar nodded. "Yes, for them," he connected the traders to them with a slight movement of his hand, "and for the rest of your life you will have to choose who to sacrifice and who to spare."

It was not a choice he relished and he had no doubt that she didn't either. She opened her palm, bringing her hands up and froze in mid-turn as coils of white-hot fire radiated from her fingers.

The lightning fire sped across the water exploding vegetation as the water bubbled and boiled. Jets of steaming water – purple, blue and green – shot into the air; the large petals burst and rained down on the shiny green leaves like droplets of a rainbow as the water continued to bubble and steam cooking the wilting lilies.

A cloud of mist settled over the area and small aquatic animals suddenly floated to the surface. They bobbed amongst the leaves several times before floating on the surface cooking gently in the steaming water. Aliedori examined her hand as if she expected it to belong to someone else and that its acts were beyond her control.

A trader, never one to let an opportunity pass by, paddled into the now cooling water grabbing the spoils of Aliedori's little fire display.

A grin spread across Waifyn's face, he unfurled himself from where he was sitting with a youngling on his lap.

"Now that's magnificent, I knew it was there somewhere."

She shifted her gaze from her hand to glare at Waifyn in reply. But he didn't see it. His attention, like those of the traders, was drawn to the sudden rainbow that followed Aliedori's water display. The water continued to steam and the vegetation cook long after all the spoils were gathered and the rainbow had faded.

Chapter 47

Moving the people was not as difficult as Aliedori first thought. The traders were at home in the water, and they took the lead, she simply furnished them with what they needed. In the burning heat of the midday sun, they soon found themselves several kilometres away from the small little hillock where they had spent the night.

Aliedori had the ability to conjure something from nothing; she just needed the raw material. At the bottom of the Jurong Fell wetland were centuries of wood and canoes, all she had to do was bring them from their watery resting place and make them whole again.

She did this with ease; by the time the canoes were raised to the surface, they were repaired, dry, and ready for use as they bobbed about in the gentle wash. She used the same incantation to make a raft large enough for the three of them as well as the three dracs.

Once everyone was safely in a canoe and rowing away from the island, Aliedori, Maldar, and Waifyn, along with the dracs, climbed on board the raft. She had hardly spoken half a dozen words since the incident. A trader or two tried to thank her, but all she did was gave them a curt nod.

While it was easy to get the settlers on their way, the waterway through the vegetation was not easy to navigate, oars caught up easily with the lilies and other aquatic plants. There were frequent curses from both Maldar and Waifyn each time either had to pull the oar from the water and shake or pull of a mass of tangled reeds from the end.

When Aliedori couldn't ignore the curses anymore, she cast a charm to clear the path as soon as the oar touched the water. The traders didn't have the same difficulty, and they appeared to be gliding through the water almost as serenely as the Cyons. To make their lives a little easier, Aliedori cast another charm to make the raft glide easily through the water. With their task easier, Maldar began copying the traders and started fishing over the side.

By the time they stopped at another small, unoccupied island, there were several Jurong Stripes; the striped eels with extended fins thrashed about on the raft before becoming still. They came upon a channel cut through the think aquatic vegetation, which was about four metres wide. They stopped at the hottest part of the day, and the island provided only a singular tree with tinted blue flowers, its roots dangling in the water. They tethered the boats and raft and climbed ashore. The traders were chatty and full of laughter, the ordeal of the night before all but forgotten. They even appeared to be a little less suspicious and afraid of their rescuers.

"How did you do that?"

Aliedori blinked and used her hand to shield her eyes from the glare of the sun to better see the person who had asked the question. The manchild stooped down in front of Aliedori. His skin was darker than hers, Maldar's, and even his own people. His large brown eyes were as wide as the sun and full of curiosity.

"Who cut that channel?" Aliedori asked.

They had stopped on an island where a channel could be seen in the distance; her back was resting against the tree.

"A mage started it for large boats, it was meant to connect the Fell people to the East."

The manchild had no interest in the channel but felt he must in order to get his question answered.

"Why was it not completed?"

The manchild shrugged his shoulders he didn't know or simply didn't care.

"The forest was frozen, the East lost many, many things," an older trader holding one of the youngsters in his arms spoke.

"And the mage?" Maldar asked.

As one, the entire traders' heads turned to Maldar, but no one answered the question. Maldar felt himself wilt under the strange gazes. He turned his attention to the dracs just to give himself something to do, but continued to feel their gaze on his back. Only Aliedori, it would seem, had the right to ask questions and had the right to an answer.

"How did you do that without a conductor I mean?" the manchild asked Aliedori.

He was surveying he papyrus with care. He made up his mind and selected one; then, upon taking a small knife from his belt, he cut the chosen papyrus and began trimming it.

Aliedori had drawn herself up and rested her head against the tree to have a better look at the child.

"I do not know, I have never used a conductor, I have never needed one."

"Are there many mages who don't use conductors?"

"A few," she replied.

"Can you go from using a conductor to not using one?"

"I do not know, you are asking the wrong person."

After a short pause the boy asked, "Are you very angry?" He was looking directly at her for the first time, but Aliedori couldn't see his face without shading her eyes.

"No, not angry, upset perhaps, sad but not angry; I had to do an awful thing." She reconsidered then said, "Yes, I am very, very angry."

"You saved us, saved the young ones, so does it matter the 'awful' thing you had to do?"

Aliedori shaded her eyes and studied the child carefully. He was closer to a man than a child in age. She pushed herself off the ground and stood; both Maldar and Waifyn waited then let out a collective sigh of relief.

"It should matter, to you of all people."

Standing up as well but keeping his head lowered, he said, "I did not mean that in quite the way it sounded."

"Whatever way it sounded, taking a life should not come easy not to you, not to me, not to anyone."

The boy stood silent, she didn't know if he was thinking about what she had said, or whether he thought his apologies warranted a different response. Aliedori doused the fire with a small hand gesture and the traders began to stir.

"We should get moving," Aliedori said to Maldar and Waifyn who had never left the raft.

The light had long since faded from the skies when the small group of sailing vessels rounded a bend and emerged into a clearing. Up ahead of them were networks of small islands far enough apart for watercraft to sail the narrow lanes. The channel skirted the settlement going off to the right and away from the Knolls housing the settlers. Maldar and Waifyn rowed the raft between the dwellings and away from the channel into narrow lily-filled water lanes.

"How can thirty-five people be accommodated? There doesn't

seem to be any spare islands to build on. Is this population control?"

Maldar felt a sudden anger at the thought, was the leader sending their people off to be turned into Greys?

Aliedori stood up to get a better look at the dwellings; they were simply huts made from the surrounding materials, papyrus grass, wood and mud.

"There are enough," Aliedori said, and the rushing sound of water could suddenly be heard all around them.

"That dwelling over there is different from the others," Waifyn said, taking his attention away from the small knolls rising out of the water.

He pointed in the direction of the dwelling occupying the largest knoll surrounded on all sides by cypress trees. The path from the tiny jetty was paved with bricks also and a small dragon boat was moored. All the other buildings that could be seen were of either papyrus or wood for wattle and daub with conical-shaped roofs.

"I have the feeling that none of us are going to be made welcome," said Waifyn.

"You sense that too?" Aliedori said. "It does explain the sinking of the knolls."

"You didn't just conjure them up then?"

"No, magic... alchemy... was used to sink them, I just reversed the charm, it was quite a simple one really."

Maldar did not care whether the people of the Fell liked or trusted them. Aliedori cared for them and that was good enough for him. As the raft approached the large dwelling a figure came onto the jetty holding aloft a luminous orb. The slender young woman held the orb higher to get a better look at the travellers.

Then her eyes drifted beyond her people and a look of disgust curled her thin lips. Aliedori walked to the front of the raft and stood facing the young woman. They were of the same age and also the same height, but the newcomer stood high above her. The jetty was deliberately built for her to look down and more importantly for her people to look up to her.

"Your people were trapped in a trader fortress but I believe that you already knew that." Aliedori's voice was steady; there was a new strength that was not there before.

The young woman turned her terrible gaze on Aliedori; a sneer curled her lips.

"There is a gateway but it's now closed, at least for the moment, and your people are back safe." Aliedori clasped the back of her hand and rubbed her thumb over her palm as if trying to remove a particularly stubborn stain.

"As you say they are my people, I do with them as I see fit." With that, the three on the raft were dismissed with a gesture of her head. She became silhouetted against the shadows along the path and was gone.

"If you knew that they were abandoned why did you bring them back here?" Both Maldar and Waifyn were by her side, but she was unsure who spoke.

"Because this is where they belong and because now they have a mage. Mages have always been the rightful leaders even in the Fells; he is a level three… Maldar."

"Hmmm."

"You can let go of my elbow now." Maldar dropped her hand as if it was suddenly scorching her flesh.

"Sorry… I just didn't want you doing anything to her."

Aliedori laughed; somehow, she could see the humour in it.

"Thank you. I will make sure my people keep away from that part of the forest."

It was the manchild that Maldar overheard asking questions about her abilities. Now he understood why Aliedori was so willing to accommodate him.

"They are not your people yet, and remember what I said," Aliedori said.

"If you continue along the channel it will take you to the town of Jurong Kass. But you can rejoin the forest after the end of the second day," the boy said ignoring Aliedori's words.

"What will you do now?" It was Waifyn who wanted to know.

"I have always been very good at building; the islands will be occupied by the end of the night."

He pulled from beneath his robe the green papyrus stem; the delicate long feathery umbrella head was broken back. The feathery head was between seven to ten centimetres and formed a perfect star shape. Aliedori reached out and touched the conductor; the manchild caught his breath and said thank you then continued, "We're naturally distrusting, and I am not sure if you can be trusted, but I wish you well."

He appeared to have addressed Maldar, and it was obvious the conversation was over as he waved his people on.

"I do not know your name; will you not exchange names at least?" Aliedori enquired.

The manchild raised his hand and the canoe halted it slow pace. He held himself with pride in the certainty of his secret, head held high as he spoke.

"We do not give our names freely; we believe that knowledge of our names can be used against us by our enemies."

Aliedori spoke with the same certainty and pride.

"We are not your enemy. That is closer to home." She paused and half turned before turning back to face the manchild. "We do not share your belief, my name is Aliedori Nasryn, this is Waifyn Nymph of Bryn-le-Fenir, and Maldar Nasryn, Dragon Warrior. We are of the Southern Realm."

Maldar and Waifyn inclined their heads as they used the little jetty to push their oars against and set the raft moving again.

"He is not likely to forget us."

"*That's the point*," she said in a low voice, "Goodbye Mage No-Name."

She smiled as the raft spun and they were facing away from the settlement heading back to the channel. They took turns in manoeuvring the clunky raft on the slow moving water; while one slept the other two pushed and pulled the raft along the channel.

True to his words No-Name Mage's forest was indeed found close to nightfall at the end of the second day on the raft.

"Why did we need to go through that for a bunch of superstitious ingrates?"

Maldar sat stoking a small fire as they waited for some root vegetable to roast. He was hungry, and when he was hungry he became irritable, and Aliedori was still refusing to talk about what happened when she was alone in the woods.

"He is a mage," Waifyn reminded Maldar.

"Yes a mage, but of what, a few huts in the middle of the fell? So what?" Maldar was not ready to let it go.

"He is the true leader of Jurong Fell, not just the wetlands. When they hear that the Intendant and two warriors brought their leader back to them they will be beyond grateful."

"You think! Is he the only mage in the district?" Maldar asked.

"You really need to visit the falls and soon," she said.

"I hear that the waterfalls are very beautiful especially this time of the cycle," Waifyn said.

Maldar made a hissing sound through his teeth.

"Do not be a cynic Maldar. That is not who you are. Besides you have always wanted to see the falls."

"Not anymore." Maldar was petulant.

"Oh do feed him, Fyn, please. If we don't he will only get worse."

This plea brought much needed laughter and even Maldar joined in.

It was their second night in the woods, and their journey did appear to be moving away from the West and heading in a southerly direction. Aliedori stood and dusted off her clothes as she walked around the fire to Maldar. She leant over and kissed him on the top of his head; it was a gesture that he had almost forgotten. It was Aliedori's way of making things better.

She started kissing him on the top of his head the first time he rushed in the playroom with a bump the size of a small dragon's egg.

He shed enough tears to fill the ocean-lake to overflowing; the bump disappeared with the kiss but the tears remained a lot longer. For two cycles he'd steadfastly refused to grow, and everyone had shot up, heads and shoulders above him. She was tall, lanky and mean, but not to him, never to him. Aliedori fought for her brother until he was tall enough, but she never used magic and for two cycles she drove her handmaidens to despair as they tried to come up with inventive ways to hide Aliedori's bruises from sight.

"You sometimes forget that you have a kind heart. Never forget that you have a kind heart, Mal, and you would do the same again."

"Not if it means you have to face those things on your own again. He squeezed her hand.

"It is just the way it is and will always be from time to time, and those times I will talk less."

"We have always talked about everything Dori, that's what we do."

311

"I know." Her nails suddenly became worthy of inspection. "It cannot be helped, for the moment but we will talk again soon."

She kissed the top of his head again and gave them both a dazzling smile.

"I am going to pick some fruits to have after our roasted roots and Jurong Stripes."

They watched her go, catching her hair up in her hand and twisting it into a bun before securing it. She turned and grinned, raised her hand and dispelling the safe barrier she had *erected* around them. Then she was lost amongst the trees.

Waifyn's voice grew lazy as if drifting off to sleep.

"She is right, you know. You two will talk again, but right now she needs to do this on her own."

"That has always been my worry, that one day she will not need me."

"Maldar, you are her brother. She will always need you and will always want you in her life."

This simple statement made Maldar blink, and he found himself looking at Waifyn in disbelief.

"It is just what I wanted to hear, a lie, I need lies a little longer," Maldar uttered.

"It's not a lie, Mal.; Aliedori needs you more than ever now."

"I have always known that Aliedori has never needed me, it's me who needs her. To teach me charms, to save my life, to show me how to live, while I learn and develop a sense of myself. Waifyn, thank you for that, I need lies a little bit longer."

"Mal, I love you, oh, so very much, you know that, but you can be a drac's arse sometimes. Aliedori needs you; she always has and always will. You save her every day, you have taught her how to be humankind, to love, to understand, to care. Do you have any idea what kind of humankind she would have become without you there to guide her, to show her the way?"

Maldar balked at the idea

"You can't be serious. She knew about my nature even before I knew for sure. One hot summer's day she said, "Do not encourage Galina, Maldar, when you know that your nature lies elsewhere. And in that instant I knew where my true nature lay and that females held no interest for me. Later that very week I met Kryspyn, my first romance, and it lasted all summer until he had to return to academy and continued his studies," Maldar insisted.

"That may be so, Maldar, but would she have known any of that if you had not been there to show her?" Waifyn argued.

Maldar closed his eyes and rested back on his elbows. He was thinking over what Waifyn had said. Before Waifyn it was always him, Aliedori and Keidrop and dragon makes three – now dragon makes four. A sudden strange cry penetrated his consciousness shattering his thoughts into fragments.

The drac's screech, their braying cry echoed around the forest. Maldar snapped his eyes open. Waifyn was running in the direction Aliedori had gone, an arrow already nocked. At first, his shout did not make sense to Maldar then it became clear what Waifyn was shouting, "She is gone, she is gone. Aliedori is gone." Waifyn had already disappeared; Maldar grabbed his sword and gave chase.

ABOUT THE AUTHOR

I was brought up on stories, tales of adventures of far off places, of princesses in peril and their princes rescuing them, they filled my head and sparked my imagination from an early age. I have very fond memories of "Lloyd Brown" or "Lloydy" as he was known to us children, telling the most wonderful stories. The only time he didn't stutter was when he was telling stories, I would travel with him to those far off places from the Grimm fairy tales and just around the corner of the "Anansi" stories of Jamaican fables, these were amongst my favourites. By the time I had to swap the Jamaican sunshine for the winter "watery" sun of England at the age of almost eleven years old. My head was already crammed full of stories to accompany me on my very own adventure to far off England.

I may have spent my formative years in the Jamaican country side with the wild green woods and perfectly clear rivers but I grew up in London. Long winter days and darkened evenings would find me with my head in a book, the Lion the Witch and the Wardrobe, Arabian Nights and closer to home Enid Blyton's Famous Five were later replaced but not forgotten by Mervyn Peake's Gormenghast, and Sterling E Lanier's Hiero's Journey.

I was a shy introverted child but while at school I was regarded as one of the "cool" kids; I was a real Jamaican with the accent to prove it. Libraries became my playground; they helped to fuel my imagination where adventure after adventure played out again and again in my head. I could be anywhere, any place, anytime from my little corner of the local library. I lived in my head; my stories gave me a sense of belonging, they sustained me and now somehow one of my adventures found its way onto the page and is about the be shared with others.

OTHER TITLES FROM IMZADI PUBLISHING

Gabriel's Wing

Going to California

I Found My Heart in Prague

The Hedgerows of June

The Other Vietnam War

The Rain Song

The Swamps of Jersey

Vietnam Again

The Blackstar Gambit

A Game Called Dead

Staring Into the Blizzard

The Weight of Living

www.imzadipublishing.com

Lightning Source UK Ltd.
Milton Keynes UK
UKOW04f0637120917
309040UK00001B/103/P